PRAISE FOR

Bound and Determined

"A searing, frolicking adventure of suspense, love, and passion!"
—Lora Leigh, #1 *New York Times* bestselling author

"[A] hot, sexy, fun romance . . . Whew! We're talking fire hoses. That's what you'll need when you read this book. Lots of cool water because you're going to be hot. The sex is great and fun, fun, fun . . . Seriously, this is a fun, erotic book . . . and highly recommended." —*Fresh Fiction*

"A witty, deeply sensual take on the classic love story plot . . . Be sure to pick this one up!" —*The Romance Readers Connection*

"[Shelley] Bradley has outdone herself with this highly entertaining read. Falling in love should be so much fun!"
—*RT Book Reviews* (Top Pick)

"A flawless story that grips a reader from page one and doesn't let up . . . Ms. Bradley's imaginative story lines and irresistible characters keep her readers coming back for more . . . Don't miss it!" —*Road to Romance*

"Had me laughing out loud one minute and reaching for a glass of ice water the next . . . a definite Perfect 10." —*Romance Reviews Today*

"Ms. Bradley simply shines . . . A fabulous book I'm not likely to forget in a hurry." —*Just Erotic Romance Reviews*

Titles by Shayla Black

The Wicked Lovers Novels

WICKED TIES

DECADENT

DELICIOUS

SURRENDER TO ME

BELONG TO ME

MINE TO HOLD

OURS TO LOVE

Anthologies

FOUR PLAY
(with Maya Banks)

HOT IN HANDCUFFS
(with Sylvia Day and Shiloh Walker)

WICKED AND DANGEROUS
(with Rhyannon Byrd)

Specials

HER FANTASY MEN

Titles by Shayla Black writing as Shelley Bradley

BOUND AND DETERMINED

STRIP SEARCH

Bound and Determined

SHAYLA BLACK

writing as

SHELLEY BRADLEY

HEAT, NEW YORK

THE BERKLEY PUBLISHING GROUP
Published by the Penguin Group
Penguin Group (USA) LLC
375 Hudson Street, New York, New York 10014, USA

USA | Canada | UK | Ireland | Australia | New Zealand | India | South Africa | China

Penguin Books Ltd., Registered Offices: 80 Strand, London WC2R 0RL, England
For more information about the Penguin Group, visit penguin.com.

This book is an original publication of The Berkley Publishing Group.

Library of Congress Cataloging-in-Publication Data

Bradley, Shelley.
Bound and determined / Shayla Black writing as Shelley Bradley.
p. cm.
ISBN 978-0-425-26821-6
I. Title.
PS3602.L325245B68 2013
813'.6—dc23
2013008548

PUBLISHING HISTORY
Berkley Sensation mass-market edition / January 2006
First Heat trade paperback edition / March 2009
Second Heat trade paperback edition / October 2013

PRINTED IN THE UNITED STATES OF AMERICA

10 9 8 7 6 5 4 3 2 1

Cover photograph by Edwin Tse.
Cover design by Marc Cohen.
Text design by Tiffany Estreicher.

Bound and Determined

Chapter One

A woman thought of just one thing when she looked at a man like Rafael Dawson—and it had nothing to do with firewalls and passwords.

Oh, my. Kerry Sullivan watched him prowl into the baggage claim at Tampa's International Airport with a restless, sexual grace. He looked good enough to eat . . . or at least nibble on for prolonged periods.

Not the most intelligent way to regard the man she had to abduct in the next two minutes.

Grimacing, she tugged down the little black miniskirt Jason had insisted would distract Dawson. Looking at her prey, Kerry feared she would be the one hard-pressed to focus. He was far more devastating than his little black-and-white picture—or his annoyed voice on the phone telling her to seek professional help—had implied. "Nerdy" was the last word she'd use to describe him, not with that wide, sensual mouth and cheekbones that could have been chiseled from a work of art. Damn it, he was supposed to be a techno-geek.

Unfortunately for her, she didn't see a pair of thick glasses or a pocket protector anywhere.

Kerry watched as Dawson retrieved his black hanging bag from the serpentine carousel and slung it over one wide shoulder. He gripped his laptop case with his other hand and scanned the signs the chauffeurs around her held up.

Now it's up to me.

The bank hadn't sent a driver. Kerry had invented one for her purposes and made a sign to lure her quarry. All she had to do was raise it—when she found her nerve.

I am woman. I am strong . . . I am way outta my league!

How was *she* going to coax a major melt-in-your-mouth hottie like Rafe Dawson, especially if he recognized her voice from their previous . . . misunderstandings? Even if he suspected nothing, she doubted he'd give her a first glance, much less a second. And if he knew she had absolutely no experience with men, she would have two chances of interesting him: slim and none. Already, Slim was packing its bags.

A virgin at twenty-three, she felt like a freak.

Even if he did look at her, couldn't place her voice, and fell for her plans, what then?

Her brother Mark and the possible prison term in his future forced her to ignore the vise of self-doubt and fear cramping her stomach. Screw what the FBI and her brother's boss, that tyrant, Mr. Smikins, thought. Mark was innocent. She owed it to him to persuade Dawson to help her prove it. The good news was that she was much more articulate face-to-face than she ever could have been over the phone. The bad news: Rafe was already one pissed-off puppy.

No, she had to put some positive energy into her thoughts. Her plan would enable her to get Dawson's undivided attention. Then he would understand she'd been right about Mark and not press charges. She hoped. Damn, she was breaking something like ten laws here.

Kerry sighed. Her first instinct had been right: This was a stupid, stupid plan.

But Rafael Dawson had refused to listen to her pleadings during any of her calls. Mr. I-Only-Take-Corporate-Clients had blocked her number, too. Since then, the brainstorm fairy hadn't gifted her with a brilliant plan, and time was slipping away. This was it.

In a way, Dawson's abduction was his own fault. If he'd only listened when she called, they could have worked *something* out! Well, okay . . . a teeny, tiny bit was her fault, too. Being less rattled would have helped, but still . . . His personal assistant screened his calls so thoroughly, Kerry wondered if the woman was a talking Doberman.

The first time he had answered the phone himself, presumably after the rabid canine's departure for the day, had been the most successful. Of course, he'd accepted the job to shore up Standard National Bank's electronic security some weeks prior and had assumed she was a bank representative. Once she'd corrected him . . . well, he'd disconnected the call. The next time she called, he'd barely listened. Her coworker's four-year-old with ADHD stayed tuned in longer. The third time, she'd been smarter. She'd pretended to be calling from another company and asked him if he did any investigative work. He'd covered his list of impressive credentials and client list—FBI and tons of Fortune 500 companies. She had no doubt he could prove her big brother innocent of embezzlement. Dawson definitely played in the big leagues. The price per hour he'd quoted her confirmed it. Kerry had nearly dropped the phone and started crying. Trial attorneys were less compensated. Much less.

She sighed. But the fourth conversation . . . That one had gone *really* badly. Even now, she could hear his deep growl . . .

"You *again*?"

"Consider me a fan." She'd done her best to put a smile in her voice.

"As often as you call, you've fallen into the obsessive groupie category. Should I worry that you're going to show up at my apartment angry and armed? Or are you the other kind of psycho who stalks a guy completely naked?"

Kerry paused, considering. "Those are strategies I hadn't thought of."

"Forget I said anything. I didn't mean to give you ideas. You don't work for Standard National Bank or eBay, do you?"

"No, but I can explain."

"At this point, I don't care who you are or what you want."

"Actually, I'm—"

"Seriously, don't tell me. I'm better off not knowing."

She'd gripped the phone tightly, feeling opportunity slipping away. Mark had practically raised her. She had to make this work.

"Just listen to me, please. I need help in the worst way."

"Oh, I figured that out a while back. But since I don't wear a white coat, I don't think I'm the right choice. Stop hounding me."

"Don't hang up. Please! I'm desperate. Our lawyer is awful, the FBI won't listen . . ."

She'd tried to keep it together, truly. But the date for her brother's trial had just been set, and the enormity of their problem had made her . . . well, emotional. Which was why she'd rambled. And cried. At the same time.

"No one will listen, and he's never even had a speeding ticket. If the pain of chemotherapy didn't make him a criminal, why would anyone assume getting married would?"

"I have no idea, nor do I want to." A brief pause later, Dawson added, "Don't call again."

He'd hung up, leaving her to plot something far more forceful and devious. Kerry really wasn't good at either. So here she was, in the frigid airport, determined to tie the man down—literally—to enlist his help.

With a resolute breath, Kerry raised the sign with Rafe Dawson's name printed in permanent black ink. Perspiration broke out under her hairline. Her hands shook. Would he recognize her voice? Or guess that she was up to no good?

He saw the sign and moved closer, luggage in tow. Then Dawson shifted his gaze to her. And didn't look away. She swallowed as he discreetly took her in, his gaze brushing her curve-hugging red halter, skimming her bare midriff, grazing her microscopic miniskirt and almost-bare thighs.

Kerry was sorely tempted to make sure her siren red lipstick hadn't smudged, that the Florida humidity hadn't detonated her sleek style into its usual curly tumble, and that she still showed signs of cleavage above her indecently tight top.

As his focus returned to her face, a bad-boy smile curled the edges of his mouth. The heat in his to-die-for gray eyes was ferocious enough to liquefy her knees in world-record time. Despite his unfriendly demeanor on the phone, Kerry was stunned that she had no trouble imagining herself running her hands across the yummy width of his chest . . .

Down, girl, down!

Dawson came closer, now a breath shy of infringing on her personal space. His heat pulsed at her in a palpable wave. She drew in a deep breath, and his killer scent enveloped her. It wasn't manufactured. The man simply smelled like black silk midnight wrapped in velvet sin. The scent totally matched his voice.

Yikes, she was in major trouble here—for so many reasons.

"Mr. Dawson," she greeted, keeping her voice breathy to disguise it.

He nodded, his gaze glued to her. Nothing in his face hinted that her voice seemed familiar. Yeah! So far, the goddess of bad and illegal plans was smiling on her.

But Rafe wore a hint of a smile, too.

Staring at him sent her pulse into a circus-like frenzy. She could make an obsession out of wondering how well muscled he was beneath his pricey linen shirt, considering the amount of hair dusting his broad chest, pondering whether he wore boxers or briefs. Or went commando altogether.

Stop! Kerry chastised herself. Being attracted to the jerk wasn't a good idea, but apparently she had no control over that. Still, distracting the man so she could successfully abduct him would be impossible if she was too busy drooling. Nor would he find it alluring.

She had to get ahold of herself. Mark's fate rested in her hands.

Why couldn't Mark have another sister, one who wasn't curvier than current fashion dictated? One with more confidence? A sister who didn't have to persuade a man she'd already irritated to help her?

"Welcome to Tampa," she forced out in her best Marilyn Monroe voice, fidgeting with the sign.

He raised a surprised brow. "You're my driver?"

Kerry hesitated, biting her lip again. Could she say this? When she had conceived this plan, the words had sounded so simple. But Dawson didn't look like an idiot. In fact, he looked more like a shrewd sex god, put on this earth to make her mind mush. Worse, what if he figured out who she was before she had him bound? Kerry pushed aside the fear that her plan had less than zero chance of succeeding. *Positive energy*, she reminded herself.

"Your driver is in the car. Think of me as a . . . hostess."

"Hostess?"

Kerry had no idea if his tone indicated disbelief or intrigue, but she pushed on. "I understand this is your first trip to Tampa. We—that is, everyone at Standard National Bank—thought you might appreciate a tour guide of sorts."

Did he recognize her voice? Believe her? Impossible to tell. Instead, Dawson watched her, adjusting his burgundy silk tie with dark, elegant fingers. Her gaze climbed to the sharp angle of his jaw, the sculpted temptation of his lips. She'd bet last week's tips the man knew how to do fantastic things with that mouth. Not that she would ever find out.

He screamed New York polish in his thousand-dollar suit. The scent of money wafted from him like a subtle cologne. She, on the other hand, probably still smelled like today's lunch special of a double cheeseburger and onion rings.

"Lead the way." He gestured her before him.

A new battalion of nerves attacked her with the force of a blitzkrieg. For her plan to work, she needed to get him comfortable, at least. Hot and bothered wasn't necessary. In fact, it wasn't even likely if he really listened to her—or looked at her hips. But comfortable she could do.

"It's pretty hot today. Humid, too. You might want to lose the coat or you'll swelter."

With a shrug, he rested his hanging bag over the back of a nearby chair and removed his suit coat. Beneath, his crisp white shirt, comfortably creased from his travel, strained to encompass a pair of shoulders so broad, Kerry would have been hard-pressed to pry her gaze away with a crowbar. Mr. Unpleasant sure was easy on the eyes.

He retrieved his garment bag, gaze discreetly scanning her. Then he paused. Looking as if he was suppressing a grin, he handed her his suit coat. She took it with numb fingers. Lord, it smelled like him—musky, mysterious, manly.

"You can wear that if you like," he offered.

Kerry stared at him with a puzzled frown. "Thanks, but it's way too hot."

His hot gray gaze drifted away from her face, down her body for a moment. He glanced away, wearing a ghost of a smile. "Suit yourself."

What did the man see, goose bumps all over her body? Yes, the air-conditioning in the airport was set on subzero, but they'd soon be outside. Scowling, Kerry looked down at her body—and found her nipples puckered prominently against the form-fitting halter top Jason's girlfriend had told her could stop traffic. Too bad it hadn't stopped her nipples from being as obvious as a neon sign.

As she turned away, mortification rolled over her in a heated wave.

With a sigh, she slung his coat over her shoulders and drew the lapels together with a tight fist. A hint of a laugh sounded from behind her. She ignored it.

"This way, Mr. Dawson." She marched toward the door.

"Rafe," he corrected, following her with a long-legged stride. "And if you're going to be my guide, shouldn't I know your name?"

Surprised that he asked—or cared—she blurted the truth. "Kerry, with a K." Thankfully, she'd never had a good opportunity to give him her name when they'd spoken on the phone.

"Nice to meet you, Kerry with a K. Since I have no meetings until tomorrow, are you scheduled to show me around this evening?"

"I'll be . . . with you for the duration of your visit." Kerry swallowed past the half-truth. She'd be with him, all right. He just had no notion that he'd spend the next few days not tied up in meetings . . .

But tied to a bed.

The thought made her stomach churn again—and not unpleasantly. The image of a man of his size and power being completely at her mercy set her imagination spinning. As for the flow of her juices . . . thinking about that now simply wasn't a good idea.

As they walked outside, the sultry May weather hit them with a gust of hot, damp air. Warm raindrops clung to every car in sight, and heavy gray clouds hovering above promised more.

Rafe sucked in a breath and loosened his dark tie with a grimace. "Wow, you weren't kidding. This is like August in New York."

"Yeah, well, we hang Christmas lights in shorts and tank tops, so there's a trade-off."

Rafe laughed. The deep tones vibrated down her spine, igniting a spark within her. Lord, when the man smiled, he was downright edible. Other than a hot glance or two—maybe even imagined on her part—he did not seem nearly as affected by her. And any minute now, he was going to hear something in her voice, which she was desperately trying to disguise, and realize she was his psycho "fan."

Damn it, positive energy! Where was it today?

"I'll take the coat now, if you're no longer cold," he offered, grinning.

Kerry risked a quick peek down. Nope, her nipples still stood straight up as if saluting a superior officer. Odd, considering the warmth curling through her at the sight of his smile. In fact, the tips of her breasts rasped against the filmy top with every breath she took, so sensitive and tight . . . and damn it all, even arousing. She couldn't remember anything like it. The whole problem was downright embarrassing.

"I—I'll keep it for a bit," she stammered, mentally cursing her fair skin. Her cheeks were likely just a shade lighter than the average fire engine. "So you don't have to carry it."

His knowing gaze coasted down, to where she clutched his coat over her chest. "Very considerate of you."

She sent him a weak smile. He had to at least suspect he was the cause of her little issue.

Oh, yeah. She had control of this abduction. No problem.

Kerry cursed under her breath. Why didn't she have a Plan B?

Thankfully, she arrived at the limo, Rafe just a few steps behind. Jason, Mark's best friend and coworker at the bank, stood there, hat pulled low over his blue eyes.

I can't do this, Kerry mouthed to Jason.

He nodded—and took over.

"Good afternoon, Mr. Dawson." Jason stepped forward to retrieve his garment bag.

"Hello," Rafe answered.

"Any other bags?"

"This is all I need."

Jason nodded and opened the door to the backseat, slinging the bag over his shoulder. Kerry stood close to her brother's buddy.

After Rafe climbed in the car and sat, Jason shut the door. Kerry felt her pleasant mask dissolve as panic took over.

"You *can* do this," Jason whispered, squeezing her hand. "Just get in the limo. I've already made his drink."

She was in over her head here. "With what?"

Jason hesitated. "Flunitrazepam, better known as Rohypnol. It's a benzodiazepine."

"Huh?"

"The date-rape drug. Think Valium with a big kick. He's not likely to remember much tomorrow." Jason shrugged. "One of the perks of your family living overseas is that they can send things the U.S. government doesn't like."

"The drug is illegal?" Kerry buried her face in her hands. "Oh, this is bad. Hollywood makes comedies about stupid plans like this, and they never end well."

"Do you want to prove Mark innocent? You know he's been framed. Dawson is one of the top electronic security experts in the country. I didn't schmooze Smikins to get his name so that you could back out. Dawson is your best option to prove Mark didn't steal a dime."

"But—"

"This is your opportunity. School just ended, Pops gave you a couple of days off from the diner. The timing doesn't get any better than this. All you have to do now is distract him so that he doesn't realize we're headed away from his hotel. Or wait until he passes out. Once we reach the cottage, you're home free."

Kerry shook her head. "Did you see the man? There's no way I can distract a guy like him with mere small talk. He's like—like Antonio Banderas crossed with Brad Pitt . . . only taller, bigger. And if he recognizes my voice, I'm hosed."

"It's fine. He's not suspicious, and trust me, he looked his share." Jason's buck-up stare cut through her insecurity. "You don't have to have sex with the guy. A little light flirtation will most likely work. If not, do . . . the minimum and move on."

No, she had no plans to have actual sex—not that a guy like Dawson would seriously look at her as a potential bedmate. He might flirt a little, but that didn't mean he wanted to get down and dirty. Still, Kerry had visions of what the "minimum" might entail, assuming he actually was interested, and in every scenario, tempting him to such an act required more knowledge than her limited experience allowed. Hell, she'd never even seen a naked penis in person. What if he wanted a blow job?

She couldn't think about that now. *Positive energy!*

"You're right. I came up with this plan and I'll finish it. When I get him alone, I will persuade him to help Mark. Somehow."

"You'll be fine. Just present Mark's case as logically as you can. Don't get emotional."

Kerry rolled her eyes. "That's like telling the sun not to rise."

Jason conceded the point with a shrug. "Do your best. Now lose the coat."

Yes, she wanted to be unafraid of her sexuality, be bold, be brave—but being liberated was harder than it sounded. Kerry shook her head, clutching the lapels of the coat tighter.

He sighed. "Dawson can't be distracted by what he can't see."

Jason had a point, damn him.

Reluctantly, Kerry removed the coat, resisting the urge to cover herself with her arms.

"You look hot," Jason assured her, giving her a quick grin.

Her, hot? Yeah, she had guys clamoring at her door. In her dreams . . .

Okay, so she hadn't had time for a relationship yet. Mark's bout with cancer had begun just after she'd left her last hellish foster home. Kerry had been trying to put herself through school and working, taking care of Mark after the chemo—all that had taken a toll on her social calendar. But Mark had been healthy for a while. Why, oh why, hadn't she found *someone* to date? Or at least have a quickie? Once upon a time, Jason might have been a candidate . . . except he was like another brother to her. And Mark would have killed him.

So now she got to have her first sexual experience since Richard and the nightmare of her prom. And she got to acquire this new experience with a veritable god. Granted, she didn't intend to have sex with him . . . but coaxing him to the cottage without touching him—or him touching her—seemed unlikely.

Lord, what if she started hyperventilating?

"Hot? I'm packed into this outfit like a sausage. I'm all boobs and hips."

"And that's a bad thing because . . . ?" Jason smiled at her hesitation. "Besides, I doubt he's thinking about sausage when he looks at you, Kerry. You look great."

She took a deep breath. "Okay, I can do this. I'll just keep him talking for now."

"Between conversation and that damn near see-through handkerchief you're wearing, that really ought to be enough."

Hope sparked. Likely Jason was right. She could handle it. She *would*. Positive energy.

Besides, what choice did she have? It was either survive this humiliation, or see her brother go to prison.

* * *

IT hadn't escaped Rafe's notice that Kerry with a K was one very sexy woman.

Or that she was a nervous one.

He sipped on a Black Irish, his drink of choice, grimacing with pleasure as the whiskey and Kahlua burned a sweet path down his throat. Very nice. Most limo services didn't pay that kind of attention to detail. Then again, Standard National, after a recent security breach in which an employee had electronically embezzled nearly three million dollars, was worried enough to pay through the nose for his services to tighten things up.

Desperate enough to hire a limo, complete with his own personal "hostess."

And since Rafe didn't live in Mayberry, he was pretty sure he knew what "hostess" meant. Interesting for a bank, usually conservative to the core, to have sent such a woman . . . but who was he to look a gift horse in the mouth?

Except that fair-skinned, wide-eyed Kerry didn't act like a woman who fucked for a paycheck.

So what the hell was she?

Generally, Rafe dated worldly women. A little conversation, maybe an evening at the theater, lots of experienced sex, then an air kiss or two goodbye. No scenes if he encountered them later by chance on the street. No tears, no regrets, no messy emotional shit.

Kerry wasn't sophisticated. In her, he sensed an odd sort of innocence that went beyond the appearance of her pink-bowed mouth smeared with too-dark lipstick and the artless sunshine ringlets beginning to overtake her hairstyle. Hell, for someone who "entertained" men for a living, she'd certainly covered up a pair of hard, heart-stopping nipples faster than a preacher's wife.

Getting naked with someone hired for the job had never appealed to him in the least.

Getting naked with Kerry . . . very appealing—as the hearty erection south of his belt buckle could prove.

Where did that leave him with Kerry? He pondered, swallowing more of his cold, tangy drink. Was she a sure thing? He couldn't possibly have misread the situation, right? No one wore a fuck-me skirt with boots like that, along with a top so small it made a bikini look like nun's garb, if she wasn't a sure thing.

It sounded logical, but that question niggled in his mind: Why was she so nervous?

Then again, why question the situation? This simple job with Standard National would finally put him over the five-million-dollar revenue mark. He'd worked two bartending jobs to afford college and damn near starved through his first year in business—all without the help of his father's money—just to reach this milestone before his thirtieth birthday. And he'd make it with two weeks to spare. He'd be someone in his own right then, more successful than Benton Dawson III had ever been. Screw the past—and his old man.

The car door opened and Kerry slid into the backseat with him. She sat close—but definitely kept air between them. A tense silence ensued as the driver took his seat, started the car, and drove away. Sipping at his drink, Rafe studied Kerry. She couldn't be a day over twenty-two, twenty-three tops. Why was she working as a glorified hooker? And her breathy, starlet-on-Valium voice? He shrugged. Maybe she thought it was sexy.

His thoughts scattered when she scooted closer and leaned in, providing a spectacular view straight down the front of that tiny red halter, which instantly confirmed two curiosities: Yes, her breasts were naturally large, and no, she wasn't wearing a bra.

Rafe bit back an insane urge to tear the tiny scraps of her clothing away and persuade her to dance the horizontal mambo with him in the limo's backseat. Now. His cock got even harder at the thought she might oblige him.

He closed his eyes. Where was his self-control? Normally, he didn't take the Neanderthal approach—stupid and ineffective. But Kerry made him feel surprisingly primal.

Rafe searched his memory for the last time he'd had sex—and came up empty. Two, three, four weeks ago? Hell, he couldn't remember. Not after being treated to a view of the best breasts he'd ever seen.

Wearing a wobbly smile, Kerry with a K tapped one of her fingers to his chest and began tracing a light, random pattern. Where did her teasing sugary vanilla scent come from? That alone made his mouth water. Coupled with her touch, his heart started chugging.

If she smelled that good, how fabulous would she taste?

Kerry stared, batting thick, dark lashes over huge green eyes. "We're going to be busy tonight—lots to see and do. If you have someone to call, someone you should check in with, now is the time. We'll be much too busy later."

The words sounded sexy and ripe with promise. His cock certainly stood at even greater attention. But the look on her face did not say *come hither*. More like *now what?* When the privacy panel between the two of them and the driver slowly rose with an electronic buzz, her sweet-faced confusion turned to dread. She crossed her arms over her chest self-consciously.

Again, he wondered just who she was and what she was doing here. Kerry didn't seem comfortable alone with him or with exposing her . . . assets. And was she asking if he was single? Would a real professional "hostess" care?

He blinked, feeling suddenly too tired to solve the riddle. Too little sleep and too little coffee were not a good recipe for a late night with a beautiful woman.

"Nope," he answered. "No one to check in with. My mother died years ago and my friends don't bother me when I work."

"Great news—about the friends." She smiled, showing a sweet pair of dimples. "I'm sorry to hear about your mother."

Whoever sent Kerry his way must have read his fantasies. He was a sucker for blondes with dimples . . . Would she surrender herself completely? The question rolled around his mind the way candy rolls on the tongue. He'd give his right arm to be inside her in the next five minutes, but the reticence she was trying to hide made that doubtful, no matter her occupation. Instead, he sipped the last of his cocktail and fished around for another tactic.

His sluggish brain took a while to cooperate. "So Kerry, what's a nice girl like you doing in a skirt like that?"

He tossed the question at her playfully. Her defensive stare took him aback.

"What do you mean?"

Rafe sighed. "You seem awfully nervous. I won't bite . . . unless you want me to."

She sent a stilted, dimpled smile his way but said nothing.

Damn it, his head was beginning to hurt. A nap before dinner would probably be a good idea.

"You don't . . . entertain men regularly, do you?"

Those green eyes widened to big-screen proportions. "I—I . . ."

"First day on the job?" he guessed.

"Exactly." She nodded vigorously, emerging curls bobbing.

Oddly, her answer pleased him. So she wasn't a hooker and she *was* having second thoughts. Which was good. He didn't like the idea of another man pawing her in the back of this limousine. For some reason, the image pissed him off.

Lord, he must be tired to be caught up in a woman he'd met all of fifteen minutes ago. What was wrong with him?

Still, his thoughts continued to spin in his oddly lethargic brain. Why had she felt compelled to take a job she obviously did not want? Was she in some sort of trouble?

"This job is more difficult than I thought. I—I'm sorry if you were expecting someone sexier." Her apology broke into his contemplation, startling him.

Forcing himself to focus, he peered across the inches separating them. Kerry had bowed her head and apparently taken up hand-wringing as a new hobby.

Something—compassion, empathy?—stirred to life within him. He placed a gentle hand beneath her chin and lifted her gaze to his. Tears shimmered in her eyes, disturbing him.

"If you were any sexier, I couldn't restrain myself. You already blow my mind."

Kerry's jaw dropped. She blinked once, twice. "Me?"

Rafe nodded—and noticed a lock of stray golden hair curling about her moist bottom lip. Slowly, he lifted his hand to brush the hair away. Kerry didn't flinch, didn't tense.

Was her silent acquiescence a green light to touch her more?

Fighting off a wave of exhaustion, he smiled and dragged his thumb along the edge of her full, red-painted lips. Damn, how would she taste? He was dying to know.

"Yes, you. Very sexy. If you don't hear that often, the men in your life are stupid and should be beaten."

That sweet pink flush crept into her cheeks again. She tried to reproach him with her stare, but that low-lashed gaze caressed more than punished him. A hint of a sexy smile played at her pretty mouth.

She was an amazing combination of angel and temptress. And he wanted her under him, legs splayed wide, in the worst way. But jet lag and an oddly fuzzy brain were beginning to spoil the moment. And damn, it was hot in here. Wincing, Rafe loosened his tie.

"I'm sure my brother has never considered whether or not I'm sexy."

"Your boyfriend?" he prodded, stifling a yawn.

Why was he asking her this? The guy was likely a loser who simply couldn't appreciate Kerry with a K the way he ought to. What kind of guy would let his woman "entertain" other men for a living?

Sleep. He needed sleep. That would restore his common sense.

"No boyfriend," Kerry whispered.

Rafe grinned, despite his weariness. "That's a shame."

His teasing made her laugh, and her dimples came out to play once more. A bleary-eyed moment ruined it, and he knew he would need that nap before dinner whether he wanted it or not. He really should have eaten lunch during his layover in Baltimore . . .

Hell, why did he have to give out now?

No. He would not fold like a cheap tent—not without tasting her.

"Kiss me, Kerry," he blurted, aghast to hear his words slurring.

She appeared not to notice. Instead, she sent him a shy nod. Rafe grasped both of her arms like a lifeline and pulled her close, dragging her firm, fine ass onto his lap. Kerry gasped. Refusing to acknowledge his utter exhaustion and his screwed-up speech, he pressed on. His raging erection demanded attention. He wanted Kerry to ache the way he did.

Odd that he should be tired and aroused at the same time . . . but who cared when he had a beautiful blonde on his lap?

Rafe settled one hand low on the curve of her hip. The other he thrust into the soft silk of her hair. He wanted to kiss her, touch her, until she was desperate to have his cock inside her. Hell, he wanted to inhale and savor her at once.

And he would make it happen now . . . if his growing headache weren't slamming him between the eyes and the need for sleep weren't shutting down his brain.

He felt freakin' weird. What was happening to him?

Apparently, he was going to have to settle for inhaling Kerry—quickly.

Rafe covered her incredible lips with his mouth. She was soft, as he had suspected. But he needed more. Everything. He plunged his way inside. Her sweet taste, like summer-ripe cherries, exploded on his tongue as she opened for him. Kerry kissed shyly, but somewhere in his lust-fogged brain, he heard her moan. If a kiss could do that, he wondered what sort of amazing sounds she might give off when he laved her clit with his tongue.

He was dying to know. And if he didn't get closer to her in the next few seconds, he was going to combust.

As he swept through her mouth for another searing kiss, Rafe lifted Kerry and shifted her to straddle him. Her inner thighs hugged his middle. Her skirt inched up around her hips, revealing the fact she wore tiny, very sheer black panties. No question, she was a natural blonde.

"Wanna touch you, rip your panties off," he breathed against her neck. "Then taste you."

Kerry shivered in his arms.

A new wave of weariness followed. He ruthlessly squashed it.

Cupping her delectable ass in his hands, he urged her hips forward until he felt the damp heat of her pressed against his tented trousers. Unable to stop himself, he broke the kiss and threw his head back. She arched into him, too, a cry rising from her lips. Raw pleasure clawed up his spine, crashing between his legs. God, the woman was killing him.

Breath coming in harsh pants, Rafe looked back to her, the disheveled hair, the swollen mouth and flushed skin. Her green eyes looked darker, dilated. Hunger tore at his belly. She would be a goddess in bed.

"Want you," he grunted. "Damn bad."

Where the hell had his ability to speak gone? Was he getting sick? Or was the light-headed feeling the result of all his blood rushing below his navel?

Fighting suddenly heavy arms, Rafe found the little bows holding her halter together. The one between her shoulder blades wasn't too difficult. One quick tug . . . *Ah, magic,* he thought, sliding one hand around to cup her breast, tease her distended nipple.

Kerry bit her lip at his touch, her lashes fluttering closed.

"So sexy," he murmured, faltering about for the next tie. After a Herculean effort, he raised his free hand to her nape and found it. The tug required to set the top loose exhausted him. But once it fell free of her body, having her breasts bared at mouth level . . . worth the effort.

Determined to stay awake long enough to enjoy the sharpest arousal he could remember—and the woman who had caused it—he stroked both nipples with thumbs and forefingers. The sweet mewling sounds from the back of her throat encouraged him. He latched on to her with his mouth, sucking hard on her flushed, rosy nipple, nipping gently with his teeth. Her sigh became a groan.

"Skin so soft," he muttered, taking the other nipple in his mouth.

Somewhere in the back of his mind, he registered the fact Kerry had sunk her fingers into his hair and was holding him in place. That suited him. He laved her again, then looked down at her panties. They were damp. *Perfect.*

But once focused down, his eyes refused to lift again. He gave up. Sight wasn't as important as touch or taste right now.

"Here," he rasped. "Now. Can't wait to be inside you . . ."

"Yes," she moaned in his ear.

Triumph spiked briefly as he reached for his belt buckle. He would have all her slick heat closing around his cock. For a while, the goddess would be exclusively his to take in every way he ached for. But consciousness became harder to grasp. What the hell was wrong with him? Heat poured over him in inferno-like waves. Sweat rolled down his temple. Rafe fumbled around to find the button that would roll down a window. No luck. Nausea hit him. Damn, he'd never been sick like this before. Never. Why now?

Kerry shimmied against him, those fabulous breasts swaying near his face. Determined to press on, Rafe slid a hand between them to tug down his zipper . . . then his world went black.

* * *

WHEN Jason stopped the car fifteen minutes later and opened the limo door, Kerry had composed herself . . . somewhat.

"We're here," he said unnecessarily, watching her.

Avoiding his searching gaze, Kerry stared past him, toward the cottage lounging in isolation on the serene shore of the Gulf of Mexico. Not a soul dotted the private, white sand beach. The small dwelling of pale peach stucco glimmered in twilight's glow, mirrored by the turquoise sea. Any other time, Kerry would have been thrilled to stay for an undetermined number of glorious sun-filled days in a place of such charm and seclusion. But now . . .

The memory of Rafe Dawson's hot mouth lingered on her swollen, tingling lips and tight nipples. Despite folding her hands in her lap, they trembled with the sharp edge of arousal. Dwelling on the minuscule panties clinging wetly to the sensitive flesh between her legs only accelerated the speed of the memories assaulting her brain.

What on earth had she done with Rafe Dawson?

She'd said *yes*. To a virtual stranger. To a man she now had to spend her days—and nights—completely alone with. The man she had already annoyed, abducted, drugged . . . now had to be persuaded to help her free her brother.

Talk about impossible tasks. Screw positive energy. What she needed was a miracle. Kerry closed her eyes.

"You okay?" Jason said.

She answered with a jerky nod. "So this is infamous Uncle Dave's Love Shack?"

"The one and only."

Great. She looked forward to seeing all of Dominating Dave's bondage equipment—about as much as she looked forward to dealing with her captive when he regained consciousness.

Why had she said yes to Dawson? Instead of "No" or "Stop" or "Where in the hell do you think you're putting that mouth?" She'd been seduced by the rush of sensations and bright emotions so new, so alluring, she'd wanted them to go on just a moment more.

"Kerry, are you okay? You look pale. He didn't hurt you—"

"No," she promised, avoiding his frown of concern as she stepped from the car.

"Or force you?"

Force? She'd all but volunteered to strip for the jerk with bad phone etiquette. "No, I'm all right."

Rafe's kisses, as addicting as her favorite Mexican food, coaxed, drawing her out with the hot demands of his mouth, the long-fingered genius of his hands . . . all while he'd been under the influence of an illegal drug. What if he'd been stone sober and actually trying?

Thirty minutes alone with the man had been overpowering. How would she survive an entire day? Or night? Without climbing on top of him and begging?

Jason's blue eyes darkened with worry. "Then what, sweetheart? He unnerved you."

Damn, she was too easy to read. She had to gather herself and stop focusing on the fact that one kiss from Rafael Dawson had overwhelmed her senses. She was a big girl now, and lack of sexual experience or not, she was going to have to make this plan work.

"Nothing I can't handle. Really, don't worry."

Liar, liar, pants on fire—in more ways than one, said a voice in the back of her head.

"I'm sorry." He took her hand. "I should have interrupted or something. I didn't think he could do much damage in so little time."

Well, Rafe had wrenched a *yes* out of her. And in that moment, shockingly, Kerry had meant that yes with every beat of her pounding heart.

Should she be embarrassed? Horrified? Or jubilant that she'd finally found a man who not only flipped her switch, but ignited every red-blooded cell in her body? *None of the above,* she reminded herself sternly. Dawson was here to help Mark, not distract her by lighting her up like a Fourth of July celebration with his sure hands and velvet voice.

"It's all good, I swear," she said finally, pasting on a plastic smile. She judiciously avoided looking at Rafe passed out cold behind her.

Jason had no such qualms and leaned in to look at their victim. "He can't disturb you for the next twelve hours at least, likely much longer." Then he frowned. "You know, I don't think red is his shade of lipstick. Much better on you."

Kerry tried her best to smile at the jest. "Come on, let's get him in the house so you can get out of here."

"Maybe I should stay—"

"We need your inside information at the bank. Besides, you don't want to risk that butthead Smikins firing you if you fail to show up tomorrow."

"I could stay for a while, make sure he doesn't give you any trouble."

A tempting offer, but not a smart one. "Too risky. Once you leave here, you're done with this. I'll swear until the end of time you had nothing to do with my scheme. Staying will only implicate you more."

Jason raked a hand through his hair. "Yeah, I just hate leaving you with this guy. It was one thing when I thought he was a passive computer nerd. But Dawson isn't passive. And he upset you."

"He just surprised me," she protested. "I've got his number now. Please stop worrying about me."

"You can still call the whole thing off, you know."

Kerry shook her head, long ends of hair brushing the tips of her shoulders. "As you pointed out earlier, what are my more appealing options? Watching Mark go to prison so I can avoid a few hours of hanging around an attractive genius who happened to catch me at an off moment?"

Jason conceded the point with a reluctant nod and began retrieving Rafe's belongings from the trunk. Kerry leaned in and grabbed her small suitcase. After a quick check to ensure their captive was still in dreamland, they made their way to the Love Shack. A wave of stifling air hit them as Jason unlocked the door and stepped into the small entryway. Muttering an apology, he pumped up the air-conditioning. Kerry followed.

Surprisingly, the Love Shack's living room décor was not gaudy. A brick fireplace with a dark wood mantel dominated one corner. Across the small room, a blue sofa sat, dotted by nautical-themed pillows. A similarly styled rug graced the gleaming blond hardwood floors. Ahead of her, a kitchen with simple white cabinets attached to the living room.

Kerry wandered into the room, charmed, despite knowing that Dominating Dave liked to bring his girlfriends here—away from his wife's prying eyes. The place was full of clean lines and warmth. She touched a red leather chair that sat near the sofa. Beyond that, she saw the hall, which led to two doors.

"The bedroom and adjacent bathroom are down here. The closet is across the hall," Jason said as he disappeared down the opening and shoved open the first door.

Out of curiosity, Kerry peeked her head into the bathroom—and gasped. It was bigger than her bedroom. Complete with a sunken Jacuzzi tub for two and a separate dual-headed shower stall tiled in shimmering shades of lapis and cream. Bright, fluffy towels graced the intricate gold rods on the walls. A towering silk flower arrangement added color from its Grecian pedestal in the corner. Mirrors covered nearly every wall. Infamous Uncle Dave had himself a real lovers' paradise.

Nerves stretched tighter than a centerfold's bra, Kerry turned and made her way out the lavish room's other door, which led directly to the bedroom.

It didn't look like a dominator's pleasure den of leather and spikes, but rather like a tasteful New Orleans boudoir, complete with an elaborate iron bed. A soft wine-shaded comforter trimmed in some heinously expensive lace covered the massive bed. Mosquito netting fell softly over the scene. Candles of all colors and shapes lay in every corner of the room, waiting to be lit. The room looked like a version of every woman's romantic fantasy. Not at all what she had expected from Dominating Dave.

"Nice, huh?" Jason said, setting Rafe's luggage in the closet in the corner.

Kerry followed suit. "Yeah."

"Don't be fooled." Jason grinned. "Wait here."

Shrugging, Kerry took off her stiletto slut boots—she hated anything more binding than flip-flops—and strolled around the room, touching a soft cherry wood armoire, then filtering the netting over the bed between her fingers. The soft chenille rug cushioned her bare feet. Getting used to a place like this would be no hardship at all.

At least she thought so until five-foot-seven-inch Jason stumbled in, staggering as he carried Rafe, who was well over six feet, on his shoulder fireman style. The shade of her accomplice's sweat-beaded face resembled the color of a very ripe grape.

"Oh, let me help!" She rushed over to Jason, just as he lumbered about and sagged against the bed, depositing Rafe across it.

No surprise that he dwarfed the bed.

Jason stood, panting. "Damn, he's not light."

"Next time, tell me you need help. I'm more than willing—"

"I know. I got it." He stretched a muscle between his neck and shoulder. "I'm glad we're nearly done situating ol' Paul Bunyan here."

"Done? He's just lying across the bed. The minute he wakes up—What are you doing?"

As Jason removed Rafe's shoes, socks, and tie, then dumped them beside the bed, Kerry watched with annoyance. Restraining an unconscious man—before he awoke—seemed far more important than seeing to his comfort. Then Jason started on Rafe's shirt, one small white button at a time. And the view became . . . incredible. Firm. Taut. Muscled. Silky dark hair lightly dusted incredible pecs. Flat brown nipples taunted her. Real six-pack abs. Kerry's eyes threatened to pop from her head.

"I'm situating him," Jason said, as he swiped at the sweat running down his face. "Can you get me a bottle of water from the fridge?"

Had Jason spoken? Oh, Rafe had endless golden skin, yummy bulging shoulders, and—

"Kerry, water?" Jason prompted, annoyed. "Fridge."

"Oh, yeah." Kerry reluctantly peeled her eyes away and back-tracked down the hall.

Inside the small kitchen brimming with New England charm, a white refrigerator gleamed. Yanking on the handle, Kerry opened the appliance to find water and a host of other staples. Apparently Dominating Dave liked to be well nourished when he tied up his girlfriends.

Grabbing two bottles of water, Kerry returned to the bedroom—and stopped.

Rafe lay completely, beautifully naked except for a scrap of sheet covering a distinct bulge just below his lean waist and above well-muscled thighs.

Jason grabbed his water from her nearly limp hand. Absently, Kerry brought hers to her mouth and swallowed deeply. Seeing the lust of your life damn near naked called for large quantities of Evian.

He shoved Rafe's shirt, pants, and boxer-briefs into her hands, leaving his socks, shoes, and tie beside the bed. "Put these in the closet, where he can't get to them."

"W-why is Dawson naked?"

"A naked man is less likely to run down the road looking for help, don't you think?"

And more likely to turn my mind to utter mush every time we're in the same room. "I suppose." Kerry glanced down at the pile on the floor beside the bed. "What about his socks, shoes, and tie?"

The mischievous grin Kerry knew well flashed across Jason's face. "Leave them there. If he finds a way to escape, at least his feet are covered."

Logic, anyone? "And the necktie?"

"A man's got to have some dignity."

Sometimes Kerry could only shake her head at Jason's sense of humor. “Great. I thought you’d restrain him . . . or something. Not strip him. I don’t see how—”

“One set of restraints, coming up.” Jason paused. “If you really think you can handle him. If not, we’ll pack him back in the car and deliver him to his hotel.”

Couldn’t every twenty-three-year-old virgin handle a rich, sex-on-a-stick guy? “No problem.”

Chapter Two

RAFE awoke—and wished he hadn't. The painful gong of a pounding headache reverberated down to his toes. He groaned. Had the Yankees been using his head for batting practice? He grimaced as blinding sunlight stabbed his eyes through closed lids. No way was he ready to open them; that would be asking for torture. An ache gouged him lower as well. His bladder felt so full he swore he'd swallowed half the Atlantic. Fuzzy creatures had taken up residence on his tongue. His general misery reminded him of that raucous Pearl Jam concert during his college days where he'd cozied up to a bottle of tequila and a hot brunette.

No, on second thought, this felt worse.

What the hell had he done last night? One would hope that, despite nearing the age of thirty, he could remember the great party that had given him a hangover of mythic proportions. But only a flash of memory tantalized him: a blonde with dimples and to-die-for breasts wearing a barely legal outfit. Kerry with a K. His memory couldn't grasp a damn thing beyond her.

Light footsteps echoed across the floor, drawing nearer. Rafe struggled to open his eyes. A quick glance showed a blonde in denim shorts, face scrubbed clean. A golden ponytail of ringlets swirled between her shoulder blades. Kerry?

Sunlight slashed his skull more effectively than Freddy Krueger with his best pickax. Groaning once again, Rafe closed his eyes.

"I brought you some aspirin," she whispered. "And water."

Blindly, Rafe reached out and took them, grimacing as he swallowed. "How long have I been out?"

"Most of thirty-six hours. Just rest awhile. Wait for those to work."

"Can't." His croaky voice sounded akin to a ninety-year-old with emphysema. "Bathroom?"

"Um . . . yeah. Need help?"

With what, holding it? "No."

Eyes still closed, Rafe threw back the covers and stood. His ankles and wrists moved with him, but felt oddly tethered. Cool air assaulted him everywhere. Hangover and all, his eyes flew open.

About two seconds later, Rafe caught on to the fact he was totally naked and restrained by wrists and ankles. The line connected to his cuffs tied him directly to the bed.

Nothing like shock to catapult a man awake.

He glared at her, testing the pulley motion of his restraints. With a tug, he could create some slack in the line, but without effort, the slack quickly retracted. "What the hell—"

"I can explain!"

That voice. It wasn't the phony purr from last night, but it sounded familiar. Where had he heard it? On the plane? No. Before that, recently. But when? A spike of pain stabbed his head, preventing any further thought.

He focused on the blonde and her wary stare instead. At least it was wary until her gaze fell, focusing on parts south that stood at rigid attention—the morning usual. As a blush stained her cheeks, she looked away.

Women still blushed? He'd never met one who did. Was she embarrassed? Odd, considering they'd had wild sex last night. Hadn't they?

Rafe scowled, brain fuzzy, confused. "Kerry, right?"

"You remembered." Surprise lit her green eyes as she returned his gaze.

Just as abruptly, the smile disappeared.

She looked way different from last night, so much so he would never have found her in a crowd. The sex siren had disappeared, replaced the red halter with a simple lavender T-shirt. Low-rise denim shorts hugged the smooth curves of her hips, baring firm, tanned thighs. Bare feet dotted with pink toenails peeked over the edge of a chenille throw rug. Today, Kerry looked clean and innocent enough to be someone's teenaged sister . . . except for her come-hither hourglass figure.

Despite his hangover, he couldn't forget her straddling his lap, her flushed nipples bare, as she said yes to more. With any luck there'd be lots more of that in their future . . . once he figured out why she sounded familiar and why he was strapped to a bed like a dizzy damsel in a bad B movie.

Pulling at the binds around his wrists again, he confirmed that they were retractable and set up on some sort of pulley system. Same with his ankles. "Is this your idea of kinky or something? If it is, I've got to tell you, I usually prefer to be on the other side."

"Kinky?" Color rushed to her fair face. "No. I mean, I guess people do that, but I've never—" She shook her head, as if to clear it. "No, and I'm really, really sorry."

Okay, so this wasn't her idea of kinky, which was a good thing . . . except that her voice sounded weirdly familiar and something about her apology signaled that her agenda wasn't sexual. Even her stolen glances seemed more curious than lusty. That sucked because having Kerry completely, watching her pale face flush to orgasm—once his colossal headache abated—sounded mighty fine. And this time, damn it, he'd remember.

"Want to give me my clothes, untie me, and tell me why you're sorry?"

"I can't do the first two." She bit her lip, gaze brushing over his morning erection again before leaping back to his face, eyes wide.

Rafe finally registered her very real skittishness and reached for the sheet to cover the essentials. He'd already guessed that Kerry wasn't a wild, booty call kind of girl. Today, she seemed downright shy, despite the fact they weren't sexual strangers. Kerry sure as hell never had spent any time as a "hostess." So why the ruse?

"Because . . . ?"

"I abducted you," she blurted.

He couldn't possibly have heard that right. "As in *kidnapped*?" At her nod, incredulity jolted him. "You kidnapped me?"

"Yes."

Had he landed in some alternate universe? Was he hallucinating? "Seriously?"

Kerry winced. "I'm afraid so. I really tried to talk to you, make you understand, but you—"

Her identity—the familiar voice—snapped into place. His jaw dropped. "You! The ditz on the phone!"

"Ditz?" She anchored her hands on her luscious hips and glared at him. "Maybe I was a little emotional that day. And nervous. Okay, a lot emotional and a lot nervous. But you have a lousy phone demeanor. You don't listen. At all. I realized that to get you to actually hear me, I had to kidnap you."

Kidnap. The word sank in, as did her attitude. She was serious. Why? Given her phone calls, he was sure he didn't want to know. How long did she plan to keep him leashed like a yard dog? What did she want, a kidney to sell on the black market? No, that was an urban legend.

"Damn you!" He lunged at her.

She backed away, nearly out of the room, green eyes wide. Her pulse pounded at her throat. The little twit ought to be scared. When he got his hands on her . . .

Rafe raked his hands through his hair, cursing at the retracting restraints around his wrists. He had a job on the table. If he didn't show up soon, Standard National might withdraw their very lucrative offer and tell him to screw himself. If that happened, he would fail to make five million by age thirty, fail to trump his bastard of a father. His business could suffer. Reputation was everything, and the economy was still iffy. What if he lost all he'd worked for?

He refused to be set back all those years. He refused to fail, since he knew too well where that path led. Failures crawled into a bottle of gin and pissed everything away.

His anger spiked like Mount Saint Helens. Where the hell was he, anyway? And why? Suddenly, nausea annoyed him like a bad case of the flu, and his bladder kicked in again.

This just got worse and worse.

Rafe shifted his weight and stared at his captor. Captress? Was there such a word? Either way, he should have suspected something fishy from Kerry's behavior last night. He'd known her voice wasn't real, but he'd been too distracted to give her subterfuge much thought. A "hostess," was she? First night on the job? Yeah, right. No wonder she had seemed nervous in the limo. She'd been breaking the law!

Slowly, Kerry edged toward him again. "If you'll just let me explain—"

Snarling, he charged toward her again. Gasping and wide-eyed, Kerry stepped just beyond the reach of his bonds once more. When he came up inches short of her, Rafe cursed, something low and ugly.

"If my business and my reputation are ruined because of you, because I didn't show up for the Standard National job, I swear what I'll do to you will make murder look like a kids' game."

"You don't have to threaten me," she shouted. "I'm not going to hurt you, and I won't take much of your time."

Rafe resisted the urge to pound his fist on something. "Is this about money?"

"No," she assured. "Like I tried to tell you, I need your help. I'm not going to hurt you, if that's what you're worried about. And—and I'm so sorry about drugging and tying you up—"

"Drugging—" He hadn't even earned this lousy hangover the fun way? "No wonder I feel so crappy. We didn't have sex, did we?"

Her cheeks flushed pink again. "No."

As strange as Kerry was, part of him wished they had. Really wished it.

Had someone beat him with the stupid stick last night? She'd duped him, distracted him with that minuscule red halter and tantalizingly brief skirt in order to slip something in his drink so she could abduct him. And he, brainless bastard that he was, hadn't quite forgotten her addictive kisses. Apparently, every last one of them had been a lie. That infuriated him as much as the abduction itself. And her weird phone calls over the last few weeks. The day—hell, his life—was deteriorating faster than a Trojan virus could eat a hard drive's contents. And Kerry was responsible.

"Can I get you something? Breakfast?" Kerry sounded so earnest, as if intent on pleasing a houseguest.

"To hell with breakfast! Unlatch these and let me go."

Regret softened the oval of her face. "I can't. You're my best hope."

Her imploring tone did not mix well with the anger churning in his gut—or the fact he still needed the bathroom. "I'm your best hope for what? Your sanity? Let me give you a clue, this scheme has convinced me you don't have any."

Annoyance tightened her face. "I'm perfectly sane, just trying to keep my brother out of prison. I really tried to explain that on the phone, not that you listened."

"I was supposed to get that from your ramblings about someone having chemotherapy and getting married?" This just got stranger and stranger. "So, what? You're holding me in exchange for his freedom?"

She shook her head. "I think you can prove him innocent. I just need—"

"*What?*" Rafe took a deep breath and counted to ten. "Look, I'm not anyone's hope and I can't help you with your brother. Release these damn restraints now. I've got a job to do."

"I know, fixing the security at Standard National. That's why you're here. Mark, my brother, is the employee accused of embezzling."

Ah, now he was getting somewhere. "And you want me to doctor some files to make him look innocent?"

"Of course not! He *is* innocent. You don't have to doctor anything, just find out how he was framed."

Rafe scoffed. "What makes you so sure he isn't guilty?"

Kerry's mouth tightened, her eyes narrowing. No doubt, he'd genuinely pissed her off. Good, then. That made them even.

"Mark is too honest. He would *never*—"

"Sweetheart, you're talking about three million dollars. For that kind of cash, a lot of men would look the other way when their ethics came calling."

"Not Mark. *Never* Mark!" Kerry crossed her arms over her chest and glared. "Look, I only need a little bit of your time. I know next to nothing about computers, you only take corporate clients and charge an arm and a leg. I figured that someone with your reputation and background who would already have access to Standard National's files would be my best chance to help Mark. I mean, you hacked into the CIA at nineteen, so digging through bank records to help—"

"How did you find that out?" The event, and the subsequent deep shit he'd landed himself in, wasn't something he advertised.

"That's not important now." At his glower, she went on, "Look, I know I've done something terrible—"

"Try illegal," he ground out. "Which I'll make sure you pay for."

"I truly am sorry for all the trouble—"

"The minute I get free, I'm making sure your ass rots in jail, right along with your brother."

"Please! You are the only way I could think to save Mark. With your skill, you should be able to find out why the bank is so convinced he's guilty."

"Did the fact he probably is ever, even for a second, cross your mind?"

"Absolutely not!"

"Right," he drawled. "What are you, Pollyanna with a rap sheet?"

"I know you're angry, but I'm desperate. I just need a little help. Please."

Her big green eyes, framed by naked, golden lashes and sunshine curls, made him hesitate. If anything, his erection stiffened even more. No doubt, helping Kerry with a whole lot of things—like out of her clothes—would be no hardship.

Then, with a shake of his head, he remembered the problem. "Help you take away my freedom and commit a crime? Hell no! If I tamper with bank records like that, what the government will do to me will make your brother's prison term look like playtime in Mister Rogers' neighborhood. You're certifiable if you think I'm going to let you push me into something stupid and against the law. I'll give you a clue, sweetheart: I. Will. Not!"

Kerry stepped closer, face imploring. Lord, she smelled good, like sunshine and sea salt and vanilla.

Damn it, he'd been kidnapped by a ditz, and his libido chose now to notice how great she smelled? How back asswards was that?

Think, he demanded of himself. How could he get out of here? Rafe glanced around the room, not seeing a single weapon in sight. A quick glance down Kerry's body confirmed she wasn't concealing anything on her luscious person. He gritted his teeth. At least that added credence to her assertion that she meant him no harm. Besides, according to her, he'd been out for thirty-six hours. If that was the case, she'd had plenty of time to strangle him or carve him up or whatever a psycho might do. It made sense that she'd concocted this crazy scheme to get his assistance, rather than do him in. Maybe he just had to keep talking, play her game, in order to win his freedom. Certainly, trying to jump on her again wasn't the way to make nice.

"I'm not asking you to tamper, just to look. If you don't, my brother will go to prison. He's all I have, I love him, and I owe him for damn near raising me."

Rafe started to interrupt, but Kerry's eyes misted over. Her chin wobbled as she fought tears. Whatever he could say about her—and he could say plenty—she was genuinely distraught. He swallowed his smart-ass comment and tried to figure out what to do, how to use her distress against her.

Uncomfortable silence filled the room. Her beseeching stare morphed into a glare.

"Are you listening? I've gathered that's not one of your skills. If you don't hear anything else I say, believe that Mark would never steal from the bank. He loved that job."

She was criticizing him? She rambled like a loon and somehow that was his fault? "Forgive me if I don't take the word of a kidnapper that her brother isn't a thief!"

"Do you need to yell? I know you're angry, and I don't blame you." She shook her head, regret and a snit of temper etched on her face. "But yelling won't help."

"I think I'm pretty calm, considering the fact you're trying to screw up my life and my professional reputation." He flung his arms wide. "Not to mention that you've got me restrained like some drooling lunatic in an asylum."

Kerry went all wide-eyed and pink. What was wrong with her? A moment later, he realized that, in the heat of his speech, he'd dropped the sheet. He should cover up, he supposed, but if his nudity brought her some measure of discomfort, well, score one for him.

He cocked his head and smiled. "Or are you a dominatrix and I'm your new plaything? You got the handcuffs going on, and I see you staring . . ."

With an angry glare, Kerry turned away. "You wish. We'll talk about this when you're calm. If you still need the bathroom, it's through that door"—she pointed two feet to the right—"along with your toothbrush and toiletries. Your restraints should allow you to walk about ten feet, more than enough to go to that bathroom."

Damn it, he wanted to finish this conversation now, but Mother Nature wasn't about to wait another moment.

And neither was Kerry, he realized when she walked out the door and slammed it behind her.

* * *

NO clocks. No books. No TV. No radio, even. And damn it, no computer. Rafe hadn't been away from e-mail this long since high school. Frozen honey moved quicker than time here, wherever here was. Hours passed. He knew that because the sun was finally sinking over the spectacular ocean view his little prison provided. He had only his thoughts to keep him occupied in the brittle silence of Kerry's little dominatrix den. And they weren't happy thoughts.

Leaping from the bed, he paced to a little window, ignoring the swaying palms, the white sand, and the whisper of the ocean. He opened the panes and let in the waning golden sunshine—but he could not let himself out, not without a pair of wire cutters or the perfect-sized wrench. Short of such tools, his restraints would stay firmly in place.

Already, he'd done all he could within his bounds, made full use of the bathroom, including the decadent shower, inspected the bedroom and adjacent sitting room. He'd even tried to make his way down the long hall, only to be stopped short, just before the closet, which he'd bet held his clothes. Rafe assumed Kerry was somewhere beyond his reach, still sexy, silent, and avoiding him. Not that it mattered. Her interest in him had never been more than pretend.

Rafe wished he could say the same. Why he should sweat every time he came within five feet of the little criminal, despite his anger, was beyond him. But he couldn't deny that she made him hot.

"Kerry?"

Nothing. The woman had refined the cold shoulder into an art form, dripping with icicles.

Silence usually suited him. He lived alone. He often worked alone. Cool by him. But silence from Kerry went beyond cool, to something more like the frigid depths of the North Pole under a hundred-foot sheet of ice. Graveyards were livelier than this place. Damn it, how long would the woman just leave him here to die of boredom?

"Kerry!" he shouted.

Still nothing. Rafe cursed. She was one stubborn woman, part grudge-holder, part mule. She was here—he felt her, heard snatches of her whispered voice as she talked on the phone, heard her slamming around the kitchen.

"Damn it, woman! This is ridiculous. I have a job to do!"

More time passed in utter silence. Could have been an hour, could have been three minutes. Apparently, she didn't care for his opinion or his agitation.

Rafe flopped down on the bed again. Now what? She'd made herself clear that she wasn't going to speak to him again until he stopped shouting and listened to her inane suggestion that he help her brother, who was probably as innocent as Al Capone.

People could be so unreasonable and unbalanced. One of the reasons he preferred computers. At least when machines became unstable, you could fix or ignore them. People . . . they never worked that way. They only got more annoying.

A click and a turn of the knob announced Kerry's entrance. He looked up to find her standing in the doorway with a wary gaze. Anger bubbled at the surface . . . until an involuntary jolt of lust surged through him at the sight of her, sizzling him all the way to his toes. Apparently he responded to her from more than five feet away. Wasn't he lucky?

Despite feeling like a panting idiot, he couldn't look away. The pale innocence of her face contrasted with the bare curve of her hip, visible between her low-rise jean shorts and brief tee, looking provocative as hell. She was part angel . . . mostly devil. Holy sucker punch to the gut.

He couldn't remember the last time a woman got to him this way. Besides being sexy, Kerry was inventive and determined—as his abduction proved. Even though she'd turned those talents to incarcerating him, he had to give her credit for grit. And she was damn loyal to this brother of hers, risking her own neck to try to save his. Stupid, since the guy was probably beyond guilty, but she'd sure put herself on the line. Had he ever known anyone so devoted?

"Would you like something to eat?" she said without preamble.

"Yes, I'm starving."

"Fine."

"Fine."

"You don't have to snap at me."

Rafe glared at her. "You kidnapped me, remember? Pardon me if being the victim of a crime doesn't put me in a great mood."

Kerry rolled her eyes. "Please, I don't have a weapon, so I couldn't hurt you if I tried, and we both know it. You're not exactly a victim, more like a temporary, albeit unwilling, houseguest."

"That's like saying someone is slightly dead."

With a huff, she exited the room, returning a few minutes later with a plate of scrambled eggs and toast slathered with strawberry jam. Not exactly Sardi's, but he quickly ate the eggs, then started in on the toast when the orange sun inched closer to the horizon. Fiery rays slanted into the room—into his eyes, adding bitter to his already sour mood. Rafe cursed and squinted.

"I'll fix it."

Kerry murmured as she made her way to the window. She turned her back to him. *Perfect.* He could launch himself at her, take her down from behind. Rafe dropped the toast, preparing to strike. Once he had her under control, he'd force her to . . .

Kerry stretched for the string to close the blinds, baring the smooth nip of her waist. His plan dissolved as lust stung him, burned his brain. Did she have any idea what she did to him? Likely, yeah. And more likely she just didn't care.

"Can't quite reach," she muttered to herself, stretching higher.

More of the lean length of her leg appeared as she stepped on tiptoe. Golden curls streamed down her back and brushed the little denim shorts that cupped her derriere, tempting him. Blood left his brain and rushed directly south, where he felt his cock stiffen under the sheet. Kerry extended a bit farther for the short lead string, and her top edged up until he swore he could see the shadow of her breast on her rib cage. Sweat broke out across his chest.

Damn! He wanted her, no question. Wanted her like a starving man at an all-you-can-eat buffet. Rafe had never had a thing for crazy women, but he wanted this one naked, writhing, covered with a fine sheen of perspiration and begging him to satisfy the ache he'd created after a leisurely feast on her body. All she could think about was keeping him captive to help her brother. Did she even remember half of what they'd done together in the limo?

Why couldn't he just forget about that, and remember that she'd kidnapped him, risking his future?

Rafe told himself to tackle her and force her to release him, to stop salivating over the enemy. And he would. Any minute now.

Finally, she yanked on the right string. The blinds snapped closed and a golden-edged darkness enveloped them. Perfect for romance or great sex—or both.

She turned to face him with a tentative smile. And Rafe realized he'd let a perfectly good opportunity to overpower her and gain his freedom pass. Damn it, what was the matter with him?

"Better?" she asked.

No. He was furious with himself and hard as hell. Worse, he'd bet she used that sweet tone when talking to her brother. The thought pissed him off. How could he have such a raging erection for a woman who was so oblivious to him? A woman who'd abducted him? Appetite gone, he set the remainder of his breakfast aside.

"Peachy. I love being tied up in the dark when there's no sex involved."

"You've got quite a mouth on you. Anyone ever tell you that?"

"My dad, every day from the time I was twelve until the day I left at eighteen. I hope you weren't planning to enact some whacked-out nurturer's fantasy and lecture me about it. I don't need a mommy."

"Aren't you a bright ray of sunshine? Do you kick kittens as a hobby?" Kerry cocked her head. "I'd hoped that time to cool down would make you more civilized. I guess not."

She'd taken him from his life and job, bound him at ankle and wrist like some damned sacrifice, and she expected him to be civilized about it? "Where are you from, Planet Unrealistic?"

"I'll come back later when you've had more time to—"

"No!"

Round one to Kerry. He couldn't take any more boredom. Besides, the longer he was tied up and left alone, the less likely he could escape. And the less likely he could take her down . . . or touch her. Unfortunately for him, those two needs both ate at him.

Much as he hated it, he was going to have to rein in his temper and play her game. Otherwise, escape would be next to impossible.

Rafe sighed. "I will try not to snap at you."

Kerry nodded. She should be relieved, but watching her captive lounging, mouthwatering and half-naked, filled her with several feelings. Relief wasn't one of them. Lord, she could barely think with her gaze roving the hard width of his bronzed chest and abs that put a six-pack to shame. The sight of him awake, tousled, and tied to the bed gave her ideas she'd never before imagined and simply couldn't afford. And all the while, Rafe kept his eyes glued to her, like he remembered . . .

Kerry looked away, focusing on the French doors—anything to gather her wits so she didn't drool on the man.

"Kerry?"

That whiskey voice of his sent a shiver down her spine. She swallowed and turned back to him too eagerly. "Yes?"

"Look at me for a minute."

Her gaze flipped to his, startled by his request. He knew what looking at him did to her blood pressure. He had to know. And stupidly, she played right into his hands, staring a path from his dark eyes, down to linger on his decadent mouth, then lower again to touch those enticing pectorals that made her want to caress him all over.

Get a grip. Kerry sighed, raised a hand to the chain suspended between her collarbones. Was her hand actually trembling? She toyed with the dangling handcuff key, an increasingly nervous habit.

"Yes?" she croaked.

Rafe watched, devoured her all the while with his dark eyes. Kerry swung the key back and forth on its chain faster as a fresh rush of heat suffused her, along with a tingling his nearness inspired.

Rafe suddenly smiled, a wide, naughty grin. "I have an idea, a way for you to get what you want . . . and what I want."

His casual, out-of-nowhere suggestion snapped her attention back to business. "Pardon?"

"Well, you want me to help your brother, right?"

"Uh-huh."

"And I"—he leaned forward, the sheet dropping dangerously low on his naked hips as he fixed her with a wicked stare—"I want you."

Kerry swallowed. Heat and tingles tore through her belly. She opened her mouth to respond but no words came out. Was he serious . . . or just trying to give her a taste of her own medicine and distract her?

"I want to finish what we started in the limo," he murmured, his voice a sexy rumble.

Rafe shifted again, leaning back against the headboard and raising his arms over his head. The muscles of his rounded shoulders and biceps bulged with quiet power. The hard ridges of his pectorals tightened. Kerry's heartbeat raced.

Why had she kidnapped the most beautiful man she'd ever seen? The only one she'd ever met who could make her dang near witless without a word?

"I want to kiss your mouth over and over. I need to taste your breasts and those beaded nipples again. I'm dying to know the feel of you, hot and tight, around me."

Liquid heat flooded between her legs as her belly exploded with dangerous sensation. Just sitting there, the man rattled her. But when he talked like that, he was lethal to her common sense.

Pacing, Kerry forced herself to look away. Rafe couldn't know how much he affected her. If she'd met him any other time and place, she'd likely run, not walk, down this avenue. But as angry as he'd been all day, his sudden about-face made her more than suspicious. Touching him was just stupid. Captor and captive—that would keep their arrangement tidy and easy. Once he'd helped her prove Mark innocent, he could go.

Her gaze slid back to him. If she took him up on his startling, heart-stopping suggestion, their relationship would be anything but easy. But bottom line, he was her key to helping Mark.

"At least I think that's what I want," he said into her silence.

"Excuse me?" Had she heard him right?

He shrugged, the muscles under his golden brown skin flexing deliciously. "In the limo I was drugged. What if memory doesn't serve correctly? What if I only thought we sizzled together?"

What he said made sense . . . in a way that made her nervous. "What are you saying?"

"I need to know for sure before I agree to any sort of bargain."

"Bargain?" He was talking too fast for her hormone-charged brain. She had a feeling Rafe was scheming to pull a fast one, but he'd overheated her too much with his seductive words.

"You want to help your brother. I want you."

He was direct and completely unapologetic about that fact. Kerry wondered if women today ever swooned like they did in the historical romances she sometimes read. She hoped so, because much more of that talk and there would be a full-on faint in her near future.

"I was thinking a bargain made sense. You agree to be all mine for forty-eight hours—"

"Yours?" Her tongue wet her suddenly dry lips at the possibilities his words inspired.

He leaned again, until she could smell the tang of his woodsy, musky scent with visceral clarity, until all she had to do to touch him was lean forward, too.

His dark eyes drilled her with a carnal stare. "Mine to do with as I want, anything I want. For forty-eight hours."

Oh my, that gave her a visual, one folks would definitely have to be over seventeen to see in a theater. Kerry flushed hot from her belly to her feet and swallowed hard. "And?"

"I'll look into your brother's situation."

"That's wrong. That's extortion!" She frowned both at his suggestion and her very politically incorrect excitement.

"That's commerce." He smiled, gray eyes gleaming. "I didn't think a kidnapper would be so sensitive about morals."

Kerry shook her head. "It's a bad idea."

"Bad as in mistaken, or bad as in naughty?"

"Both."

His smile turned lascivious. When had her heart started chugging like a freight train? Why did he have to look at her as if he'd become the Big Bad Wolf and she, Little Red Riding Hood, wearing only a garter belt? For some perverse reason, despite his brazen, not-so-nice suggestion, she was oh-so-tempted.

"So what do you say? Are you game for a little audition?" he whispered, the stark white sheet caressing then exposing the bronzed ridges of his belly.

"Audition?"

"Just kissing, and a little touch here or there."

Just? Kerry didn't believe Rafe had anything that mild in mind. Lord, she felt faint.

"No sex," he clarified. "Yet."

She struggled for her next breath. "And this will prove that you want me?"

He nodded. "And if I want you as bad in ten minutes as I did in the limo, I'm all for a bargain. What do you say?"

"You'll help my brother if I agree to this insane idea."

"If I'm getting what I want, you'll get what you want."

Thoughts raced through her brain faster than headlines changed on cable news. His suggestion was unconventional at best, exploitive at worst. So why did it arouse her? She was a modern woman. Okay, so she had a few old-fashioned tendencies. Despite that, letting a man call all the shots settled about as well as static cling with her. But somehow, the idea of giving herself over to someone as sexy and dangerous as Rafe had inexplicable, undeniable appeal.

Lord, did that make her as bubble-headed as Mark's wife, Tiffany?

Kerry's gaze strayed to his hands and stubbornly stayed. What would he do to her with those? Caress down her spine, plump her breast, squeeze her nipples, probe the part of her that was growing wetter with each passing second? And if the theory about judging the size of a man's penis by his fingers was true, then Rafe's intelligence wasn't the only thing above average. Hell, she knew it was true; she'd seen every hard inch of him with her own eyes.

"The clock is ticking," he reminded her. "Where is your brother now?"

Kerry closed her eyes, reality slamming her again. "The Pinellas County Jail, awaiting trial."

"Which starts . . . ?"

She swallowed. "In less than two weeks."

"And you're waiting for what? I'm asking for a simple yes or no. It's completely your choice. If you're not interested, just say so."

The bargain should be that simple, but it was also that complicated. She bit her lip. What would he say if he learned she was a virgin? He'd think she was an undersexed freak. And not that she'd been saving herself for marriage, but the idea of trading it away pricked her with disappointment. Yeah, she was going to have to lose it sometime—hopefully soon. But bartering it to keep her brother out of prison wasn't what she'd had in mind. She wanted it to mean something to the guy she gave it to. Losing it here in Dominating Dave's Love Shack seemed as unromantic as doing it in a bathroom stall at Denny's.

And then there was Rafe himself. She didn't know him well, and allowing him anything and everything . . . well, that meant giving a lot of trust.

"What is it? You look worried. Talk to me." Gone was the wicked grin, replaced by something serious, edged with concern.

"I—I'm thinking."

Suddenly, he reached for her hand and took it in his warm grasp, thumb caressing her knuckles. "No apologies. When I see something I want, I go after it. But I know that no means no, Kerry. I'd never hurt you."

"And this isn't about revenge?"

He glanced down at the tented sheet. "Do you think I'd rather have revenge or sex?"

She met his gaze, thick with lust and anticipation. But she saw sincerity beneath it all. For some bizarre reason, gut reaction maybe, she believed him.

Helping Mark was her priority, without question. But after sleeping less than three minutes since she'd arrived at the cottage, damp sheets haunted by the remembrance of Rafe's mouth on her, Kerry could not deny that she wanted another taste of the man.

"A-all right."

"Yes?"

She nodded, feeling suddenly emboldened and shy at once. Finally, she'd know more about a man's touch than drunken pawing at the prom. But what would he expect? What should she do?

"I'll need a hand free, sweetheart."

That demand set her suspicions on alert. "No."

"Yes, or I can't touch you the way I want to. Gotta touch you. I'm dying for it."

Obviously he thought she'd been born in the last five minutes. "You're just saying that to persuade me to uncuff you."

Rafe laughed, something mirthless. "Did you fail to look down?"

Kerry looked again and found the sheet tented up by an erection that, if anything, had become more impressive. Her eyes widened. "Oh, my."

"Manipulating you would not put me in this state. I assure you, it's all about the idea of touching you. And I've got to tell, I won't be able to do that well with this thing around my wrist."

Faced with such irrefutable evidence, she felt herself caving in. Shocking that a hunk of man like Rafael Dawson would get so thoroughly aroused by her, particularly after her ranting over the phone and abducting him. Miracles never ceased.

"I'll even give you my left hand." He held it out.

She'd bet he could manage plenty of sensual devastation with that hand.

Kerry hesitated. She didn't know Rafe, shouldn't trust him. But how many choices did she have?

She looked at his hands, his fingers. Why did her body remember his touch? She felt like a radio tuned in only to his frequency. Butterflies danced in her stomach.

Damn, she needed to focus her thoughts on abduction, not seduction.

"Kerry? You want to help your brother. I want you. Yes or no?"

Rafe was right.

Slowly, she lifted the chain from her neck and thrust the little key into the hole. The cuff came unhinged with a quiet click. Quickly, she deposited the key on the far side of the sitting area, directly on the windowsill. The spot was just beyond his reach, even with the pulleys fully extended. Still, she watched him for anything suspicious.

Rafe seemed to ignore her, instead flexing his fingers. "Much better."

By his side again, Kerry sent him a lame nod. Silence fell. What now?

Then Rafe sent a stare her way—scorching with sexual promise, possessive even. The inky spikes of his lashes fanned up toward the sweep of his dark brows, framing unforgettable eyes that gleamed like brushed silver.

At that look, Kerry forgot to breathe. The butterflies had suddenly grown by leaps and bounds, either that or taken up air hockey. She wasn't scared or intimidated. Nervous, definitely. She couldn't even claim she was out of practice, since she'd never had much in the first place.

"I've thought about this all day," he murmured.

Her stomach coiled so tight, Kerry wondered if she'd ever be able to eat again.

"But," he added, "I've also had something else on my mind." The wicked grin captured his mouth again, signaling the return of the devil inside him.

"Oh?" Kerry held her breath.

"One of the things I remember most vividly about the limo ride is your sheer little black panties. I want to see you in those."

Kerry sucked in a breath. "You do?"

"Yeah," he said in a voice now sandpaper rough. "And nothing else."

Chapter Three

KERRY knew her eyes widened like a kid's at a horror movie, but she couldn't stop the reaction. "N-now?"

"Right now." His gaze consumed her.

Her stomach plummeted to her toes. Why, oh why, had she done laundry last night when she couldn't sleep? Why had she put those little panties on again this morning? No reason, except they made her feel daring, wanton, in control of her sexuality. Like the kind of woman who could handle abducting a sinfully attractive man. The kind of woman she wanted to be.

Kerry tried to drown out the voice in her head that cursed her harebrained theories. It was too late to back out. A deal was a deal. Anything and everything, he'd said. All she had to do to help Mark—and help herself to a big dish of Rafe's sex appeal—was cooperate.

He wanted her to strip for him. Scary, yes. But oddly arousing, too—wildly so. A tingling took up residence between her legs, as confidence and curiosity converged in her chest.

"All right." Her voice never wavered.

He smiled, his stare devouring and challenging her at once. "Excellent."

His cocky expression told her he didn't believe she would follow through, and normally Kerry feared he'd be right. But she'd be damned if she'd allow herself to be outdone by a man wearing nothing more than a sheet, handcuffs, and a killer smile. He could make demands, true, but she had the power. If nothing else, given her lingerie, she had the element of surprise.

Shooting him a daring stare, raking her gaze over his naked, bronzed chest, Kerry kicked aside her sandals. She hesitated only a fraction of a second before she reached for the bottom of her T-shirt.

"You're wearing them now?" His hot stare drilled into her composure.

Biting her lip, she nodded.

"Even better." Rafe smiled like a man contemplating a whole lot of sin. "Go on."

Feeling a flush crawl up her neck, Kerry grabbed the hem of her T-shirt again, eased it over her head, and flung it away. Instantly, the refrigerated air whisked over her heated skin, cascaded over her nipples. He could nearly see them, Kerry knew, peeking over the top of the sheer lace black demibra that all but presented her breasts like an offering.

The smug smile slid off Rafe's face. He stilled, gaze fixed and intent, then sat up. The sheet dropped to his hips, revealing the ripple of hard abs . . . and barely covering the rest of his remarkable equipment.

The bold appreciation in his stare made her forget the fact she stood half-naked before a virtual stranger, forget everything but him. His rapt body language replaced nerves with confidence. And unexpected liberation. The harder he stared, the more arousal tightened in her belly, heating her in every place suddenly aching for his touch. Her heart pounded like a heavy metal drummer out of control. Her panties . . . How could a man's mere stare make them so damp? Kerry had never imagined that getting naked on command would flip her switch. Apparently, it did.

"Damn, woman."

"Problem?" She feigned innocence, her self-assurance growing.

"No problem at all, babe," he whispered. "I love a woman with real thighs, instead of twigs."

Kerry felt as if she were glowing, as if she were enormously beautiful, not the woman who had grumbled about her hips while struggling into her size twelve shorts.

Suddenly, his mischievous smile returned. "The rest, please."

At his prompt, she reached for the snap at her shorts with trembling hands, their gazes fused in heat. A pool of desire swirled low in Kerry's belly, trickling between her thighs as she eased down the zipper, the rasp of the metal teeth like a crescendo in the silence punctuated by her aroused breaths. The merest slice of those black panties appeared. His pupils dilated. Oh, she had his rapt attention. Her confidence—and her arousal—soared.

High on the surge of her feminine power, Kerry slid the shorts down the curve of her hips with an exaggerated wriggle. The denim caressed her thighs, then stopped in a heap at her feet.

She wore only sheer black undergarments, which hid absolutely nothing, and a brazen smile.

Her heartbeat pounded as perspiration gathered between her breasts, thrust together by the deceptively sturdy lace bra. And Rafe's expression . . . hot, unblinking, intent. It alone made her melt. What would happen when he actually touched her?

"And that delectable little bra now . . ." he prompted, motioning with long, dark fingers.

Kerry's heart chugged faster as she reached behind her, torn between a new attack of her nerves and sharp arousal. One, two . . . The hooks came undone, the bra fell forward. By some instinct, she caught the cups in her hands, barely covering her breasts.

Rafe's chest rose and fell a bit more rapidly. He leaned forward until he came to his knees on the mattress, exposing a lean hip, the top of a muscular thigh. His gaze was now melded onto her. For a moment, Kerry closed her eyes but the stark appreciation in Rafe's stare burned its way into her brain, scorched a path from her belly to her vagina. He wanted her—no question. In a fierce, reckless way, she wanted him, too, more than she ever would've imagined possible, given the circumstances. Arousal thickened inside her, dampening her black panties. Was it having a man of his size and power at her mercy or knowing that she affected him on the most basic level that turned her on?

"Kerry?" His growl demanded she look at him.

She opened her eyes, taunted him with a come-hither stare—and dropped the bra.

Her nipples beaded under his sizzling gaze, now unbearably tight. Power, need, fear all swirled together. They played a dangerous game, and still Kerry wanted it, wanted his touch.

"Come here."

Said the spider to the fly . . .

Refusing to back down, to be afraid, Kerry put one foot in front of the other, keenly aware of the gentle bobbing of her breasts as she stepped to the edge of the bed.

"Closer," he whispered, finger crooked. "Where I can kiss you and touch every inch of your skin."

Kerry hesitated, then wondered why. She had the upper hand. The key to the handcuffs lay far across the room, his BlackBerry tucked away in a closet he couldn't reach. He did, however, have what she needed to gratify the hot ache bubbling inside her.

Drawing in a shallow breath, she sat on the edge of the bed, near his knee.

Rafe wrapped heated fingers around her arm, and her heart went into overdrive. Oh, even that touch felt like heaven. Desire coiled deep in her belly, winding even tighter when he caressed her arm up and down, thumb brushing the side swell of her breast.

"You're so soft," he murmured, moving in.

Closer he came, closer . . . He leaned toward her, his potent gaze focused on her mouth. She tingled with anticipation as she closed her eyes.

His skin felt as hot as a furnace as their chests met. His breath fanned across her cheek as he whispered, "I can't wait to devour you."

Kerry didn't think it possible, but her heart beat even more wildly, the coil in the pit of her belly pulled tighter, the need between her legs ached deeper.

Then he kissed her. Nothing gentle or tentative. Rafe conquered her mouth, not with force but persuasion. His kiss seduced her until she yearned to open to him and give him everything he wanted. The soft command of his lips over hers, his tongue luring her into the recklessly building fire between them, was too compelling to resist. He cupped her face and groaned, a sound that reverberated all through her body.

God, she was lost. Was there anything more decadent than having such a man's single-minded attention, his rampant desire? If there was, she'd never felt it.

And he had yet to do more than kiss her.

Breathing hard, Rafe lay his forehead against hers. "Lie down beside me."

His request . . . dangerous. *No, no, no,* her mind chanted. But who wanted to listen to reason at a time like this? The need he roused in her flared pure fire across her skin. No doubt, he could burn her all the way to the core if she wasn't cautious.

But damn it, she'd been cautious her whole life. No one had ever incited this hot, wild feeling in her, made her so aware of herself as a woman. No man, especially not puking Richard of prom party fame, had ever made her ache with his very first touch.

Yes! her body shouted.

A few shallow breaths later, Kerry succumbed to curiosity and the broiling flame in her belly and lay on her back, staring at him through slumberous, watchful eyes.

"You want to know what I'm going to do, don't you?" The small smile on his face teased her with possibilities.

Her heart pounded out a frantic rhythm. “Yes.”

His smile widened as he cupped her breast. His fingers warmed the sensitive skin beneath. Kerry caught her breath, then recovered . . . until he flicked a thumb across her distended nipple. Yes, she’d been touched here, touched herself even. But it was nothing like this.

Kerry gasped as he repeated the process. Her nipples tightened to hard nubs. She felt her breasts swelling, the pleasure spreading. Then he started on the other. She caught her breath.

“So sensitive. So sexy,” he whispered against her nipple.

Rafe caught both the nubs between thumbs and fingers and rolled them in his firm grip. His touch was rife with pleasure . . . and a hint of pain. The sting of it ignited her, zinging fire through her belly, straight between her legs. Lord, what else would he do to her?

As if he could read her thoughts, he reached around him to the bedside table. Puzzled, Kerry watched as he swiped the jelly off the corner of the toast she’d brought earlier. He rubbed it onto her breast, over her nipple. The cool sensation jolted her with a fresh jab of desire. Swallowing, Kerry knew what would come next, knew, and wanted it more than her next breath.

But no imagining or remembrance prepared her for his hot mouth covering her nipple, tongue swirling, teeth nipping, lips suckling, until Kerry thought she’d come out of her skin with pleasure. She gasped, thrashing on the bed as her arousal climbed to dizzying heights.

He reached around for another swipe of jelly, applying it to her other breast.

“Yes!” she shouted at the feel of his mouth on her freshly coated nipple.

In answer, he merely groaned, sending delicious vibrations through her body. She felt so tightly strung, so in need of release.

“You want to come?” he murmured into the valley between her breasts, dusting kisses on her abdomen.

Kerry hesitated, watching him. Did she answer yes, say she

wanted to come more than anything? She wanted to, but had no experience with this kind of thing. Would he think her too brazen if she admitted aloud how much she wanted an orgasm?

"Don't be afraid to say what you want," he whispered, as if he understood her hesitation. Then he laved her nipple with his tongue. "Tell me everything you want. I want to give it to you."

As his voice dropped to a wicked rasp, the fire in her belly raged hotter at his words. His teeth gently teased her nipple, his palm skimming the surface of her belly and hip. Pleasure burst and spread until she could hardly breathe.

"Yes," she admitted raggedly as he sucked her nipple into his mouth again. "But . . . but I—oh, that feels good . . ."

He chuckled. "You were saying?"

"I thought . . ." Kerry tried to gather her thoughts in the face of such enormous pleasure. "I should be auditioning for you, not the other way around."

Lifting his head for a moment, Rafe smiled with both mirth and warmth. "You are."

"What?" she breathed.

His smile turned downright sinful. "I want to know that you can come for me. Readily and loudly. Half my pleasure is in feeling yours."

Before Kerry could reply, Rafe lowered his head again, and the delicious rasp of his tongue over the sensitive curve of her breast coiled the desire inside her even tighter.

"Shouldn't I be—Lord, I can't think when . . . when you do that," she stammered.

"So don't think."

Fighting the mounting confusion and desire, Kerry thrashed her head from side to side. "I should be arousing you."

"Oh, you are. I can't wait to hear you scream." Rafe kissed a path up to her neck, nibbling until he sent shivers down her spine. "Grab the headboard."

Kerry surrendered, a thousand erotic images swirling in her

head. Before she could question his demand, he yanked on the ties of her little panties and tossed the black wisp of fabric to the ground. She was still gasping as he took another dollop of jam from the toast. Their eyes met, the jolt shaking her all the way to the soles of her feet.

With a very naughty grin, Rafe eased to the end of the bed, nudged her thighs apart with his shoulders, and dabbed the cool jam directly on her clitoris. Would he really . . . ?

"Wait, Rafe—Ohmigod!"

The sensation of his hot mouth around the sensitive button, tongue toying with it, then delving inside her . . . words couldn't describe. Kerry's brain shut down entirely. Sensation flooded in a hot, wet rush. The swelling, the moisture gathering, his talented mouth everywhere.

He eased his finger inside her, filling her with wicked delight. Seconds later, he found a sensitive spot and rubbed without pause or mercy. Tingles soon became an aching pressure, a need for more. He dragged his tongue through her wet slit in a slow, mind-blowing stroke. She cried out, arched off the bed. A storm swirled behind her navel, at the base of her spine, gathering strength as it converged everywhere he touched her. Her every muscle tensed. She forgot to breathe and held on to the iron swirls of the headboard like a life preserver in a raging sea.

"That's it," he encouraged. "Swollen breasts, flushed skin." He breathed against her slick folds, adding fuel to the fire. "So responsive."

He turned his attention back to her clitoris, dragging his tongue over the hard button with enough leisurely pressure that Kerry thought she'd rocket off the bed and into space any second.

"Rafe!" she panted.

"Come for me—now." With another swipe of his tongue, Rafe's finger found the needy spot deep inside her, applied the perfect pressure that had her gasping.

The storm clouds within Kerry clashed, creating one explosion that crested to unbelievable heights. The warm, liquid honey of satisfaction rolled through her limbs even as her back arched off the bed. Pleasure rocked her, vibrating through her body seemingly without end. She screamed. And still Rafe didn't stop, probing and tasting her as the sensations raged endlessly.

As the contractions finally subsided, Kerry lay on the bed, slick with sweat, breathing heavily. Rafe eased away, moving to her left. She was too tired to even open her eyes, much less move, but she could die a happy woman after this. Certainly nothing could be better.

"Wow," she breathed.

"Yeah, wow," he whispered in her ear, lips pressed softly to the sensitive spot below her ear. "You're so intriguing, I'm almost sorry for this."

"For what?" she asked, words slurred.

Then she felt the clamp of fabric tether her wrists together, then another tug jerking her arms up.

Alarm raced down her spine, shattering her rosy, lazy glow.

"What the—" Kerry craned her head back to see her wrists tied to the wrought-iron headboard in some complicated knot—all secured with his discarded necktie. "Rafe, what are you doing?"

He waved at her with his unrestrained hand. "Did I forget to mention that I was a Boy Scout, and a left-handed one at that?"

* * *

KERRY might look like innocence and spun sugar, but inside she was a firecracker waiting to explode. Damn, she ignited him more than his last three girlfriends put together. Rafe took a deep breath to right his pulse, then another. A quick glance down confirmed his cock at full staff . . . and now that he'd used this bargain to trick her, he figured his chances of getting inside Kerry were nil. His father was more likely to give up booze.

Besides, his mission had been securing the handcuff key and freedom, not getting a good lay. Unfortunately for him, the head to the south disagreed violently.

"This is so not according to plan. This can't—" She grunted and tugged at her bonds. "I can't . . ." The knot didn't give. "No! Untie me, you son of a bitch!"

Normally, Rafe would say he deserved that, but once Kerry had abducted him, all bets were off. Sure, she thought she had justifications, but he had work to accomplish in order to meet his five-million-dollar goal and prove to Benton Dawson III that he was a success. He didn't like being duped. It pissed him off to admit that his own libido—and his weakness for blondes with dimples—had gotten him into this mess. Worse yet, that same irresponsible libido was shouting that he wasn't done with Kerry.

His libido wasn't going to get its way.

"Not gonna happen. I think it's your turn to lie here, helpless and bound, for a while."

Apprehension slid across her rosy face. "I know you're angry with me. You have every right to be mad but . . . don't you dare hurt me!"

Her bravado in the face of her bound vulnerability intrigued him nearly as much as her beautiful breasts. Still, the thought she believed he would hurt her disturbed him.

"I'm not going to hurt you. I'm not a bully and I don't get off on a woman's pain."

"You can't go anywhere!"

"Watch me."

Rafe frowned as he crossed the room and stretched to retrieve the handcuff key he'd seen her set there earlier. No matter how he tugged and pulled, he was two inches too short to reach that damned windowsill.

"I put the key there because you can't get to it," Kerry pointed out, a hint of smugness in her voice.

Nope, he wasn't giving up. There had to be some way . . . *any* way.

By sitting on his ass and reaching with his toes, he came closer, but still no cigar. Behind him, he heard Kerry sigh in relief. Damn her!

Gaze circling the room, Rafe looked for a hanger, a pen. Something long and sturdy would do the trick. He saw nothing to fit that description except his dick, still standing straight and tall and looking for action. Too bad it didn't qualify.

Finally, he resorted to faint hope and the skills he'd picked up playing high school baseball. Grabbing one of his shoes from the floor, Rafe took aim at the necklace and tossed it. One of his black Italian wingtips made a loud *whack* as it hit the window. It thudded down on the hardwood floor.

Rafe smiled. The key fell that final two inches closer. He reached until he grasped it in his palm.

Kerry gasped. "Ohmigod . . . No! You're leaving, aren't you? You can't leave!"

Quickly, Rafe unlatched Kerry's necklace, setting the chain aside, then made quick work of his remaining shackle. It gave way with the sound of a metal crunch. He let it retract all the way back to the bed's special compartments and smiled.

"Sure I can. Are my clothes in the closet?"

"Someone will come looking for me."

"Good, then I won't have to worry about you getting free after I'm gone."

"What about our bargain?" she demanded. "Forty-eight hours and all that?"

Rafe shrugged. He hadn't really meant that. He would have promised her a round-trip ticket to Fiji if he'd thought that would have lured her close enough to beat her at her own bondage game. Despite the fact his scheme had enabled him to touch Kerry—something he'd damn near been dying to do—bartering his services for sex hadn't been his plan. But Kerry's voice induced him to look at her.

Big mistake. She was amazing naked and bound. Soft, slender neck, round breasts that fit his palms so perfectly, hard berry nipples. He held in a groan, but even as he did, her body drew his eyes down over her gently rounded abdomen, the flare of a woman's hips, to the downy pale thatch that protected the slick confection of her core.

"Please," she called. "You have every right to be mad at me. I should not have kidnapped you—"

"That's right," he growled. "I told you to leave me alone over the phone for a reason."

"But I need your help. No one will listen to me. Not the police, not Mark's boss. I tried to hire a detective, but I couldn't afford one on a waitress's pay. I didn't know what else to do. I couldn't just stand around while my brother went to prison."

Her voice trembled. Rafe jerked his gaze back to her face. She didn't cry. But the resolution hardening her face, shining from her mossy green eyes, shocked him. Even naked and at a virtual stranger's mercy, Kerry didn't think of herself. She didn't think anything of her pride. Instead, her every thought was for the brother she loved. Kerry had risked her future, her safety, even wagered her body to help Mark.

Again, the depth of her caring and loyalty stunned him. He'd never known anyone that steadfast. Certainly, he'd always known if his father had to choose between booze and paying attention to his only son . . . well, Dad's hangover would attest to his choice. Either Kerry was very selfless or very stupid. Rafe wanted to be angry with her for her scheme. He wanted to want revenge. But he didn't. The amazingly loyal, sexy woman, even if she had her ditzy moments, really intrigued him on a level he couldn't remember experiencing before.

"I'll give you forty-eight hours, anything you want." Kerry looked him straight in the eyes. She swallowed, but in no other way did she betray any nervousness. "Just don't leave yet. Hear me out."

Rafe sucked in a sharp breath as he hardened yet more. So fucking tempting, the idea of taking complete control of her body here, in the bed built by someone with a wide dominant streak . . . but he had a job to do. Standard National expected him for a preliminary meeting.

He shook his head, dropping his gaze from her pleading stare, and retrieved her clothes from the floor.

Without waiting for her reaction, he turned toward the closet to set her clothes out of reach and find his own. But her desperation filled the air, and guilt prickled down his spine. Guilt, of all things! Damn it, he didn't owe Kerry a thing. He'd given her thousands of dollars' worth of his critical time, as well as a hearty orgasm. Why should he feel anything but sure that his time to exit had come?

In the closet, he found his boxer-briefs folded on top of a built-in dresser. He quickly donned them over his still raging erection, then found his suit pants neatly hung and his shirt freshly pressed. A quick sniff told him Kerry had washed it as well. A captress who doubled as laundry service? Wow, she'd done a better job than his five-dollar-per-shirt dry cleaners.

"Rafe?" she called.

He heard her thrashing against her bonds, cursing softly under her breath, but he didn't answer. Getting out of here was top priority, before he lost this lucrative job with Standard National and his shot at reaching the five-million-dollar mark prior to his birthday . . . before he succumbed to the odd urge to help her, or gave in to his desire to know every inch of her body in every way.

Instead, he reached into his suit coat. His BlackBerry still rested in one pocket. Quickly, he checked for messages. One from a former client asking for advice, two messages from his assistant, Regina, and one from an old girlfriend he vaguely recalled had labeled him an antisocial, computer-centric great lay. Not to mention three messages from Mr. Smikins at Standard National Bank wondering why he hadn't appeared for their lunch meeting. At that, Rafe swore long and hard. Damn Kerry and her scheme to save her likely worthless brother.

He pounded the bank's number into his phone's keypad, cursing himself under his breath. A woman kidnapping him and keeping him from business should royally piss him off. The hell of it was, he couldn't muster much more than a sting of annoyance. As the reality of her bondage had occurred to her, in the face of his possible retribution, she hadn't asked once for mercy for herself. Nope, she'd thought only of her brother. God, the prick better deserve such loyalty.

Finally, a recording informed him the branch had closed at 4 P.M. and would be open at 9 A.M. on Monday. Monday? *Today was Saturday?* The date on his BlackBerry said so. Shit, he really had been out for thirty-six hours.

At the prompt, he entered Smikins's extension. At the tone, Rafe left the branch manager a message, one full of crappy lies about being sick and missing his plane. Ending the call with a grimace, Rafe sighed. Why wasn't he calling the police? Why hadn't he told Smikins that the sister of their former employee-turned-thief had abducted him?

He couldn't—not yet. Hell, he wasn't any sort of hero. But the truth couldn't be ignored: Kerry already had plenty of trouble.

For some damn reason, he just couldn't make himself turn her in and add to her mounting difficulties. Maybe because once upon a time, someone had given him a second chance and saved him from the tank when he'd hacked into the CIA. That had turned his entire life around. Maybe because the thought that he might actually be refusing to prevent an innocent man from going to prison didn't rest well with him. Hell, most likely it was because it was Saturday evening, and Smikins wouldn't be available for a while . . . and Kerry could be his until then.

Everything south of his waistline approved of the plan. No doubt, he was in deep.

"Anything I want, is that what you said?" he asked softly, hungry stare raking her as he returned to the bedroom.

She swallowed hard and met his stare. "If you'll help my brother, then yes, anything."

Agreeing to this probably didn't make him a nice guy. Rafe smiled. So sue him. How often did an average guy get a chance to be both noble and get laid—and by a woman who sizzled and burned him when they touched?

Whoa! His mind reeled. What the hell was he thinking? Or more to the point, which head was doing it?

"I've got to be honest, Kerry. I can only look into his situation. I can't change anything. If your brother has truly been framed, I can help you find evidence, but I won't fabricate any. Tampering with files could send me to prison for a long, long time."

The smile that broke out across her face, the hope that jumped into her eyes, settled someplace in his chest. She brightened like a Christmas tree in the snow, all glowing and wondrous. Even though she wore not a shred of makeup, her red-rimmed eyes bespoke an utter lack of sleep, and her hair tumbled across one shoulder in a wild fall, Rafe couldn't remember ever seeing a more beautiful woman than Kerry when she smiled. He also couldn't deny that he liked being the cause of her happiness.

"You won't have to fabricate anything, I promise. Once you see the facts of the case, you'll know he's been set up and help me find a way to prove it to the police." She gazed into his eyes, held his stare for a long moment. "I knew you could do it. That's why I picked you. I swear you won't be sorry. Mark's a good cause."

Rafe doubted that, but now wasn't the time to argue. "Fine. Before we agree to anything, I want you to be very clear on what I'm saying." He moved closer, sat on the edge of the bed . . . and couldn't keep his hands to himself. "Anything, Kerry." He reached up, fingers tracing the side swell of her breast, drifting under to cup her, rising to tease her nipple. "Or maybe I should say everything." He held her gaze with the force of his. "Before this is over, I'll have you under me, legs spread wide. I'll want you on top, riding me hard. I'll want your sweet mouth all over me. I'll take you from behind, from the side, standing up. I'll fuck you indoors, outdoors, with toys and without. I'll see you bound, wanton and screaming my name. I swear I'll never hurt you, but I want total control. That means trusting me, which I know won't come easy, but if you can't handle that, we don't have any business making this arrangement."

Kerry's face changed with his every word. Her eyes widened, her face flushed from delicate pink to a deep rose. And her pulse, pounding faster—*gong, gong, gong*—at the base of her throat.

She said nothing for what seemed eons. He'd bet her feet were getting colder by the nanosecond. Likely, she would back down. Part of Rafe knew it would be the sane thing for both of them. They could part ways and pretend this bizarre incident had never taken place. Still, he hoped like hell she didn't refuse. For reasons Rafe didn't want to examine too closely, he didn't think he could let go of Kerry without having her at least once.

"What do you say, Kerry?"

Chapter Four

BREATH held, Rafe remained still as Kerry's gaze skated across his face, down his bare chest, to the hard-as-a-hammer erection tenting his boxer-briefs.

"Do you need more time to think about it?" He gritted his teeth against the searing arousal and smoothed a lock of long, sunny hair away from her face. "Take it if you need it. I want you to be really sure before you answer."

Cheeks flushed, she looked away. "No."

Unexpected disappointment gouged Rafe in the gut. His first impression of Kerry had made him suspect she was psycho, and he should be cool with the fact she didn't want to have forty-eight hours of wild, steamy, anything goes, burn-you-to-your-toes sex. Rafe sighed. Problem was, he wanted it bad—with her. The feeling was illogical and inexplicable, but real.

Still, her decision was probably smart. Who really bedded down with a virtual stranger to save their brother's ass? It was above and beyond the call of familial duty. But he didn't like her refusal. Their chemistry sizzled, and he had an instinct that sex with Kerry would blow them both away.

"I don't need to think," she murmured into the silence, raising soft green eyes brimming with hot curiosity up to him. "I understand what you're saying. And I agree. To everything."

She said yes? Yes! Lust slammed his gut, sizzling so strongly that for a moment, he couldn't draw a breath. Instantly, his imagination took over, incorporating all the interesting gadgets and toys he'd discovered while trying to break free of the bed Kerry now occupied. Yeah, those little goodies might come in handy. But the real thrill of their agreement would be her body—soft, sweet, curved in the right places. He could hardly wait.

"Say something." Kerry's voice broke on the request.

She nibbled nervously on her bottom lip, shifted her green eyes away.

The pang of softness that hit him square in the chest at her vulnerability should have seemed really odd, considering his compulsion to climb between her thighs. It should have seemed as weird as listening to Bob Marley at the Louvre or eating jalapeños on chocolate ice cream.

With Kerry, it seemed normal.

Aware of the darkness that had overcome the cottage with the sunset, Rafe flipped on the small lamp beside the bed. Soft yellow light cast a halo over Kerry. The tumble of her sunshine curls and her soft, swollen mouth urged gentleness with the same intensity that her naked, bound body inspired a pounding need to fuck her.

"Seriously," he said in between harsh breaths. "Yes? You're sure?"

She hesitated a mere instant. "Yes."

Her soft assurance nearly did him in. It wasn't smart to be so wrapped up in this game, he knew, but at the moment, he and his dick of steel didn't give a shit.

A smile stole across his mouth as he took her face in his hands. "I'm going to do my best to make you one satisfied woman."

Kerry gave him a shaky nod as he lay beside her and covered

half of her bare body with his chest. Heat fused their skin. She singed him, no question. An instant later, he took possession of her mouth, stealing inside. Oh, she tasted honey-sweet, her lips pliant and warm. Addicting.

The little catch of her breath ringing in his ears, he made another thorough sweep inside with his tongue. Forget ambrosia, Kerry was like the creamiest, richest latte ever.

Every red-blooded cell in his body leapt for joy that she'd said yes. *But only to help her brother,* reminded the nasty voice in his head. *Not because she wants you.*

Rafe broke off the kiss and swallowed that bitter reality. Looming above her, breathing hard, he clutched her hip with greedy fingers.

Okay, her agreement might be about saving her sorry-ass brother now, but he'd find a way to change that. Her verbal yes wasn't the green light he wanted; only her body could give him the go-ahead. It was up to him to earn her yes, and to give her such blinding pleasure that she'd never regret agreeing to this bargain.

Rafe rose and sidestepped to the headboard. Just above Kerry's right shoulder, he found the first handcuff he sought—the one that had bound him less than twenty minutes ago. He released her wrists from the necktie binding them, then substituted the cuffs around one delicate wrist with a satisfying click. He repeated the process on her other.

"What are you doing?"

"You gave me total control, remember?"

Kerry pursed her rosy mouth closed with a jerky nod. She all but shook with nerves. "Okay, wh—what do you want?"

"Such unbridled enthusiasm," he teased. "Damn, that gets me hot."

She bit her lip, then smiled. "Sorry. I'm nervous."

"I know." He caressed the side of her face. "At this point, you're not sure if I'm your brother's savior or some sex-crazed creep. Hell, I'm probably both. But we're going to be fine. It's going to be good, I promise. Now kiss me."

Kerry propped herself up on her elbows, inching closer to him. Under his boxer-briefs, his cock throbbed in rhythm to his heartbeat. He burned to take her now, take her later, again and again.

Finally, she touched her mouth to his gently, tentatively. Rafe fought not to dominate the kiss, forced patience to see where she would take it. Soft, so soft, like butterfly wings—there, but barely. Damn, he wanted, needed, more. He was losing his freaking mind.

"Harder. Open your mouth to me," he whispered against her lips.

Instantly, she complied, her mouth under his again, now with more pressure. She parted her lips. Still, Rafe waited to see what she wanted, what she might do.

Then Kerry's instincts seemed to take over. She tilted her head, fused their lips together in a wet kiss, her tongue teasing his bottom lip.

Rafe groaned. Her kiss didn't demand or submit. It invited, lured, teased with enough of her taste to whet his appetite, but not enough to satisfy.

He tensed, trying to hold back his urge to take control. He wanted more, so much more. *Patience,* he willed himself.

Soon, she rewarded him by opening fully to him, her tongue shyly swirling around his before retreating, as if tempting him to follow. He resisted—barely. Kerry arched to him, her naked breasts enticing against his chest. And those catchy little moans in the back of her throat as he raised a hand to her nape, took the rubber band from her hair, and filtered his fingers through the shining golden curls . . . those moans sent a hot chill of need shivering up his spine.

He gave in to the urge to nibble on the bee-stung fullness of her bottom lip, plunder through her mouth as if he could lap up all of her sweetness in one kiss.

Using the give in the cuffs' pulleys, she clutched his shoulders and deepened the kiss even more, the pressure almost rough now. Rafe felt sure he'd lose his mind at any moment.

But he couldn't.

Though Kerry's aptitude for passion in this situation was certainly exceeding his expectations, by not jumping on her like an out-of-control teenager, he would put her at ease, establish a bit of trust.

His plan was working . . . until she hooked one calf around his thigh and ground her hips against his. At that point, he admitted the effort to be slow and patient was damn near killing him.

Rafe tried to resist her nonverbal invitation, but his palm itched to cover her breasts, toy with the nipples he felt swelling, hardening against his chest. Impulse won out.

With a dip of his head, Rafe lowered his mouth to her neck. He nibbled on the sensitive joining with her shoulder. She rewarded him with a shiver.

"I can't wait to get inside you," he whispered against her skin. "It's going to be incredible."

In response, Kerry threaded her fingers through his hair, then began a trek lower. She caressed his nape, slid a soft palm down the length of his back, curved a warm hand over his ass.

"This feels so good," she whispered between kisses. "I never knew . . . It's like I'm burning up all over."

Kerry didn't say more; she didn't have to. The fact she'd never felt this way before made his internal temperature skyrocket.

Rafe knew their kind of sizzling chemistry came along as often as snow in Tampa. That he was so hot over such an unusual woman surprised him, but what the hell.

Arching against him, Kerry's breath hitched. He dipped his head lower still, caught one swelling nipple in between his lips. He planned to toy with it. Lips and tongue alternating, no suction yet. But once that hard, pink little bead met his lips, all his plans went to hell.

Rafe inhaled her, capturing her nipple deep in his mouth, sucking, flicking her with his tongue, rolling the other bud between his fingers. Those catching noises in her throat became full-blown moans.

"Rafe!" she cried as she wriggled against him.

Damn, she felt good. Drowning in lust took on a whole new meaning when Kerry was the woman in the center of the pool. Patience was losing out—fast.

Scooping one hand under her back, Rafe shifted her until his cock pressed against her core. Even through his boxer-briefs, he felt her damp heat. Dear God, what the woman did to his imagination, to his body, shocked him. The threads of his control . . . Rafe felt them unraveling.

Kerry kissed her way down his jaw to nibble on his neck. It was like adding gasoline to a blaze. She nipped softly at him with gentle bites, then smoothed over his sensitive skin with open-mouthed kisses. She repeated the process on his shoulder and chest, inching down his body, sliding her soft skin across him.

Without warning, she took his nipple in the hot cavern of her mouth. He groaned, realizing quickly what little control he possessed around Kerry was just about exhausted. The only urge he had was to rip away the damn underwear confining him and set a world record for thrusting inside her.

It isn't a race, he reminded himself. *Think baseball stats, HTML tags, reruns of* I Love Lucy . . . *anything!*

The hungry animal in him wouldn't focus on anything but getting inside Kerry in the next five seconds—and he knew that slamming into her without any preliminaries, then lasting thirty seconds, wasn't going to earn him any brownie points.

Rafe drew in a harsh breath, then another. He swore softly. His cock was swollen, hard to the point of pain. For some odd reason, he'd wanted his zany abductor the first time he saw her, and the urge to touch, taste, possess her, now, seized him mercilessly. If he didn't take the edge off this need, he wouldn't have the control to make it last, to give her the pleasure necessary to make her scream his name.

Had he ever wanted a woman this much? Must be the unusual circumstances. Clearly, the bargain got him hotter than he'd anticipated.

"Kerry," he got out between harsh breaths. "Kerry."

Slowly, she lifted her mouth from his throbbing nipple and looked at him through dreamy, dilated eyes. Her flushed cheeks and swollen mouth only tightened the knot of desire in his gut. Instinctively, he pressed his cloth-clad erection into the folds between her legs. Telltale tingles brewed at the base of his spine.

"I want to make this good for you, but there's no way I'm going to last," he confessed. "I want you too much."

She nodded. The lust clouding her green eyes only made him crazier. Definitely time to act—now.

With a roll, Rafe flipped their positions, his back now on the mattress, Kerry lying on her side at his left. An impatient flick of his wrist later, his boxer-briefs found a new home on the floor. He took her hand in his and kissed her palm. Then, using the give in the pulleys tethering her wrists, he drew her fingers down to his cock.

Quickly, she gripped him in her small hands. He groaned at the feel of her tentative grip. Somewhere in his thick haze of desire, he heard her gasp. To his delight, she didn't stay idle. Those clever fingers caressed his length, first with a light brush, a tease. Up, then slowly down. Her thumb swiped the top of the swollen purple head.

Rafe gritted his teeth. "That touch of yours is driving me to the brink of sanity."

"I like the thought of making you insane."

Another one of her sweet strokes brought him perilously close to the edge. When he wasn't so out of his mind with lust, he'd worry about his lack of control. "You've about convinced me that sanity is overrated."

Her throaty laugh had him digging his heels, taking deep breaths—anything to draw out the pleasure, make it last. The sight of her bare breasts only added to her considerable appeal and his uncharacteristic lapse in control.

Then she squeezed her hand around him in a firm grip and began to stroke.

Seconds later, Rafe knew Kerry's deft touch would be the death of him. If he was going to go . . . well, he wanted to go in style. "I want your mouth on me."

She stilled for a moment. He saw a hint of wariness in her eyes, along with sizzling arousal and more of that curiosity that ramped up his blood pressure.

She dropped her gaze to his cock, then lifted it back to his face. "You—you'll have to tell me what, you know, you like. I've never . . . done this."

"Really?" Had all her past boyfriends been eunuchs? The thought of being the first man inside her mouth made him wild.

Shyly, she nodded. "If I do something wrong, you'll tell me?"

Wrong? At this point, as long as she didn't try to pull a Lorena Bobbit with her teeth, she was going to be perfect.

"Yeah." Rafe barely recognized the scratchy voice as his own.

How the hell had a woman as lush and gorgeous as Kerry gone her whole adult life without knowing this intimacy? Which led him to wonder . . .

"Has any other lover performed orally on you?"

She flushed a darker shade of pink. "No."

Another first. Amazing. Arousing. What other delights could he show her? The visions in his head were plentiful and definitely not fit for youngsters or those with heart conditions.

"There will be lots more of that," he promised. "Later."

A tremulous smile tilted up the corners of her mouth. "Guess I know what you want now."

"God, I hope so."

"You'll tell me, right?"

"Absolu—ahhh." The silken heat of her mouth slid over the head of his penis, her tongue hugging the underside. With a delicate swirl, she covered him from base to swollen purple head. Filtering his fingers through the thick tangle of her curls, Rafe moved the pale curtain aside and anchored his hand on her nape to watch the erotic sight of her sampling his cock.

White-hot sensations jolted through his gut. They spread at the incredible suction of her mouth rising up his length. "Yes."

Kerry repeated the process, once, twice, so fucking slow he felt each swipe of her tongue, every inch of her hot mouth. Ah, heaven.

Soon, she raised one bound hand, pulleys extending, to grip his base. With the other hand, she traced an intricate pattern inside his thighs, in the crease between his leg and groin. Between the sight of her submissive pose and the feel of her hot mouth, he couldn't hold back the moan rumbling from his chest. She gave a little answering sound that vibrated down his cock. Could a man die of pleasure? If he wasn't careful, Kerry would help him prove that possible.

Rafe barely had the time to note that the rest of the blood in his body had rushed into his erection before his entire body tensed. Tingles danced up and down his spine. Just another heartbeat, another breath . . . He gripped the sheet in one tight fist, Kerry's hair in the other—and felt his world explode.

Pleasure drenched every crevice of his body, swirling like a heavy liquor in his limbs, robbing him of breath, of thought. Not only was he about to die, he was dying happy.

Wow. If that blow job had been all about saving her brother and nothing else, he admired Kerry's gusto. For an amateur, she'd certainly handled it all like a pro. But given the fact her gorgeous green eyes looked to him for approval, he knew better. Another warm pang took up residence in his chest.

Blow jobs didn't usually make him feel warm and fuzzy. Relaxed and mellow, yes. Prepped him for round two—every time. Again, Kerry proved she affected him in some odd way that defied the logical universe as he knew it. Kind of like the woman herself.

His first urge was to bring her close, hold her against him.

"At the risk of sounding clichéd," she murmured, "was it good for you?"

Rafe couldn't hold in his laugh. A long, loud one, which earned him a half-serious punch in the stomach.

Kerry frowned and withdrew to the other side of the bed. "Hey! Be nice."

"Nice isn't something I'm noted for," he admitted and pulled her close against him, her side tucked under his arm, her body nestled against his. This felt weirdly right.

But she struggled in his grip, reaching for the sheet to cover herself. "You know what? I don't care if it was good. I don't care if I improve. I'm not going to be laughed at—"

He kicked the sheet away and framed her round cheeks in his hands. "You were wonderful. I'm not laughing at you. Well, I'm laughing at your line. I mean, you have to ask yourself, did I moan? Yes. Did I last long? No. Did I come like there's no tomorrow? Oh, yeah. Mission accomplished, I swear."

Kerry smiled and relaxed. "Good. Will you move your legs so I can have the sheet?"

"Cold?"

"No." A delicate flush spread across her face. "I just don't lounge naked in front of guys."

She did now. "If you're mine for forty-eight hours, I want you naked. No sheet."

With a less than graceful sigh, Kerry accepted his edict. "You're bossy, you know that?"

"Yeah."

"Maybe I should ask you to cover up, then."

"Not in the mood," he quipped. "It would only be a waste of time when I decide I want you again."

"Oh, what about when I want you? I mean, my sister-in-law told me oral sex was awful. But that was fun. I enjoyed having you in the palm of my hand—literally."

"Liked the power, huh? The control."

Kerry flushed and flashed him a smile that was half-coquette, half-sin. "Did I like knowing I could turn Mr. Big and Bad into Play-Doh? Sure."

“Don’t get used to it,” he warned. “I have ways of making you scream my name.”

She laughed and curled up against him, as if she belonged there and nowhere else. Damn if she didn’t feel that way to him, too. God, had someone dropped him into the Twilight Zone? What was next, Marilyn Manson as President? He never liked to “cuddle” afterward. Cuddling was for kids with teddy bears.

But Kerry was . . . Kerry. She was as sunshiny as her hair. Somehow she kept him guessing, got him laughing—things he hadn’t done with a woman in a long time. Maybe not ever. It seemed impossible that he was actually liking the nutcase who’d abducted him.

“We’ll see,” she breathed against his chest. “In the meantime, I might call Tiffany and tell her she’s wrong about oral sex. Of course, since she’s married to my brother, having that conversation with her makes me think of her doing it to Mark, then I get grossed out.”

Rafe frowned at that logic. “If your brother is married, don’t you think he’s having sex?”

“I just didn’t want to think about it. *Eeewww!* That’s like imagining grandparents going at it.”

Again, he laughed. “I never thought of it quite like that, but okay, I get your point.”

“Thank you. Can we drop the whole Mark-having-sex thing?”

“You brought it up.”

Kerry paused, clearly thinking. “Oh, I did. Sorry. It’s forgotten.”

“Good . . . I guess.”

Silence followed. Rafe found himself smiling as he stroked her bare back and enjoyed the smooth line of her spine, the swell of her buttocks under his palm. Kerry the kidnapper was proving to be one interesting woman.

“Why did you agree to forty-eight hours of sex just to save your brother?” Rafe couldn’t hold back the question. “Why not wait and see how the trial goes first?”

“You’re not exactly a hardship,” she admitted with a smile.

“Even so.” He had to smile at her backhanded compliment.

"Kidnapping me, agreeing to have sex with me; they're big steps to help someone you don't know for sure a jury will find guilty."

Kerry shook her head. "He has no one on his side. The investigator has decided he's found his man. The public defender is overworked and, I think, out of his league. Mark had plenty of access to the money and ample motive. His wife is overwrought and not equipped for the stress. He has no one to help him except me, so I'm going to do what I can. I owe him that."

"Owe him how? Because you share blood?"

"He practically raised me. Our dad died in a car accident when I was two. So Mark, my mom, and I were tight. When I was little, we lived in this teeny apartment near the mall. Not the best neighborhood, but all Mom could afford." Kerry paused, swallowed. "When I was eleven, I was really sick; high temperature, sore throat, the works. My mom ran to the corner convenience store at, like, midnight to get me some cough syrup."

She got quiet, teared up. Rafe had a bad feeling he knew where this story was going.

"Asshole with a gun?" he asked gently.

Kerry nodded. "The robbery was in progress. He shot her twice, and that was it. Her life was over. I remember thinking at her funeral that mine was, too. I still miss her so much."

Rafe understood. The words clogged in his throat, so he just kept stroking her back, offering silent comfort.

After a sniffle, she went on. "The foster system got ahold of us after that. At least they kept us together. Mark sheltered me from everything bad. He helped me with homework, protected me from school bullies who threatened me, beat up guys who thought I was an easy target. I still remember him trying to explain my period to me when he barely understood it." Her shimmer of a smile brimmed with affection. "He taught me physics, how to play football. Mark did his best to be both a mom and dad, even though he's only four years older.

"When he turned nineteen, he scraped together some money

and petitioned the courts for custody. At the time, he was working for a bank, so he got custody. It was so great to be out of the system, away from people who never let you forget for an instant that the only reason you lived in their house was because the state paid them."

Without thought, Rafe tightened his arms around her. She'd had a tough childhood, and her brother, guilty or not, clearly meant a lot to her.

"You and Mark are real close, it sounds like."

"Mark is all the family I have left. I'd do anything to help him."

"I got that." He caressed her shoulder. "So he took you in when you were fifteen, and things have been peaceful until recently?"

"I wish." Using the cuffs' retractable feature, Kerry sat up and curled her knees up to her chest, securing them to her with her arms. "Just before I turned seventeen, Mark was diagnosed with an advanced form of melanoma. He lost his job because he missed so much work. That meant he lost his insurance, too. I took afternoon and weekend jobs to pay rent, buy food, pay bills. It wasn't enough, not even close. I felt like I let him down."

Rafe grasped her face between his hands, forcing her to look at him. "You were a kid. You couldn't have done more."

She shrugged. "When Mark recovered from cancer two years ago, I thought he finally had a second chance at life. He was beginning to pay off his medical bills, though it's going to take years. I'm helping him as best I can. And he married Tiffany six months ago. She makes my neighbor's poodle look like Einstein, but Mark loves her, I guess. His life should finally be happy. Instead, he's facing this crap." She shook her head. "It just not fair. He sacrificed so much to see me happy. Once, he even sold the stamp collection he'd had since he was really little to buy me a birthday present. He's a great person, not a thief."

If even half of what Kerry said was true, Mark was a hell of a guy. It was possible she was deluded. Often family members really didn't know as much about their loved ones as they imagined. But as crazy as Kerry could be, she didn't strike him as stupid.

In fact, she struck him as brave and unbelievably loyal. What kind of courage did it take for a woman to break the law and abduct a guy half her size just to help a loved one?

Oh, he still wasn't pleased at being drugged, dragged, and bound, lied to and manipulated. The edge of anger still festered in his gut, though a great orgasm had taken the bite out of his fury. Rafe couldn't deny, though, that he understood Kerry's reasoning a whole lot better now.

"Mark deserves a fresh start—not to be in prison with a hairy boyfriend named Bubba! I can't afford to hire a private investigator, and the FBI won't help. Everything Mark's boss uncovers makes him look that much worse. But I know they're wrong. My brother is innocent."

"Why didn't you say any of this over the phone? You might have saved us a lot of trouble."

"I was nervous and emotional. I didn't know you. Your assistant all but read me the riot act when I tried to talk to her. Besides, would you really have listened and helped?"

Rafe hesitated, then admitted, "Probably not."

Kerry shot him an I-told-you-so glance.

He'd been so driven for so many years to prove his success and abilities, both to himself and his old man. Listening to Kerry babbling over the phone about sibling love and loyalty would never have registered. Not until he met her, started to understand her.

"So," he began, "I'm listening now. Tell me about your brother's case. I need dates, events, and the FBI's theory. If you have any of the reports, that would really help."

Thank you, she mouthed, her green eyes luminous and soft.

Just one look and Rafe felt something inside him melt like plastic under a blowtorch. He held Kerry closer. This really meant a lot to her, and for the great sex he knew they would have, the few hours of his time it would take to look into Mark's situation was nothing. He'd definitely negotiated the better part of the deal. Kerry's agreement to be available to him in any and every way far surpassed the sacrifice he would make in rummaging through a few files. Despite his abduction, which in his book put a lot of points in his favor, maybe this deal was unfair. Should Kerry really have to scrape together the trust to open her body to any and all invasions he could think of just to help her brother?

His mind quickly approached an answer his body didn't like.

"In the closet in the hall is a built-in dresser. In the top drawer, I have a file of everything you need," Kerry indicated, breaking into his thoughts.

After a quick jaunt down the hall and into the closet, Rafe found exactly what he was looking for. Kerry kept all the papers together . . . the arrest record, police reports, copies of transaction evidence from the bank.

"I'll start this tonight."

Swallowing, she nodded, then leaned in to kiss him on the cheek. "I don't have to tell you how much this means to me."

"No." The picture was sharper than the fifty-two-inch plasma TV he'd bought last month. "I get what you're saying."

Electronic music suddenly filled the air. The theme from *Harry Potter*? What the . . .

"Oh, my phone. It's in the front room. I need that." She held up her manacled wrists.

He wasn't nearly ready to release her. "Let it go to voice mail."

"It's Jason. If I don't answer—oh, just go get it, please."

Rafe sighed and launched himself out of the bed, pulling on his boxer-briefs as the second ring began. Why was he doing this? And who in the hell was Jason?

Maybe she did have a boyfriend . . .

Sitting on the pale wood of the coffee table, her phone chirped the mysterious music once more. Rafe picked it up and walked back to the bedroom, handing it to Kerry.

Answering the phone, she nodded at him. "Hi, Jason."

"What took so long? Are you okay?" Rafe heard the other man say.

"Fine. Great. Phone was in the other room."

"Oh." Jason hesitated. "Everything all right?"

"Everything is fine. Wonderful, in fact."

"Yeah, you sound pleased. What's going on? Does that mean Paul Bunyan is less crabby today?"

Paul Bunyan? Rafe frowned at Kerry. She ignored him.

"We're . . . coming to an understanding," she hedged.

"Really? Are you sure, sweetheart? If you need my help, I'm there for you. You know that."

Sweetheart? Sounded like boyfriend material. Irritation clamped Rafe's gut. One blow job did not a relationship make, and he knew it. But damn it, for the next forty-something hours Kerry was supposed to be his, fairness or lack thereof aside. Rafe didn't give a shit if this guy had any prior claim. In fact, if Jason was stupid enough to allow the woman he liked/loved/wanted to bone within five feet of another guy, especially a naked stranger trapped in a remote cottage . . . well, Rafe would be happy to make sure ol' Jason learned a hard lesson. Rafe also planned to make sure that "Sweetheart" didn't forget him anytime soon.

Kerry smiled into the phone, annoying him even more. "I'm okay, really. Rafe is going to help."

"Just like that? Did he finally listen to reason?"

She hesitated, flicking an uncertain gaze his way. "We understand each other now."

"What does that mean?" Jason sounded unconvinced. "I know the guy gave you a really hard time both before and after he woke. He's not scaring you, coming on too strong? Maybe I should come out there."

"Thanks for your concern, but it's not necessary. We've just about got everything worked out. The plan worked perfectly after all."

"You're sure? I can be there in forty-five minutes—"

Done listening to Jason's posturing, Rafe grabbed the phone. "Look, asshole. It's under control. I agreed to help. Back off. She'll call you if she needs you."

Glowering at the phone, Rafe pressed the Off button and tossed it on the bed.

"What was that about?" Kerry asked with a scowl. "He's just concerned."

He snorted. "Concerned with finding a way into your pretty panties, I'd guess. Is he your boyfriend, Kerry?"

Fighting the urge to ball his hands into fists, he stared at her, waiting. The bitter feeling churning in his gut was totally unfamiliar, but he recognized it as jealousy. The thought of this Jason guy calling her sweetheart and maneuvering his way into her lingerie pissed him off.

"I told you in the limo—not that you probably remember—but I don't have a boyfriend."

Oh, he remembered. "I'm guessing Jason would be happy to volunteer."

Kerry shook her head, frowning. "No. He has a girlfriend. Mara is great. I think he's going to propose soon, in fact. Jason is just Mark's best friend. I've known him for, like, five years. He's never even made a pass at me. And even if he was interested, Mark made it clear to Jason that I'm off-limits. Seriously, I'm pretty sure Jason thinks of me as a sister by default."

Staring at Kerry's pretty, pink-tipped breasts, the enticing curve of her waist, the beauty of her smile, the soft exterior that hid true female grit, Rafe couldn't imagine how any red-blooded man could look at Kerry and think *sister.* Even her delicate feet were graceful. Was Jason blind? Stupid? Tempestuous, zany Kerry was one of the most interesting women Rafe had ever met.

"Okay, stop with the skeptical expression," she said. "I'm going to have to tell you something, and I didn't want to. It will only freak you out."

"I'm already freaked out. You're out of your mind if you believe Jason isn't looking for a way between your legs. If your 'friend' is a typical guy, he's going to look for any opportunity to get laid, girlfriend or no. Don't you know that about guys?"

Something in her face closed up. "Thanks for the 411. Now get the hell away from me."

What? No sooner had she turned her back on him, than he grabbed her shoulders and pinned her to the mattress. "I'm trying to explain Jason's motives to you. How does that make me the bad guy?"

She cast her gaze on the wall over his shoulder, refusing to look at him. The gesture crawled under his skin.

"You're not. You're just telling me about guys. Thanks." Her voice sounded anything but appreciative.

Suddenly, Rafe got it. He took hold of her face and blocked her view of the wall behind him. Now she had nowhere to look but at him. "I didn't mean me."

"You are a guy."

"I'm not going to apologize for wanting you. Yeah, I want to nail you. So what? A few minutes ago it seemed pretty mutual. If it makes you feel any better, I don't have a wife or a girlfriend. I'm just not keen on the idea that you might be attached. I generally don't poach."

Bullshit, the voice inside him said. It wasn't the idea that he might be poaching that annoyed him; it was the idea of any other man touching her.

What in the hell was wrong with him?

"Goody for you. Someone get the guy a medal," she muttered.

Rafe tossed up his hands and stood with a sigh. "Look, I'm just trying to make sure you understand that Jason's motives aren't as pure as you think. I've delivered my warning. If you want him fucking you when we're through here, I guess that's your business. Hell, for all I know, maybe he already has."

Kerry squirmed away from him, thrashing for freedom. "You're an idiot! Jason hasn't done anything to me."

She stood on the other side of the bed, her manacles allowing her that much autonomy. Then she grabbed the sheet and covered herself from neck to knee, directly defying his earlier request. Her thoroughly pissed-off glare told him her disobedience was intentional.

"Jason hasn't ever touched me." Then suddenly, she looked away. "No one has. I'm a virgin."

Chapter Five

SHOCK coursed through Rafe like a jolt from a power line. He said nothing for a full thirty seconds.

He had been born and raised in New York City and frequently walked through Times Square. The place seemed to spawn the unusual. He ignored street preachers screaming about the coming of eternal hell and damnation with the same ease he disregarded contortionists making their living out of a tip cup. Generally, nothing surprised him.

Except, once again, Kerry.

“Virgin,” he said finally. “As in never had a man’s cock inside your pussy?”

Kerry rolled her eyes. “That’s a lovely way of putting it. You are one smooth talker.”

Her sarcasm rubbed his raw nerves with all the softness of steel wool. “Hey, I could have asked if you’d ever been fucked. But you haven’t?”

Clutching the sheet to her, Kerry frowned. "That isn't exactly the way I would have put it either, but no, I haven't."

Seriously? Maybe not . . . But in their short acquaintance, Kerry hadn't exactly received awards for her honesty, Rafe reminded himself. "How do I know that's the truth?"

"Why would I lie about something this embarrassing?"

She had a point. What would lying accomplish? And as much as he didn't want to, Rafe believed her. Her virginity explained so many things, like why she looked both fuckable and undeniably sweet in that short skirt she'd worn the night they'd met, why she blushed after a few wicked words. It also explained the hint of inexperience he'd caught in her kiss and why she'd never given or received oral sex before him.

And she had agreed to allow him to be the first man deep inside her body.

"Why?"

"Why what? Why wouldn't I put it that way? I'm not fond of dropping F-bombs. I mean, I sometimes lose my temper—"

"Why now? Why me?" Rafe swallowed against the thread of impatience he heard in his voice. "Why the hell did you agree to this bargain when you didn't even know what you were signing up for?"

"I'm a virgin, not a moron. I know what sex is."

"That's not the same as having it. That's like saying you could handle a tiger because you've read about them."

"Siegfried and Roy thought they could handle tigers after twenty years' experience. You see how well that worked out."

"You're impossible." He sighed.

Kerry sank to the edge of the bed, turning her back to him. "And you're freaked out. I knew it. That's why I didn't want to tell you."

"You were going to let me find out the hard way?"

"It would have been over and done in a minute, no big deal. It isn't like I saved my virginity for some shining wedding night. I just never . . . I never met anyone I wanted to be with. Between being shuffled from foster home to foster home and Mark getting cancer, losing it just seemed like a low priority."

Rafe crossed his arms over his bare chest. "And you weren't going to tell me. That would have been a fun discovery. What if, for our first time, I'd started reaming you from behind and smacking your ass for the hell of it?"

"What if you had?"

"It's not a virgin sort of way to have sex."

"There's only certain positions virgins are allowed to use?"

Staring at the ceiling, Rafe started counting to ten. "Seriously, you never had a single boyfriend volunteer for virginity patrol?"

"It's not like I broadcast the fact. Look, I had plans to lose it on prom night, but my date was more interested in the bottle of vodka he smuggled into the dance."

"Too drunk to perform?"

"Too busy vomiting on my dress—while he had his hand down the front of it. That was the extent of my experience. At least until you."

Rafe felt like his head was about to explode. He'd never wanted the responsibility of being the first man inside a woman and showing her all about sex. It seemed too time consuming, first of all. He preferred a woman who knew what she wanted and wasn't shy about asking for it. He liked women who understood how to please a man.

Being a woman's first seemed so intimate, inevitably creating emotional ties he didn't want. Women were sentimental about their firsts, or so he'd been told, and he didn't want anyone sentimental about him.

Kerry inspired anxiety . . . but not the kind he expected. The responsibility bothered him, but in a different way. What if he hurt her? Hell, he would; it was simple biology. But the rest of the thoughts jumbling inside his head were totally unexpected. Rafe *wanted* to teach her about her pleasure, about his. He planned to do everything he could to make sure she remembered him. Even the thought of Kerry remembering him sentimentally didn't disturb him. He relished the idea of being inside her, where no one else had been. And for as long as he was with her, no one else would be. Was that territorial? It felt suspiciously so.

Why?

He needed to think, to breathe some air not swarming with her teasing sugar-sunshine scent. He had to find some view somewhere in this two-by-two cracker box not teeming with views of Kerry—or his memories of her touch.

"Is my laptop here?" he said.

"You're angry about this." Her beautiful, bare shoulders slumped. "What can I say? I'm sorry. Look on the bright side; I'm disease-free."

How could he want to castigate, comfort, and screw her all at once? What the hell was she doing to him and his normally rational brain? He closed his eyes and counted to ten—again.

Rafe had to pick one emotion, so he chose the safest. "Kerry, when have you not tried to manipulate me? Everything you said in the limo was a lie. You drugged me, kidnapped me, stripped me down, tied me up—"

"And I'm sorry for it all. I am. Believe me, I'm really not like that under normal circumstances."

Her apology barely registered. "You tell me Jason isn't your boyfriend—"

"He isn't."

"And that he doesn't want to get into your panties. I still think you're feeding me bullshit designed to throw me off track somehow. Then you agree to have sex with me, while having no intention of telling me you're a virgin. What's next? Are you from outer space? Or having Elvis's love child via immaculate conception?"

She huffed out an angry sigh. "Elvis is dead and I'm not green or pregnant."

"With you, I'm not sure that's proof of anything."

"Oh, get over it." She smiled. "At least you know I can't pull a fast one on you à la *The Crying Game*."

He glared.

"Okay, okay. No more surprises," she promised.

"Right. You want me to investigate this case of your brother's, who you swear is innocent. And you've given me tons of reasons to believe that."

"You're angry. I got it. You have a right to be angry. But I did everything to help Mark. I would *never* lie about him. Helping him is too important. And before you forget, you're the one who came up with this little sexual blue-light special. Don't act like I twisted your arm here."

As much as the truth pissed him off, Rafe couldn't refute that. In the moments since she'd agreed to their hot sex bargain, he'd been desperate to touch her, taste her, take her. He'd been far less angry about his abduction and far more focused on how her wet slit would grip his cock and what sort of noises she would make when she came. Worse, even after a great blow job, he still felt that desperate urge to know every part of her body intimately.

Shit.

Rafe made his way down the hall, to the closet. He quickly dressed in his slacks and dress shirt. "Where is my laptop?"

As he reappeared in the bedroom door fully dressed, panic tightened Kerry's face, widened her eyes. "Rafe, can't we talk about this? I know you're angry, but—"

"Where the hell is my laptop?"

"In the living room, next to the TV," she murmured, tears welling in her green eyes. "Are you leaving now?"

He should. He should. He knew he should . . . but somehow he didn't want to, not until he savored her every delight . . . and tortured her a bit with her own medicine.

Mind spinning with possibilities, he approached her and reached for the handcuff key. "I promised to look into your brother's situation. You promised me forty-eight hours of sex. I'm going to work on my end of the deal now. I'm uncuffing you so you can rest and live up to yours later. Until I come to you, leave me the hell alone."

* * *

FOR three hours, Kerry listened to Rafe in the front room, trying to imagine what he was doing on her brother's behalf. It beat trying to forget everything they'd done together in this rumpled bed. The orgasm he'd given her had made her body explode with such force, Kerry was stunned her brain hadn't burst with it. The feel of his tongue rasping over her slick flesh while his finger prodded the bundle of nerves inside her . . . even the memory electrified her more than a light parade at Disney World.

Equally enticing was the freedom and power she'd had with Rafe's body. Like velvet steel under her hands, his skin enthralled her. He wasn't one of those bodybuilders whose biceps exceeded their brain cells. He was lean, like a swimmer. The salty-musky man scent and taste of him had her hormones doing the Macarena. Tiffany really had given oral sex a bad rap. What a rush! Feeling Rafe tense, hearing him groan as he clutched her hair in his fingers, gentle yet aggressive. That's how Rafe kissed her, touched her. If he took her to bed in that same fashion . . . Well, the thought made her shiver.

Again, he'd persuaded her through his touch, his kiss, to say yes. Even after he'd given her plenty of opportunity to say no. How was that possible? She wasn't easy, except with him.

In a weird way, she trusted him. He had no reason to be kind. When he had stayed with her after managing to trick her and tie her down, she'd been stunned. Of course, he must actually want her. Guys couldn't fake an erection—at least not that she was aware of.

And there was no denying that, despite everything, she wanted him.

"What the hell?" Kerry heard him mutter down the hall.

The tapping of the keyboard and a few soft curses later, he rose to pace the hardwood floors. None of that sounded promising, and Kerry wished she knew more about computers than surfing AOL required. Jason had always called it Internet with training wheels. Maybe she should have tried to come out of her cybershell. Too late now. It was up to Rafe.

Could he find anything to help Mark?

Before the abduction, Kerry had been certain that an expert like the esteemed Rafael Dawson could find the proof needed to free her brother. So certain, she would have bet a lung. Now she wondered. Maybe it wasn't that easy. Could someone alter, freeze, or heaven forbid, erase the files that might prove Mark innocent?

Positive energy, she told herself. Rafe was the best; he'd find something.

Tiptoeing down the hall, Kerry peeked into the front room—and drew in a sharp breath.

Rafe sat, gorgeous and shirtless, in the cottage's red leather chair. Muscles rippled along his bronzed shoulders and back, around the sizable width of his arms, every time he moved. A pulse of heat beat low in her belly, and Kerry chastised herself. No matter how yummy, now was not the time to indulge her overactive hormones with Rafe. Biting her lip, she held in a sigh.

His laptop rested on the ottoman. Rafe's gaze alternated between her file folder full of Mark's case information and the square color screen. Kerry didn't want to disturb him, but the suspense was killing her. She also didn't want to endure another tongue-lashing. Suffering Rafe's sarcastic temper was not her idea of fun.

"You don't follow directions well, do you?" he asked, not looking up from his work.

He'd heard her? Tugging the lavender shirt over the short shorts she'd donned, she asked, "How did you know I was here?"

Casting a glance over his shoulder, Rafe shot her a sardonic glance. "Let's just say you shouldn't apply to work undercover."

"I can't be that loud. I have bare feet," she protested while wiggling her toes.

He snorted. "I grew up listening for the sounds of sneaky servants and my father. If I didn't listen hard enough and move fast enough, there was hell to pay."

"In trouble a lot as a kid? I can picture that."

"My fair share, anyway." He shrugged.

Kerry's imagination provided an image of Rafe, all dark razor-cut hair and fancy prep school uniform framing silver eyes full of mischief. The only thing that had changed since then was his clothes . . . or lack thereof. Damn it all, why didn't the man put on a shirt so she could think straight?

"Find anything yet?" she asked.

Rafe glanced over his shoulder, that hot silver gaze zeroing in on her. "You mean other than the fact you're wearing clothes when I told you not to?"

"I mean about my brother." She anchored her hands on her hips.

He shrugged. "Still looking into it. Tell me, was Mark a smart guy in school?"

"Honors all the way. He was a whiz with math and science. Without him, I would never have made it through my first semester in college. Algebra Two nearly did me in."

The smile Rafe tried to suppress showed through. "What about computers? Does he know much about them?"

"Only what he learned at the bank. Jason had been teaching him some . . . before his arrest. Mark had just been promoted to assistant manager and needed more computer skills."

Something in Rafe's gaze sharpened. "Do you know what Jason taught him?"

Kerry shook her head. "It all sounded like Greek to me. If I was at Mark's house when he and Jason talked cybergoo, I usually found my sister-in-law, Tiffany. She's always good for chats about *General Hospital* and the merits of nail polish."

"Hmm."

"What's that mean?" she demanded.

"Maybe nothing. I don't know yet." Rafe twisted in the red leather chair and riveted her in place with a challenge of a stare. "Let's talk about you. Let's talk about the fact you're dressed in more than your birthday suit."

"Well, I . . ." she sputtered, as caught off guard by his tone as by the tension coiling low in her belly. "I assumed that since you weren't in the room—"

"Don't assume. I have total control, right?"

Was he serious? And was she actually aroused already? "Yeah."

"Naked means naked. Off with it. Now."

Blinking, Kerry paused. "In the middle of the living room?"

"Whenever, wherever, and however I say. So, now, here, strip."

God, she should hate this. She took orders for her meager living, for Pete's sake. Oh, but she'd never taken orders like this, from someone as sexy as Rafe. With a few words, her pulse began to skitter. Her nipples beaded. He could see, Kerry knew. She'd opted against a bra, and even now his gaze caressed the hard tips. They only got harder as he stared.

Her body might be on autopilot to Orgasm Land, but her brain still had a little autonomy. And it wanted him just as hard.

Reaching for the hem of her T-shirt, Kerry lifted it slowly up her torso. Cool air glided over her abdomen, her ribs, finally rushing across her breasts. Her nipples tightened even more.

"No bra." His raspy voice more than hinted that he wasn't immune.

Kerry looked right at Rafe, met his molten stare. The connection of their gazes whipped through her like a live wire carrying twenty thousand volts. Her body tingled, her vagina dampened and clenched just from his mere stare. She wondered how much longer her watery knees would support her. Likely not past his first touch.

"No bra," she murmured.

"I approve. I hope you didn't disappoint me by wearing panties."

Swallowing, she bit her lip nervously.

"That's mine to bite," he warned. "Don't play with it. In fact, don't play with any part of your body without my permission."

His quiet commands drilled through her composure, past the veneer of civilization. She'd always pictured that she'd like a nice guy and they'd have nice sex. Nothing about Rafe was nice, including her scorching reaction to him. The likelihood they'd have nice sex ranked up there with the Loch Ness monster suddenly walking on land, or Tiffany joining a think tank.

"Yes." She had the oddest urge to add on *sir,* or *master,* or something.

"You're wearing panties, aren't you?"

Resisting the nervous urge to bite her lip, she answered, "Yes."

"Bad girl. Until we're done here, you don't wear them anymore. You don't wear anything at all."

He crossed his arms over his massive chest and stared at her with an arrogant brow raised, as if he were some sultan making a pronouncement. Her mind rejected the idea of being totally submissive, despite how much her libido was enjoying it. Still, she'd made a bargain . . .

"Are you this way with all women?"

"Not really." He hesitated and seemed to have something to say. In the end, he just shook his head. "No."

Kerry frowned. A wealth of meaning lay in that nonanswer. She had no idea what, though. Why would he treat her differently than other women?

"Stop stalling. As hot as those swollen nipples are, I want it all. And you're still half-dressed."

Closing her eyes, Kerry felt her pulse pounding between her thighs. He just didn't give up. And she couldn't stop liking this dominating side of him—a little too much for her comfort. Was it him? Was it her? Did she have some sex fever she'd never heard of?

With shaking fingers, she plucked at the button of her denim shorts. The slow rasp of the zipper followed, the sound magnified by the utter silence. In its aftermath, she heard her shallow breathing, heard her heartbeat in her ears.

Wait! This shouldn't be one-sided. She'd never been easy before. Why start now?

Raising her chin, Kerry stripped off the low-rise shorts—and only the shorts. She crossed her arms over her naked breasts to drive home the point that her little black bikini panties would stay firmly in place. Never mind that the two triangles of fabric barely covered the essentials. Never mind they were completely transparent. They were a bit like a bad birthday gift—it was the thought that counted.

"Defying me already?" Rafe wore a shark's smile, tinged with a hint of sin.

Kerry's knees went weak, and she leaned against the wall for support. "Yeah. So?"

"You're proving to be a very naughty girl who needs to be punished."

Cocking her head, she regarded him with a barely concealed smile. "You'd like to be the guy to dish it out, wouldn't you?"

"Yes, I would." He rose to his feet, his sizzling stare wiping the smile off her face and nailing her to the floor.

"Take them off." His whisper whipped desire through her every nerve.

"What if I don't want to?"

"You want to."

She did her best to look affronted, though she could feel her nipples hardening again under her forearms. "That's awfully presumptuous."

"Not really." Rafe lowered his gaze to the panties, zeroing in on the patch at the front. "You've made those panties so wet, they're clinging to you."

His stare challenged her to deny it. She couldn't.

"Now, be a good girl," he murmured, walking closer, closer, until he pinned her back flat against the wall and covered her bare chest with his own. His fingers locked in hers as he held her arms above her head.

Kerry gasped at the heat.

"Take them off," he whispered, eyes scorching.

Drawing in a shaky breath, Kerry closed her eyes, trying to absorb the overload of sensations and emotions Rafe elicited. His heat and musk enveloped her, while his voice inflamed her. No, that wasn't all. He made her feel sexy.

For the first time in her life, a smart, stylish guy like Rafe wanted her. She wasn't from Fantasyland; she knew it wasn't forever. But to imagine that she could intrigue him enough to persuade him to stay and help her, that he would desire her as hotly as his eyes claimed . . . it was her own for-now fantasy. And she was determined to enjoy it.

She wriggled one hand free of Rafe's grasp and plucked at the strings holding up her panties. The sheer black scrap fell to the ground, leaving her completely bare.

Rafe took half a step back and devoured her with silver eyes that all but glowed with lust.

"You make me crazy," he whispered as he closed in and wrapped his hand around her nape.

His mouth came crashing down on hers. Nothing about his kiss was tentative. He took her mouth in a deep, possessive claiming from the first touch. Kerry opened to him like a drowning woman welcomed a life raft. Instead of saving her, though, his touch created waves of desire that tugged her under, where common sense no longer applied, where nothing but this man and the way they felt together mattered.

His mouth left hers, nipping at the sensitive spot where her neck met her shoulder, before traveling down to hover over her breast. He licked the hard point of her nipple with a quick rasp of his tongue, then dragged the edge of his fingertip over the sensitive flesh. He finished with a puff of cool air.

Lightning streaked through her body. Kerry cried out.

"I love how responsive you are. You could come for me in the next two minutes, couldn't you?"

Before she could answer, Rafe massaged her nipple from root to tip once, twice, before his fingers glided their way down her belly and into the soft nest of curls between her thighs. It took him less than an instant to find her clit, now beyond wet and throbbing. With sure fingers, he began caressing her with wicked, circling strokes.

Kerry gasped, her head falling back against the wall as pleasure drenched her, stealing her voice, buckling her knees. Rafe held her up, silently demanding she take what he gave her.

He used his feet to spread her legs farther apart, opening her more fully to him. "You're going to come for me, aren't you?"

Whimpering in answer, Kerry lifted her hips toward his magic fingers, praying he didn't stop. Sensation built, spiraling into need, into something she would have begged for if she could find the words.

When he pressed his fingers inside her, she gasped in shock, in pleasure.

"You're so incredibly tight," he whispered. "I can only imagine what it would be like to be inside you, thrusting with long, slow strokes that constantly drag my cock over this spot right here." He found the bundle of nerves, and his fingers imitated his words. In seconds, he had her trembling and gritting her teeth against the monster orgasm mounting just out of reach. "I'd love to be inside you," he continued. "You'd be all tight and hot, pulsing around me when you come. Just like . . . now."

The building dam of sensations inside Kerry burst. Vaguely, she heard herself cry out. But mostly she felt Rafe all around her—his fingers inside her clenching vagina, the hot slabs of his chest rasping against her nipples, so heavy and swollen.

Rafe planted warm lips on her neck as she began to come down. "You look beautiful in pleasure. I can't wait to see you come again."

He kissed her mouth gently, lingeringly. Kerry returned the kiss tiredly, then lay her head against his shoulder, her body slumped against his.

She could hardly deny that she felt sated. Orgasms so intense they caused black spots in her vision weren't an everyday occurrence in her admittedly short years of masturbation. But somehow, it was more. It was Rafe, who for all his big, bad words and whispered demands made her feel safe and desired.

And she'd bet that beat nice sex with a nice guy any day of the week.

* * *

BY 1:18 A.M., Rafe was forced to admit two things: Kerry looked both amazingly sweet and touchable while curled on her side sleeping naked, and there was a very real chance she'd been telling the truth about her brother.

Heaving a tired sigh, he sank to the edge of the bed and removed his socks. He couldn't resist looking over his shoulder at his temporary love slave. Moonlight glowed on her oval face, illuminated the enticing curve of her lush rosy mouth. At the sight, his dick stood due north, as it did anytime she was near. He'd had a stiff johnson for lots of women in his life, so that was nothing new.

The gooey sweet feeling in his chest felt totally unfamiliar. She was getting under his skin, and he wasn't sure why. On the surface, she was a waitress with a half-finished college education, without a complete grasp of common sense, and had a family member who might soon be spending hard time in prison. But Kerry wasn't the kind of woman he could see merely at a surface level. The lengths she'd gone to in order to help Mark still astounded him. The fact she'd plotted and flawlessly executed his abduction amazed him. Then she, the woman with next to zero sexual experience, had nearly seduced him . . . more than once.

Rafe saw in Kerry a loyal, warm-hearted beauty where he'd only assumed to find a ditz. He glanced at the time on his BlackBerry: 1:20 A.M. Kerry was his to touch and explore at will for roughly the next forty-two hours.

If he held her to the bargain.

His conscience warred with his libido. He wished he could tell them both to pound sand.

He almost regretted persuading her to strip earlier. Almost. But seeing her reaction had been too important. He had to know, could Kerry handle a sexual relationship under these odd circumstances? To her credit, she hadn't cried or pleaded or passed out. Not Kerry. Instead, she'd toyed with him, teased—and responded beyond his wildest expectations. Rafe couldn't shake the memory of her flying apart with his fingers deep inside her, her cry resounding in his ears. Still, he wasn't sure about her readiness to have a two-day fling. Her body was ripe, no doubt, but emotionally . . .

Emotionally? Rafe frowned. When had he ever worried much about a lover's emotions? Sex was recreation. It was like eating ice cream—great for the short while it lasted. When you got tired of one flavor, you moved on to the next. Ice cream never cared whether you wanted it now or later, or even at all. It never wanted to get to know you, hear your feelings. It never demanded that you "share yourself." So why should he worry overmuch about a woman he wouldn't be with in two days' time?

Without an answer to that question, he cursed softly and stood. None too gently, he tugged at the fastenings of his slacks and shucked them, kicking them aside, along with his boxer-briefs.

"Rafe?" Kerry whispered in the dark.

His entire body tensed at her voice. Lust, anger, more complex feelings he couldn't name all swirled in his gut.

"Sorry to disturb you. Go back to sleep."

Instead, she sat up and pushed a curly lock of pale hair from her face. Her green eyes shone soft, sleepy in the moonlight. He read trust in that expression. Amazing.

"What did you find?" she whispered.

Might as well get this discussion over with now. "If you're telling me the truth, that Mark is a smart guy who knows only a little about computers, there's no way he did this."

Sleep left Kerry's face, to be replaced by a luminous smile and a deepening of the trust in her expression that seemed to blow a hole in his chest. “Thank God.” She took his hand. “Thank *you*. What made you decide he’s innocent?”

“I didn’t say he was, exactly. But . . .”

Kerry snatched her hand away and crossed her arms over those beautiful naked breasts. “What does that mean?”

Shaking his head, Rafe urged her to sit back against the headboard, then handed her the bedsheet. If she wanted to discuss e-security and the transactions in question, looking at the enticing curve of her breasts and her soft sex—while seeing all the trust in her eyes—would not help him to be coherent. She cuddled up with the luxurious Egyptian cotton without comment.

Willing his stiff cock to stand down, he sat beside her. “Let me start at the beginning. In a case like this, one of the first questions I have to answer is, was the job done from the inside or the outside? In this case, the bank’s software at the time of the theft looks fairly up to date and most of the key security patches had been installed. Their software wasn’t configured very well, and I’ll fix that, since that’s part of my job. But it would still take someone with a fair amount of skill to hack into that system, and even then, they couldn’t frame an employee in this way without having some inside information.”

“Okay.”

“Since I didn’t find any evidence of firewall tampering around these transactions, I’m ruling out external theft. I agree with the FBI here. That makes this an inside job.

“Different questions arise when you’re dealing with an insider. How did it happen? Did the criminals trick an employee into giving away vital information? It’s one of the easiest ways to steal because companies don’t train their employees to spot cons. Someone slick can call an employee, claim they’re from IT, and ask for sensitive information. A lot of well-meaning people don’t think twice about a request like that.”

“Oh, that makes sense. Do you think that happened here?”

"Hard to say. It's always a possibility that someone unwittingly assisted a criminal, and since we only know from Swift Codes that the money went to Grand Cayman after it left Standard National, we can't follow that lead. Another possibility is that someone on the inside performed the transactions via an unauthorized access point."

"Huh?"

Against his will, Rafe smiled. "It's not uncommon for an employee to get fed up with the amount of time it takes their company's IT department to obtain and install the equipment they feel is necessary to do their job. This means they circumvent the process by bringing their own from home or buying new equipment from their department budget. They install it themselves and hook it up to the network."

"People know how to do this?"

Rafe sneered. "Yeah, there's always one wise guy wherever you go."

"And the people monitoring the network for the company don't know the new equipment is there?"

"If they aren't paying real close attention, no. I'm not ruling this out as a possibility; it goes hand in hand with weak electronic transfer controls."

She frowned. "You're losing me with the Techese, Spock. Could we have this discussion in English?"

Rafe grinned. "When businesses began doing more things via computers and e-mail to eliminate paperwork, they unwittingly circumvented a lot of the approval processes, as well as the paper trail. They frequently lose track of all the people approving transactions. That may not have happened here, but I suspect it may have played a role in the reason money was stolen on multiple occasions with Mark's ID before anyone discovered it missing."

"Oh. That fits. Mark said that half the time Smikins had no idea what was going on. He often delegated things that he was supposed to do himself."

"Peachy." Rafe's voice rang with sarcasm. "Another common issue is crappy password policies."

"Like an e-mail password?"

He nodded. "But think larger. Passwords are required for most every system. There's one required to log on to the funds transfer system used at Standard National Bank. That's how they pointed the finger at Mark. Whoever did this used his ID. They had to have his password to do that. Unless you're so mentally challenged you make Paris Hilton look like a genius, anyone seriously trying to embezzle money doesn't leave this obvious an electronic trail. A neon sign is more subtle."

"But someone framing Mark would want it to be obvious."

"Exactly. Who had access to his passwords? Do you know?"

"Mr. Smikins for sure. Mark used to complain that he insisted on keeping a current list of everyone's passwords, even though it was against company policy to share passwords with anyone. That's why I've suspected him all along. He hated Mark with a massive purple passion."

"Because . . . ?"

"Smikins is an autocrat with short man's disease and all the sex appeal of a kumquat. And he wanted Tiffany bad. But Mark, who could pass for a Viking in the right clothes, landed her."

"That could be a motive, I guess. Who else had access to Mark's passwords?"

"I'm guessing that Tiffany, his wife, might have his passwords. She works at the bank, too. That's where they met, in fact."

"Any motive there?"

Kerry hesitated. "How can I say this nicely? It seems like you'd have to be really sharp to carry off a plan like this. That isn't Tiff. Sweet, yes, and caring. She's a Hallmark Movie of the Week fan. She collects Precious Moments figurines. Master thief seems like a big stretch."

"She could be helping someone on the outside."

"I can't think who. She doesn't have any family. Her girlfriends seem as sweet and nonthreatening as she is. Truly, when I look at the lot of them, I think shoe fiends and Build-a-Bear lovers way before I think greedy criminals."

"It could be an act." Rafe sighed. "Or maybe she was duped by someone on the outside into revealing Mark's passwords."

"That's totally possible. Like I said, sweet . . . just not the brightest star in the sky. If you're a model-thin redhead, you don't have to be."

"I prefer blondes with dimples," he murmured hotly.

Kerry flushed a pretty pink. "You're saying that to make me feel better."

"No, I'm not," he vowed, pressing a soft kiss to her mouth. Lord, he wanted to jump her. "The first time I saw you smile, I wondered if whoever sent you had been reading my fantasies."

She sent him a supernova smile in reward.

Rafe cleared his throat. Best to finish this discussion before an alluring smile and a great pair of bare breasts derailed him. Besides, as tired as he was, he needed sleep before having any sort of sex.

"Anyone else who might have Mark's passwords?"

She hesitated. "Jason."

"Ah." Rafe sent her a brittle smile. "Your esteemed, purely platonic friend."

Kerry rolled her eyes. "He is! He has been so there for me since Mark's arrest."

"I'll bet. No chance he knew that Mark was your champion and support system and decided to eliminate him, while gaining a bunch of money—and you—in the process?"

"No. Jason has had hundreds of opportunities to hit on me and he never has."

"I find that hard to believe. Maybe you're just not picking up on his cues."

"Maybe you're just delusional."

Or maybe she shared Stevie Wonder's visual capabilities, Rafe thought, but he let it go—for now. But good ol' Jason, no doubt, warranted a lot of further investigation. No red-blooded man could look at Kerry without sex crossing his mind at some point. And getting closer to Kerry seemed like plenty of motive to Rafe.

* * *

AN overwhelming wave of heat awoke Kerry a few hours later. She tried to kick off the offending blankets, only to find she had none.

At her movement, a hand around her waist tightened. Heat flowed from that hand onto her bare skin, exuded from the arm slung over her, radiated from the equally naked body pressed against her back. The granite erection pressing against her butt scorched her.

Rafe.

She swallowed. After their half-English, half-Techese discussion, he'd claimed exhaustion and settled down beside her. Besides the whole sex thing, she'd never literally slept with a man. Especially not a naked one. It was a sensual experience in itself, heated skin, soft breaths, human comfort.

Kerry sighed and curled against Rafe. His hard chest, his textured palm, his lightly hair-roughened legs tangled with hers. His breath teased her neck. He represented danger, a man who had bargained with her for sex . . . yet with him she felt safe. A luxurious feeling she'd rarely had the opportunity to embrace during her chaotic life.

Get a grip! Her imagination was way out of hand. Rafe was no safer than your average lion prowling the savannah.

Usually, a safe man didn't make a girl tingle in all the right places with one glance. Rafe did that. Kisses from a safe man had never inspired immediate thoughts of lying on her back and spreading her legs. Rafe did that, too. Something about him not only called to her and ruled her sexuality, but connected with her on a lot of unexpected levels. He was scary and exhilarating at once.

And she was sounding like a candidate for the loony bin.

Frowning, Kerry opened one eye enough to see that sunrise was a promise on the horizon. Too early to be awake. She closed her eyes again, only to realize she really needed to pee and wasn't likely to sleep again.

After answering nature's call and grabbing a quick shower, she wrapped her towel around her and wandered back into the bedroom, over to the window that overlooked the stunning ocean view. Dawn swept over the salt-drenched seascape in lush blues, pinks, and oranges. Lovely, really. But all she could think about was Rafe. The man swirled in her head, his musky, masculine scent all in the air. His kiss drove her insane, and now he believed her brother was likely innocent. She sighed. Prince Charming, yes—but not hers to keep. She owed him the sex he wanted. She could like him okay, but nothing more.

"What's wrong?"

Kerry whirled at the sound of his sleep-roughened voice. "How long have you been awake?"

"Since you left the bed. Is something wrong?" Propping his back against his pillows, he cocked his gorgeous, sleep-rumpled head, silver eyes examining her in the soft light. "You look worried."

As if she would tell a guy like Rafe that she was liking him more than sexually and fearing that letting him go would be tougher than expected. Yeah, she'd rather cut off her right hand with a rusty knife. No doubt he had loads of sophisticated New York City women falling at his feet. He'd never be interested in more than a good time from a suburban Florida virgin.

His soft curse interrupted her thought. "Never mind. I know why you're worried."

She turned away and closed her eyes. Please God, don't let her every emotion be written all over her face, as usual. Mark had always teased her that her face wasn't an actual open book, but a kindergarten-level reader.

Where is the nearest pit of quicksand when I need it?

Behind her, she heard Rafe rise. He settled warm hands on her bare shoulders. "What do you say we forget about having sex?"

Chapter Six

FORGET about having sex? Had she heard that right?

Shock scattered the earlier tumble of her thoughts, momentarily numbing her brain like a shot of Novocain. A faraway buzzing rang in her ears. The sting of rejection slid between her ribs like a knife.

He doesn't want me.

Was there some reason that the only two men she'd ever thought of having sex with both choked before the "big game"? The difference was, Richard had mostly disappointed her by vomiting on a dress she'd loved. But she truly wanted Rafe. Really, really wanted him.

Kerry couldn't deny that the only thing she had in common with a beauty like Kate Hudson was hair color. Still, perfectly average women managed to find love all the time. She wasn't asking for undying devotion from Rafe. Certainly a half hour of his time and a little passion weren't too much to hope for.

Apparently, a suburban Florida virgin wasn't even good enough for a good time.

Well, if Rafe didn't want her, she didn't need him. She didn't need any man, damn it.

Fighting the sting of tears in her eyes, Kerry jerked from his touch and spun around to find the door. Big mistake. Rafe blocked her way, looking so scrumptious this morning wearing nothing more than his boxer-briefs. He looked even yummier now than he did in his thousand-dollar suits. His inky hair had a soft, rumpled look that tempted her fingers. With dark sideburns that melded into a morning-after shadow, he unconsciously flaunted his dangerous, bad-boy appeal. A pang cut into her like a bleeding wound from a bad slasher flick.

"Move," she demanded.

Rafe stood unyielding, tall against the sunlight beaming through the window, illuminating the golden skin smoothed over his bulging shoulders and the defined ridges of his chest. And his eyes, softer than usual, were filled with something she feared was pity.

Curling up and dying had never sounded more appealing.

He crossed his arms over his wide chest. "No."

Cooperative as usual. Great.

"Fine," Kerry bit out, chin raised. She would not cry, she would not cry, she would not cry. "But what about Mark? If not having sex with you means not gaining your help for him—"

"I'll help," Rafe assured her. "He needs it."

So what was he now, a philanthropist, suddenly willing to give of his time to help the needy, as long as it meant avoiding the horizontal mambo with her? "If you'll help Mark and you want to forget the sex, then we'll forget it."

He frowned. "Look, I just don't want you to feel obligated to do something you'll regret."

Now he was worried about that? She'd thought a smart guy like Rafe would know that she wouldn't have agreed to their bargain if she thought she'd regret it later. "This is about you," she accused. "Have you gotten enough of what you wanted, so you're just done with me?"

Rafe's frown became a sinful half-smile.

She clutched the skimpy black towel closer to her chest, achingly aware of his gaze touching her bare shoulders. If he didn't want her anymore, why did he look? That unwavering stare made her toes curl even when he dismissed her. Pathetic! Her body needed to stop pumping out the come-and-get-me pheromones!

"You think I've gotten enough of you?"

His hot silver stare touched its way down her body, pausing at her breasts as if he could see through her towel and picture her as naked as a centerfold. Her nipples instinctively beaded under his gaze. Kerry drew in a stunned breath as he made a visual path down to her belly, her barely covered femininity, touching her with every glance.

Bewildered by the unmistakable lust sharpening his features, Kerry took a step back. Now able to see Rafe's barely clad body, she noted that he sported a really impressive erection. Even through his boxer-briefs, it looked even more insistent than his stare.

The words coming out of his mouth and the state of his arousal matched as well as a pink mini with orange and brown mules. Okay, what on earth was going on?

"I . . . I thought—"

"Oh, babe. I've only had a little taste of you. It wasn't nearly enough. I could be inside you morning, noon, and night for the next two days. I guarantee it wouldn't be enough."

As his hot gaze confirmed his desire, the knot of dismay in her belly eased—until she realized he still wasn't coming closer to touch her, to take her. Then he dropped the blazing stare and turned away.

The view of his taut backside in black boxer-briefs was so fabulous, it took Kerry a moment to focus on his words.

"Listen, I suggested this bargain when I was incredibly aroused and thoroughly pissed off. I didn't believe you'd accept. I didn't think about what would happen if you did. And then when you told me about your inexperience . . ." He turned back to her with a shrug. "I'm just thinking sex isn't a good idea."

Understanding dawned—and really ticked her off. "It's the virginity thing, isn't it?"

"Not . . . exactly." Hands on narrow hips, Rafe stared at the ceiling and heaved a long sigh. "Well, in a way. But—"

"Look, if you're worried I'll cling like a vine afterward, don't. I tell time well enough to know when forty-eight hours ends."

"Kerry, that's not it."

Okay . . . "Then what? There are plenty of condoms. I checked."

An unexpected smile softened his face. "Yeah, I saw them, too." Then he sobered. "But there's more to this than condoms or lack thereof."

What? If he really did want her and wasn't worried about her having all the suction of a Hoover when this was over, what was the matter? No doubt, he could perform. They were alone. She'd shaved just that morning. So what was the issue? Oh, she was so confused. And men thought women were hard to figure out?

Turning away, Kerry stared back out at the white-sand shore, thoughts racing.

Damn it, she ached so bad with the need to touch Rafe, to experience the incredible pleasure she sensed he could give her. Dangerous as it was, she loved the idea of feeling closer to him, pretending he was her man, even if for a little while.

No matter what he said, his sudden disinterest in sex with her had to be the virginity. She'd just known it was going to freak him out.

Did it ever occur to him that she felt like a mutant? Maybe she should tell him that she wanted him because he made her feel both aroused and safe at the same time. Because she felt so drawn to him. Or was he too weirded out by the whole adult-virgin thing to care?

The towel suddenly felt too skimpy, mortification heated her face in the most uncomfortable way, and her head hurt.

"I know this is about my virginity. And you know what? I don't want it any more than you do." She reached for her phone and turned toward the door to find the closet and her clothes. "I'm going to put an end to this. In two hours, I can have it taken care of so neither one of us has to deal with it again."

"What does that mean?" Rafe's eyes narrowed.

"Well, if you're right about Jason, I can just call, have him pick me up and take me to my place—"

Before she could reach the door, Rafe clamped hard fingers around her wrist. She whipped her gaze up to his face, then winced at his fierce expression. He'd clenched his jaw so tight, she wondered if he could break diamonds with his teeth.

"Put the fucking phone down."

With every sharp word, his eyes turned more molten—swirling with lust and fury. Thick tension churned in her belly at that look.

She dropped the phone on the floor, barely noticing when it thudded on the soft area rug. She'd handled that badly, she supposed. Did Emily Post have a chapter on suggesting alternate lovers to a current one for the breaking of one's hymen?

"You'd actually have sex with Jason to get rid of your virginity? And then what? Come back here and think that solved the problem so we could go back to Plan A?"

Okay, so maybe she was the Queen of Crazy Ideas lately.

"Maybe. No." With a sigh, Kerry's shoulders slumped. "I don't know."

"Do you want him?" Rafe demanded to know.

"No." She shook her head. "But I'm not celibate by choice exactly; I certainly don't want to be celibate by force. I want to experience more of the passion and pleasure you've given me a taste of."

"So if I don't have sex with you, any other penis will do?" he growled.

No. In her heart, Kerry knew that. She wanted Rafe. But her temper urged her on. "How would I know?"

Anger exploded all over his face. "Give me a break! You're obviously not the kind of woman who just fucks anyone. You've been waiting for something special. I know that."

"Suddenly you're a sensitive guy?"

He stalked closer. Kerry held her breath, heart pounding, as he breached her personal space. She felt the heat of Rafe's body as he drew nearer. Then he reached out, clutched her shoulders. Her skin burned beneath his fingers.

"Let's get a few things straight, shall we? One, I only volunteered to release you from our agreement because you shouldn't have to sleep with a guy you've only known for a few days just to get help for your brother, especially when it's entirely possible he's innocent. Apologizing probably makes me look like a hypocrite, but what the hell? No one should be coerced into sex, especially not the first time."

"But I—"

"Damn it, let me finish. I'm trying to be decent here. I've said I'll help your brother, no matter what happens between us." He shrugged. "I'd just rather not have you call me three kinds of a son of a bitch and hate me later."

Kerry stared at Rafe in stunned silence. He'd backed off for her? Not because he didn't want her. Not entirely because she was a virgin. Because he was afraid *she* would hate *him*? Talk about an alternate reality. So the big, bad wolf actually had a conscience.

"Two," he went on, his gaze zeroing in on her face, his stare forcing her to meet his. "It's not that I don't want you or your virginity. I want you." He closed his eyes for a moment. "So fucking bad I can barely think of anything else." Rafe opened his eyes again, and the feral want in those eyes blasted a bolt of need right to her core. "I want to sink down into you, deep, be the one to open you to pleasure. I want to hear you scream my name in orgasm, knowing I'm the first man your body's ever enveloped while you come."

Kerry drew in a sharp breath as desire tore through her belly. His blistering stare matched his words as he lowered his hands to her hips and dragged her against him.

Once again, she felt the fact he had the erection to do all the things he'd just uttered.

"And if you call Jason right now, I'll find him and break both his legs."

Was he jealous? There was no mistaking the possession in his gaze. Wonders never ceased. Surprise bloomed inside her, and she bit her lip to hold in a smile.

"Very mature," she teased.

He shrugged. "Sue me."

So . . . he'd put the choice in her hands. Usually it took Kerry a long while to make a decision. Not today. She drew in a breath and gathered her courage.

"I'd rather have my wicked way with you." She shot him her best interpretation of a come-hither stare.

He swallowed hard, gaze riveted to her. "Be really sure, Kerry. Once it's done, there's no taking it back."

His concern swelled warmth in her chest as she raised a hand to his face. "Don't get me wrong. I'm thrilled to have you on Mark's side. I think, in time, you'll be as convinced of Mark's innocence as I am. But I'm not just a sister, I'm a woman, too." She dragged the pad of her thumb over his lower lip even as anxiety churned in her stomach. "I didn't agree to that bargain solely to help my brother. I agreed because I—I want you." Fighting a blush, she went on. "You being first, me being yours for two days . . . it's exciting. It feels right."

"You're really willing to keep our agreement?"

How many times did a girl have to say yes? Lord, she'd been as subtle as a wrecking ball in a room full of crystal. Rafe wanting her to think about it and be sure was very sweet . . . but unnecessary. Despite everything she'd put him through, he'd been amazingly decent. She thought the fact he was capable of incredible things with his mouth and hands was a big plus, too.

Kerry didn't lie to herself; this wasn't the beginning of a long-term relationship. A worldly, wealthy man like Rafe would never actually *care* about her. Besides, she had to lose her virginity to someone someday. Why not Mr. Make-Me-Sizzle?

"More than willing," she whispered.

At her words, his gaze brightened, glittered. He smiled, somehow managing to look both sinful and reassuring at once. That expression made her heart beat in a rhythm that would go over big in a salsa dance club.

"I'm more than willing, too." Then he leaned closer and whispered against her mouth, "Trust me."

Kerry felt the smile stretch across her face. "Glad to hear it. I was afraid I was going to have to tie you down again."

One of his hands meandered over her hip, to the small of her back, over the swell of her butt. "Interesting possibilities . . . for later. Now, I want you all to myself, altogether naked, all day long."

Staring at his soft, sculpted lips, anticipation beating at her like a prizefighter on speed, she nodded.

"You're wearing too much again."

Kerry frowned. "It's a bath towel."

"It's too much." Lifting his hand from her ass, he grabbed the black terry cloth at her back in his fist and gave a gentle tug.

That quickly, Kerry found herself wearing nothing but goose bumps.

Rafe's restless gaze roved over her every curve and swell, from her pink-painted toenails, to her tightly clenched thighs, over the flare of her hips to her breasts and their hard rosy tips.

Finally, he curled his hand around her nape and raised his gaze to her wide eyes. "Remember, anything. Everything."

"I'll hold you to that."

A smile quirked the side of his mouth. "You won't be holding anything while you're bound spread-eagle to the bed. But that's later, too . . ."

Kerry gasped but the sound never made it past her lips before Rafe covered them with his own. He took advantage of her open mouth, sliding his tongue inside.

His kiss heated her from zero to three-fifty in about two seconds. Lips mating, tongues sliding in a teasing dance, Kerry lost herself to the taste of Rafe. An ache of desire spiked in her belly at the demand in his kiss. His possession of her mouth told her that he would make few concessions to her inexperience. He wanted a full partner in pleasure and intended to drive her to the brink of her inhibitions—and beyond.

His hands cascaded down her back in a long, smooth stroke, bringing her skin alive beneath his touch. One gentle finger played at the curve of her buttocks, at the cleft in between, leaving tingles in his wake, before skating across her hip, drifting up to her waist.

Rafe stoked a restless feeling in her belly, between her legs. Kerry wriggled against him. When his thumbs skimmed down her hipbones, then to the tops of her thighs, tracing maddening little circles so close to her ache, she drew in a ragged breath of air.

With tender, biting kisses, Rafe lowered his mouth across her jaw, down her neck. Kerry swayed into him, want making her hazy, crazy, making her burn.

He nipped at her lobe as his thumb traced the vee of her mound. "So hot, so sweet. I'm dying to touch you everywhere, get the taste of you on my tongue, memorize the feel of you closing around my cock."

His words inspired a mental picture that had Kerry moaning. She took his face between her hands and crushed her lips to his again. In true Rafe fashion, he invited himself inside and lingered, prowling as if he owned her mouth, her every breath.

With a sweep of one arm down her back, Rafe cupped his hand beneath her ass and lifted her against him. Her legs parted around his hips, her mound pressed flush against his erection. The only thing stopping them now was the thin cotton of his underwear.

A guttural groan tore from his chest as he clutched her hips and pressed her against his hot length. He crushed her mouth under his again in another ravaging kiss. Lost in sensation, awash with a want stronger than anything in her imagination, Kerry felt nothing except his hands, knew nothing except his mouth as he kissed her and made wicked, whispered promises of never-ending pleasure.

Until she felt the rumpled sheets of the bed at her back.

Rafe followed her down to the bed, then lifted himself up on his elbows. "We're going to be so good together, babe."

Nodding, Kerry ran a hand up the bulge on his biceps, the hard ridge of his shoulder. His warm solid flesh and uneven breaths reassured her. "I'm already breathless."

A smile of pure sin dominated his face. "Just wait."

With one finger he began to trace large, lazy circles around one breast, never quite reaching her areola, never touching her nipple. Kerry watched him as he stared at her nipples while they beaded and swelled. He swiped his tongue along his lower lip, as if anticipating the taste of her. She couldn't wait to feel his molten mouth close around the sensitive tip again. Anticipation burning her alive, she arched up to him, offering him everything.

He ignored her invitation.

"Close your eyes," he whispered instead, his voice thick, rough.

"Why?"

"I can't give you what we both want if you don't trust me. If you can't do that, this stops now."

Trust him? Oddly, yes, she did. Utterly, in fact. She hesitated only a moment before she allowed her eyes to drift shut.

"Excellent. Keep them closed."

"I will if you'll hurry this along."

"Wanting this over with?"

"Wanting more of these great feelings."

"Then I definitely won't keep you waiting," he whispered against her ear, sending shivers across her skin, down her spine. "Just long enough to need it."

Rafe shifted his weight then. She heard something open, close. The temptation to peek, to brace herself for whatever he planned, nearly overwhelmed her, but she didn't want to ruin it. Besides, she trusted him. In fact, she was startled to realize that the only person she'd ever trusted more was her brother.

Before Kerry could ponder that thought further, something soft whispered across her nipple, so light she wondered if she had imagined the sensation. The tingling afterward told her otherwise. He repeated the action to her other nipple. The sensations were delicious and enticing but . . .

"Rafe." She gasped. "More."

"Like this?" he taunted, barely dragging the soft item over her sensitive, swelling skin again.

Kerry moaned. "No. More."

"How about this?"

He skimmed the underside of her breast with the pad of this thumb, circling to the top of her breast, before trailing away.

"More, damn it."

"Such impatience." He kept on with that soft, teasing something. "Lie back. Enjoy this. I'm enjoying the hell out of watching you wriggle and flush and swell."

"I need . . ." Kerry struggled to find the words to express what her body craved. "I need . . ."

He grasped her nipple and gave a firm squeeze. Liquid fire shot straight from her breast to her vagina, lighting her up like a Roman candle. "Oh, yes. That's it!"

He laughed again as he pinched her other nipple. She struggled for her next breath. Then the delicious pressure was gone.

That maddeningly soft something caressed the undersides of her breasts again, then bisected her stomach. A feather, she finally realized at he swirled its tip inside her navel. Her stomach tightened as Rafe drew the supple fronds at the line where her lower abdomen met her pubic mound.

For long moments, he tickled her, tormented her right there . . . but not quite where she needed him, with enough pressure to inflame . . . but not enough to satisfy. Everything between her thighs came alive, pushing beyond a restless ache to a need for satisfaction.

"Spread your legs," he demanded.

"Rafe," she breathed. "You're tormenting me."

His sin-inspiring laugh told her she'd hit upon the truth. "That's the plan. Now do it."

Biting back a reply, Kerry eased her thighs apart a few inches.

"More."

She hesitated. Her mind raced. Could she take much more of his teasing? Already she was so aroused. Tingles danced across her skin like little pinpricks, concentrating near all her most sensitive spots.

"Kerry, spread wider."

Drawing in a shaky breath, she complied, granting him another few inches.

His weight disappeared as he shifted to the edge of the bed. "Yes. So pretty. So pink and slick and pouting. Spread completely."

That raspy, needy note in his voice compelled Kerry to push lingering modesty aside and open those last few inches.

"Perfect."

Rafe dipped the feather lightly over her folds, making her arch and gasp. Lord, she was going to lose her mind with these barely there touches and wondering what he might do next.

"Rafe, stop teasing me. I want you now."

"You're not ready yet."

She sighed, wishing she could see his face. Was he even half as aroused as she was? "If I get any more ready, I'll die."

He chuckled. "Matters aren't that drastic. Yet. Be good and bend your knees."

"Why?"

"It doesn't matter. This is about trust. You've got to trust me."

"You're so bossy," she got out between gritted teeth, torn between the urge to scream with frustration and wail with the ascending pleasure.

"Yes."

"You like it that way."

"I do. Now, are you going to follow directions or be naughty and disobey me?"

As Rafe took another swipe at her slick, sensitive core with his feather, Kerry managed to gasp out, "What if I want to be naughty?"

"Next time. I'm trying to be gentle. If you push me past my limit . . ."

Kerry's pulse skittered at the thought he would soon touch her, even take her and show her the pleasure she'd only fantasized about. Slowly, she drew her knees up, opening for him like a flower.

"I wanted to see every bit of you, Kerry. Now I can."

The feather drifted over the damp heat of her vagina, growing wetter by the moment. He dragged the tip of the feather over the swollen hood of her clit. The reply Kerry had formed died in her throat.

He repeated the process again. And again. And again, suddenly alternating the barely there glide of the feather with a heated pinch of her nipples. The subtle ache of desire mingled with a bare hint of pain. The contrast overloaded her senses until Kerry felt delirious. Desire charged inside her like bulls running in Pamplona. Perspiration filmed her forehead as the sensual torture went on and on, just like her pleasure-filled cries.

Suddenly, he stopped. Kerry's heart chugged out of control as she felt Rafe loom closer.

"Open your eyes." His voice was like sandpaper over gravel, deep and rough.

Lifting her lashes, Kerry opened her eyes and focused on Rafe. The blast of demand in his eyes scorched her with another swath of fire through her belly, between her legs.

"Let me touch you," she whispered.

"Later," he growled, then bent his head.

He fit his hot mouth over one stunningly sensitive breast. His tongue swirled, his teeth nipped. She'd no more than gasped when she felt two of Rafe's fingers skim over her swollen vulva. He coated his skin in her juices and traced an unhurried, maddening path around her clit, bringing it alive until she swore every nerve ending in her body was focused on her nipples or vagina.

The inklings of climax began brewing low in her belly, deep in her core. She felt tingles down her legs, swirling up her spine. And still he continued slow circles around her aching clit.

His teeth nipped at her tender nipples as his thumb swiped a deliberate path over the swollen bud between her legs. Her eyes flew open. Close. So, so close to an orgasm so powerful it was going to drown her, swallow her whole.

She wanted it more than a red BMW Z4. More than a lifetime supply of chocolate. Way more.

"Rafe." She arched her hips to him, trying to draw in a whole breath.

Twin flags of red swathed his dark cheeks, proving he, too, was aroused. His gray eyes looked like melted silver. Kerry took comfort in that, though it wasn't enough to drive her over the edge when he dragged his thumb over her clit once more.

"Do you want to come?"

"Yes," she admitted, lifting her head to steal a quick, wet kiss across his lips.

"Then close your eyes again."

Everything inside her yearned to throw her arms around him and drag him down against her, wrap her legs around him until he had nowhere to go but deep inside her. She suspected, however, that only obedience would get her the release of tension she needed.

Slowly, she closed her eyes.

Like a drowning man, Rafe sank into the depths of her mouth and began to kiss her as if she was the sweetest treat in the world. Ecstasy frothed inside her as he licked at her lower lip, swirled his tongue through her mouth. He groaned into her, tunneled his fingers through her curls, held her close.

Urgency surged inside her as he mastered her mouth, kiss by endless kiss. Every sweep of his lips over hers brought new heat, new need. She arched into him, silently pleading for more. Rafe denied her. The anticipation built, the knot in her belly tightening.

Then he moved to her left. She heard something tear and

peeked in time to see him rolling a condom over his thick erection, starting with the engorged purple head, then down his long, vein-bulging length. Seeing his flesh in his own hand somehow aroused her.

He settled his weight over her again, taking her hips in his grip, thumbs stealing back to her wet vagina again, raking gently over her clit. On instinct, she spread her legs even wider in invitation. Her orgasm teetered again, right on the brink.

Then she felt the head of his penis at her entrance. He waited a heartbeat, two. "Now open your eyes."

His intimate whisper reached into Kerry and turned her inside out. As she looked into his compelling silver eyes, burning with demand, desire, edged in tenderness, she melted.

"I'm sorry," he rasped.

"Why?"

He didn't answer with words. Instead, Rafe drew his hips back, then plunged forward, inside her. Her virgin barrier gave way under the force of his thrust. A sharp pain ignited between her legs. With a cry, she tried to pull away. He clutched her hips, keeping her in place. Kerry gasped at the discomfort, but still he kept on, burrowing farther into her.

Until he reached the hilt.

"That's why." He paused between deep, uneven breaths. "I knew it would hurt."

It had. But as he slid back, nearly to the point of withdrawing, then eased into her again, it hurt less. The third time, much less. By stroke number six, it was all good. She arched up to him. The sense of being full, completed, only added to Kerry's sparking arousal.

"That's it," he gasped. "So hot, so unbelievably tight." Rafe smoothed away a curl that clung to her cheek. "I'm dying to be inside you when you come. You're heaven."

Sweat beaded at his temples as he fitted his hands beneath her butt and tilted her up. His stroke changed, and he moved with short digs into her. The head of his penis dragged repeatedly, quickly, over that one oh-so-sensitive spot.

Lord, she was going to instantly combust. Kerry clung to his broad shoulders, kissing his neck, his jaw, as she raised her hips to his thrusts. She was going to explode into a thousand, million pieces, and she could only hope Rafe would be there to catch her when she did.

"Oh, God. Yes." She tossed her head from side to side. "Yes!"

He raised her desire with each smooth stroke. It built like a storm in her belly, swirling, growing, hovering on the edge of release.

The scent of sex brewed between them: sweat, straining need, female musk. Blood sizzled along her nerve endings every time he sank into her. Her throat ached from crying out. Still she clung to him, his hard bronzed shoulders, his wide back rippling with every stroke. And those silver eyes bright with hunger mesmerizing her, connecting more than their bodies, telling her as loudly as a shout how damn good she felt underneath him.

His thrusts came hard, fast now. Rafe touched the mouth of her womb each time he sank deep, shooting off sparks of pleasure so sublime, Kerry thought she'd go blind. Her body instinctively tightened around him, as if wanting to keep him inside her, and the friction pushed her perilously close to the edge.

And still Rafe's shimmering gaze sank into her, seeing everything, persuading her with his hot stare to open herself and show him everything.

Arousal built, robbing her of breath. Lord, why had she waited so long to experience something so wonderful?

Then Rafe reached a hand between them, squeezed a thumb between her legs and dragged it across her clit again.

The sensation sent her into the stratosphere.

She cried out, feeling the thick stalk of his erection inside her as she contracted around his steel-hard length. Pleasure roared, her heartbeat drumming into her ears, along with his harsh breath as he tried to keep pace around her clasping walls.

The burst of ecstasy tapered off slowly. When she finally regained some sanity and a breath, Kerry pried open her eyes and peered at Rafe. Sweat rolled off his brow as he clenched his teeth, muttering choice words under his breath.

"Rafe, you didn't come?"

"Not yet. Not time."

Replete, satiated, Kerry shook her head. "I don't think I can take more now."

In response, he bent his head and dragged his velvet wet tongue across one nipple, then the other. They beaded to life again instantly. They stood at rigid attention when he tweaked them again.

"You can," he vowed between strained breaths. "You will."

She shook her head.

Then he began to barrage her with slow, intense strokes. Deep thrusts that proved how sensitive her tissues still were, how easily he could reawaken her desire.

He sank down, down into her body, each plunge of his cock inside her turning up the heat of the sweet, urgent need reemerging inside her. She felt her body clasping at him, clutching him as if she never wanted to let go. Fire licked her clit, fueled by that insistent thumb of his.

Suddenly the impossible was not only probable but imminent as sensation skyrocketed, spurred on by his insistent gaze. His unyielding stare encouraged her to take more, give more, even as his body demanded it.

Orgasm hammered her with pleasure again as she exploded, contracting around him with twice the force. A wave of dizziness flattened her, amazed her with the potency of her climax. Above her, Rafe gritted his teeth between fast, pounding strokes. He swelled inside her, stiffened, and let go of his control. Kerry heard her own cry, loud and hoarse, now mingled with his.

Breathing hard, Kerry lay back against the bed and closed her eyes, feeling the out-of-control beat of her heart slowly return to normal. A part of her wondered if the rest of her would ever be normal again.

Rafe lay over her, cocooning her head between his elbows. Beyond satisfaction, the seductive feeling of being safe and protected remained, quietly growing in strength.

They exhaled as one.

"Look at me," he murmured.

Slowly, she opened her eyes. Nerves assailed her suddenly. Gee, it was a little late to be worried and anxious. The deed was done. That realization didn't stop the butterflies from kicking the walls of her stomach like contestants at one of Mark's martial arts tournaments. What did Rafe think? What would he say?

When she met his gaze, the nerves disappeared. His gaze burned molten with knowledge and satisfaction and promise. Despite the perspiration dampening his sideburns and the rumpled state of his hair, he looked amazing to her. Her heart tripped at the tenderness on his face.

Down, girl! Rafe was a fantasy. Not Mr. Right, just Mr. Right Now. She had to keep her heart out of this agreement. He would leave soon, probably no later than Wednesday. Their bargain would end even sooner. Getting tied up in the guy was just stupid, stupid, stupid.

And something she couldn't afford.

"Amazing," he whispered. He brushed her mouth with a soft kiss.

With that soft word, Kerry felt her heart trip again.

* * *

OH. My. God.

Thoughts spun in Rafe's brain. Unfortunately, that was one of the few functional parts of him at the moment. His legs? Not a chance.

Again, Kerry staggered him. Yes, she'd been incredibly tight—but he'd been expecting that. Predictably, her body had enclosed him, clasping with a wet suction he'd damn near felt to his toes and curdled his mind against everything except the moment he could get inside her again. She'd blown him away with her enthusiastic acceptance and boisterous participation, and the incredible trust she had placed in his hands. Her uptilted green eyes were a window to her every thought, every reaction. She concealed nothing, offered everything. He'd never known anything like it. Hell, it wouldn't surprise him to learn he'd been more nervous than her. Because from where he lay—standing was still out of the question—she seemed a lot braver than he'd imagined possible.

"Wow," she breathed. "No wonder people write songs and books about sex." She slanted him a dimpled smile from a face flushed with latent passion. "This makes me question Oprah and her first book club selections. Who would choose to read that depressing stuff? Maybe she needs to talk to Stedman about what he's doing wrong in the bedroom."

Rafe laughed. How had she gone from orgasms to Oprah in one thought? Only Kerry . . .

"You're a crazy woman."

"Oh?" She arched a brow. "You're the one still lying on top of me . . . and growing harder by the moment, if I'm not mistaken. What does that say about you?"

"That I'm the village idiot, no doubt."

Victory shone in her satisfied smile. "I love to hear a man admit his faults. I wish you could teach that skill to my brother." Suddenly, the light dimmed in her eyes. "But you won't be here that long."

"No, I won't."

Kerry's deflated expression warned Rafe that things between them would get tangled if he wasn't careful. Encouraging her wasn't smart. They were here to fuck and help her brother, and these short hours together weren't reality. They both had lives—over a thousand miles apart. Besides, he sucked at relationships. Why bother? Good times, good sex, an easy parting; that was his speed.

That didn't mean, however, he wanted Kerry to regret what they had just done. Or to have done it only to bail her brother out of trouble.

"I'm, um, going to grab a quick shower. Can you let me up?"

Her withdrawal was nearly palpable. She focused on a spot on the ceiling, just over his shoulder. Still braced on top of her, Rafe found himself reluctant to let Kerry go. But doing so was the only smart move.

Slowly, he rolled away and watched as she grabbed her discarded towel, wrapped it around her gorgeous curves, and disappeared into the bathroom. If she'd slammed the door, that would have given him some indication of her mood, but no. Tears, anger, and blame he'd halfway expected. Only a quiet click heralded her exit.

He frowned. Maybe she wasn't pissed or regretful—just a little replete. That he could handle.

With a grimace, he pulled off the condom. Traces of blood reddened the latex. With a frown, he deposited it in the nearby trash can. Though he'd come like a geyser and he couldn't deny concern for Kerry, Rafe's cock stood hard as granite again. All it had taken was a glimpse of Kerry's bare thigh and shoulders, still rosy in the aftermath of passion, and he was ready for more.

Well, they'd agreed to forty-eight hours of unrestrained sex. They'd just proven their encounters would be completely mind-blowing. Hell, try beyond his comprehension. Reality could come later—much later. The only thing he wanted coming now was Kerry, followed closely by himself.

With a smile, he stood on shaky legs. He wandered to the nightstand and grabbed a fresh condom, then hesitated. Imagining Kerry naked and against a wall in a steam-filled shower made his cock jerk and rise even harder against his belly. He grabbed a second condom, just in case.

Whistling a cheerful tune, he made his way down the hall. He grabbed the doorknob and turned.

It was locked.

What was up with that? The blood on his condom sparked a memory. Was she hurt, by chance? Or more upset than he'd thought?

"Kerry?"

No response.

He knocked. "Okay in there?"

Nothing. Shit. What if she was crying, or God forbid, seriously bleeding? He knew more about origami than virgins, and that wasn't saying much. Maybe he'd hurt her somehow.

Again, he banged on the door. "Kerry?"

Still nothing.

Quickly, he retrieved a wire hanger from the closet and twisted it up with a curse. Seconds after applying it to the lock, the catch gave way. His anxiety stayed firmly in place as he shoved the door open . . . only to find Kerry gloriously naked in the huge, glass-enclosed shower. The hot, dual-headed spray of water kissed her body, front and back. Would he love to set one of those sprays right on her honey spot and watch her throw her head back and gasp as her pleasure spiked . . . He set the condoms on the bathroom counter and closed the door.

"How did you get in here?" Her voice held a startled note as she turned away.

Rafe tossed the mangled hanger onto the floor, opened the shower, and stepped inside.

"Picked the lock. You're okay?" he asked as warm water hammered tense muscles.

"Yes."

The word itself implied *fine*. The tone . . . slightly arctic. Relief and confusion tumbled over one another. She was okay but locking doors against him? And why would she be mad? No wonder he was bad at relationships; women were so confusing. Why didn't they come with manuals or a help file he could access by pressing F1?

" 'Yes'? That's it?" He glared at her in question.

"I just wanted a few minutes alone to think."

"Why the locked door? You can't think unless you've got a dead bolt between us?"

"P-R-I-V-A-C-Y. Or didn't they teach you to spell at St. Bovine's Academy for the Insanely Overprivileged?"

Despite his irritation and concern, he couldn't hold in a laugh. "St. Bovine's? Catholics don't worship cows."

"Whatever."

"Actually, dear old Dad sent me to The Beekman School in Manhattan. And yes, they taught me to spell . . . for the most part."

"Is it the concept of privacy you're having trouble with? Should I explain?"

What the hell was up with her? Rafe made it a policy never to know too much about the inner workings of the female mind, but this he had to figure out. "How did I know you weren't hurt?"

She heaved an exasperated sigh. "I would have told you. Can't a girl be alone?"

He thought about that. Granted, the few minutes it took her to shower didn't represent a significant chunk of the time they had to spend together. Why object if she wanted a few minutes to herself? Call him a caveman, but he did object.

"If you're only going to use it to dredge up reasons to be pissed off, then no locked doors, Kerry. Until tomorrow night, you're mine to take anytime I want, anywhere I want, any way I want. You're clear on that, right?"

"You've reminded me plenty of times. I get it." She turned a cold shoulder to him. "But I didn't sign up for Big Brother."

Attitude. That, along with Kerry's stay-away body language, told him that something was troubling her. The sex? She'd seemed pretty focused on the pleasure at the time but . . . was she thinking of Mark and his problems now? Wishing she hadn't gone through with this, after all?

No. She'd been fine, until that comment about his not being here to teach her brother to acknowledge his faults. So she was upset by the realization this affair couldn't last? He hoped she was smarter than that, but she was barely experienced and might be listening to her emotions more than her logic. Or he might be totally confused and utterly screwed.

As he stared at her truly amazing backside, Rafe did something he found himself often forced to do in Kerry's company: He counted to ten.

"I'm not your brother," he reminded her harshly.

She hesitated. "Good thing, too, or that would make pretty much everything we just did illegal in fifty states."

Was this even the same woman who'd been in his bed panting his name fifteen minutes ago? Rafe brushed the question away. She'd promised to make herself available, and he wanted her now. She wasn't shutting any more doors against him, not when they had a lot more sex to have. End of story.

"Why are you standing in the shower with me? I mean, okay, you're not my brother. So what are you? My own personal Peeping Tom?"

"Yeah. Peeping, touching, stroking, fucking. But if you're upset about something, spill it. Don't make me guess. I can't read your mind and I won't try."

Kerry hesitated, then sighed. "I don't mean to be witchy. The last few days have just been a lot, you know? Sex was heavier than I thought. I just wanted a minute alone."

Suddenly, guilt gnawed at him. She'd had a big day already and it wasn't even nine.

"Sorry. Look." He turned her to face him, fascinated by the haphazard upsweep of her sunny curls, the little drops of water running down her fair skin . . . the vulnerable expression he'd never seen her wear. That made him want to hold her—something he usually saw as a big waste of time. "We've got a lot of hours ahead of us to enjoy. Let's not worry about anything else now, all right? Later will take care of itself."

With a gentle touch to his shoulder, she nodded. “You’re right. Sorry if I growled.”

“No sweat. Let me find the soap and do my thing. Then I’ll leave you alone for a while.”

“It’s okay. Stay,” Kerry whispered, stepping closer, nearly into his arms.

She didn’t have to ask him twice.

Rafe closed the distance between them and looked at her. Just looked, wishing he could read her mind. Did she really want time alone for space, or was she already putting distance between them? That thought bothered him. After all, one time together relieved her of her virginity. Maybe that was all she wanted, or she hoped that put an end to their bargain.

Not even close.

Kerry met his glance with a question in her soft green eyes. Rafe lifted a hand to her cheek. He couldn’t stop himself. Not touching her was impossible at that moment. And it wasn’t just about getting inside her, though God knew he loved that idea, too. For now, he just wanted her near. Wanted to kiss her.

With a dip of his head, he took gentle possession of her sweet lips. She yielded, opened, feeling so damn good. She moaned softly into his mouth. Something warm and honeyed spread inside him as he leaned against her. From chest to thigh, they touched. He pressed her against the water-warmed tile and kissed her as if tomorrow didn’t exist. In a way, he wished it didn’t.

A sudden mechanical *whoosh* startled them both. Shit, was someone here?

On alert and in battle mode, Rafe clapped his hand over Kerry’s gasp and gazed around the small shower, looking for the source of the noise. It was more than water spraying. More than the drain taking water away. Too close to be a door opening in the rest of the cottage.

He looked around the small black cubicle and found the source of the sound.

At the far end of the shower, a panel in the wall had retracted, revealing a hidden eighteen-by-eighteen compartment all decked out in matching black marble tile—and filled with items that alternately had him holding in both laughter and drool.

With a crooked smile, he glanced between the treasure trove and his still-sweet Kerry. "Oh, babe. This party's about to get a lot more interesting."

Chapter Seven

INTERESTING? Mischief lit Rafe's gaze as he reached around Kerry, blocking her view of the open compartment.

When he wore an expression like that, she trusted a used car salesman more. "Define interesting."

"I'd rather show you."

His crooked smile made her heart pick up speed. She noticed a telltale moistening of parts south. Lord, what this man did to her. And she'd locked him out of her shower. What *had* she been thinking?

Of the future, of going on without him. Of the hour close at hand when she'd no longer have Rafe's touch, see his smile. Surprisingly, she found these very unhappy thoughts.

She wasn't in love with him or anything. Maybe having sex with the incarnation of all her fantasies had fried her brain worse than an overdone egg on the breakfast platter she served at the diner.

Ya think? the little voice in her head mocked. She told it to shut up.

Seriously, being with him felt a lot like she imagined a relationship should be. They laughed together, teased each other, argued passionately, had amazing sex before they started all over. Somehow she doubted she could ever get bored. And while he challenged her, she never felt unsafe, as if he might hurt her or push too far. She'd never clicked with any guy on so many levels. For sure, she'd miss the connection.

But Rafe was right—worrying about that now was pointless.

"You're all about showing me, aren't you?" She smiled.

"Every chance I get, babe." He looked back at her with a wink. "And if you don't give me chances, I'll make them."

With that, he grabbed something into his sizable hand. "Now, this is what I call soap."

He opened his fist to reveal a pale, palm-sized soap shaped like a lush breast, complete with a turgid berry nipple. He rubbed it slowly across his chest, down his abdomen. Bubbles clung to his taut golden skin, sliding down, down . . . Kerry's breath caught in her chest as he eased the soap between his legs, swiping the breast back and forth over his testicles—all while his gaze pinned her in place. His hands swept up over the hard erection jutting up. She swallowed as she watched him slowly encircle his penis, now thick as her wrist and standing nearly to his navel, and soap himself, stroke himself. He moaned softly. She had no idea why the sight turned her on; it just did.

Mesmerized, Kerry pushed his hand aside. She clutched the hot width of his penis with her fingers instead, stroking him up and down. He was like silk, like steel, solid, amazing, so male. Touching him, watching pleasure spread across the hard angles of his face, thrilled her. She wanted to see him come, see his expression when he found satisfaction. She wanted to be the one to give it to him.

Her brazen behavior shocked her a bit, but not enough to stop.

With a kittenish smile, she increased the tempo of her strokes.

Eyes closed, Rafe dropped his head against the wall. "Damn, woman. You get me there."

His rapid breaths, followed by moans, escalated her arousal. Her own breathing wasn't too steady. Neither were her knees, for that matter. All she knew was that Rafe's thighs and chest tensed, the muscles in his wide shoulders rippled with every movement, his erection stiffened even further in her hands. He had to be close . . .

"Not now." The strain in his voice was evident as he shoved her hand from his shaft. "Not like this."

"Why not? I was having fun," she protested.

"Much more of that would have put an end to the fun. Now it's your turn for a little soap," he whispered as he reached past her again. His voice sent a shiver of anticipation sliding down her spine.

This time, he extracted a small soap in the shape of a man's penis—and a very hard one with pinkish testicles.

Kerry burst out laughing. "Dominating Dave strikes again. He thinks of everything."

"Who?"

"Jason's uncle. This place—we call it the Love Shack—belongs to him. He's a wealthy real estate developer on the West Coast, but he built this retreat so he can bring his girlfriends and tie them up for hours of bondage heaven. Apparently his wife isn't into that sort of thing."

"Hmmm. Well, Dave keeps his Love Shack really well equipped. Collars and cuffs and paddles, oh my."

"Oh my, is right." She giggled, took the penis soap, and began washing up, laughing again when she nearly dropped the slippery sucker. "Now I know why I didn't find the soap earlier today. You must have leaned me against a button on the wall or something."

"You're right." He felt the wall behind her and found the switch. The panel closed.

Kerry reached behind her and opened it again. She took a few half-steps to the corner of the shower and peeked inside. "What other goodies are in there?"

Rafe pulled her back. "You know what they say about curiosity and the cat."

She snorted. "Killer sex toys? Dave is extreme, but come on. Let me see."

"I'd rather surprise you."

But she already had her hands on something big and purple. She turned it over. Rafe groaned.

"Butt Buddy." She read the name on the bottom of the six-inch rocket-shaped plug. She looked up at him with a grin. "Want to make friends?"

"Want to get real? Now if you'd like to become acquainted—"

"No thanks." She shuddered. "No more than one new orifice per day, I always say."

Rafe's rueful smile had her grinning. "When did you start saying that?"

"Now?"

"I figured. In that case . . ." He grabbed the anal plug from her grasp and moved toward the compartment. He put the purple rocket away, then extracted something else, shielding her view with his body.

"All right. What are you hiding?"

"A little something you may find . . . tempting." He turned and presented her with an item that made her drop her jaw in the vicinity of her knees.

Kerry stared at nine inches of red shimmer jelly goo shaped like a well-hung, very hard erection and burst out laughing. "Little? Are you serious? That would stretch any woman out more than her first yoga class."

Wearing a roguish smile, Rafe lifted the screamingly bright dildo and examined it. "You're not impressed by"—he read the wording at the base—"Glitter Dong?"

Holding her laughter in was not an option. "Is that really its name?"

"Check it out for yourself." He held it out to her.

With a shake of her head, Kerry shied away. "I'll take your word for it."

"Want to make friends?" he teased, turning her words back on her.

"I have plenty of friends, thanks. And I wouldn't classify something intended to prowl any and all of my orifices as one."

"Glitter Dong may surprise you."

The sin in Rafe's voice stopped her. Did he want to use it on her? Watch her masturbate with it? She'd heard some guys were into that. At the thought Rafe might demand a little floor show here in the shower, fear and excitement blended into an exquisite shiver. Could she do it?

Rafe brought out the daring in her, the woman in her. Yet she always felt safe, never rushed, never threatened. Being with him was so easy . . . especially when pure thrill pumped through her blood.

"How will it surprise me?" She scoffed. "By making me glow?"

"If the orgasm is good enough . . ."

"Oh, stop. Seriously."

His smile teased her. "Glitter Dong has special features." Rafe grabbed her hand, brought it forward, and placed the dildo in her grasp.

Its texture was definitely artificial and warm only where he had touched it. When Tiffany had received something similar at a bachelorette party, Kerry had only had one thought—tackier than a rusted truck on cinder blocks in the front yard of a double-wide. Why would any bride-to-be want such a thing when she could have a flesh-and-blood man? But the idea of using it to drive that flesh-and-blood man mad with want put a whole new spin on the concept of owning this little toy.

"Oh, and what would those features be?"

"Obviously its size and color."

"Obviously." She rolled her eyes.

"It's harness compatible, I'm guessing."

"Excuse me?"

"Let's just say it provides a female the ability to strap this sucker on and see what it's like to be the driving force during sex."

"For real?" Kerry knew she looked like the wide-eyed naïve virgin she'd been until an hour ago. Oh, well. "I could attach this to some sort of harness and . . ."

"Fuck someone? Yeah."

"Male or female?" What a strange, amazing thought.

"You got it."

"Who dreams up this stuff? Clearly someone with a mind more wicked than mine."

Rafe laughed. Not surprising, really. He'd probably known more about sex toys by the time he was twelve than she did today.

"See these suction cups?" At her nod, he fastened it to the black marble bench in the large shower. "If you were so inclined to sit there, it wouldn't move while you took your pleasure."

"And you'd watch?" Heat crept up Kerry's cheeks when her purely informational question came out like a personalized invitation to a voyeur.

"In a heartbeat, babe. I'd love to watch."

Kerry's mind raced. Her blood churned until she could hear it racing in her ears. Could she do something so personal with an audience?

"I don't know if I can—"

"You can. Try," he whispered, hands clasping her hips. "I want to see you."

With hot fingers, he guided her to the shower bench, then lifted her onto it with little effort. Hard tile met her knees. Kerry trembled as she glanced down to see the dildo rising tall and thick between her legs.

Arousal tangled with fear, heightened by a dash of the forbidden. The feeling was so familiar when Rafe was near. Kerry swallowed. She felt herself hesitate and moisten at once. Harsh breaths pumped her chest once, twice.

"What if it hurts?"

"Then you'll tell me and we'll stop."

She stared at him, into his silver eyes. There she saw not just heat, but warmth. He wanted her, wanted her pleasure, yes. But he would keep her safe, too.

There was no denying he knew how to make her feel incredibly good. And that the thought of driving him mad with desire held huge appeal.

"Kerry?"

Biting her lip, she nodded, earning her a wicked smile.

Slowly, he began urging her hips down with the gentle vise of his fingers.

Lord, her friends would say she had to be twenty kinds of crazy to take on an oversize dildo just so she could arouse the man who watched. But as her vagina, now slick beyond belief, touched the red penis-shaped toy, the expression on his face heated like a solar flare—hot, lashing, not to be denied.

An answering flash of lust burned between her legs. Her clit throbbed.

She continued lower, down, feeling the dildo stretch her fully. Rafe lifted one hand to her shoulder and eased her down another inch. She whimpered at the pleasure/pain.

"Almost there, babe."

She closed her eyes, shaking her head. "No. No more."

With fingers biting into her hips, Rafe helped her rise until she stood on her knees again, then he urged her down once more, taking a bit more of the dildo into her. "Ease into it."

She gasped at the sensations, burning, pressure, pleasure. Still, Rafe had filled her equally. A glance at his erection, now right in front of her, confirmed the comparison.

Kerry repeated the motions again, finding a rhythm and depth that pleased her. Pleased? Heck, drove her mad. Thick pleasure rose and swelled, threatening to crest and overtake her like a riptide to a drowning victim.

"Touch yourself," Rafe whispered, caressing his way up her torso to palm her breast. "Show me how you drive yourself wild."

His inflaming words arced through her, burning away any

shyness. Caught up in the fervor, she lowered her fingers to the pale thatch of curls between her legs and swirled them over her clit. Rafe watched, his eyes darkened with approval, with a promise to drive her higher.

"Yes," he whispered against her ear. "You're so damn sexy."

Need flowed through her body. Her muscles clasped the dildo, her gaze helplessly locked on Rafe's, knowing he watched every movement. Her thighs trembled with effort. So, so close . . . She groaned. The fact Rafe appeared to grow harder with every stroke only sent her toward the precipice faster.

He bent and captured her lips then and plunged his way inside, deep, deep in her mouth. She tasted the sizzle of desire in his kiss. The bite of his fingers into her hips, the crash of his mouth on hers, the ragged drag of air into his lungs—those all paled in comparison to the feral, sexual promise in his gaze when he pulled away, panting hard.

Kerry didn't want to come alone, which was a serious possibility unless she did something soon.

When he stood before her, rolling each of her pointed nipples between his fingers, Kerry did the first, most effective thing that came to mind: She lowered her mouth to his cock. His musky scent mixed with the water sluicing all around her. The tang of salt rasped on her tongue. And his groan . . . as wonderful to hear as a favorite song.

"Oh, Kerry. Oh, yeah, babe. That's it." His sizable hands slipped into damp hair, wrapping strands around his fingers, guiding her up and down. "So good."

Encouraged by his verbal appreciation, she ran her tongue on the underside of his erection, slipping over the engorged head. Swirling, licking, savoring, she sucked him until her cheeks hollowed, until she saw his thighs tremble. Until he stiffened against her tongue.

Suddenly, he groaned and withdrew his penis from her mouth. "Gotta be inside you. Now."

With his left hand, he reached out of the shower and grabbed a condom from the counter. With his right, he extracted the big red toy from her body and tossed it to the tiled floor with a clatter. So close to orgasm, she cried out. Rafe's look silenced her. His nostrils flared as he devoured her with a silver gaze so intent, anticipation licked like fire up her spine.

Here stood a man who wanted her, a man who would not take no for an answer, a man who intended to possess her so thoroughly she would never forget it. The thought made the tension in her belly ratchet up a notch.

"Rafe—"

"Gotta feel you, tight and slick. Gotta get deep into you." He tore open the condom's packet and sheathed himself. In one quick motion, he turned her around, her back to his chest, and lifted her leg until her foot rested on the bench.

Like this? Would he really take her like this? Kerry's heart beat with a wild rhythm as her body throbbed in time. Finding her next breath definitely took a backseat to getting Rafe to touch her, fill her. The sharp arousal in her belly gouged her restraint. The ache . . . God, she needed him inside her, around her, whispering his every desire in her ear.

His fingers found her clit at the same time Kerry felt the head of his penis meet her slick opening. She whimpered and lowered herself down as much as her bent knees would allow. Her greedy body clasped onto the head of his thick stalk, trying to suck him inside. Those fingers circling the button of nerves above her entrance had her crying out his name.

With a firm grasp on her hips, Rafe surged up in one quick thrust, stretching through pliant muscle and tissue. He drove home, all the way, his tip probing at the entrance of her womb. In this position, she felt him everywhere, stretching her wide with a delicious bite.

Rafe withdrew slowly, so slowly it was pure torture. Then he rocketed back inside her, grazing her tingling, ultrasensitive flesh. Then he slanted the showerhead in front of her, right at her clit. The pound of the warm spray hit the needy bud with a steady, insistent rhythm. She gasped at the staggering sensation. Her head fell back against his shoulder.

Tunneling farther inside her, Rafe shaped a calloused hand over a taut breast, pulling at the hard point of her nipple. Every roll and pinch shot arrows of sensation straight between her legs. His lips moved on her neck, nipping gently, sending shivers of thrill down her spine. Kerry rocked back against him in silent pleading.

"You feel me inside you?" He nipped at her lobe, breathed over her neck.

"Yes," she moaned. "God, yes."

"There's nothing like this." He grabbed her hips and began pistoning in and out of her. "Nothing like the feel of you hot and tight and mewling when I get deep inside. Come for me."

With his words and the feel of his hard body claiming her in a relentless pound of pleasure, Kerry's arousal soared. As every inch of him poured into her like liquid lust, he ignited all her sensitive nerve endings. Her heartbeat roared in her ears so loudly, it drummed out the pounding of the water, everything around her except Rafe's panting demand.

Tighter and tighter the pleasure strung, coiling into an orgasm so violent, she wondered if she'd survive it. The power of it built and built, towering above anything she'd ever known. Her body throbbed for release. Even her pebbled nipples pleaded into the warm haven of his hand.

"Oh, Rafe." She was on fire, burning . . . consumed. "More."

And he obliged.

His next thrust buried him so far inside her, Kerry could nearly taste the overwhelming rapture. Hard and heavy, he filled her faster than lightning, branding her. The mounting orgasm screamed just under her burning skin. It was going to swallow her whole, and she wanted it more than anything. Behind her, his chest heaved with effort. He grew harder still and doubled his effort, filling her fiercely, deeper with each jackhammer stroke.

Every time he filled her, Rafe stole away her sanity. As the tension escalated again, Kerry whimpered. And then she exploded, disintegrated, fell apart in his arms as the pleasure swept her away to the oblivion of ecstasy. Rafe pulsed inside her contracting walls, tightened his fingers on her, and shouted out his release.

Lava-hot pleasure spiked again, and Kerry could only soar with it as the exquisite sensations burst through her. She cried out, the stars alighting in her vision, bright, exhilarating, full of promise.

Then the stars faded. She exhaled once, twice, trying to catch her breath. Heck, trying to remember her name.

A minute passed, maybe two. Neither moved.

Doing her best to ignore the sudden vulnerability that crowded her worse than shoppers at a Christmas Eve sale, Kerry concentrated on the now lukewarm water pelting her shoulders. But the need for Rafe to hold her overwhelmed her and would not go away. Somehow, he'd possessed her so thoroughly, he had laid bare her soul. She felt too open, completely without defenses, as if the only thing that would heal her now was his touch.

As if he felt her yearning, Rafe planted his palm on her abdomen and curled his body around hers in something close to a hug. Grateful for the contact, she closed her eyes and sank back against him. Even as the water cooled a degree more, his warmth seeped into her. Tears pricked the tired sockets of her eyes.

She shouldn't think about what would happen later, not today. But later she wouldn't have this anymore. Rafe would be gone from her life as quickly as he'd entered it.

"You amaze me," he whispered as he turned off the water, then planted a gentle kiss on her shoulder, on her neck.

She amazed him? *He* was the one who dared her within the safety of his arms to scream with pleasure until her throat felt raw, then left her emotions spilling out of her like a wound in need of a tourniquet. Talk about amazed. Tears scalded her eyes as he continued to plant slow, sweet kisses along her shoulder blade, her nape. Besides the fact his half-hard penis was still lodged inside her, he'd connected their bodies from shoulder to ankle, as if he wanted to touch every part of her. His body heat combined with steam in the shower cubicle, the slight rasp of his body hair everywhere, and the tender stroke of his fingers over her belly, overwhelmed her.

Why was he so gentle? When he was like this, stopping the fantasy that Rafe was her man was impossible. He made it too easy to pretend he cared, that they could have a future. She had no defenses against him. The possibility of falling in love felt a little too real.

Oh, God. Was she sinking slowly, giving her heart to him bit by bit? Another tear fell.

No, no, no. This was just sex. The emotion must stem from the suddenness, the unexpected jolt of the naked connection between two sexual partners. That had to be it. She knew next to nothing about him except that he was intelligent, sexy as hell, and liked to sleep in the middle of the bed. That didn't add up to love. Lust? Oh, yeah. With him, she could see a major orgasm addiction being a problem. The tears, they had to come from lack of sleep, of food. *Of common sense,* that pesky voice told her.

Shut up! she silently told it.

Falling in love with someone as unattainable as Rafe made playing in traffic look downright brilliant. And she wasn't stupid. After all, he came from money, was geographically undesirable, and probably had more women clinging to him than roadkill has flies.

Falling in love had probably never crossed his mind—and it shouldn't. As a couple, they were as inconceivable as a sumo wrestler modeling for Victoria's Secret.

There, now she felt better. Really. And if she kept telling herself that enough, maybe it would eventually be true.

"You okay?" he asked.

Kerry gathered her thoughts long enough to nod and hoped he would mistake the tear that rolled from her cheek and onto the forearm he'd slung across her chest for mere water. If he found her crying, she'd be more embarrassed than the time she'd had to wear a secondhand dress on her first day of high school.

"Fine."

"If I pushed you too far, I'm sorry. With you . . . I lose my mind."

If she wasn't careful, with him . . . she'd lose her heart.

Another soundless tear tracked down her cheek. Another dribbled to her chin. Her throat ached as she held the rest in. How could she keep opening herself to him again and again?

Yet how could she refuse him after promising him forty-eight hours of commitment-free sex?

* * *

FROWNING at Kerry's weirdly quiet mood, Rafe set her omelet on the table, along with a piece of toast. Both times now she'd been reserved after sex.

That same thing had happened once before, years ago, with a college girlfriend. Rather than deal with her emotional crap, which likely would have filled a pair of Samsonites, he'd stopped calling.

Failing to solve the puzzle back then meant he now had to guess Kerry's problem. Normally, he wouldn't bother. But with her, something was . . . different. More intense inside, beyond the pleasure he derived from the sex—though he felt plenty of that. Some unusual connection jumped between them when they touched. And even after the sex, he was loath to release her, to let go of that link, even if he didn't understand it.

Shoveling his hands through damp hair, Rafe grimaced and tried to guess at Kerry's feelings. Guilt? Regret? She didn't seem the type who'd drown in self-recrimination. Fear? Nah, none manifested in the heat of the moment. Insecurity? While most modeling agencies would find her too curvaceous for *Cosmo,* Rafe thought her body was perfect. Maybe he ought to tell her so. Or was she sad because she'd wanted her first lover to love her? Ouch.

If he was smart, he'd give up guessing, wait until her mood passed. Or he could just focus on Mark and leave Kerry be.

Other than his brain, the rest of him thought that idea sucked.

For now, she was all his. He wanted her. No way he was going to give it up because she was feeling moody.

"Breakfast," he called down the hall.

The bathroom door opened, and Kerry stepped into the hall, wearing his slightly rumpled dress shirt, which brushed the tops of her thighs—and a plastic smile, sans those dimples he adored. As she approached, he let the fact she was dressed slide for the moment and focused on her slightly puffy eyes. Had she been crying? His guess, yes. The thought made his gut churn, as if he'd eaten something rancid.

"What's wrong?" He took her hand as she hovered at the edge of the little kitchen.

Right on cue, her Tupperware smile appeared again. Gently, she pulled free. "A little tired. Hungry."

Yeah, and he was Santa Claus's cousin, twice removed.

Since asking if she was okay had only earned him the equivalent of "fine," obviously it was time for Plan B. He just had to think of it first.

"You cook?" she asked, looking at the steaming food, pale brow raised.

"A man's gotta eat. Too much fast food is like throwing garbage down your body. I'm no gourmet, though."

She hesitated. "Did your mother teach you before she passed away?"

"No. I taught myself out of necessity."

"Good skill to have," she murmured as she retreated to the little two-seater pine table against the wall, eyes downcast.

Rafe stayed silent as he watched her with a frown. Something wasn't right. "What are you thinking?"

Weird. Normally, he didn't care what anyone thought. If they wanted to share, fine. If not, well, most of the time the thought wasn't earth-shattering anyway. Why was she different?

"Nothing." She punctuated that word with another fake smile and began picking at her omelet. For a supposedly hungry woman, she wasn't eating much. In fact, she seemed more withdrawn now than when she'd first entered the kitchen. Because he wouldn't talk about his mother?

Or . . . was she upset because she'd been having sex with a virtual stranger? Did she want to know more about him just to say she did? It wasn't logical, but maybe it was a woman thing. And Kerry wasn't known for possessing lots of logic anyway. Warmth? Yes. She was giving and loyal and fun. Logic seemed farther down the list of her qualities.

"You want to know about my mom?" he asked—and could have kicked himself for doing it. Sex was just fine when conversation was relegated to the bedroom. Why mess with a good thing?

Because he was a schmuck and he wanted to see her smile again.

"It'd be nice to know something about you, other than your occupation."

So his hunch had been right. But questions about his mother—it was a topic he never discussed, along with most of his personal life. His private business was private. He wasn't keen on a trip down memory lane. The journey wasn't pleasant. Being a woman's lover didn't entitle her to know everything about his life. But as Kerry buttered her toast with a vulnerable, almost lost expression, he realized that she'd been an open book about her life, given a lot of herself—starting with her virginity. The only thing he'd given her was a lot of smart-alecky comebacks and an erection.

He sighed. "My mom didn't teach me to cook because she died when I was eleven, just like you. Private plane crash. She and my dad weren't living together anymore. If she had lived, it would have been an ugly divorce." Rafe tried to shrug, to shove back memories of his father shouting the same insult over and over, the one that always made her cry. "I got tired of hearing him call her a gold-digging Puerto Rican whore. I guess she did, too."

Shock stilled her for a long moment. "I'm so sorry. I didn't mean to dredge up bad stuff with my question." She took a bite of her omelet. "This is good. Thanks for cooking."

Watching her shove the rest around on her plate, Rafe thought her compliment on his cooking was a thin way of changing the subject. For some reason, he didn't mind so much telling her something about himself, now that he'd started.

"My mom was going back to Puerto Rico to see her priest, to ask how she might have her marriage annulled in the Church. I would have been with her if I hadn't had a big test the day she left."

Kerry gasped. "Oh, God. Were you at school when you heard?"

He nodded. "I'd just finished my English test. Aced it, too." And he remembered the first time he'd cried after her death was the day he'd received his exam score . . . then realized the one person he could have shared it with, who would have been the proudest of him, was gone.

"That's awful." She took a small bite of her toast and ate it. "What about your dad? Did you two get along?"

Rafe abandoned the idea of eating and watched Kerry. The starch seemed to melt out of her with every word he spoke. If all he had to do to make her happy was keep talking, he could manage. Talking to Kerry was pretty easy, actually. Besides, whom would she tell? After Tuesday, he'd probably never see her again.

Scowling, he shoved that thought away.

"Not to this day. Dad was born to wealth. His grandmother was a Vanderbilt. When he got my mother pregnant while spending the summer in Puerto Rico, my maternal grandfather insisted they marry. I never knew why Dad hated me until she died."

Kerry, too, pushed aside her plate, leaning across the table toward him. "Certainly he didn't hate you. How can anyone hate their own child?"

"Ah, but he wasn't convinced I was his. I look just like her, except the eyes, which seemed to come from nowhere. That was enough to convince my dad she'd been sleeping around while he got stuck with the bill. A week after Mom's death he drove me to a hospital two states away for a paternity test."

With a gasp, Kerry's jaw dropped to her chest. "Did it matter at that point? You were eleven."

"Sure it mattered. My mother had been poor and ethnic. If he could rid himself of his last link to her, all the better for him. But Mom had the last laugh. Test proved a ninety-nine point nine nine eight percent possibility that good ol' Dad had indeed sired me. Pissed him off, too. But since he was stuck with me, he was determined to make a better man out of me."

"At eleven?"

He shrugged. "It was a place to start."

"That's awful."

"Dad decided I should go to Harvard and marry well, hobnob in the Hamptons. Wasn't happening. I was never cooperative on my best days, but the following summer I discovered computers and everything changed. I played games, surfed the Internet when there wasn't much out there to surf. I discovered chat rooms, wrote viruses. The more he hated it, the more I did it. It was so easy to shut him out. Of course, he ripped the phone jack out of my room. I just hung out with other guys who were plugged in and stopped coming home."

The tone came out blasé, and Rafe prided himself on that. But he remembered that shitty summer, the first time he'd lived with his dad in almost two years. The constant shouting, followed by silences so cold they could freeze out a polar bear. That summer he'd cried himself to sleep more than once, missing a mother who would never come back, hating the father who hated him. God, he'd been twelve going on twenty.

"That's awful." She reached across the table for his hand.

"That's a theme for you." He shot her a halfhearted smile.

Continuing with the tale wasn't on his list of favorite things to do, but Kerry was responding to him again, looking him in the eye, expressing her emotions using her sweet face and kiss-swollen mouth, touching him.

While he hated baring his childhood bullshit, he'd do it if it kept her near and responding.

"Long story short," he concluded, "Dad was a bitter man who couldn't accept that the marriage he thought had ruined him was his own fault. He fell into a bottle of gin while I was in high school and pretty much drowned. We didn't talk much while I was in college. I refused to take money from him. With a few student loans and grants, I put myself through Columbia, which also pissed him off. In 2000 he put most of his fortune into dot-coms and they all went south. That sealed the deal. Today, he's an alcoholic with only a fraction of his fortune left. I help him out sometimes, but he still likes to pretend I'm not his."

"That's . . . awful. I know I've said it before, but really, it is." She covered her heart with a hand, eyes swimming with empathy. "His pride hurt you both so much."

Encouraged, Rafe went on. "It's one reason I wanted the Standard National job so bad. With their check, I would be over the five-million-dollar mark just before my thirtieth birthday, and I'd have earned every dime on my own. And for every time he called me worthless, I'd now have a comeback. Five million of them, in fact."

She stilled. "I took that away from you with this stupid abduction plan. Oh, I'm so sorry."

"I want to go to the bank tomorrow and see Mr. Smikins, ask a few questions about Mark's situation. The job will work itself out somehow, some way." At least he hoped it would. This was one goal he would not, could not, let go of.

"I'm sure." She gave him a sad, rueful smile. "Just don't tell him you actually know me or think Mark might be innocent. He loathes Mark, but I've hounded and accused him since my brother's arrest. I doubt he'll be inviting me to Christmas dinner."

Rafe couldn't stop himself from touching her, gliding the backs of his fingers over her soft, bare cheek. "Your brother is lucky to have you. I've never known anyone so loyal."

And that was the rub. As a kid, he'd have given up every one of his Hot Wheels and his Nintendo games to have anyone care about him like Kerry cared about Mark. Yes, his mom had loved him, but every memory he had of her was tainted with the anger and despair his father had constantly driven her to. As an adult, he saw that she'd spent a decade trying to make the bitter bastard love her. Instead, his father had only broken her heart a little more each day. With his mom gone, Benton Dawson III hadn't had anyone else to torture, so Rafe had become his verbal whipping boy.

"I'm more than lucky to have Mark." Kerry turned into his touch, kissed his fingertips. She sent him a wistful smile. "Tell me more about you."

"You mean, like, facts?"

At her nod, he opened his mouth. He wasn't sure where to start, now that she'd heard his major life trauma, such as it was. Why not the beginning?

"I was born May eighteenth, 1979, which I'm told makes me a Taurus. My—"

"May eighteenth? You'll be thirty in less than two weeks?"

Like he wanted to be reminded of that. "Yeah. Lucky me."

"You going to have a big bash with friends?"

"No."

She frowned at his quick answer. "Why not? Even if you don't want one, your friends should foist a party off on you. It's their duty."

"Not my friends. I've got a few I play basketball with during the week. You know, guys from the gym. My college roommate and I still get together for a two A.M. cup of coffee every now and then. I have a few friends online from around the world. None are the throw-a-bash type."

"What about holidays? Who do you spend them with?"

"Holidays have never been a big deal to me. Turkey TV dinners and a new computer virus to solve give me plenty of cheer."

Kerry frowned, her eyes going all soft. Rafe tried not to wince at how empty it must sound to her, given her bond with her brother and all. No wonder he hated Christmas.

Kerry frowned. "Who do you tell your secrets to? Who do you talk to when you really need it? What about *those* friends?"

Did he really have anyone he considered a friend in the true meaning of the word?

He shrugged. "I don't have many secrets that need telling. I guess the closest person would be Regina, my assistant."

"The pit bull on the phone?"

"Yeah. Been with me for four years." He smiled. "She's great at screening calls."

"I'll say. So you talk to her?"

Was that note in her voice curiosity or jealousy? After the shit she'd given him about Jason, he ought to give it back. But he couldn't. "She's part superassistant, part mom. She doesn't let me forget my dry cleaning before a trip. About once a month she asks me if I've had someone clean my apartment lately. She's got a couple kids, I think in college. Anyway, she pretty much views me as just an older version of her sons."

"Oh." That one syllable was rife with relief. "Met her kids?"

"No. I think the older one goes to NYU." Rafe searched his memory for their names. "His name is Alan. No, Alex." He frowned as he drew a blank. "Maybe he's the younger one. I can't remember."

"So she has two boys?"

"Yeah." Or three. He couldn't remember that, either. Regina talked about them periodically, but he'd never really tuned in much. Yeah, she was more than an employee, but not someone to whom he wanted to spill his every secret.

"Is Regina married?"

She had been at one time. Right after she'd started working for him, she'd invited him to a party to celebrate her wedding anniversary. The twentieth? Rafe hadn't gone, and he had no idea if she and what's-his-name were still married. He figured it was none of his business.

Why did he suddenly feel like a real prick?

"I guess so." He shifted uncomfortably in his chair.

"What do you talk to Regina about?"

Besides business and schedules, equipment and invoices?

"She knows about my brush with the CIA." Rafe latched on to that. Of course, he'd told her because doing so was ethical . . . but he had told her something he didn't tell many. "She knows I like black coffee. Starbucks, if given a choice. She baked me a birthday cake a few years back."

Kerry's expression held . . . pity. She thought his life was empty; that was written all over her face. Well, it wasn't. He had work, basketball, an occasional date, and his computers.

"You don't have to look at me like that. I like my life. It's uncomplicated."

But he had no one special in his life. In her roundabout way, that's what Kerry wanted to know. The truth was as much of a newsflash to him as it was to her. It had never bothered him before. Why did it bother him now?

"Didn't mean to look at you like anything. Sorry." She wore another smile so artificial, it could have come straight from DuPont.

So she didn't believe him. Fine. In the end, no one's opinion but his mattered anyway.

Scowling, Rafe left the table. He wandered to the bedroom, walked past the rumpled bed, to stare out the picture window at the gently rolling ocean.

His life had never bothered him because he never cultivated the people who wanted to get close. Pushing them away was easier, safer. In the end, someone would only disappoint someone. There would be drama and crap. Or they would just drift apart, leaving a gouge in everyone's heart.

Why *did* his life bother him now?

Kerry drifted into the bedroom then, her expression questioning. He met her gaze in silence as she made her way across the room and hugged him. Nothing else. No kisses, no preludes to sex. Just wrapping her arms around him, filtering soft fingers into his hair, breathing in tempo with him and offering warmth.

He wanted to resist. He didn't need anyone. But withstanding her allure was like a computer junkie turning down the opportunity to debug a new Windows platform. In the end, he squeezed his eyes tightly shut and hugged back.

His insides felt as mushy as a bowl of oatmeal. He wanted to tell himself that he wasn't clinging to her. It was a lie. How had one ringlet-laden, slightly off-center blonde reached so deep inside him that she'd dredged up both his ugly past and most of his guts all in the same day?

Now Rafe knew why being alone had never bothered him; he didn't like being vulnerable. He'd never liked it. But he'd never had anything like this, like her. Never known anyone so impossible to resist. Most likely, Kerry would leave a hole in his heart after he'd gone. But for the first time, he wondered if having the experience, the memory of her warmth, just might be worth it.

Chapter Eight

KERRY watched Rafe wander out the bedroom's double French doors, to the awaiting beach. Once his bare feet hit the sand, he started walking the shoreline, staring out at the water.

He had not invited her along, but she hadn't expected it. Mark, when confronted with heavy subjects, often retreated to "get his head screwed back on straight," as he liked to put it. She recognized the signs. And wanted to kick herself. What on earth had possessed her to ask him personal questions? Clearly, he would rather have had a root canal without Novocain. If she had just gotten over her emotional spell in the shower and shut up, he'd be here, and they'd be laughing or having sex . . . or both.

But no. She'd been as smooth as a stuttering man in a singles' bar.

It was equally clear that Rafael Dawson was a lonely man. A man who had no one. Sure, he had money. That didn't change the fact his father was an ass, his assistant was nothing more than an employee, and his pals only friends on the surface. Rafe would return to New York soon, back to his half-life. Without her. But she meant to give him one great memory of their time together, so her next course of action was as obvious as a black thong under thin white shorts.

A box of Twinkies, a bit of red food coloring, and a dozen condoms later, Kerry stood back and surveyed her handiwork with a smile.

* * *

"SURPRISE!" Kerry shouted as Rafe walked back through the French doors some forty-five minutes later.

Startled, he looked from her dimpled smile to the shadowy bedroom beyond. A lone black crepe streamer ran the length of the far window, barely visible in the dimly lit room.

A black streamer? She'd half-decorated for a funeral? If she was shouting "surprise" at him, did that mean he was the guest of honor?

"What's this?" he asked.

Kerry slapped her palm against her forehead. Darting to the French doors behind him, she slammed them shut and, with a flick of her wrists, she threw back the sheers. Sunlight spilled in, illuminating the bedroom in a golden glow.

The black streamer was actually purple. So it wasn't a funeral. That was good news. But he was now puzzled by the oddly oval-shaped balloons in different colors that decorated the floor. What the heck was going on?

"It's a birthday party, goof—or at least the best I could manage in less than an hour. If your friends aren't going to give you a party . . . well, I wanted you to have one. Happy almost-thirtieth birthday."

As she grabbed his hand and squeezed, amazement dropped his jaw. Kerry had organized a birthday party? Out of the clear blue sky? For him?

Something warm exploded in his chest.

"I didn't have a lot to work with," she hedged. "I only found one length of streamer, but I used it. The balloons . . ."

Peering down, Rafe really looked at the inflatable décor. "Condoms?"

She grinned. "I found a box of multicolored ones and I thought, *What the hell.* Well, except when I nearly hyperventilated blowing them all up."

Her laughter was infectious, and he repressed a smile to deliver his dry return. "You realize that's a waste of perfectly good condoms."

"It's your birthday. There are plenty of other condoms for *those* occasions," she scolded. "Now your cake . . . I had to improvise—a lot."

She pointed to the little table by the bed. A lumpy rectangular blob sat on a plate, smothered in whipped topping. Red lettering on top read HAPPY BIRTHDAY RAFE, though his name was a little smaller than the rest, so it would all fit.

It was the funniest-looking cake he'd ever seen. Despite that, joy raced through his system, scraping down his nerve endings, mingling with other feelings he didn't understand. When was the last time he'd had a birthday party? Rafe frowned, counting back the years. He drew mostly a blank, until he thought of his mother. She'd thrown him a party for his eleventh birthday in May before she'd died that October.

"The cake is ten Twinkies held together by some whipped topping." Kerry bit her lip, looking nervous. "I—I found a little food coloring and dyed some of the topping red for the writing. Hard to spread. You probably can't read it." Her shoulders drooped. "You look unamused. Maybe this was a bad idea."

His gaze flew to her, zeroing in on her uncertain face. She thought he was unamused after she'd done something so amazing for him? "I'm stunned. It's the nicest thing anyone has done for me in years."

With those simple words, a smile blossomed across her face.

Pink tinged her makeup-free cheeks. Her mossy green eyes sparkled with delight. Standing there in his rumpled shirt with her pale curls shoved half-up, half-down in a haphazard clip, Rafe was sure she was the most beautiful woman he knew. Certainly, she was the warmest. Amazing that no one had taken advantage of her tender heart. Or that she still had it, given her childhood. But he admired the hell out of her for it. Most people he knew, himself included, would be scared shitless to expose that much of themselves to anyone.

Not Kerry.

The warm something that had exploded in his chest earlier was still swimming around and making mush of his insides. It urged him to grab her and hold her close.

Still holding her hand, Rafe used it to pull her into his embrace. "Thank you."

"You're very welcome. Should I sing to you? I found a candle and a book of matches in the kitchen."

"Can you sing? Would Simon Cowell throw you off the stage?"

From the corner of her eye, she slanted him a guilty look. "In a heartbeat."

He couldn't hold back a smile. "That's honest. You were willing to embarrass yourself?"

"It's for a good cause."

"Let's skip the singing, shall we?"

"Good call." She snuggled deeper into his arms. "Want cake?"

Glancing askance at the cake, he winced. "Is it poisonous? How long have those . . . ingredients been sitting around here?"

"Well, I can't answer one way or the other. I can only say the Cool Whip wasn't growing anything, so that was encouraging. The Twinkies, I don't worry about. Did you know they have no expiration date? And take it from me, someone with my hips is an authority on that subject."

Rafe felt a crooked grin cross his face. "Would you be offended if I said I was far more interested in getting my mouth on your hips . . . or any spot nearby, than that cake?"

"You mean, all that effort going to waste?" She gaped at him in mock outrage.

"Just call me an asshole. I doubt it would be the first time."

"Not exactly." She giggled. "So let's talk instead about a gift."

Kerry's sugar sunshine scent teased him to distraction, and he began nibbling on the soft skin of her neck. "Gift? That sounds promising."

"Don't get excited. First, I'm a waitress, and when last I looked, your occupation brings home a lot more than mine. Second—stop that," she giggled as he licked her sensitive lobe and breathed in her ear.

Rafe ignored her. What was it about this woman that revved up his libido? He was operating on very little food or sleep and a whole lot of sex. But it was more than mere sex. He'd walked the beach, contemplative, grim, thinking about his life. Two minutes with Kerry and he felt high on her, somehow light, optimistic even—a definite first for him. He'd love to bottle this sensation and gulp it down whenever he'd had a shitty day. Something about her made everyone around her more carefree. It was hard not to like a girl who could make you laugh, make you horny, and make you think—all in the same day.

"Second," she went on, "there's no store anywhere near, so you'll have to be creative in asking for a gift."

"Creative." He unlatched the top button of the shirt she wore and whispered, "That sounds suspiciously like an invitation."

"Maybe."

Kerry was all coquette now, and Rafe liked it. The tease in her was even more interesting when she ran her palm up his thigh, narrowly missing his stirring erection.

"Maybe not," she countered.

In response, Rafe unhooked another button on her shirt and slid the white cotton off her bare shoulder and brushed a thumb over the swell of her breast, just above her nipple. "I certainly don't want to take anything you're not willing to give."

"Of course not."

He touched her again, this time caressing the side of her breast and narrowly missing the tip. She sighed, her eyes closing.

She looked pretty willing at the moment.

Rafe smiled. "So how about this: I only give you what you beg me for."

Her eyes perked open. "Excuse me?"

"That's what I want for my birthday. I want to touch you until I drive you insane with want. I'm not going to give in—or give you anything—until you beg."

"You asking me to beg defeats the purpose, doesn't it?"

"Oh, I fully anticipate that you'll hold out as long as you can." The expectation raced through his system faster than ants to spilled sugar. "You're no pushover."

"Think you can make me beg? Pretty cocky, aren't you?"

Laughing, despite the lust tearing through his system, Rafe tilted his hips against hers, letting her feel him at full staff. "With you, always."

"You have no shame."

Neither did she, apparently. She wriggled her hips against his until his cock met her mound. Her mock scold was lost on him. In response, he released the third button on her shirt and stole a glance at the newly exposed swells of her breasts. "Why bother?"

"I'll have you know I'm pretty stubborn."

"I figured that out already." Softly, he slid a pair of fingers over the downy skin between her breasts, curled his touch to the hidden underside of one swell. "That's why this will be fun. What do you say? Up to the challenge?"

"Absolutely. I'm looking forward to it."

"Let the games begin," he murmured against her mouth.

Her lips, lush, soft, rosy, lay just beneath his. Her eyes closed, and Rafe sensed not just her desire but her trust. Hunger surged inside him, greedy, insistent, as he claimed her mouth. Hard to believe he'd already had her twice today and it was barely noon. And that his blood was pumping a hot demand for more through his veins already. God, what was it about this woman?

Her taste. As soon as she opened to him and he swept his tongue inside, her flavor hit him. Sugary whipped topping and the tang of orange juice combined with a hint of cherry to create something addicting, something uniquely her. One kiss wasn't enough. Nor was two.

Kerry soothed and comforted him like a cheery firelit home. But as always, she was a dichotomy. Even as she contented him, she incited him, made him wild. When he touched her, his blood raged, molten and unrelenting with need. He had to have more. He needed her open to him, wet for him, entreating him—now.

Damn, he was becoming a greedy bastard. He had to take it easy on her. She was new at this.

Pulling her closer, flush against his straining erection, he could only hope she wasn't too sore from rounds one and two. Of course, if she was, he could always kiss it and make it better . . .

He eased one hand down her back, over the sweet curve of her ass, then lifted the tail of his shirt. Her bare bottom warmed his palm, even as he parted the shirt farther over her breasts with his other hand. The garment's shoulder fell down to the crook of her elbow, exposing her right breast. A simple flick of his thumb over her nipple caused a thrilling catch in her breath. A second brush elicited a moan. The caress of his finger between the firm cheeks of her ass had her gasping.

Rafe found the remaining buttons of the shirt and flicked them away, working his mouth down her neck. He nipped at her shoulders, slid his tongue over her collarbone—and kept heading south, sliding the shirt down, down as he went. Finally, it swept past her hips to puddle on the floor at her feet, leaving her wonderfully, gloriously naked.

"You have the most lush body," he whispered against the swell of her breast. "Ripe, pliant. All woman."

She sighed. "A little too ripe."

"Because you have curves? I prefer to make love to a woman, not someone with all the shape of a twelve-year-old boy. You"—he kissed the side of her breast lightly, grazing her with his tongue—"have everything a man could want."

At that, Kerry drew in a ragged breath and mercifully dropped the subject. They had much more important things to concentrate on.

Rafe continued his quest down her body. He bypassed her nipple, which hardened as he passed above her, grazing the sensitive flesh with morning stubble on his chin. He followed that with a hot breath. Kerry's head fell back, and she exhaled.

He hid a smile. No doubt, she'd be wet already, and he wanted to test the waters, so to speak—hell, he wanted to taste them, but not yet. Not until he drove her as crazy as he was.

"Let's move to the bed," he murmured.

Before she could reply, he guided her to the rumpled mound of covers and pillows and shoved them all to the floor with an impatient sweep of his arm.

At her surprised little gasp, he took her face in his hands and anchored his gaze to her. "I don't want anything covering you, anything getting in the way of what I'm going to do to you. If you want me to do something for you, to you, ask me using very precise words. And say please."

Kerry stared back with wide mossy eyes, dilated yet defiant. "I won't."

"We'll see," he promised softly. "I have all afternoon to change your mind. Lie on your back."

She crossed her arms over her chest. "No."

At her challenging, almost smug expression, Rafe knew she was going to enjoy the friendly rivalry almost as much as he was. "Then we'll do this the hard way."

Wearing a crooked smile, Rafe dropped to his knees on the chenille rug and planted a kiss low on her belly. He glided his fingertips up the back of her thigh, a ghost of a touch. Goose bumps broke out on her arms. Already he could scent the wetness between her thighs.

Another kiss to her belly, moving lower. She caught her breath, then bit her lip to stop the small gasp. He smiled as he lifted her foot into his hand and massaged her instep, opening her flushed, slick flesh to his gaze. He wanted to touch Kerry, taste her, slide so far into her that she would never remember the feel of her body without him.

By some miracle, he managed to keep his stare away from her damp curls and focused on rubbing her foot. Just as she started to relax again, he planted his next kiss on her body, this one the lowest yet, so close to her honey spot. He dragged a fingertip up the inside of her calf, idling up to her thigh, slowing as he approached her pussy. But he never quite touched it. Her thighs tensed. Her breathing quickened.

"I'm going to make you feel so good," he breathed against her wet flesh. "All you have to do is lie back and say please."

"No."

Her refusal sounded more like a weak cry. Rafe lowered her foot to the outside of his thigh, leaving her legs slightly spread. God, what he wouldn't do to get closer, be deep inside her in the next ten seconds. Instead, he beat back his impatience and brushed soft fingertips over her damp mound, back and forth, back and forth. Kerry drew in another rough breath. Her knees began to buckle. Perfect.

Kneeling at her feet, Rafe reached up her body and grasped both of her nipples, rolling them between a firm thumb and forefinger. He swiped her clit with his tongue.

Kerry let loose a sharp cry. Her knees gave out beneath her, and she fell back on the bed.

"You look beautiful on your back," he murmured against her inner thigh as he climbed his way up her body. "Spread your legs."

"No." Her refusal barely climbed above a whisper.

"Tsk, tsk. Not very obedient today, huh?"

"Or any day," she shot back.

Rafe smiled, imagining her statement was entirely true. But he knew her body now, knew how to make her hot and compliant.

He slid his knuckles across the top of her folds, just above the hood of her clit. "You drive me wild when your legs are open to me. C'mon . . ."

She hesitated, then shook her head.

"You want to," he whispered. "You want to show me every slick, pouting curve."

"Rafe . . ."

Ah, not a yes or a no. Making progress. Still, he took the decision out of her hands.

Taking one of her knees in each hand, Rafe spread her quickly and wide. She fought briefly, but not convincingly. With no leverage—or real desire to keep him away—the battle didn't last long. He leaned in between her thighs, his torso keeping her open to him.

"Perfect," he murmured.

He caressed her inner thighs with the back of his hand while breathing so close to her mound she no doubt felt every warm exhalation. He swiped a thumb over her slick lips, gratified to note she was extremely wet.

Fisting the sheet in her hand, Kerry tensed, as if expecting him to devour her as voraciously as a wild animal would its prey. He chuckled.

A swipe of his tongue over her hard clit had her gasping, writhing. He drew away. She tensed and whimpered.

"If you want something, all you have to do is ask."

Eyes tightly closed, Kerry answered, "No."

He laved her clit with this tongue again, then drew it into his mouth and sucked. Meanwhile, his fingers continued to work her nipples, which swelled and hardened more with each touch. She let loose a sharp gasp.

"You want something. Tell me what." He punctuated his demand with a light, butterfly touch to the sensitive tissues on either side of her clit.

Kerry was so pink and swollen now. She wanted, no question. But so did he. In a bad way. Perspiration beaded on his forehead, his back. His cock was so hard, he felt sure it could double as a battering ram. Damn, he wanted to rip these constricting pants off. He needed to get inside her, feel her explode around him.

Why could he never seem to get enough of her?

Rafe nibbled the tender flesh of her inner thigh. “I gotta know what you want. Do you want to come?”

She hesitated.

“Say it.”

“Rafe . . .”

“I’ll only toy with you until you say it.” To prove his point, he trailed a pair of fingers down her belly, right back to her clit, circling. She hardened under his touch, and when he slid those same digits inside her, he could feel the tensing, the fluttering of her flesh.

A whimper. A pause. “I want to come.”

The coil of desire tightened in his gut, put a stranglehold on his cock. He loved hearing her say those words to him.

“How do you want it?”

“You know.” Voice breathy, she struggled to get the words out.

“I don’t have ESP, babe. Tell me.”

Rafe waited. Nothing. In the silence, he wriggled his fingers inside her and found her G-spot. With an incessant, slow pace, he rubbed. Kerry gasped, arched. The pale skin of her neck and breasts flushed with fresh excitement. Her nipples were now ripe berries, red, succulent. She swelled around his fingers even more, squeezing. Slow pulses rippled with more power. Orgasm was so, so close.

He stopped. But he was sweating.

“Rafe! Oh . . .”

“Oh” was right. At this rate, he was going to lose his fucking mind. Impatience seized him, and he tamped it down with every ounce of self-control. Damn, he’d set out to conquer her. Instead, she tested him to the limit of his endurance.

"Touch me," she cried, despite her heavy breathing and trembling thighs.

Got her talking. Almost there. "I got my fingers on your nipples. I'm touching you."

But he couldn't resist squeezing the hard peaks of her breasts and raking his tongue through her slit once more, dragging slowly over the hard bud of her clit.

She gasped. "That. More of that."

"This?" He rolled her nipples between his fingers again.

"No," she wailed.

He stopped.

"Yes, that. But your tongue, too . . ."

"What about it?" he breathed against her sensitive mound.

If he wasn't mistaken, she swelled again, pink flesh turning a definite rosy red. She had to be on the razor's edge.

She panted once, twice. "Lick me."

Her voice was quieter than her exhalations, but Rafe realized she'd just taken a major step. Why it was important that she verbalize her desires to him, he wasn't exactly sure. Maybe he wanted her comfortable enough with him to say anything. He wanted her to trust him with what she needed and believe he would give it to her.

"Lick you here?" He gave her a lazy swipe of his tongue near her knee.

"No!"

"You're going to have to tell me where, babe." He nipped her thigh with his teeth.

"Lick me here . . ." With trembling fingers, she reached down and parted the delicate folds of her flesh for him. Rafe's heart stopped. He'd wanted words, but the temptation she presented . . . Dewy, swollen flesh crying out that he satisfy her ache. Kerry offering herself to him with her own hands. No way he could resist. This was better than his hottest teenage wet dream.

Arousal tight in his belly, Rafe slid two fingers inside her once more, rubbing that sensitive bundle of nerves as he leaned in and tongued her tender clit from side to side in an insistent but unhurried taste.

She tightened around his fingers again, more. Her thighs trembled, and one hand found its way to his hair and fisted, keeping him close. Not that he had any desire to be anywhere else. He loved the power of giving her an orgasm, but he also loved her enthusiastic appreciation.

"Oh, Rafe. Ohmigod!" she panted. "It's big. I can't—"

But she could. And as his fingers kept working inside her, he sucked in the hard nub of her clit and gently raked it with his teeth to prove she could take it.

Powerful contractions gripped his fingers. Her clit seemed to explode on his tongue as she let loose a high-pitched, keening cry and shouted out her climax.

Rafe helped her ride it all the way to the end. For interminable seconds, the pleasure seemed to roll on. If his mouth hadn't been so busy, he would have smiled.

When Kerry quieted and fell limp, he kissed his way up her belly, absently flicking his tongue over a nipple before whispering in her ear, "Damn, I forgot to make you say please."

Kerry gave a tired laugh and planted a kiss on his neck. "I'll try to remember my manners next time."

Teasing aside, Rafe edged the hard ridge of his cock against her wet mound. "I need to be inside you, Kerry."

"Well, it's your birthday, and I'm pretty sure I got the gift with that last round. So it's time for you to tell me what you want. Oh, maybe I should make you beg."

He tried to appreciate her humor. Difficult when sweat poured off him and he felt tied up in more knots than ropes on a sailboat. "Babe, I'm begging now."

Reaching into the bedside table, Rafe extracted a condom and handed it to her. He looked right in her eyes, deep. "Touch me. But go easy on me. I'm dying here."

Teasing aside, Kerry caressed his length, rubbing her thumb

across the sensitive tip where he was already slick with seeping moisture. He hissed in a breath. A happy little smile brought her dimples out to play. Yeah, she liked knowing she affected him. Minx.

All thought disappeared as she secured the condom over the head of his penis, rolling it down the granite length bulging with veins. Her gaze hardly left his. Rafe drowned in a sea of tempestuous green. Her warm gaze reassured and teased at once. He stared back, unable to look away. Did his own stare display all the crazy feelings he couldn't put a name to? He didn't care. What she saw was irrelevant as long as she took him inside her now.

Once she had the condom in place, she stroked his inner thigh and placed a little kiss on his mouth.

Rafe gave her no more time for gentle play before he lay down beside her and lifted her over him, until she straddled his hips. They met chest to chest, belly to belly. He devoured her mouth, sinking deep into the sweet recesses, even as he bent his knees, lifted his hips, and slammed home.

Into his mouth, Kerry gasped. And from underneath, he rode her. Hard. One long, pounding stroke blurred into the next. She met him thrust for thrust, her sweet body welcoming him, closing around him in such perfect wet heat, the sensation had him gritting his teeth against the rush of a pending orgasm.

Despite feeling on the edge, scraped raw, he wanted more. He wanted to hear her scream again and know she was as out of control as he.

Gripping her hips, Rafe adjusted beneath her enough to hit her G-spot with his next stroke. She gasped in his ear. With a grim smile, he repeated the process. Yeah, he might be going over the edge and losing his mind shortly, but he damn well wouldn't go alone. He wasn't going to be the only one to give up all control.

One thrust bled into the next, all bound by a white-hot haze of pleasure. Kerry's nails dug into his shoulders. She met him thrust for thrust as he pumped inside her. There, he felt her tighten, tighten. She began to ripple around him.

"Come!" he growled.

Kerry screamed in his ear even as her body began to milk his. His gut tightened into a knot of ecstasy that burst through his body, exploding down his legs, up his chest, to the base of his spine.

"Yes. Fuck, yes!"

The orgasm seemed to last forever. Long after he ceased coming, he could feel the ripple of Kerry's aftershocks. They triggered the pulse of new pleasure within. He sighed, too tired and too content to move.

"It's always so intense." Her shaky voice sounded in his ear. "Another day of this is going to do me in."

Him, too. Kerry was making him lose his mind. Or worse . . . was she showing him his heart, then stealing it, all at once?

* * *

BY four that afternoon, they were both famished. Kerry heated up frozen burritos and tossed together several cans of fruit to make a dinner no one on Food TV would ever feature. Rafe ate without complaint, then, oddly quiet, settled in with his laptop on the red leather chair in the adjoining den.

Kerry cleaned up after the meal. Feeling on edge, she watched as Rafe raced through some e-mails. Her gaze caressed his profile, the broad splendor of his golden shirtless torso. Like his lovemaking, he was intense, focused. But he could be gentle. They'd been here at the Love Shack only a few days, but it felt much longer. With every hour, her sense of connection to Rafe grew until it felt bigger than Godzilla. Wondering again how she would cope after he was gone disturbed her. She was as clueless about that as Tiffany was about something like quantum physics. But Rafe was not hers to keep.

All she could do was enjoy him while he was here.

She didn't dare wonder what, if anything, he felt. Likely not much besides gladness that they had great sex together.

As Rafe let himself into Standard National's system through a back door—one he'd created himself—Kerry watched, her relief and warm joy that he was indeed helping Mark somehow bittersweet in the face of the reality of the ticking clock. In a little more than twenty-four hours, Rafe would no longer be in her life.

Kerry swallowed a pang of anguish that nearly brought her to her knees.

For now, she had to focus on the fact that she'd kept her end of the bargain; now Rafe was going to keep his.

This arrangement between them wasn't about her Disney Princess wishes for the future. She'd always hoped her prince would come someday. Kerry wondered if she'd actually found him, but she pushed the thought aside. This was about Mark. Had to be about Mark.

Impatiently, she flipped through magazines and outdated Christmas catalogs, tapping her foot against the hardwood floor. She tried to look busy as he scanned the screen, wrote frantic notes, clicked all over the place, read the police report, and cursed a blue streak.

After the fifth "What the hell?" in as many minutes, Kerry couldn't stand it anymore. "What's wrong? You're trying to find something to help Mark, right? Is it that bad?"

"Hang on." He fended her off with a murmur and the wave of his hand.

Click. Frown. Click. Frown. Click. Frown.

"Holy shit!"

Her feigned nonchalance disappeared faster than the liver and onions special on Senior Day at the diner. "What? Something that will help Mark?"

"Is Mark's terminal number 4389?" he asked suddenly.

Kerry paused. "I don't know."

"Did he ever mention a terminal ID number?"

"No, but I don't work there, so even if he told me . . ." She shrugged. "He could have told me how to take apart a manifold and it would have the same effect."

With a nod, he conceded that point. "Who might know his terminal ID?"

"Tiffany, for sure."

"Call her. Ask her. I think I see something . . ."

Excitement bubbling in her belly, Kerry dialed. "Okay."

Tiffany didn't answer. Instead the machine picked up. "This is Mark and Tiffany. We're gone or busy doing what newlyweds do. Leave a message and we'll call later. Might be much later." *Beep.*

Surprisingly choked up over hearing her brother's voice, Kerry hung up. Keeping the resulting tears inside hurt. Her throat constricted. She felt as if a two-ton weight now lay on her chest. Then again, Rafe had her in such a jumble, she'd probably cry at feminine hygiene commercials.

Worry underscored it all. What if Tiffany didn't know the answer to Rafe's question? What if nothing helped and Mark ended up in Leavenworth or some other awful federal destination?

"No?" Rafe asked.

"She's not home." Kerry sighed. She had to stay focused, positive. Crying wouldn't help Mark now—even if it would make her feel a whole lot better for ten minutes. "Jason might know."

Rafe gritted his teeth. Jaw locked, he looked as happy as someone who'd been told the neighbor's dog had dug up his yard.

"Call him."

Pretty sure that she'd heard Rafe mutter an unpleasant word that started with an F and rhymed with truck, Kerry winced and called Jason. He answered on the second ring.

"Are you okay, sweetheart? Do you need me?"

Rafe's frown became an oppressive scowl at Jason's endearment. Kerry resolved to keep things as simple as possible. Sure, people couldn't shed blood over the phone, but somehow she sensed that wouldn't keep Rafe from trying.

"I'm fine. You?"

"Worried about you."

Nice to know she still had friends. A hint of a smile curved her lips. "I need your help. Is Mark's mainframe terminal number 4389?"

"His terminal address? No. I'm pretty sure it's 4119. Why?"

Rafe held out his hand for the phone. "Let me ask him a few questions."

Kerry hesitated. The tension between Jason and Rafe made no sense. Neither had any reason to be jealous. But Rafe in particular acted as if she were one bone and the guys were both mean junkyard dogs.

Then again, if their growling could in any way help Mark, let them terrorize each other.

"4119?" Rafe repeated. "Yeah. I see that terminal here. Who does 4389 belong to?"

"What have you been doing to her?" Jason accused. "She sounds exhausted."

Kerry rolled her eyes as the line of Rafe's jaw tightened even more. "None of your business. I'll take care of Kerry. You want to help your friend or argue over his sister?"

"You're a prick," Jason snarled.

"Feeling's mutual. At least I've been up front about what I want from her. How many years have you been lying to her about being just her friend?"

"Bastard! If you've so much as thought about getting her in bed, I'm going to shoot you."

"Start loading your gun, hotshot."

Her belly did a vicious flip as she grabbed the phone from Rafe. "Stop it! Both of you! I feel like a piece of meat. We're here to help Mark."

"Sorry," Rafe murmured, managing to look at least somewhat contrite.

"Watch yourself," Jason advised.

"Let's worry about Mark. Do you know who terminal 4389 belongs to?"

"I don't think I've ever heard of it."

Disappointment plummeted Kerry's stomach to her toes. "That's not Smikins's machine?"

"No. He's 4115. At least, I think so. But call Tiff. She's got a complete list of all the terminal IDs since she's been filling in until he gets a new assistant."

"Thanks."

"Anytime, sweetheart. You know I'm here for you."

"I appreciate it."

"Seriously, be careful with Dawson."

"I'm fine."

Before he could say anything else, Kerry hung up. Then she glared at Rafe. "What's with you?"

His eyes blazed silver sparks as he glared at her, lips thin with anger. "I don't want him crawling all over you once I'm gone. He's been lying to you for years about his intentions, and it's bullshit."

Unable to stop herself, Kerry rolled her eyes. "Whatever. Let's talk about Mark. What's the deal with this terminal 4389? Did you find something?"

His annoyed sigh let her know she hadn't heard the last about Jason, but he let it go for now. "Maybe. Each instance of the thefts took place from a terminal that looks like 4119, but there's something weird here in the file allocation tables at the kernel level. It looks like someone changed the terminal IDs and buried it deep in code. And that's not something just anyone can amend. To get into those, you have to have the Admin ID and password or be one hell of a hacker."

Was that even English? "Are you saying that someone took this 4389 and did something to the system to make it look like Mark's terminal when it wasn't?"

"Exactly."

Hope and skepticism churned in her stomach. "Why didn't the FBI find it?"

"Because of where the real thief buried the code. The bank's mainframe system is built on AS400 hardware with a UNIX platform and—"

"Don't do your Spock routine again. Please."

Rafe took a deep breath and started again. "UNIX is like a Windows operating system for mainframes. Make sense?" At her nod, he went on. "Like any computer, you put software on it. But the software can't work unless it's installed on a computer that already has an operating system in place. The software on the bank's system is clean. No bugs, viruses, or anomalies. This is where the FBI probably looked because most people would have created some way at the software level to frame Mark. Not this guy."

"Maybe this guy did it someplace else because it would be less obvious."

"I'm sure. Since the software wasn't tampered with, then you'd look to the next level: the operating platform. None of the UNIX code looks as if it's been screwed with either. So you go down a level again, to the very bones of the system. But getting the corrupt code way down where it looks like he put it . . . That takes someone with a lot of knowledge. Or someone with the System Admin's I-am-mainframe-god password. But even using the System Admin password would leave a trail. At the very least, anyone looking at the records would see them log in and out. But the System Admin password wasn't used anywhere near the time frame of the first theft. Or the third. It just doesn't add up."

"So this person is a hacker?"

"On the inside. That's my guess. Review for me again our short list of suspects. Is Smikins hacker material?"

"I don't know. I'm not sure what his computer proficiency is. He doesn't seem that smart, but that may just be because I loathe the little toad."

Rafe nodded. "We'll keep him as a maybe. Your sister-in-law?"

Kerry scoffed. "Tiff hardly knows how to work an ATM without someone talking her through it."

"Which could be an act."

"Of Oscar proportions?"

"I'm not ruling her out yet. If she's guilty, the last thing in the world she wants to do is let anyone know she's smart enough to pull this off." Rafe drilled her with a hard stare. "And your little wannabe fuck buddy? Didn't you say he knew a thing or two about computers and code?"

"Oh, stop. Even if Jason wanted to sleep with me, which I'm not convinced he does, saying that he's guilty of framing his best friend seems totally off the wall. I just don't see it."

"Yeah, and if he's guilty, he's banking on that."

Chapter Nine

MORNING came, and with it, reality. Monday. Her bargain with Rafe ended tonight. And surprise, surprise, the thought of him leaving had the same effect on her stomach as receiving notification of an IRS audit—pure, deep dread.

As soft gray light filtered through the sheers of the Love Shack's bedroom, Kerry snuggled her back against the warm furnace of Rafe's chest. He spooned her, one hand on her belly as he breathed deeply and evenly against her neck.

A lingering shiver of pleasure vibrated through her body when she remembered the previous night. After their predinner sex and, of course, the freezer-burned, preservative-laden meal itself, they'd had postargument sex—hot and wild on the little kitchen table. They had agreed in the most pleasant way possible to disagree about Jason. Exhausted by then, Kerry had retired to bed and fallen asleep . . . only to feel Rafe's tongue on her nipple and his lips wending their way up her throat a short while later. "Can you, just one more time?" His whisper had sounded so much like a plea, Kerry relented. Okay, reveled. They came as midnight did.

Now contentment and safety—the two things she'd always wanted most in life—she had right at this moment. Was it too greedy of her to wish she could keep it longer? Of course she no longer slept with one eye open, wondering if her current foster parents would show their true colors as thugs or perverts while she was at her most vulnerable. Being alone was better, yes. Just not what she ultimately wanted out of life.

She sighed and forced her mind to the present. Today was not only Monday, but the day she and Rafe had decided to go to Standard National armed with the information they'd found in the bank's own system. Kerry admitted she had never been a regular churchgoer, but now seemed like a good time to start praying. Mark deserved every bit of positive energy she could drum up, and divine energy seemed like the very best.

"I can almost hear the thoughts whirling in that pretty head of yours," Rafe murmured, voice smoky with sleep.

Kerry smiled. How was it possible she knew so much about him after a weekend? Why did that make her feel all melty inside, like a warm batch of chocolate chip cookies?

"Guilty." She covered his warm hand on her belly with her own.

"Nickel for your thoughts."

"A nickel?"

"I'd give you a penny, but inflation and all." He laughed.

"I'm thinking about Mark." *Mostly*. "I'm hoping today we're able to prove he deserves to be free. Then, although you still have every right to be furious with me for kidnapping you, it will all have been worth it to me. I hope to you, too, since you'd be so instrumental in freeing an innocent man."

Behind her, Rafe tensed. "For your sake, and your brother's, I hope it's that easy. But I speak from experience when I say that dealing with the Feds can sometimes be like talking to mud. They both listen about the same. What we have now is something suspicious, but nothing conclusive. Until we have hard proof . . . I don't know. Don't get your hopes up too high yet."

Nodding, Kerry swallowed her apprehension. Rafe was right. She knew it. She just didn't want to hear it.

"Maybe we'll find hard proof at the bank. Or maybe what we've found will trigger someone's memory."

"I'll cross my fingers that happens."

"Thanks." Kerry snuggled against him again, and encountered a very healthy morning erection. She cast a surprised glance over her shoulder.

"Would you settle for me crossing my fingers a bit later?" he asked, then brought their joined hands over her breast. He guided her finger over her nipple, watching with hungry, heavy-lidded eyes as she brushed it, back and forth, with the tip.

Okay, she'd touched herself here before, but not with a man, a lover, watching. A twinge of innate modesty poked at her, but the arousal leaping in her body squashed it. The peak of her breast hardened so quickly, light speed would seem a snail's pace. Down south . . . she was moist, yes. What woman wouldn't be continually ready with a lover as attentive and fabulous as Rafe? But his great prowess and stamina overwhelmed her novice tissues.

"It's not happening now, buster. Not without a shower and some breakfast first."

He trailed his fingers down to her vagina. "Feeling tender, babe?"

"After the deflowering in the bed, the boogie in the shower, your birthday present, the little stunt on the kitchen table and ringing in the new day, ya think?"

"I get the message. I'd say I was sorry, but for that I'd have to be a saint."

Kerry scoffed. "As if."

"My point exactly."

"Even if you don't qualify for sainthood, it wasn't all you. I think you would have eased up if I said I was too sore."

"But you knew that would have been no fun." One of his fingers toyed with her navel.

"True, but this morning, we must pay for our frolicking with a bit of waiting."

Rafe nodded. "Fair enough. Wanna guess what I want for lunch?"

She gave him a rueful shake of her head. "Talk about a one-track mind."

"That is not true. I'm the evolved species of man. I have two tracks: computers *and* sex."

She laughed. "Impressive."

"Not necessarily in that order, mind you. And since one track far exceeds the other at this moment"—he pressed the length of his cock against the cheeks of her backside—"and you're out of commission, would you do me a little favor?"

Arching a brow at him, she said, "Men are so predictable. A blow job, right?"

"I wouldn't turn it down if you're offering." He grinned. "But I had something else in mind . . ."

* * *

RAFE and Kerry arrived at Standard National's doorstep at eleven. He did his best to focus on the upcoming visit . . . but everything about the morning was surprising the hell out of him.

First, the fact Kerry had brought her car—and he used that word loosely—to the Love Shack and stashed it in the garage even before his abduction—just in case. The black limo he barely remembered from the airport was parked next to her car. Had he known transportation lay within reach, he would have tried twice as hard to get away, even if her 1991 blue Honda looked more suited to a stunt car show than the highway.

If he'd succeeded in escaping, though, he would have missed out on the greatest weekend in memory.

Second, the fact she had consented to his little favor. Even knowing what she wore under that baggy shirt made him sweat, to say nothing of the secretive smile curving her mouth each time she'd looked his way on the drive over.

Finally, the bank itself. Small and regional, he'd known that about Standard National. Catering mostly to the remaining small-town and suburban interests in Hillsborough County and surrounding areas, as well as small business owners, it wasn't a huge multibranch operation. He hadn't expected one, really. But he'd imagined something more than the size of a fast-food joint with three tellers, two loan officers, and a few others with unknown titles.

Beside him, Kerry bit her lip and looked around. "I don't see Smikins at the moment." She took a few steps, peered around a wall to a desk in the corner under a flickering fluorescent light. "But there's Tiff."

Suspect one. Rafe trailed behind Kerry—admiring the view—as she crossed the faux marble floor, across aging gray carpet, and stopped before a tall redhead wearing a very conservative brown suit perched behind a desk twice her size.

"Tiffany!" Kerry smiled in greeting to her sister-in-law.

Model-thin redhead had been the perfect description. From the looks of it, Tiffany and Calista Flockhart could have shared a closet. Wide blue eyes and fair, barely freckled skin made her look like a waifish creature of the runway. Though such women had never appealed to Rafe—who wanted hipbones poking you during sex?—he saw where Smikins, suspect number two, might want her. Kerry could easily be right about unrequited lust/love being Smikins's motive . . . if he was guilty.

"There you are!" Tiffany greeted. "I called and called last night. Are you okay?"

"Fine." She looked in Rafe's direction. "Just busy."

"Something you want to talk about? If listening can help, I'm all ears."

"I appreciate it, but all is well. You?"

"Good." Tiffany sighed, then bit a plump lip smeared with sheer gloss. "Well, mostly. I misplaced my house key. Did I leave it with you, by chance?"

"No, haven't seen it."

Her shoulders drooped. "I was afraid of that. I'll just keep looking."

Kerry smiled. "You'll find it." After Tiffany's murmur of thanks, she continued. "Where's Smikins?"

"Pouting in his office. The e-security guy he hired is supposed to show this morning, and Shorty says he wants to make him wait as long as the consultant made him wait. So he's hiding in his office and 'isn't to be disturbed.' " She dropped her voice, imitating Smikins.

"What a geek! Let me intro—"

"Oh! Before I forget, I somehow undid whatever you did to fix the remote controls. I know you had them all programmed into one, but I can't keep it straight. When I tried to use them to record *General Hospital,* I ended up with an hour of some documentary about deadly plants."

"Ouch. Sure, I'll help you."

"Mark always teased me when I did something like this. I suppose it's kind of funny if you think about it. I'm just not in the mood to laugh." Tiffany shrugged.

"Hey, what are sisters-in-law for? Besides, you're always feeding me and listening to me whine about school."

"I like hearing about your school stuff. Helps take me away from . . . everything else."

The catch in her voice caught Rafe's attention. Tiffany looked down toward the sleek high-heeled pumps on her feet. Was she hiding tears?

Kerry slid a gaze to Rafe, then took Tiffany's small hand in hers. "How about I come tomorrow to fix the remote?"

With a sniffle, Tiffany lifted her head and managed an awkward smile. "Tomorrow is great. Sorry to be a burden. I'm just a little distracted these days." She raised her gaze, moisture shimmering in the corner of her blue eyes. "Mark's absence is getting to me more and more."

"I know." Kerry squeezed her sister-in-law's hand.

While Rafe imagined Mark's arrest hadn't been easy on the young bride emotionally, Tiffany struck him as the kind of woman who floated through life leaning on everyone around her and never saw anything wrong with it. He shook his head. The external package might be tempting, but not enough existed between the ears to interest him. But Smikins might be another case. Was it possible that, in addition to a husband, she had a man who potentially wanted her enough to commit a crime to have her?

Well, he had to give Kerry credit for her assessment. While he wasn't ruling anyone out as the party guilty of framing Mark, her description of Tiffany as someone not likely to join a think tank seemed reasonable. Personally, it wouldn't surprise him to know that Tiffany had married Mark to help her with electronic gadgets and find her keys. If that was the case, why would she want him in prison? And could she possibly bury code in the kernels of a mainframe system?

Then again, looks could be deceiving. Maybe, somehow, in an alternate universe yet to be explained, Tiffany was actually very bright.

"We all depend on Mark," Kerry murmured sympathetically. "We all love him."

Tiffany's eyes widened as if she suddenly remembered something. "Oh, speaking of Mark, he asked about you when I visited on Friday. Jason said you were away over the weekend?"

Kerry flushed thirty shades of red. "Yeah, which reminds me, this is Rafe Dawson. He's—"

"Just the person I wanted to see," said a male voice behind them.

They both turned. Somewhat short, angry blue eyes, narrow face. Definitely not smiling.

"Jason, I didn't see you when we came in." Kerry moved toward him.

Suspect three.

Rafe watched as she approached the shorter man and embraced him. The sting of a hundred hornets pricked at his stomach as he watched Jason's arms curve around his woman.

His woman?

Figure of speech.

Kerry cast both men a nervous glance. "Rafe, Jason. Jason, Rafe. You two . . . know each other. Sort of."

Rafe stared at Jason. He glared back. Neither offered a hand to the other. After a long stare-down during which Rafe thought he could feel his blood boil, Jason looked away first as Tiffany's phone rang. Brow furrowed at the silent spectacle, she excused herself to get it. Kerry seemed to take that as an opening.

"How's work?" Kerry asked.

Jason faced her with a smile that made Rafe grit his teeth. "The usual. How are you, sweetheart?"

"Great. You?"

He stabbed Rafe with a glance. "Worried about you."

"Don't bother. She's in good hands." Rafe gritted his teeth.

"Is this where I'm supposed to mimic your smarmy New York accent and ask if you're Allstate or something?"

Rafe crossed his arms over his chest and took the brief, petty enjoyment of looking down his nose at the shorter man. "If trite jokes are your speed, go for it."

"Can you two speak a civil word to each other?" she hissed in a heated whisper.

Jason fumed. Rafe brooded. Neither answered.

Kerry shook her head. "Great. In one corner, we have Immature the Idiot. In the other, Juvenile Jerk-off. Can you two please put a cork in it for an hour? We're here for a reason. So let's play nicely."

At Jason's stiff nod, she went on. "Okay, is this your break? Can you talk now?"

"Got an hour," Jason confirmed. "I think we should talk away from this place."

"Good point," said Kerry. "Smikins could come out of his office any minute."

The tense trio walked to a nearby taco chain, Kerry between them. She sat with a salad and a diet soda. Rafe picked at a couple of tacos and some rice. Jason seemed to have ordered one of everything.

Kerry ignored the enormous amount of food on his plate, as if it was commonplace, which only led Rafe to imagine it was.

"Did you manage to find the list of terminal IDs and who they're assigned to?" Kerry asked the minute they'd all sat down.

Jason looked around the room as if searching for spies. Rafe resisted the urge to roll his eyes.

"Yeah."

"And?" Rafe snapped.

Jason glared at him before turning back to Kerry. "There's no 4389 listed."

"What? That's not possible!" she asserted. "It exists. We know it. Rafe saw it in—"

"Here, look." Jason thrust a folded scrap of paper across the table at them.

Rafe laid the page out flat. Beside him, Kerry stared at it, too. No 4389.

"Have you looked at older records?" Rafe cut in. "Gone back a year or two?"

Jason hesitated, clearly debating between his desire to help his best friend and piss off his competition. "Those records don't exist anymore. When his old assistant left in a huff after Smikins passed her up for another promotion in favor of Tiffany, she deleted every file on her computer and half the files on his. She took stuff off the server, renamed documents so they were impossible to find, you name it."

"So, as far as records go, the terminal doesn't exist."

"Pretty much."

"Another dead end." Kerry squinted, clearly fighting tears.

She looked his way. Unshed tears lent a glossy appearance to her green eyes, eyes that pleaded to him for help. God, he would've done anything to help her, just to make those damned tears go away. For now, all he could do was squeeze her hand.

She squeezed back. "So what do we do now?"

* * *

SO far, this day wasn't turning out as she'd hoped.

During a silent walk back to the bank, Kerry let her thoughts wander. Her stomach twisted, tears threatened again. She had so many questions buzzing through her brain, they drowned out rational thought. But when Jason had gone for a refill of his drink, Rafe had cautioned her to leave the details of the programming oddities he'd discovered a secret, at least until he could rule Jason out as a suspect.

Rafe's tone indicated he didn't think that would happen soon. Kerry wished he'd get over his odd dislike and suspicion of Mark's best friend.

Upon arrival at the bank, they entered its cool, muted interior. Jason kissed Kerry on the cheek, as usual, then went back to his window. Beside her, Rafe tensed, clenched one fist.

"Why does it bother you when Jason kisses me on the cheek? It's just a sweet, friendly thing to do."

"We've been over this. All I'm going to say now is that I don't like liars."

Rafe's voice was flat. But his eyes . . . they were alive with anger and passion, like clouds churning over a storm-filled sea. Was it possible he cared, at least a little?

Stupid, stupid wishing. His plane left tomorrow afternoon. By then, he'd be long done with her. In a month or two, he'd likely completely forget her. She'd better not, for a moment, lose sight of that.

"Fine. Then explain to me why the FBI didn't notice the fact terminal 4389 doesn't appear to exist? That's an anomaly, right? They didn't question that."

"They didn't know about 4389, babe. I just found it in the code last night, remember? The programming made it look as if every transaction occurred from Mark's machine. Even if they found it, it's possible they would have surmised that with the last secretary being as destructive as she was, the terminal used to be in service. Mark would have known it and simply used it for his purposes."

"By programming it to make himself look guilty?"

Rafe shrugged. "Or making it look like someone else was trying to frame him. Or something else entirely. Who knows?"

"This circular logic is giving me a headache."

He planted a gentle kiss on her mouth. "I can take your mind off it. Are you still wearing—"

"Yes."

"Ah, you're killing me here." He discreetly adjusted the front of his expanding slacks.

"You want to see, don't you?" She flashed him a teasing smile.

"You know I do," he whispered as a customer, an older man in overalls, passed them by. "I want you to wear them tonight . . . all night."

"I'll think about it."

"I'll persuade you."

"You're welcome to try."

Rafe flashed her a killer smile, one that not only made her knees go weak, but seemed to burn itself in her brain. For the rest of her life, when she thought of him, somehow she knew she would remember that smile.

"Go talk to Tiffany. I'm going to see if Smikins came out of his office while we were away. Oh, and I need your car keys to get my laptop."

Kerry handed the keys over. Rafe raised a brow when he looked at her conglomeration of key chains.

"Universal Studios, Tampa Bay Buccaneers, Elvis, SpongeBob SquarePants, Phantom of the Opera, holy cow! Is this Justin Timberlake?"

"Are you blind? It's Orlando Bloom."

"You think he's . . . what? Cute?"

"Well, duh!"

"Probably gay."

Kerry stared at him in amusement. "Why is that the universal male response? Any man considered incredibly good looking automatically needs bashing by every other man. Feeling threatened?"

Rafe rolled his eyes. "By a pretty boy? Hardly. I just think I'm far more likely to be interested in what you're wearing under that shirt than some dude named after a tourist town. Can we find a quiet corner so that I can see? Just take a quick peek?"

Still snugly in place, they made Kerry very aware of her own body, of the little edge of arousal simmering each moment she wore them. "No."

"Knowing what you're wearing," he whispered, "is making me so damn hard. And since I ended up with tacos for lunch, instead of you, I'll definitely want a fulfilling dinner."

"Kind of a glutton, aren't you?" Kerry resisted the urge to laugh.

"Where you're involved, yeah."

A middle-aged woman passed close on her way out the door. As she stared, Kerry wondered how much of their conversation she'd heard and understood. Rafe apparently wondered the same thing when he changed the subject.

"Why so many key chains? Do you use this as a hand weight in your spare time? Do biceps curls from the car to the door?"

"Funny. No, I collect key chains. Friends give them to me as gifts when they go places or I buy ones that I think are interesting. What do you collect?"

He thought about it for a minute. "Gadgets. I never put much furniture in my apartment, just lots of electronic . . . stuff."

"Oh, sounds like you could be featured in *Better Homes and Computers*."

Smiling, he walked out the door. Kerry meandered toward Tiffany's desk, watching as Rafe walked toward the parking lot. A glance told her Tiff was still on the phone and looking stressed. Mark had always complained about unreasonable customers wanting to circumvent the bank's policies for their convenience. Likely, her sister-in-law was feeling that heat now.

A minute later, Rafe returned from the car, laptop case in hand. "Where is Smikins's office?"

She pointed him to the appropriate door.

"Thanks." He winked and set off. "I think I'll just go knock and make suspect number two see me."

Once he'd gone, Tiffany stepped up behind her in a cloud of Chantilly. Tension showed in the lines of her mouth. "He's very handsome. Who is he?"

"Rafe Dawson."

At Tiffany's blank look, Kerry supplied, "You know, the guy the bank hired to shore up electronic security."

The lightbulb finally went off. "Oh, that guy. How did you meet him?"

She hesitated, Rafe's warning about telling their suspects sounding silly. But hey, she could follow directions as well as the next chump. "Long story. Something wrong? You look upset by that phone call."

Tiffany looked this way and that, all around. "Not important. So where did Rafe go?"

"To talk to Smikins, hopefully."

"Has he been looking for some way to prove Mark's innocence? Has he found anything?"

"Rafe is looking." Impulsively, Kerry hugged her sister-in-law. "I want Mark back as much as you do. So that's got to be enough for now."

Tears shimmered in Tiffany's eyes. "I want him back so bad, but Kerry, what if Mark really is guilty? And, oh God, what if Rafe only proves that?"

"No!" She was sure incredulity showed on every line of her face. "Mark's not a thief!"

"He's definitely not. Usually. I—I just mean, who could blame him for being desperate? Such staggering medical bills at so young an age. Before his arrest, we talked about having kids next year but he decided we just couldn't afford them. That really broke him up."

"Tiff, I know that must have hurt you both, but I don't think Mark would steal under any circumstance. Don't even think that. Don't let anything that grouch D'Nanza of the FBI says confuse you." She grabbed Tiffany's hands. "And don't lose faith. Rafe is the best at what he does. He'll figure it out."

Kerry refused to believe anything else.

* * *

RAFE entered Smikins's office shortly after noon. An overstarched white shirt contrasted with a slick of brown hair that lay flat and in perfect place. Gray slacks, a nondescript blue-and-gray tie. Black shoes polished to such a high shine, Rafe wondered if Smikins used them as mirrors. Small even teeth, a pale mouth, and round brown eyes made up the rest of an uneventful face.

Rafe stood and, towering over the man by a good eight inches, introduced himself, offering his hand.

He stared at Rafe's hand, then Rafe himself before taking the offered greeting. "Finally. Glad you're . . . feeling better. Sick, wasn't it?"

Pompous slime—Rafe's gut agreed with Kerry's perception. "As a dog. Glad to be here now, though. I was able to start some preliminary work late yesterday. I'll need you to answer a few questions. Is now a good time?"

"I'm very busy and not ready to see you just yet." His look challenged Rafe.

"Whatever you want. It's your dime since you're paying me by the hour." He shrugged. "I'll come back when you're ready."

"You're late. Perhaps I won't pay you anything."

So the yippy Chihuahua wanted to play hardball?

"If you got it covered, I'll be on a plane back to New York tonight. Just be sure to let your regional manager know you've got everything under control."

"Well . . ." Smikins backpedaled. "You *are* here for a limited time, and the security of this institution and the money our customers entrust us with is vital. Since your illness set us back at least a day, I suppose we must see to this business now. But I will be talking to my boss about your tardiness and how it affects your fee."

It was possible Smikins could paint a black enough picture to prevent or delay the bank from paying him. Rafe clenched this teeth and told himself that throttling the little bastard wouldn't solve anything.

"Talk to him." He shrugged, feigning nonchalance. "You want me at the top of my game, I have to feel well. And now that I do, let's get down to it. I have questions."

Smikins sniffed. "What do you want to know?"

In the guise of asking about the branch's security, Rafe put the man through a series of questions about firewalls, internal security, software updates, hardware, and coding. In most every instance, Smikins showed himself to be knowledgeable, far more than the average guy off the street. Apparently computers were a part-time hobby for Shorty, as Tiffany called him. The guy was a bona fide hardware junkie.

While he couldn't conclude for sure that Mark's former boss was guilty, Rafe couldn't deny Smikins probably had the knowledge to pull such a heist off. And since Smikins apparently disliked Mark because he wanted his employee's wife . . .

Speak of the devil. Tiffany bopped into the office with some mail for Smikins. Rafe watched the way the man's brown eyes followed the redhead's every move until she walked out the door.

"Pretty girl," Rafe baited.

Smikins said nothing, just stared at the closed door.

"Very pretty, in fact," Rafe added. *C'mon . . . take the bait, take it.*

At length, Smikins sighed. "Married." He shuddered. "To a big, arrogant hulk, complete with a tattoo around his biceps. A shame, if you ask me."

"No doubt. Why would such a pretty girl marry that kind of guy?"

Now that they appeared to have an opinion in common, Smikins began to warm to him. Rafe settled back to listen.

"I can only imagine he bullied her into it. Mark Sullivan is a lug. He could probably be a success in the WWE. He's the employee we arrested, you know, for embezzling. I, for one, was not surprised when all the signs pointed to him. Egotistical. Obviously disloyal. Tiffany could do so much better."

I'll bet you remind her of that—every chance you get, weasel.

"Now that he's in jail, hopefully she will."

Smikins smiled. "My thoughts exactly. Hopefully this time, she'll choose someone a bit older, a man with a bright future who's a tad more settled in life."

Is that supposed to be you? Rafe bit his tongue to keep that question inside. Clearly, the boss man had a major johnson for Tiffany Sullivan.

"I'm sorry." He shook his head. "I didn't mean to sidetrack you from business. Any other questions?"

"Just one." Rafe rubbed his chin, looking for the right phrasing. "Do you have a list of all the terminal IDs and their associated employees for the last, say, two years?"

"I don't. My former assistant left following a . . . disagreement. I subsequently discovered that she had a destructive streak, and those records are gone."

Just as Jason had said. Damn! "Do you recall any terminals that have been brought into service or retired?"

Smikins thought hard, if the sudden slant of his brows toward his nose was any indication. "Several new ones: 4104 belongs to Cassie Wilkens, and 4258 to Leon Jones." He hesitated, still thinking. "Oh, and 4389 was retired. Keyboard didn't work properly."

Bingo! Finally, some useful information. Rafe repressed a smile. He didn't know who the guilty party in all this crap was, but getting information on that terminal was a first step in clearing Mark and giving Kerry back a bit of happiness.

"Retired?"

"Indeed."

Rafe waited for elaboration, but none came. He held in an impatient sigh. "What happened to the terminal? How was it retired?"

"I'm not sure. I left that with my former assistant. Not sure what she did with it."

"But no one uses it anymore."

"That's correct."

Bullshit. "Do you have someplace I can plug in?" Rafe gestured to his laptop.

"Directly across the hall. It's a storage room now, but there's an old desk, and since it was once an office, it's fully wired. Is that all you need to improve the bank's security?"

"For the moment. Thanks."

Rafe left Smikins and crossed the hall, shutting the storage room door behind him. It was dusty and smelled like stale coffee and mildew. Boxes littered the floor in stacks, their warping cardboard illuminated by the afternoon sun slanting in.

Setting up quickly, Rafe worked into Standard National's system. He took an hour to reconfigure the bank's software, update patches, and generally tighten up security. Then he sent the particulars, along with suggested new electronic approval processes, to Smikins and the guy he'd indicated was their IT manager.

The routine side of his business complete, Rafe started looking at the software and the records from a more personal point of view. He wasn't sure what he was looking for at first. Transactional activity, patterns, something that would show an "off" pattern on the days Mark's supposed thefts from the bank had occurred. Comparing activity with the terminal numbers Jason had provided, he saw that Tiffany, Jason, and Smikins had all been logged on during those days, so he couldn't rule anyone out.

And now . . . what? Rafe didn't know and aimlessly ambled around the system, looking for *something* helpful. He had so little time left in Florida to set Kerry's world right. She'd never had a break in life, and he wanted to give her the first. For whatever reasons, he wanted to be the first in something in her life other than sex.

He couldn't stay here; it was impossible. He had a job in Jersey on Thursday morning. And what they had . . . it was more than sex. Denying that would be as stupid as saying the earth was flat. Okay, so he cared. They shared something almost too powerful. But like a supernova, it would burn out quickly under the intense heat and pressure. It had to. Especially since he sucked at relationships. Loners with crappy work schedules just didn't make good boyfriend material. As far as commitment went, who could he have learned from, his dad? Yeah, there was love for you. Rafe knew he'd never shared well, especially of himself. Beyond that, he and Kerry lived too far apart, had totally different lives. Why was he even jogging this mental path?

Shaking his head to clear it, Rafe glanced down at the screen and focused. The daily activity report. He scanned down the list quickly—then came to a dead stop.

Terminal 4389 accessed at 9:55 A.M. today, again using Mark's ID and password. *What?* That hadn't been deleted yet? Talk about a big security no-no.

Rafe then looked for a list of transactions performed at the terminal and found none. But his heart raced. Finally, he'd found something concrete. Whoever knew about terminal 4389 had been in this building this morning. Might still be here. And it wasn't Mark; he was behind bars.

He rushed down the hall to find Kerry. He pulled her away from her sister-in-law's recap of some soap, then hustled her into the storage room.

"Someone accessed the terminal today. With Mark's ID. Got any idea what time Tiffany and Jason came in?"

"They both opened, so they probably started at nine-thirty."

"From what I can gather, Smikins hid in his office all morning. He logged in about nine. Whoever accessed the terminal did it just before ten. That puts them all here. Smikins admits to knowing about the terminal but says he asked his old assistant to retire it. Jason said he didn't know anything about the terminal. He could also be lying. Did Tiffany say anything?"

"I didn't ask."

Rafe grimaced. He'd like to be working with full information, but he could start with what they knew. Asking too many questions about the terminal might alert someone's suspicions. "Jason and Smikins are more likely candidates anyway. Both probably had access to Mark's ID and password. Both know something about computers and had motive to want Mark out of the way."

"Do not tell me you still think I'm Jason's motive."

"Take off your blinders, babe. If you do, you'll see it."

"The way you do, through hallucinations?"

Rafe shot her a sarcastic smile and saved the report on his screen to his hard drive.

"Is that concrete enough for the Feds?" Kerry asked, biting her lip.

He shrugged. "It doesn't tell us who did it, but it does point out that other people might have used the same information earlier to perpetrate the crime. And that they're still on the loose. We shouldn't have to prove his innocence, just cast doubt so they'll reopen the investigation."

"I have the investigator's number. I'll call. I'll get him to believe."

Before Rafe could protest, Kerry had dialed the number.

"Robert D'Nanza," the investigator answered after the third ring.

Kerry took a deep breath. "This is Kerry Sullivan, Mark Sullivan's sister. I know why my brother is innocent."

"I've already heard your 'he's too honest' speech. I hear that from family members a lot."

"No, I have new information. You see, Rafe found a retired terminal. But the bank may not know it's still being used. The real thief is still using it, though. He used it today!"

"If the bank has a retired terminal, I don't see how that's relevant."

"Well, Mark is in jail, so he can't be using his ID and stuff, right? I mean, Smikins has access to Mark's password, and he hates my brother. Since he's really after my sister-in-law, it's obvious he's guilty."

Rafe heard the quaver in Kerry's voice, the same trembling he recognized from his very first conversation with her. She was so nervous, and she was not handling the explanation well. He squeezed her hand for support.

"What?" exclaimed D'Nanza.

Biting her lip, she looked to him with desperate green eyes. Her panicked face and reddening nose told him she was about to cry.

"And—and it's obviously someone from the inside since the system hasn't been tampered with. Rafe said so. That means—"

"That you're rambling." The investigator interrupted her, then said something else Rafe was too pissed to hear.

He grabbed the phone.

"This is Rafael Dawson, owner and CEO of Dawson Security Enterprises."

Then Rafe laid out his findings. Special Agent D'Nanza listened . . . for about two minutes.

"Look," the agent said. "We got tons of proof on this guy. Since you were hired by the accused's sister—"

"She didn't pay me a dime."

"Whatever. Point is, we've got nearly an airtight case against Sullivan, and the word of someone new to the case who's in league with a relative of the accused isn't compelling."

"Then who is still using a supposedly retired terminal? Who the hell is using Mark Sullivan's ID?"

"For all we know, the bank reassigned this terminal or they're simply testing it. There are a lot of what-if's here. Mr. Dawson, frankly, I don't have any way of knowing the veracity of this information and I don't have time to chase ghosts."

D'Nanza hung up.

Rafe cursed, harsh words that caused Kerry to wince. Her shoulders sagged in defeat. Her green eyes turned turbulent with tears.

"I'm sorry." Regret cracked his voice. "That guy . . . he wasn't going to listen."

Nothing new, unfortunately. Damn it, he'd wanted to make this better for her, resolve this for her so she could get on with her life happily. He didn't like failing. Or letting her down.

"I should have known he wasn't going to listen." Kerry slumped down in her seat and burst into tears. "You tried to warn me. And—and worse, he told me that Mark's trial has been moved up. It starts next Monday."

Chapter Ten

AT three o'clock, Kerry and Rafe climbed into her beat-up blue slug of a car and drove back to the Love Shack in the thickening traffic.

She barely saw the cars on the road as she sank deep into her thoughts. All this effort, for nothing. She'd poured weeks of planning—a challenge for her in the best of circumstances—into kidnapping Rafe. She'd taken a stranger away from his life, tied him to a bed, for Pete's sake, with every intention of forcing him to help her brother. She'd broken the law and probably prevented him from achieving a deeply personal goal.

All for nothing.

It would be a wonder if Rafe didn't resent her like a waitress does bunions for all she'd done to him.

She couldn't cry anymore. She'd been doing it all day. Now she hovered somewhere between a thick sludge of dread and sheer numbness.

Even worse than what she'd done to Rafe, she'd let Mark down.

Her brother was no closer to freedom today than he had been last week. She'd believed with her heart and soul that Rafe could help her save her brother from an awful fate. Nope.

She also couldn't seem to save herself from falling hard for a man destined to leave her.

Hot tears stung her eyes anew. Her head pounded nearly as badly as a jackhammer. Embarrassment heated her cheeks. It seemed nothing could get worse . . . until she remembered this was her last evening with Rafe. By morning, he'd be gone from her life. Forever.

As they arrived at the Love Shack, Kerry let out a shaky sigh and climbed out of the car. Rafe followed in silence, seemingly elsewhere mentally.

Of course he is, idiot. He's with beautiful women who won't drag him into their problems, break laws, and cry every two seconds. He's probably wishing himself back in New York on a hot date with a woman who can carry off a slinky black dress and a witty laugh. Who could blame him?

They walked into the shadowed interior of Dominating Dave's cottage. How familiar everything seemed. How intimate. Kerry looked at the red leather chair Rafe frequently lounged shirtless in, the kitchen table they'd made lascivious use of. So many memories here, in such a short time. How had that happened?

Yearning and regret tangled in her throat as she faced Rafe in the little living area. "I'm sorry. Incredibly sorry. For everything."

For a heartbeat he said nothing. Just stared. "You look tired. Sit down."

Kerry watched, frowning, as he went to the kitchen, opened the fridge, and poured her a glass of wine.

"Drink," he ordered after crossing the room and thrusting the glass in her hand.

She took a dutiful sip, then another . . . until she drank it all. Unfortunately, even downing the whole bottle wasn't going to make her feel better, particularly since it would only add the need to puke along with everything else. Guilt still buzzed and stung like a whole hive of killer bees. And Rafe, standing there with traces of patience and concern on his face . . . Why? Surely he understood the implications of their call to the FBI.

Her grand scheme, in which she'd illegally robbed a perfectly wonderful man of freedom and free choice, was over. Mark would likely go to prison. She had failed miserably.

She would have to live with that truth for the rest of her life.

Kerry frowned up at him. "You have every right to be furious with me for dragging you into this mess. Clearly, my hope that the FBI would listen to you, that some perfect piece of evidence to free Mark would be easy to find—it was all a dream. And now Smikins is threatening not to pay you, and I've screwed up the goal you've worked toward for years. I've ruined everything."

Disgust rolled through her as she had to fight new tears. Oh, she was pathetic.

He knelt in front of her and brushed a stray lock of hair from her cheek. "You're being too hard on yourself. You did what you thought was necessary to help Mark. I don't fault you for that. Smikins will pay me if I have to wring his scrawny neck."

A sad smile flitted across her mouth. "But what I did to you . . . it was so wrong. It's only right that I let you go now. I—I'll be happy to make you dinner if you're hungry, then I'll help you pack your things and drive you back to your hotel. You can get on with your life and forget I ever screwed it up."

He stopped. His expression closed up faster than a government office on a holiday. Traces of patience and kindness disappeared, replaced by a forbidding gathering of black brows. The air between them went still, heavy. Kerry watched, her stomach pitching and rolling—then landing somewhere in the vicinity of her shins. *Uh-oh.*

Rafe's lips thinned, nostrils flared, as he dropped his hand and stood, towering over her. "So I've served my purpose and you want me gone? How convenient for you."

Is that what he assumed she meant? "I just thought—"

"What? That you could get out of the rest of this bargain?" He stepped closer, looking down at her with an expression that bordered on menacing. "Babe, you promised me forty-eight hours of fucking. By my watch, it isn't up yet. We've been tangled in other shit, and you've put me off all day."

Tangled in other shit? Oh, just saving Mark. That was shit now? Did he assume she'd put sex before her brother? Was he angry that she hadn't? If so, he apparently assumed she had all the decision-making skills of a life-sized blow-up doll.

"I'm not settling for no anymore," he growled. "No matter how or where I want you, your answer should be yes."

Amazing—from good guy to bastard in like three seconds. "Or 'Yes, master' would be preferable, right?" Kerry stood, crossing her arms over her chest. "You talk like I'm nothing but a piece of ass."

Something ugly crossed his face. "Well, you act like I'm an expendable hacker, so I think that makes us even. Strip."

"What?" Kerry felt her heart pounding, amazement mixed with anger.

"You heard me. Off with the clothes. All of them. I've had an impossible hard-on all day, waiting for a glimpse of what's under that baggy shirt. I want to see now."

"You've got the patience of a preschooler with an ice cream sundae, and the maturity to go with it. I think we should talk instead. I'm not sure why you're angry—"

"I'm not angry; I'm horny. I want you out of your fucking clothes."

As if to prove this, Rafe grabbed her around the waist, seized the nape of her neck, and captured her mouth in a demanding, ungraceful kiss. Too angry, too confused, Kerry didn't respond. She tried to jerk away. Her brain spun with questions. She'd tried to do the right thing and let him get on with his life. Why was he angry?

Then he cupped her face, swiped at the seam of her lips with his tongue, and moaned. Heat sparked in her belly, which she did her best to ignore. Instead, she leaned away, opened her mouth to ask him if he'd lost his mind in the last three minutes or if he'd been unhinged all along. Before she got a word out, he covered her lips with his own again and poured inside. He invaded her very senses.

The first sweep of his tongue told Kerry he was determined to ignite her. The second proved that he could. Her indignation and anger started to melt under the onslaught of his mouth. Possessive. Hungry. Determined. He wanted her. He wasn't taking no for an answer.

At that point, in a contest between desire and rage . . . well, rage wasn't winning any blue ribbons.

She had no defenses against Rafe. Not when he was mad, not when he was tender, not even when he was conquering—not in any circumstance, it seemed. Not since she'd realized how much she cared for him. It was a dangerous level of care. Even in the face of his anger, the thought of him returning to New York and never seeing him again left her slightly panicky and despondent.

She did *not* want to know why.

Whatever it meant, this would be their last night together. In spite of Rafe's odd, wicked mood, part of her shouted that she should make the most of it. The saner part said she'd only sink deeper and faster into heartache.

Unable to stop her reckless heart, Kerry clasped her arms around his neck and threw herself into the kiss—all her anger, all her confusion, all her passion . . . along with the misery she feared was coming.

Rafe's hands made their way down her body, clinging to her shoulders, cupping her breasts, outlining her waist. When she tilted her pelvis to his and slid against the heavy bolt of his erection, he grasped the sides of her loose-fitting blouse in tight fists and moaned.

Breaking off the kiss, he stared at her. His sharp gray eyes clawed her with hunger.

"Strip," he demanded again, all pretense of a sensitive guy gone. He was all determined alpha male.

She'd never seen him in this mood. His playfulness gone, steely determination to have her in its place. Warmth didn't inhabit his eyes, only heat. That blazing intensity broiled her skin, her blood, letting her know that if she succumbed, he was going to do everything in his power to inundate her with pleasure.

The thought made her weak in the knees. And her tummy . . . and her head.

And it worried her.

"Maybe we should talk," she said, coming up for air.

"Talk later. Strip now."

Kerry could have told him to go to hell. She knew that in her gut. Rafe would have been pissed off, but he would have gotten over it.

Instead, she acknowledged the want enveloping her heart and churning in her body. She pushed aside the ache she knew she'd feel tomorrow after Rafe had gone, the odd mingled anger and excitement she felt tonight at his attitude, and focused on enjoying his touch tonight. She unfastened the top button of her blouse.

Then Kerry dropped her hands to her sides and slanted him a sultry stare. "Is this what you had in mind?"

He shook his head. "More skin. More quickly."

"What's the rush?" she asked with a languid rise of her hands to button number two.

Rafe swallowed as she unfastened the button between her breasts, then parted the baggy striped fabric just enough to show the inside swell of her cleavage and no more.

"Rush?" He glanced at his watch before his gaze returned to her face, aggressive and uncompromising. "It's been fifteen hours and forty-three minutes since I've been inside you. That's a third of our time together. I've been patient."

Something in the hard angle of his jaw, the steely glint in his gunmetal gray eyes, told Kerry that Rafe was done waiting. Done talking. Done with anything that didn't involve sex.

An instant later, he confirmed her suspicions by barreling toward her and hoisting her off the floor with a vise grip under her arms. Lifting her as if she weighed nothing more than the average toddler, he settled her against his chest. But the toddler theory went out the window as he held her against his full-staff erection with a hand curved under her ass.

"Wrap your legs around me," he bit out as he strode down the hall.

Automatically, she obeyed.

The friction of his rock-hard cock against her dampening folds had her moaning. Before she could finish the first sound of pleasure, Rafe captured it with his mouth. He delved inside and looted more, like her breath, her sanity. He pillaged with all the mercy of a pirate, taking, taking . . . and giving back a pleasure and expectation that left her dizzy and achy.

Inside the bedroom, he lay her against the cool sheets. Before she could say a word, he'd removed her sandals, popped the button of her khaki shorts and worked them down her hips, then tossed them across the room. They landed with a soft *whoosh* on the hardwood floor.

He spared no glance to see where they landed—or for the white cotton thong barely covering her essentials. Instead, he focused his attention on her half-unbuttoned shirt. Setting his jaw, he began the task of unbuttoning it, bottom up. His eyes narrowed with each new inch of skin revealed. First, her navel and the smooth skin of her belly. Next, her rib cage and the soft underside of her breasts. He didn't pause to look or touch the flesh he'd just exposed. No. Every scrap of his attention was focused on the last straining button holding the shirt closed over her breasts.

For a long moment, he only stared. Kerry waited, tingled. The phrase "breathless with anticipation" held infinite meaning in that moment. She ached. Need centered low in her belly, between her thighs, twisting her mercilessly. For a moment, she imagined things he might do with her, want from her. Those images tumbled, one over the other, in her mind. Each one, more erotic than the last, sent fresh blasts of heat straight to her vagina. She felt her own slick moistness dampening her white cotton thong. Rafe drew in a deep breath, and Kerry felt sure that he could scent her wetness. She shivered. Their gazes connected, locked. He stared, eyes alive with the molten heat firing his taut body.

"Undo it." He dropped his intent gaze to that last fastened button on her shirt. "Show me. The thought kept me hard all day."

A surge of power flowed through Kerry. She might be underneath a strong man, half-undressed and taking orders . . . but appearances were deceiving. Something in Rafe's face said he was barely maintaining a thread of control, one that could snap at any moment.

She smiled. "What will you give me if I do?"

Pure predator took over Rafe then, and he laid his body over hers, covering her completely. Heat assailed her at every point of contact, thighs, belly, breasts. Kerry caught her breath at the sensation. Oh, God, the ache. She *needed*, damn it. Needed the pleasure, the searing affection, Rafe gave her.

Her power dissolved in a haze of desire as she realized she was barely hanging on to her own composure.

Without rational thought, she arched her pelvis against his, grinding her aching folds against the hardness that told her he was all man and beyond ready.

"I'll give you what you want," he whispered ruthlessly in her ear. "What your body craves. Undo that damned button, and I'll press you beyond your boundaries, trip you into orgasm after orgasm all night."

His words carved out a crater of craving in her belly. Nothing on earth would please her more. Suddenly, she could hardly remember why she'd been fighting. Who knew? Who cared?

"Yes."

He raised himself a few inches from her chest. "I want to watch that last button come free. Do it."

Kerry slid her hands between them. With trembling fingers, she shoved the little disk through its corresponding opening, then all but ripped the two sides of the shirt apart, leaving her nearly naked breasts exposed . . .

Except for the small golden rings clipped gently to her taut nipples.

"Oh, yeah. I've died, and you're heaven."

Leveraging himself down her body, he pinned her to the bed, his middle now keeping her thighs spread wide. He'd positioned his mouth perfectly level with her breasts.

Kerry's heart beat erratically as he licked his lips and pierced her with a stare of scorching sexual promise.

Rafe lowered his lips to her breast, sucking her nipple into the voracious tunnel of his mouth. The tip of his tongue played with her sensitive nipple, now hyperaware from wearing the body jewelry all day. More blood rushed into her nipples, and Kerry swore her entire being was centered there, totally a captive to the pleasure Rafe bestowed upon her.

She moaned and arched into his mouth, spreading her legs wider in silent supplication. He ignored her voiceless demands for satisfaction and kept at her breast, toying with the tiny gold hoop fastened over her nipple, gently nibbling on its hard tip until the sting of pain combined with a jolt of pleasure that had her pleading.

"Rafe. Now. Please now."

"You've felt these all day, haven't you?" he whispered against her skin.

"Yes."

"Did they arouse you?"

"Yes."

"Make your nipples beyond sensitive?"

"Yes."

"Did you imagine my mouth on you, sucking, licking?" He echoed his words with actions, fastening his mouth on her again.

"God, yes." She could barely get the words out, the feel of his mouth so distracting.

"I stayed hard all day thinking about you riding me, about sinking my cock into you while my tongue worked that little loop and your nipples at once."

"Why are we waiting?" she panted.

His laugh had all the smoothness of sandpaper. "I want you wild first. I'm going to give you a night you won't forget."

Forget? Not possible. She'd always remember the way the ache inside her had grown, swelled to mammoth proportions, swallowing her heart with it. Taking a breath was almost too difficult. Pleasure had diffused her brain, now haunted her blood, until she could only want beyond anything she'd ever imagined.

"I'm wild." She scratched at his shoulders, folding her legs around his torso to prove it.

"Not yet, you're not. But I have ideas . . ."

Kerry had no clue what he meant. In the next moment, his mouth devoured her other breast, giving it the same hot sting he'd given the other. Knowing he wouldn't let up until he was good and ready, she threaded her fingers through the inky strands of his dark hair and held on.

At least until the devil inside her urged her not to take this lying down.

Drawing in a deep breath and doing her best to gather her wits, Kerry murmured, "Did you think of my nipples all day?"

"Hell, yes," he muttered against her skin before licking her sensitive tip again.

She hissed in pleasure but was not dissuaded. "Did you imagine them getting hard? Swelling?"

His mouth full of her breast, he only nodded.

"Did you think I'd be slightly aroused all day, and stay wet and ready because of it?"

"Yeah." He fixed her with a hot stare. "Were you?"

Sending him a kittenish smile, she nodded.

"You're killing me. Too sexy to refuse, too infuriating to ignore, too amazing to forget. Damn it. You're not getting away until I'm ready to let you go."

Before Kerry could decipher what those cryptic words meant, she felt his hand clamp about her wrist. He pushed it up to the head of the bed and entwined their fingers, anchoring her down. Rafe took her mouth in a drugging kiss. Already she throbbed everywhere. Now something deep inside her joined in. When they kissed, Kerry swore she could feel not just his passion, but his loneliness, and a frenzied desperation she didn't understand.

Rafe released her hand. An instant later, she felt something cool and metallic encircle her wrist. A glance showed that he'd tied her down with the first of the Love Shack's shackles. Just over the edge of the bed, he reached. And suddenly all the give in the pulley drew taut. The line held her arm immobile above her head.

While she lay in gaping shock, he repeated the process with her other wrist.

She could not move her hands an inch.

"What are you doing?" Kerry demanded.

"Showing you how thoroughly you're mine tonight. Mine." His breathing was harsh, labored. "I'm dying to have you spread out under me, mine to take. All sweet and submissive."

His words hit her like a two-ton weight, hammering the death knell to any resistance she may have had.

"Rafe—"

"No more words. Trust me."

"If I ask you to let me go, you'll do it, right?"

He licked the pad of his thumb and swiped it over one sensitive nipple. "I won't give you a reason to ask. I just need you bound and under me now."

Before she could draw another breath, he'd strapped her ankles to the bed and denied her any slack. Naked, save some nipple jewelry and a white thong, she lay spread out before him like a virgin sacrifice. His to take. All night. The thought made her shiver.

Wearing a shark's smile, Rafe rose from the bed and stripped in world-record time. Shoes flew in one direction, pants in another. Kerry had no idea where his shirt landed. She was too busy watching those washboard abs as he removed his boxer-briefs, then letting her gaze wander lower.

His cock rose to his navel, hard, thick, bulging with veins. “Aroused” only began to cover it. He looked like a man in heat, a man who wouldn’t accept no. A man who would last all night.

From the nightstand, he grabbed a handful of condoms and set them on the mahogany surface. Kerry gaped. There had to be seven or eight there.

“Feeling ambitious?”

He shook his head. “Feeling like I’m going to explode if it takes me more than three seconds to get inside you.”

Rafe ripped the thong away from her body and tossed it over his shoulder, the garment torn, forgotten. But he didn’t immediately tear open a little foil packet and put the condom to good use.

“Still sore?” His voice cracked, and Kerry suspected the edges of his control had nearly frayed beyond his ability to endure.

She began to shake her head, too aroused to know discomfort. Taking that as his green light, Rafe trailed a pair of fingers down her body, dragged them over the hard nub of her clitoris, then sank them deep into her wet heat.

Her nerve endings came alive at his touch. Kerry arched in encouragement, tilting her pelvis up since she could move nothing else.

“Good?”

On a ragged breath, she nodded.

“Take more.”

“Yes, more.”

Rafe obliged by sinking a third finger deep into her heat and teased that sweet spot inside that drove her insane. She groaned. Perspiration broke out around her hairline, between her breasts.

Kerry all but whimpered as the pleasure ramped up in her belly. A knot of need gathered between her legs, growing, congealing. How could he do this to her so easily, put her right on the ragged edge?

The question—along with all coherent thought—flew out of her head when he bent and suckled her clit into his mouth.

Pleasure pounded her in an unending assault. His clever tongue teased her to the edge of sanity, along with those long, probing fingers. He drove her to the brink of orgasm—only to pull back, concentrate kisses on her belly, her hip, her thigh.

When she'd cooled enough to catch her breath, he started over, tongue taking long, liquid swipes at the bead of her clitoris, before drawing it into his mouth.

He groaned, nearly sending her soaring . . . nearly. She panted, drawing in a deep breath, then even stopping that because it required too much effort. Close . . . so, so close.

But Rafe released her clit, withdrew those magic fingers again, simmered her down to a slow burn.

Kerry moaned. "Let me come."

"Eventually," he murmured against her slit.

Using his thumbs, he parted her folds and delved inside with his tongue. She arched as much as her restraints allowed. But Rafe's tenacious mouth remained fastened on her, giving pleasure, blowing her mind, almost enough to send her over the brink—but not quite.

And so the ramp up toward orgasm started again. A faster build, a rapid climb to mindlessness. Certainly, it required less effort on his part—a gentle swipe of his tongue over her clit, a well-placed finger or two.

"Tonight, you're mine. No leaving, no sleeping, no saying no."

"Yes."

Her thighs trembled with effort. Kerry focused all her thoughts on completing what the dark-haired devil had started. She was drenched now, dripping. So swollen, she could feel how full her folds had engorged, how taut her nipples had puckered.

But as he allowed her to cool down yet again, Kerry gritted her teeth and acknowledged that Rafe knew just how to keep her on the knife's edge.

"No!" she protested. "What are you doing to me? Why?"

"Making sure you know who's master of your body."

Before she could say a word, a determined, possessive glint fired his steely eyes. Desire knotted in her belly as he plunged a finger inside her again. Kerry nearly came off the bed when he resumed the teasing play of her clit with his tongue.

When he replaced his finger inside her with his thumb and eased his drenched digit farther down, into the unbreached depths of her anus, she moaned.

Determinedly, he pumped his fingers into her simultaneously. The wild, foreign sensation scorched every nerve ending. Rafe sucked on her pleasure bud, even as his fingers possessed her everywhere, filling her to capacity.

Oh God, he was driving her mad with a pleasure that threatened to rob her of her soul. Like the strongest storm, need raged in her, growing, expanding into the fathomless depths of desire. His touch sizzled like lightning. Down her arms and legs, up her belly, to her painfully tight nipples.

Ecstasy, pure and white hot, was upon her. Kerry's eyes flew open wide, connecting with Rafe's unrelenting gaze. Wide bronze shoulders, wicked hands, haunting eyes. All tonight, all for her, that stare said. The floodgates of pleasure burst, torrential, explosive. She was dizzy, couldn't breathe, as satisfaction swirled through her body. Black spots danced at the edge of her vision as she cried out, thighs tense, womb pulsing.

Brilliant. Endless. Somehow she doubted she'd forget this if she lived to be one hundred.

Minutes later, now limp and spent, Kerry lay with her eyes closed, wanting to sleep for a week.

A ripping sound alerted her to the fact that wasn't going to happen. She watched as Rafe rolled the condom over the surging length of his cock, then reached to the sides of the bed, near her ankles. A metal *click* on each side later, and he'd returned the slack to the pulleys spreading her legs wide.

The idea of clamping her thighs together to keep him out never occurred to her. Even if it had, Rafe grasped her knees, bent them, and pushed them wide, making way for the solid width of his muscular torso. He slid into the vee between her legs, the tip of his penis poised against her seeping entrance.

She expected him to plough inside and ease his ache right then. Instead, he lowered his lips to hers and captured her mouth in a fiery kiss. He layered his warm lips over hers, then sank into her, reaping her response from every corner with his tongue. She tasted herself in his kiss, along with his determination that he not reach orgasm alone.

He was dreaming if he thought she could manage another ten-point-plus explosion on the Richter scale again so soon.

Still, Kerry couldn't deny that with just his kiss, he'd managed to get her hormones doing the hustle again.

"Take me inside you," he pleaded, voice raspy. "Now. Tell me you can."

At a loss for words, she nodded.

Something like a growl gave her an instant's notice before Rafe fastened steely fingers on her hips and plunged inside her full throttle.

Kerry cried out. Tender, swollen tissues she'd thought immune to Rafe after the ground-shaking orgasm a few minutes ago seemed to leap in delight at the spine-tingling friction of his entrance. He filled her full of him, seemed to touch every corner of her. Lord, who cared that chocolate existed when such a man could give her something infinitely better?

"Yes," he groaned as he sank to the hilt. "Hell, yes. Are you with me? Tell me you want this."

The sensation of being filled to bursting, her aching flesh stretched pleasurably to accommodate him, all her nerves held in thrall at his touch . . . what could she say? "I want you."

"I feel you gripping my cock, your body sucking me back in every time. You're blowing my mind," he gritted through clenched teeth.

Clutching him tighter with her thighs, Kerry clung. The ride became harder, each thrust wild but precise in its ability to drag her closer to the precipice. Again, the orgasm loomed huge, receding reality as it ratcheted up and quickly stole her mind.

"You're mine." *Thrust.* "Mine." *Thrust.* "All"—*thrust*—"fucking"—*thrust*—"mine."

Before Kerry could even moan in reply, Rafe lifted her legs and tucked them into the crooks of his elbows, positioning her to take him even deeper inside her body. She swore she could feel him at the mouth of her cervix.

"Can't wait," he said, plunging into her hard, fast. "Come. With me. Now."

As if on command, Kerry became hyperaware of Rafe's cock sliding over the sensitive bundle of nerves inside her, then pushing up inside her, all the way to the tingling end of her channel. One more, two more, three more strokes like that and—

"Rafe!"

She erupted like a volcano, molten and uncontrollable, like a force of nature. The knotted desire in her abdomen released to indescribable ecstasy. It surged through her with the strength and finesse of a charging bull. Her body squeezed him, milked his cock, as he shouted in gratification.

His voice rang in her ear, and she watched the pleasure transform his face from hard angles to a replete, almost peaceful expression. He gasped for one breath, then another, as his movements slowed, then stilled, inside her.

Still panting, Rafe dropped his forehead onto hers. "Unbelievable. Every time amazes me."

"Me, too," she admitted. Why lie?

"Why is that?" He spoke as much to himself as to her.

Frowning, she had to admit that having prior experience might have made answering this question easier. On the other hand, Rafe's question seemed to indicate this was as uncommon as a seventy-five-percent-off sale at an upscale department store. Maybe some chemistry—or feeling—between them caused the riot of need every time they touched.

Kerry wanted to believe it would go away, that in time, she would find someone else equally proficient at lighting up every nerve in her body. She feared otherwise. Somehow, her body had known no other man would please her, and her excuses about not having time for sex and being too distraught . . . they didn't seem as airtight as before.

Kerry worried that Rafe had imprinted himself somehow into her body's memory and that no one would ever be able to take his place. Was that because they shared more than mere chemistry?

Rafe's BlackBerry broke into their chorus of shallow gasps moments later, shattering the peace. Reluctantly, Rafe extricated himself from her body, climbing from the tangled bedsheets.

Half-listening, Kerry soon realized he was talking to a client from California who'd accidentally erased their security patches and feared an electronic attack. Rafe dealt with the client, giving her time to regroup.

Why *did* their every time together seem to raise the roof and shoot them to the stratosphere? Kerry had only one theory left, and if she dared to say it—which she didn't—she doubted Rafe would like it any better than she did. After all, what sane man wanted to hear that a woman he'd known only a few days suspected that she loved him?

She had to get away from him soon, before she did something really stupid, like beg him to stay with her forever.

Chapter Eleven

ALMOST midnight.

Toying with the keys on his laptop, Rafe sat in the tropical luxury of the Love Shack's silver-shadowed patio overlooking the silent turquoise lap of the ocean. He guzzled a beer. It was not his first.

Kerry had suggested he leave. She wouldn't have said it unless she wanted him gone.

He gave a silent, bitter laugh. Hell, she'd offered to drive him out of her life—after making dinner, of course. Can't string a man up by his balls on an empty stomach.

Not that he blamed her, really. He'd failed her. And while he'd been getting busy in her bed—and shower and kitchen and floor—at every possible opportunity, she'd been focused on Mark. Once the FBI had disregarded the clues he'd found and refused to listen, Rafe no longer served any purpose in her grand plan. And she'd dumped him.

Had he let it be and moved on? No. He'd played Conan the Caveman, beat his chest, then carried her off by her hair for a good ravishment. Figuratively, of course. Oh, she'd been a good sport tonight, seemingly more than willing. But Kerry was a woman who kept her word, even when the bargain involved her body.

Tossing back another long swallow of beer, he sighed. Who knew what to think? Just yesterday he'd suspected her of getting too emotionally involved with him. Now he wondered if she'd cried because she felt like she'd been whoring herself for her brother. Because she had thrown away her virginity, giving it to the first stranger who might be able to help her. And he, with an ego as swollen as his ever-ready cock, had simply assumed she cared for him.

What a fucking idiot.

The other head was no better, he thought. For the first time in days, his boxer-briefs weren't tented. His flaccid state wouldn't last long around Kerry, he knew. Tying her down and inducing her to orgasm with all the protruding parts of his body hadn't been enough. An hour later he'd taken her swiftly against the wall. The savage satisfaction at hearing her cry out his name still stunned him.

He was a man with red blood cells who clamored for lush women with Kerry's sort of enthusiasm. He reveled in the kind of sexual trust she placed in him. Still, Kerry giving her body every time he crooked his finger, in any way he wanted, wasn't enough. He had her . . . but he knew very well that he didn't. Despite their bargain, she wasn't *his*.

Rafe didn't want to know why that pissed him off.

Something was very wrong. Women were meant to be lusted after, wanted. Women weren't supposed to be *needed*. And he feared very much that's where he was at the moment.

How ironic that three days ago he'd wanted nothing more than to escape the woman he'd thought just south of psycho. Now he was pretty sure he needed the psych ward far more than Kerry ever would.

Saying goodbye to her come morning . . . damn it, a part of him didn't want to. The thought lodged somewhere under his skin, irritating him like a case of the hives. The irrational part of Rafe urged him to race inside and claim her body again, in the hopes she wouldn't forget him. He had the most insane urge to imprint himself on her, ruin her for any other man.

The more sane part of him told him he was being a moron.

Behind him, French doors opened with a quiet *click*. Rafe didn't have to turn to know Kerry stood there. He felt it. Peace washed over him. And as evidenced by the fact his cock was again doing its best imitation of a flagpole, lust. Two feelings that, until Kerry, he would have sworn were mutually exclusive.

"I thought I'd find you out here," she murmured.

Doing his best to look busy, Rafe logged into Standard National's files. "Yeah."

He couldn't look at her. If he did, he'd jump her, rip off whatever she might be wearing, and find some position, comfortable or not, to get inside her, become a part of her. Drown out the clock in his head, ticking away the seconds they had left together. Or he might demand an explanation for being dumped. So he opted for pulling up account files in the bank's database.

God, he hated this shit. Relationships sucked, and he didn't want one. He had no idea how to have one anyway. This little . . . tiff with Kerry was a perfect example. She'd dismissed him, or he was pretty sure she had. His experience at interpreting emotions was less than zero. He'd be more successful at building a spaceship without instructions.

At his right, Kerry sighed, then slid into the chair next to him. "I think we should talk."

Unable to stop himself, Rafe glanced her way. Lavender V-neck top. No bra. Black lace panties tied by minuscule bows on each hip. The whole look had him salivating. Lust made him half feral, and she wanted to talk? Yeah, right after Tinkerbell sprinkled him with pixie dust and he flew away to Neverland. He gritted his teeth, willing his blood to stop rushing south.

Opting for the safe view, rather than the one that made him think of the soft cries she made as she neared orgasm, he turned back to the computer screen and hit the keys that would open the bank's transactions for the day.

"Rafe?"

He turned back and saw her face. Kerry didn't look like her usual, sunny self. A hint of something somber wrinkled her brow. Rafe figured he had something to do with it and swore under his breath.

"Talking is not painful," she pointed out.

That was her opinion.

Kerry sighed. "Look, I just want you to know I appreciate everything you did for me. We met under . . . unusual circumstances."

That was one way of putting it. Rafe raised his brows.

"Okay, I had a stupid scheme that was more desperate than smart, and after drugging you and tying you down, we met. More accurate?"

He risked another glance at her. Pale, firm thighs, crossed as if protecting the secrets he knew so well. Kerneled nipples, breeze playing with her pale curls, mouth still swollen from his kisses. Like a pale goddess she was. He could only think things like *here, mine, now*. In contrast, realizing that her first attempt hadn't gone well, Kerry was probably looking for a gentler way to dump him on his ass.

Not trusting his voice, Rafe shrugged and looked back through Standard National's records. He scrolled, looking but not seeing much.

Why the hell couldn't she deliver her Dear John speech and leave him the hell alone?

"By offering to take you home, I was trying to do the right thing and let you get back to your life. I know you have goals, and I hope you reach them. I hope you show that five-million-dollar bank account to your father and that he realizes how smart and successful you are. I wasn't dissing you, and I certainly didn't mean to upset you or bruise your male ego or whatever."

Was he that obvious? Did she suspect, as he did, that the hurt went beyond ego?

Frowning, Rafe glanced at Kerry again. Soft, white throat, sweetly curved cheek, eyes as soft and green as the grassy hills of mist-enshrouded Wiltshire he'd seen on a business trip last year. He rubbed the back of his suddenly tense neck. Now he was waxing poetic about a woman he'd walk away from in a handful of hours? Maybe more sleep would help.

He doubted it.

"I'm over it," he lied. "What are you going to do about Mark now?"

Kerry sighed, shoulders slumping. She looked exhausted. "I don't know. I'd do anything for him. You, obviously, know that. I'm just not sure how I can help my brother now. I thought about trying to encourage Tiffany to pry information out of Smikins. But I'm afraid she'd have to get down and dirty in the slime's bed, and Mark wouldn't want that. I still think Smikins is guilty, or at least knows a lot more than he lets on. I just can't prove it."

Certainly, her theory was possible. Rafe couldn't deny that wanting a woman was a powerful motivator. It was the same reason he suspected Jason was guilty. But they could both be wrong; Tiffany might be a criminal mastermind. Normally, he wouldn't think so, but normally he wouldn't believe that a grown, sensible man could be having feelings far beyond lust for an off-the-wall blonde he'd met four days ago.

At this point, he was forced to concede that he didn't know squat about this situation.

"Mark's trial starts in less than a week, right?" he said finally.

Her eyes slid shut. Her shoulders sank more. "Yes."

"You need a plan."

"I know. But I'm not good at planning. How can I plan around something I barely understand?"

Rafe opened his mouth to reply but glanced at the computer screen. There! Twenty-five separate electronic deposits into Standard National from the same small Midwestern bank that had filtered the other deposits Mark had been accused of embezzling. He sat up, leaned over his keyboard. Another few clicks later, he confirmed that the account the deposit had been made to had been established between 3:58 and 4:12 P.M. today at terminal 4389, user ID identical to Mark's.

"Holy shit!"

"What?" Kerry leaned across the table, closer to him.

Wrapping an arm around her shoulder, Rafe pulled her closer to the screen . . . and to him. "See here."

Kerry frowned as he pointed to the deposit record. "What?"

He laid the information out for her. "Here are deposits from the same bank the previous theft derived from. Look at the terminal ID and user name."

"The hidden terminal and Mark's ID." She cast a stunned green stare at him. "Ohmigod, what does that mean?"

"Maybe nothing. But Standard National receives so few deposits from this Midwestern bank. Only a handful in the last five years, except the deposits that were stolen. Now more than two dozen in one day, each just small enough to escape the need for a bank to report it to the Feds. I'm thinking whoever did this is definitely up to something."

"It sounds fishy. But we have to figure out what this person—or people—is up to, to prove anything."

"You're right. And the whole scenario is odd. If these people making the deposits knew their money had been stolen in the past, why would they keep making deposits in exactly the same way? It's like they want their money to be stolen."

"That doesn't make any sense." Kerry frowned.

"On the surface, you're right."

Rafe rubbed his chin, nearly wishing it possessed the magical power of a genie in a bottle. Maybe then he'd know what to do: Take her invitation to leave and get back to his normal, sane—and lest he forget, lucrative—life? Or stay behind another few hours to help Kerry find some way out of her dilemma?

Duh. He knew the answer before his mind had finished forming the question. All her life, people had run out on Kerry, or worse, died. She'd been alone her entire life, except for Mark. She'd endured some hard times. The one person she had always counted on was now behind solid, iron bars enjoying his free cable TV. Other than him, Kerry only had Tiffany. Oh, and in her mind, Jason, which made Rafe want to hit something. Yeah, Jason would love to help her . . . right onto her back with her legs spread. *Not gonna happen, pal.*

Besides, they were both suspects. Nope. His choices were to leave the entire mess in Kerry's lap and force her to fend for herself again, or to pitch in, hoping it would help.

Hoping she still wanted him by her side.

The smart thing would be to start packing his suitcase now. Apparently, his brain had taken a vacation.

"Assuming it's the same person or people, what could they be doing?" Kerry asked.

"Anything." He shrugged. "Money laundering, I guess. Not certain for what purpose, exactly. But I have an idea how to get some answers."

"What?" Kerry nodded, biting her kiss-swollen lower lip. "Something tells me you and ideas are dangerous together."

"Why would you think that?" He frowned.

"A hunch."

Her cheeky smile made him laugh. "Well, I *know* you and ideas are dangerous. I have the experience to prove it. Maybe we should try it my way this time."

Kerry hesitated. "I've already asked far too much of you. You don't owe me a thing. In the morning, our bargain ends and we're even."

She said the words he'd wanted to hear since waking up hungover Saturday morning. He could hardly believe the anger they engendered now.

"We're not fucking even." He stood, chair scraping across the flagstones, and pounded a fist on the table. "You can't drag me ass deep into your crap, then dismiss me like some naughty little boy when you're through."

Shock widened her mossy green eyes. She leaned forward, providing a shadowy glimpse of her downy-soft cleavage. Even when she tossed him on his ass, he wanted her.

"I can't demand that you stay and help me, either," she countered. "It's not your problem. I knew that all along and I was so desperate to do something, *anything*, that I overlooked that fact, broke laws . . . did things I'm not proud of."

"Like fucking me?" Rafe heard the sharp note in his voice. "Gee, thanks for the orgasms but I really shouldn't have—"

"Stop putting words in my mouth!" She rose to her feet, fists clenched at her sides. "What is wrong with you? Would I love for you to stay and help me through this for the days, weeks, hell, months it might take to free Mark? Yes. But I can't ask you to do that. I don't expect you to stay. You've done everything I've asked and more. It didn't work, so I'm trying to thank you for your help and let you get back to your life. And you yell at me," she muttered, then went to the door leading back to the cottage. Then she turned. "And for the record, you may think differently, but I never *fucked* you."

The conversation ended when she slammed the door.

Her blistering words rang in his ears. Was Kerry trying to say their time together had meant something besides sex? Or just protesting his language, which he knew needed improvement?

Heaving a huge sigh, Rafe sat and stared at his laptop. Smooth. Real smooth. Either way, the only person he knew for a fact who had worse relationship skills than he did was Jack the Ripper.

Leaving would be best, no matter how much he wanted to stay. The fact he'd managed to infuriate and insult her when she'd apparently been trying to do the right thing, at least in her eyes, only underscored the fact that he was severely relationship-challenged.

Humans made mistakes, yes, but only idiots made the same mistake twice in one day. He'd opened his mouth for the second time in about eight hours and inserted both feet—while wearing cement shoes. Very smooth.

At this point, his choices to help her were limited. The idea circulating in his head . . . he ought to be committed for even thinking it, much less seriously contemplating it. Not only did the notion circle his brain, it dive-bombed.

Opening a new Internet browser, Rafe ploughed around various sites until he found the information he needed. He made a phone call. It was way after hours, so Rafe wasn't surprised he had to leave a message. He could only hope it was enough of an explanation.

Grabbing his laptop, Rafe skulked inside. Kerry lay in the bed with the blankets bundled up to her chin. She did not look up at him as he entered.

"Sorry," he mumbled, setting the laptop down on the dresser and turning to face her. "I'm not good at saying what's in my head sometimes. I have a crappy temper."

"Apology accepted," she said stiffly.

"Are you trying to release me to let me get back on with my life? Or just wanting to get rid of me?" He pierced her with an insistent gray stare. "Shoot straight with me."

Kerry sat up, and her golden curls tumbled to her shoulders as she held the sheet up to her chest. "Trying to let you get on with your life. I thought that was clear."

Rafe shrugged. "I took it as a dismissal. I . . . ah, I got mad before I asked if you wanted me to stay and help before my plane leaves. It's only another eighteen hours or so, but I thought I'd offer."

Her green eyes widened with wonder. Tears pooled at the bottom edge, threatening to spill down her apple cheeks. His offer had made her cry? Damn if that little bit of man-made salt water didn't rip out his guts.

"Look, if you want me gone, fine. I can pack and be out of here—"

Kerry launched herself into his arms, cutting off his sentence. "You'd actually stay a little longer?"

"It's either that or sit around and watch boring-ass reruns until my plane leaves."

She backed away, onto the bed again. "I guess embezzlement is more interesting than reruns."

Rafe sighed. He was fucking this up, too. "I meant to say that I want to help you, not that embezzlement is more entertaining than *Friends* in syndication. You've got a big job in front of you and not much help. You've tried hard, and we can find the answer, I think. You shouldn't have to do everything alone."

The uncharacteristic tightening of her mouth told him that little speech hadn't helped either.

"What?" he demanded. "I can't be helpful now?"

"I don't need your pity."

"This has nothing to do with pity. You—you deserve help, and I think I can help you. Okay? When I leave, I'd like to know you're going to be all right."

Somewhat mollified, she nodded. "Thanks. You said earlier that you had an idea?"

"Yeah." He nodded and cleared this throat.

Time to jump off the bridge. Was he ready? Sure about this?

The hope on Kerry's face punched him in the gut. What if, when he left, he could do so knowing her brother, her anchor in life, was going to be with her again, taking care of her? Mark would make sure Kerry's future worked out. He'd already forbidden Jason to ask her out, so Rafe figured her brother had some sense.

But the risk of this scheme . . .

Might be worth it if Rafe could turn that tentative hope on her face to true happiness.

"Those deposits I showed you out on the patio, remember?" At her nod, he went on. "They add up to nearly half a million dollars. I'll bet someone in the bank, our thief, is watching that money and waiting for the opportunity to take it or transfer it elsewhere. I'm going to beat them to it."

"What?" Kerry frowned. "It sounds like you're saying that you want to steal the money."

Rafe did his best to smile. "Bingo."

* * *

KERRY felt her jaw drop somewhere in the vicinity of Miami. "You're going to steal the money? But—but that's illegal." Her mind whirled. She gasped. "And after what you did to the FBI—"

"CIA," he corrected.

"Whatever. The point is, you said yourself they'd put you away for good if you ever used your hacking illegally again. Rafe, no. It's too risky. Why would you even suggest it?"

The fact he would even bring up such a scheme appalled her . . . and touched her. Was he seriously willing to go that far out on a limb for her?

"Not steal, exactly," he clarified. "I put a call in to D'Nanza and told him that I'd opened an account in my name at another bank and would be transferring the money there. I offered to sign the money over to the Feds, if they want. Anyway, the point is, one of our three suspects will realize the money is missing and start looking for it, probably sooner rather than later. If they're clever enough to frame Mark, they'll be clever enough to see that I've taken it. They'll come looking for me and tip their hand trying to get the money back."

"But you'll be gone as of this afternoon."

"I have a feeling this will all play out before then. If not, I might be able to change my flight and stay one more day. But I'm pretty sure that by sunset, we'll know who our culprit is."

Kerry gnawed on her bottom lip. "Won't it look like a trap?"

He shrugged. "Maybe they'll think I'm a thief. If not . . . doesn't change the fact someone *will* want that money bad."

"But if you put the bank account in my name—"

Rafe shook his head. "No dice. That person is likely to come looking for you, and that's far too dangerous."

Kerry blinked, staring absently at the blanket pooled in her lap. He was planning to set himself directly between her and the thief? Himself and the Feds? Why?

She raised a gaze to him that tumbled with emotions: hope, amazement, fear, uncertainty. Everything she felt showed on her face, no doubt.

"It's dangerous for you, too. You'd be risking a lot just to help me."

Rafe winced, pulled at the back of his neck with his palm. "No big deal. Look, if you don't like the plan—"

"It could work," she conceded. "But all the risk stops at your door. You might be arrested if D'Nanza decides to be difficult. This crook might be violent. You're putting your fingerprints all over this, so that someone twisted enough to break the law repeatedly and frame an innocent man will come find you. Why?"

He shifted from one foot to the other and looked away. "Do I have to have a reason? Do we have to analyze this to death?"

His actions said that he cared, at least a little, and she wanted to believe that more than anything. But his words indicated that his caring for her made him uncomfortable. Rafe's suggestion was awfully bighearted; interrogating him about it just wasn't smart.

"I can't let you do this," she said finally. "It's too dangerous. I appreciate you wanting to join the fight, but I'll find some other way that doesn't risk you—"

Rafe turned back to the dresser, pressed a few keys on his laptop. Something flashed on the screen. Deposit records with lots of zeros suddenly disappeared. A few more strokes, and the deposits appeared again elsewhere. "Too late. It's done."

The enormity of the risk Rafe had just taken for her dropped her stomach to her knees. He'd stolen a whole lot of money just to help her. He might be arrested. Their robber might have a murderous streak. And he knew it—his face told her that. He'd done it anyway. If he'd merely wanted to see an innocent man released from sure prison time, he would have set the new account with the embezzled money up in her name. But no. He'd insisted on establishing the accounts with his name, assuming all the risks—to his freedom, his reputation as a businessman, his very safety.

Kerry felt fresh tears sting her eyes. If she'd been lying to herself before, she could no longer pretend that Denial was a river in Egypt.

She loved Rafe.

And she was equally sure that, despite his sacrifice, he didn't want to hear it. After all, he'd offered to stay a day or two, not a lifetime.

Thrusting away that reality, Kerry left the sanctuary of the bed and walked on silent feet toward him. He watched, eyes wary, hungry.

Pausing a foot away from Rafe, Kerry wordlessly tugged her shirt over her head, leaving her bare from the hips up. Surprise and lust darkened his stormy gray eyes. As his gaze roved over her shoulders and her bare breasts with their tight, swollen nipples, those same mesmerizing eyes burned.

"Kerry—"

She stretched her mouth up to his and kissed him with the bittersweet joy churning in her heart. Yes, she loved someone who would never love her. He was sophisticated city, rich, used to privilege, well educated; she . . . hopelessly unpolished, barely halfway through college, scraping by as a waitress in a greasy diner. He'd never want her beyond this adventure, and she didn't blame him.

But she had this moment, right now.

Swelling with a need to touch Rafe, Kerry kissed him, coaxing him to part his lips. In true Rafe fashion, he not only opened, but took over. He swept inside her mouth, connecting them together. She leaned into him, feeling fused to him by the pleasure his kiss gave her, by the need swirling in her heart.

The kiss seared her, every stroke of his tongue ramping up the arousal tightening her belly.

Rafe lifted his head, panting. He stared, the question hovering in his eyes.

To answer it, Kerry plucked at the ribbons holding her small lace panties in place. With the tug of the last bow, the scrap of black seduction fell to her feet. She smiled in welcome.

His eyes widened like big, shiny quarters.

"Kerry?" he whispered thickly.

Her heart gonged in her chest, reverberating with both adrenaline and love.

In answer, she caressed his cheek. "You're an amazing man. I'm lucky you didn't keep me tied to the bed and call the police when you had the chance. I'm lucky you didn't flay me alive with that sarcastic tongue when I confessed I'd kidnapped you. I'm lucky you turned out to be both brilliant and fantastic in bed." She smiled and lay a simple kiss on his lips. "Mostly, I'm lucky to have met you."

Before Rafe could react, Kerry pressed her naked body against his sleek, tightly muscled form and layered her mouth over his again. He stiffened, his body going taut. For a wild moment, Kerry feared rejection, or more specifically, that he'd realized she loved him and do a twelve-hundred-mile dash all the way back to New York.

Unless groaning "Gotta have you now" and possessing her mouth with a single devastating kiss was a new form of rejection, she need not have worried.

Even more, something in Rafe's kiss was different. Softer. The demand was still there, but a new mood tempered it. The sensation was like gentle persuasion, silent pleading, desperation. She'd felt hints of these from him before. But this . . . it was overwhelming. Reverence flowed from him to her with every touch.

His mouth seemed to worship her. With his kiss alone, he told her that he wanted her, cared enough to help her through some tough times, wanted to offer her succor in his touch.

With a smooth hand, he caressed his way down the bare skin of her sensitive neck, traced the line of her spine, feathered his palm over a hip, her buttocks. She tingled everywhere he touched with such slow certainty. She shivered when he urged her back and down to the soft welcome of the bed.

He dotted kisses along the edge of her jaw, nibbled on her neck as if he had all night to do nothing more than touch her, revel in her skin.

A hazy, pleasure-filled contentment spread through her as he moved down her body, his tongue taking lazy swipes at her nipples, sucking gently at her.

Bliss rolled through her body, softening muscles, moistening her. She brushed her fingers through the silky dark strands of his hair, delighting in the closeness. Nothing in her life had ever been perfect.

Until now.

As Rafe inched up her body, again to consume her with the fire of a languorous kiss, Kerry spread herself beneath him in invitation.

"I want you. No games, no toys. Just you."

He reached for a condom on the nightstand. "I can't think of anything better."

A rip of foil and a few movements later, Rafe tunneled inside her. She welcomed him with a sigh as he filled her, thick, pulsing, so full of life. Every muscle and nerve in her body was attuned to him, eager to have him near.

Kerry raised her hips, wrapped her legs around him, and invited him in farther.

With a groan, he accepted, burying himself to the hilt inside her. And he stayed, lingering, as if he could barely stand to leave any part of her, even to thrust.

He clasped her cheek in his hand. Their eyes met as he pressed farther into her, making her gasp.

"So good," he muttered. "So perfect."

Sweet need curled deep inside her, rolling like waves on a tranquil crystal-clear ocean, at his words. The tender caring in his eyes reached deep into her heart as he withdrew from her body. Kerry held in a whimper of protest—barely—when he clasped her hand in his, fingers entwined, and fused their mouths together. Finally, he entered her again with a slow, sure stroke.

Kerry nearly exploded in a pleasure so sublime, it didn't simply touch her body, but dug all the way down to her heart.

With gazes still locked, he eased into her again. Beyond their body connection, the intimacy of their mating gazes made her feel more attuned to him than ever. His dark face flushed with familiar arousal. Kerry could predict that the muscles of his powerful shoulders would bunch up and roll as he moved inside her. She knew what the widening of his dark pupils meant, the harsh male groans.

"Can't stay away from you," he muttered as he thrust into her again.

She met his unwavering stare. "You don't have to."

Her words seemed to unleash something inside him. His fingers tightened on her hands, matching the urgency tightening his mouth, driving his hard strokes into her. He engorged even more. Every stroke seemed to possess her more fully than the last. Pleasure blossomed, grew, spiraled, spun nearly out of control. Kerry threw her head back and moaned his name.

"That's right. Feel me. *Me* inside you."

Flesh rippling, she clamped tighter around his cock. Her breathing rushed out of control. Her heartbeat revved like a turbocharged sports car. Even more enthralling was the way he kept looking at her, thrust after thrust, as he filled her with himself.

Love swelled in her chest, threatening to choke her. Would this be the last time she held him? Desperation seized her. She was not ready for her time with him to end. But it would. In less than a day, she would be without him.

Kerry clung to Rafe, holding tight.

Her body raced out of control. Arousal flared beyond her center now, streaming up her belly, down her legs. Every breath was hard to steal. Close . . . so close.

"Babe, I can't hold out."

"Don't stop," she pleaded. *Don't ever stop.*

Every muscle in Rafe's body seemed to tighten, his back, the hard globes of his buttocks, the harsh lines of his jaw. Then she lost focus as her world exploded and ecstasy erupted inside her, obliterating all but the love she didn't dare tell him about. Rafe followed her over the edge with short, sure thrusts and a harsh cry of satisfaction.

After, he didn't roll away. Half-hard, he stayed buried inside her, stroking her hair with a tender hand as she recovered from the aftermath of mind-blowing pleasure.

But it was the love that lingered.

He wouldn't want to hear it. She was better off keeping it to herself and saving the humiliation of his quick dart to freedom, away from his crazy abductor turned nympho.

Still, the fact that he could never be hers, would never want to be, stripped away the vestiges of carnal satisfaction. A dull ache thudded in her chest, which felt hollow and painful. Tears stung her eyes, choked her.

Kerry was almost grateful when her cell phone rang. Rafe held tight as she wriggled beneath him, trying to leave the bed. After a moment's struggle, he let go. She grabbed his shirt and donned it, then walked across the room to her phone, allowing her first breath not tinged with his clean scent in an hour.

It was just as well; she would have to learn to breathe without him from now on.

Chapter Twelve

RAFE listened with half an ear as Kerry answered the phone. Three seconds into the conversation the familiar voice on the other end made him swear under his breath.

Jason. When would the idiot stop chasing Kerry?

And he wished the other guy's pursuit didn't make him want to pound someone into the ground, preferably Jason himself.

In a few hours, it wouldn't be his concern. His gut staged a revolt about that fact. Damn it, Kerry was getting under his skin.

"The investigation is going . . . well," he heard her say. After a pause, she turned her back to him and murmured, "I don't know exactly what Rafe and Smikins talked about. What? No, all Rafe said is that he's confident we'll know something soon." She paused. "Coming home? Probably tomorrow. I'll call you."

Gritting his teeth, Rafe sat up in the bed and contemplated her narrow back outlined in his shirt as she hung up the phone moments later. Yeah, Kerry was going home tomorrow, sooner rather than later. She had to, before the bitter end got . . . well, bitter, thanks to his lack of relationship skills. And now that he'd stolen the money from the thief, there would certainly be one pissed-off criminal on the prowl, looking for him. For all he knew, that someone wouldn't mind trying to extract the information and passwords for the new account out of his hide. If he had thought it through a bit more, he would have acknowledged that Kerry's safety came first and realized that transferring the money meant the beginning of the end for them.

Shit.

But before that, there was the little matter of her overly friendly "friend."

"Jason is awfully persistent. Don't you get tired of having a slobbering stalker?"

She turned and glared at him. Rafe held in a wince. Why didn't he just shut the hell up? He was good, at least in business situations, about keeping his cool. All that went out the window with Kerry. She knew where he stood about Jason, and hammering her with it every time the prick's name came up wasn't going to earn him a Mr. Congeniality award.

Yet another example of why he wasn't cut out for this relationship stuff, even if it had crossed his mind lately a time or two—or ten.

"Don't you get tired of worrying about a guy who's nothing more than a good friend?" she said finally. "Trust me, I know Jason. He's no more interested in me than I am in him."

Naïve; that was Rafe's only word for her. Kerry genuinely believed what she said. Her exasperation told him that. Which told him that she knew as much about men as he did about applying mascara. In other words, zilch.

"He asked a lot of questions about the case." A moderate change of subject, for which he mentally patted himself on the back. Proof that more thinking before he opened his mouth would help.

"Mark is his best friend. Of course he's curious."

Or guilty and wondering what we know. "Thanks for not telling him what's going on with the money. No one needs to know but us. If he had anything to do with the theft, he'll figure it out real soon."

"I figured you'd say that."

Good that she'd foreseen Rafe's desire to keep their plan quiet. But could she guess the next thing he had to say? Rafe doubted she'd have seen this one coming.

Getting the words out wouldn't be easy. His tongue stuck to the roof of his mouth. He watched her, lush curves half-visible through the Egyptian cotton of his shirt. She was breath-stealingly sexy. So warm and fun and adventurous. So loyal and loving she'd put her entire life on the line for the brother she loved.

Kerry had taught him new things about women, like the fact they weren't all shoe-happy twigs with maxed-out Macy's cards. But she'd taught him about himself, that being with someone else didn't have to be so damn annoying that he wanted to gouge his eyes out. And he'd always enjoyed sex—loved it, in fact. But with her, an extra spark made the air zing between them, gave every touch the impact of an electrical jolt. Giving that up would be a bitch. But Kerry had also reminded him about fun, about taking risks, that life wasn't just about working and making money. Sometimes people just *had* to do things. He'd gone on this crazy ride with Kerry for that very reason, and had the weekend of a lifetime.

But all good things came to an end, especially when her safety was at stake.

Gut clenching, Rafe crossed the room. Before he could stop himself, he brushed a rioting gold curl back from her face.

"Kerry, I think it's time you took me to the hotel. It's got to end."

Shock blanched across her face. She paled, but didn't make a sound. Lips pressed together, she nodded mutely as she tried to turn away.

"It's safer this way, babe," he said, grabbing her hand and bringing her face-to-face with him again. "Like you said, the thief could be some murderous psycho, and I don't want him finding you."

She stared for a long moment, eyes darkening with emotions he couldn't begin to name. "What about you?"

"I'll take care of myself. I want you out of the thief's path. To everyone who's a suspect, you act like you know nothing about the money."

Nodding, Kerry extracted her hand and backed away. "Morning soon enough for you?"

Rafe glanced at the clock. It was just past midnight. Getting into the hotel would be a pain in the ass at this hour. They might even have given his room away by now, so he'd have to call to get another. The bank was closed, so the thief would likely be unable to check the bank records until morning.

And—okay, he admitted it—he wanted to steal another few hours with Kerry.

"Yeah, morning is fine."

Another silent nod later and she retreated to the bed, slid in, turned off the bedside lamp, and shut her eyes. Her every muscle screamed with tension. She looked ready to burst. With relief? Tears? Anger?

God, he was so not equipped to guess about this woman-emotion stuff.

He crawled into bed beside her, aching to touch her while he could. "Please don't be upset. It's for the best."

"I'm not upset." Her voice was as stiff as a well-starched shirt.

And when he tried to curl up to her, her entire body turned rigid and she shifted away.

Because their bargain had more or less ended and she owed him nothing else, or because she cared and thought he was rejecting her?

Damn, he hated trying to guess. Hated worrying about how she felt. Usually other people's emotions didn't bother him. He never gave them a single thought. Kerry . . . He'd spent plenty of billable, productive hours worrying about her feelings. Hell, for all he knew, she wasn't hurt right now, but having a sudden attack of PMS. This was why he sucked at relationships.

"Be pissed if you want." He rolled away from her, onto his back.

"I said I'm not."

"Real convincing, too. I'm thinking of your safety."

"And getting back to that comfortable life where computers kept you company, no one gave you a birthday party, and you didn't have to care about anyone but you. I expected that." Anger laced her voice. "Believe me, I never expected a rich, brilliant city slicker to stay with a scale-challenged suburban waitress."

"What?"

"I mean, sex is one thing. I'm young and female, so why not, right? But I never expected to be more to you."

Had she wanted to be? Rafe put the brakes on his suddenly pounding pulse.

"You're not the kind of man to truly want a woman who's still working her way through college," Kerry went on, "who will probably never wear a single-digit size of clothing other than shoes, who resorted to crime because she couldn't afford a private investigator."

Scowling, Rafe sat up and rolled her to face him. "You make it sound as if I think you're not good enough. Or that I'm a snob, or somehow think I'm better. What kind of bullshit is that?"

"I'm just stating facts."

He snorted. "Incorrect 'facts.' I'm not better than you or anyone. I turned a hobby that nearly landed me in prison into a lucrative business. That was damned lucky." He grabbed her by the shoulders. "I'm the son of an alcoholic and a desperately unhappy woman who barely spoke English. There's a big claim to fame. And if you make one more derogatory comment about your size, I'm going to smack that ass until it turns as red as a cherry."

She rolled her eyes. "You'd probably like that."

Rafe joined her attempt to lighten the moment. "Who says you wouldn't?"

"You're impossible."

Rafe could barely stand to look at that heartbreaking mouth, her downcast eyes.

So he placed a long, still kiss on her lips and backed away. "This isn't real. You have a life; I have a life. If anything, you're too good for me. I've never known anyone with such a big heart. I don't have the ability to . . . care for people the way you do. I'm not wired that way. Relationships and I—we just don't get along."

"But just tonight, you risked everything to help me—"

"I didn't say I was a total shithead." He raked a hand through hair he already suspected looked like it had been styled by Medusa's hairdresser. "Look, you needed help, so I helped you. It's my good deed for the decade. Staying together . . . it puts you in too much danger and doesn't make sense. My flight leaves in about twelve hours."

Kerry tensed before her face settled into lines of grim acceptance. "You helped me so much. Your plan will work, I think. Mark's freedom is all I hoped for, and I'm grateful."

By unspoken agreement, they left the conversation there. Kerry curled on her side, away from him, lying so still, her breathing so light, he knew she wasn't asleep. Neither was he. But he pretended to be—and pretended he hadn't seen the hurt on her face, pretended that he didn't want to roll over, grab her, and make love to her until they were exhausted beyond walking, beyond arguing or thought.

But he couldn't do that, or anything else. So he did nothing but try to ignore the dull ache pounding away at his chest and watch the sun rise through the sheer-draped French doors, ticking away the seconds until he boarded a plane out of Kerry's life forever.

* * *

BY eight the next morning, Kerry had steered through the rush-hour traffic and pulled up with an equally silent Rafe to the circular drive in front of his palm-shaded hotel. The sprawling property resembled a tropical paradise, and she'd always wondered what staying here in a suite overlooking the Causeway would be like. The resort's beauty was totally lost on her now.

Her legs felt like lead as she crawled out to the humid morning and helped Rafe with his hanging bag. He grabbed his laptop. Neither looked at the other, and Kerry's heartbreak drummed so hard inside her, she swore it reached new decibel levels.

Thank God, he didn't seem to notice.

As they passed, the hunky valet gave her a long look and tipped his white cap. Rafe glared at him and took her hand, leading her into the refrigerated interior, complete with huge fresh flower arrangements in classic urns and a darkened bar that wouldn't see action until tonight, well after Rafe had left town.

Sudden tears lashed at her eyes, stinging the sleep-deprived sockets. Kerry looked at the ceiling, willing them away. If Rafe didn't care, thought parting as easy as flushing the toilet and that he'd forget her by nightfall, then by damn, she'd give the same impression.

Why let the man know she was going to love him for the rest of her life? He would never reciprocate.

"Here's your bag." Horrified at her breaking voice, Kerry cleared her throat. "Thanks for everything. You have my cell phone number if something happens with the money. Have a good trip back." She stuck out her hand.

Rafe looked at her as if she'd lost her mind. He dropped both bags on the cool ceramic tile and grabbed her hand. He used it to yank her forward, flush against his body. As he wound an arm around her waist, she could feel how completely aroused he was. And no one was around to care, except a small woman behind the front desk in the distance, apparently looking through paperwork.

"Kerry, I don't know what's going on in your mind, but don't give me some bullshit that you're not upset."

His gray gaze softened and delved into her, melting her heart that much more. Parting was painful beyond believing, and his tenderness would only kill her. Already, she knew it was going to take years to get over him, if she ever did. He was only making it worse . . . and better. Rafe was sweet, in his gruff way. Seeing this final display of warmth only made her love him more.

"A lot on my mind," she said, discreetly trying to wriggle free.

His grip didn't give an inch.

"If you're worried about Mark, don't be. This plan isn't perfect, but I think it will work. In the end, someone will want that money and come after it. I'll be watching." The hand at her waist splayed across her lower back as he raised the other to cup her cheek in his palm. "If you're disappointed that this . . . *thing* between us can't go on, try not to be. We had a great time. Intense, but not meant to last. I'm not good for you, babe. I don't know how to be with a woman if it involves more than sex. I'd only break your heart."

You already have. She swallowed the lump of pain in her throat, blinking to force back fresh, hot tears.

"I should go," Kerry managed to choke out.

He tensed, tightened his grip on her. But he nodded. "Yeah, I have bank deposits to monitor, phone calls to make. I want you home. You being safe, that's the most important thing."

If it was only about her safety, if Rafe truly wanted her with him, she'd risk anything to stay here, watching those deposits with him, sharing smiles, making love . . . planning a possible future. He didn't want any of that, and she'd only humiliate herself by asking.

"Bye," she murmured.

Before she could think, move, Rafe swooped down, landed a hot, openmouthed kiss on her lips. Heart bursting, flooding her body with love and need and pain, she opened to him and kissed back one last time with every ounce of feeling in her body. Suspended for long moments in emotion, the kiss felt like something out of time. No one else existed. Nothing around them mattered. Only his mouth, connecting his soul to hers, seeming to tell her that he cared and regretted their parting.

Too bad his kiss lied.

Abruptly, he lifted his head and picked up his luggage. His full lips still damp, he whispered, "Bye, babe."

* * *

KERRY barely made it to her car before the tears started to fall. The gray clouds threatened rain, but she beat them to the punch and cried all the way home. Luckily, traffic wasn't moving fast or she'd likely have been off in a ditch on the side of the road.

The dingy house she rented stood still and hot and unwelcoming. She flung herself on the lumpy secondhand couch and curled up into a ball, tears flowing.

How had it happened so fast? One minute Rafe had been just the sexy target of her scheme, the next minute the most exciting lover of her fantasies. Then, in the blink of an eye, he was the man willing to risk prison time to help her . . . but not risk his heart to stay.

A knock on the door boomed through the little room, startling her. Rafe? Surely he could have found her address on the Internet if he'd wanted to.

Drying her tears on her shirt as she raced to the door, she opened it, heart bursting with hope, only to feel it fall to her feet in one lurching rush.

"Jason?"

"I was on my way to work and thought I'd take a chance to see if you were back. You okay, sweetheart?" He rushed in, shutting the door behind him, and wiped the tears from her cheeks. "Damn it, that bastard made you cry, didn't he?"

No more tears, not unless she was alone, she vowed to herself.

Instead, she pasted on a self-deprecating smile. "My fault. The ending . . . it was just a little abrupt. I'll get over it."

There was a whopper of a lie, guaranteed to earn her a spot in Hell—if kidnapping a stranger and having amazing sex with him for days on end didn't already count.

One of Jason's hands resting on her shoulders drifted down her back. "I hate to see you hurt."

"Thanks. You're good to me."

"I always will be." Jason's blue gaze locked onto hers with surprising intensity.

He'd never looked at her like this before. Was he trying to say something?

"You know, I can help you get over him." One of his hands

drifted down her arm, thumb brushing the side of her breast as he went. "I'm here for you if you need me, however you need me."

Shock lanced her brain. She stiffened. Jason? Her buddy Jason? Was he . . . hitting on her? She felt her mouth drop open.

"You're surprised. Haven't you thought about it, even once?"

No. "I—I . . ."

"I've thought about you a million times. I stayed away because Mark wanted it that way. You seemed too innocent. But now you need someone. I can be that someone."

Jason was seriously coming on to her. *Shocking.* "You've thought about having sex with me?"

His soft laugh told her that she'd understated her question. "All the time, sweetheart. But now . . . something about you has changed. That passion I always suspected you had is all over your face. I could punch Dawson for hurting you, for touching you even, but he unlocked something inside of you I can nurture. But it's about more than sex. I want to take care of you."

Ohmigod! He was serious. Never had she suspected Jason of anything more than being a friend, or wanting more than friendship in return. Rafe had been right—she'd been blind to every clue that pointed to Jason's interest. How could she have been so wrong?

"But—but . . . Mara? I thought you were going to ask her to marry you."

"What gave you that impression?" He frowned. "I like her. She's a great person, a lot of fun. I don't care deeply for her. She doesn't fire me the way you do. Give me a chance to make everything better for you."

"You're not just talking pity sex?"

"Pity?" Jason's steady blue gaze pinned her in place. "Lust, want, caring, amazement, hope, yes. Never pity."

How had she missed the signs of Jason's interest? Rafe had sensed it right away, before even clapping eyes on her brother's best friend. If Rafe had been right about that . . . had he been right about Jason's guilt?

Kerry gasped. Could *she* actually be his motive to frame his own best friend?

When she tried to back away, Jason held firm.

"You're hurting me," she protested.

"Sorry." His grip eased slightly but he did not release her. "I'll never hurt you, not like that asshole Dawson. It kills me to be pretty damn sure that he used your body in every way possible, then crawled out of your bed and broke your heart."

Kerry flushed, embarrassment and pain washing over her in a hot wave. But she couldn't contradict Jason. At moments like this, she hated the fact she was so easy to read.

"I'd never do that," he murmured. "Well, at least not the breaking-your-heart stuff."

But he would use her body in every way possible, if she let him. Kerry did not find that thought comforting in the least.

"Um, how about coffee?" She managed to squirm free and all but sprinted to the kitchen.

He followed. Uh-oh, bad move. Her galley kitchen was both narrow and short. Jason stood in the entry, blocking the only exit.

"No thanks. Kerry—"

"What time do you have to be at work? It's already nine."

"The bank is open late on Tuesday, remember? I don't go in until eleven." He sidled closer.

Kerry swallowed. He didn't need to be in for almost two hours, and she lived only three miles from the branch.

Mind racing, she searched for some way to change the subject, or end this altogether.

"I'm really tired. Would you understand if I just wanted to go to bed—"

"I'd love the chance to go with you." He jumped forward and took her hands. "Let me be with you, ease you. I can comfort you and take your mind off Dawson."

As if to prove his point, Jason leaned in and set his lips over Kerry's. She tried to back into her rickety wood veneer cabinets, but his hand cupped the back of her head and held her still against him.

The kiss started soft and slow, proving how gentle he could be. His fingers wove tenderly through her hair.

"God, I've waited forever to touch you," he whispered against her cheek.

Her mind frighteningly blank, Kerry didn't know what to say, to do. Frozen, she felt his lips cover hers again. Even when she did not return the kiss, he groaned. Against her belly, his erection grew. She felt no arousal, only shock. Faint sadness tinged the mix. How could she have been so wrong about Jason's platonic friendship?

Did she know him at all, really?

Suddenly, he ended the kiss, stared deep into her eyes. Kerry shook her head, silently asking him to stop, since shock had frozen her throat.

"Don't say no, not without giving me a chance to show you how I feel, how good we could be together."

"No, Jas—"

He covered her mouth with an aggressive kiss that bespoke pent-up passion. The softness in his lips had been replaced by a harsh drive to possess. The tip of his tongue played at the seam of her lips.

Kerry wrenched away.

"Open up, sweetheart," he pleaded. "Please. I can make you feel so good. You'll forget him."

As he charged forward again, Kerry wedged her hands between them, flat against his chest. She pushed, sending him stumbling away.

"Stop! Mark wouldn't want this. *I* don't want this."

He tensed, paused. "I can see that I surprised you. You need time."

"Jason, you're my friend," she said, eyes imploring. "Just my friend."

He bristled, jaw tensing. "I could be a lot more if you'd let me."

"No." She swallowed. "I love Rafe."

"After a few days? It can't be real love."

"You're wrong."

His mouth pinched into a thin line. "He doesn't love you."

The truth of that statement made grief sink like a cold black stone in her gut. "That doesn't change how I feel."

"He doesn't deserve you!" His fists clenched. "He's taking your devotion and throwing it back in your face. He doesn't give a damn if he's trampling on your heart. He's going back to New York, where he'll probably never give you a second thought because he's such a jerk, and you're going to cling to his memory and not give another man, one who really wants you, a chance to form a solid relationship. Kerry, think about how wrong that is."

Put that way, she did sound dumb. But it didn't change how she felt, deep inside. Some people made decisions with their heads. She always made them with her heart. Her head told her that someday she'd have to get on with her life. Her heart told her it didn't have to be today. It knew she loved Rafe. Period.

"I can't force myself to stop loving him. I—I'm not ready to think about anyone else. And right now I have to focus on helping Mark. His trial starts in less than a week."

"Damn!" he swore and backed out of the kitchen. "You're not even willing to give me a try? I've waited—God, like four years—for the right time."

"Now isn't the time. I don't know if it ever will be. You're a good friend, but I don't think I can be more."

"This is his fault. Where is the asshole?"

"Rafe? It doesn't matter—"

"It definitely does. Where is he?"

"I'm not telling you. You'll only fight for no reason. You punching him doesn't solve anything. Think about it, Jason. It wouldn't be fair for me to come to you with someone else in my heart."

"I've had no one else but you in my heart for years, and he's clouded your mind so much that you won't even listen. If you won't tell me where to find the selfish slimeball, I'll find out for myself," he snarled. "I'm not giving you up to a user like him!"

Turning away, he stomped to the door, wrenched it open, then slammed it so loud the entire house shook.

Kerry stood, staring at the door, stunned. Trembling, she made her way to the breakfast table and sank into a chair. In a few short months, her world had started to cave in. Now, the entire foundation of her existence was disintegrating on one overcast Tuesday morning. Mark had been arrested and gone to jail, and her plan to save him hung in the balance. She'd lost her heart to a man who didn't return her feelings. She'd probably lost one of her best friends because she didn't want more than his friendship. Pops, her boss, hadn't been thrilled when she'd called in sick this morning, and she desperately needed the money working at the diner brought in. She was due to start summer school next Monday, which wasn't paid for, and her head felt ready to explode. What was she going to do?

For the moment, she opted for a shower. It wasn't a stroke of genius, but it was a place to start.

A long twenty minutes later, she combed her wet curls, wrapped herself in a thin cotton robe, and skulked to the kitchen to make a cup of tea.

As her bare feet hit the cool linoleum, she gazed at her answering machine. A flashing red light. Rafe? Or Jason?

Breathing suddenly constricted, she pressed the button. The electronic voice informed her the message had been left just before 10 A.M., mere minutes ago. Then Tiffany's voice filled the room, sounding slightly harassed.

"Hi, are you home yet? Guess not. I thought I should warn you, Smikins is looking for Mr. Dawson. He's not happy and asked me to track Mr. Dawson down. I had no idea where to start and with Shorty on a rampage . . . Can you help me out and tell me where Mr. Dawson is staying? Call me on my cell phone. Thanks!"

Smikins in one of his moods . . . A self-induced lobotomy would be more fun.

Kerry erased the message. She wasn't in the mood to talk to anyone. Her sister-in-law was such a great listener—sometimes too good. She'd want to hear every last detail, talk through every bit of the problem. Kerry didn't want to talk about the fact that her fling with Rafe was over. On the other hand, Rafe had stuck his neck on the chopping block to help Mark, so if she could do anything to make sure he got paid so he could go to his dad a five-million-dollar man, she would do it. Then she'd have her tea, a good cry, and figure out how to recover from a broken heart—one of the few repairs for which Superglue was useless, damn it.

Grabbing the phone, Kerry dialed Tiffany's cell number. Voice mail picked up immediately. *Thank goodness.* She left the name of Rafe's hotel and quickly hung up. Family obligation met for the moment.

She turned to grab some sugar for her tea and noticed the pantry door open on her right. Had it been open earlier?

Probably. Likely she'd been too distraught to notice. It had an annoying habit of popping open, and her landlord was too lazy to fix it. Normally, she'd ask Jason to look at it . . . but that was clearly out of the question now.

Refusing to travel that mental path, Kerry lifted her little red kettle from the stove and ran fresh water into it. A cup of hot tea. That would be good. That would help clear her mind. She sifted through the tea bags in the silver canister on her counter. Lemon? No, too tart. Mandarin orange? Possibilities. Peach? Too happy.

Something, a shuffling, sounded behind her. Before she could turn, she heard a *whoosh*. Pain exploded in the back of her head. Darkness crowded the edges of her vision. She tried to turn, to see what had happened.

She crumpled toward the ground instead. Then . . . nothing.

* * *

CHECK-IN went smoothly enough. Too bad, really. Rafe had hoped for someone to argue with. Instead, Isabel, as her name tag read, had been perfectly polite and professional. Damn, why did women always choose the wrong time to be accommodating?

Because the hotel wasn't full, they allowed him to check in to a room at barely nine in the morning. He paid for the night, though he'd be leaving for the airport about three-thirty. Until then, he would watch the money he'd taken from the accounts, talk to D'Nanza about being reasonable, and pray he didn't get arrested.

Such a full plate should have meant that he could go more than fifteen seconds without thinking about Kerry.

Yeah, and Shaquille O'Neal was going to take up professional ballet dancing.

As he set up his laptop on the squatty desk and sat in the uncomfortable chair, he eyed the minibar. Was just before ten in the morning too early for a beer?

His phone rang, providing enough distraction to avoid answering the question. He picked it up and looked at the caller ID. Unknown.

"Rafe Dawson," he answered.

"Special Agent Robert D'Nanza. What the hell are you doing, stealing half a million dollars?"

"Making sure someone innocent doesn't go down the river. Mark Sullivan did not commit this crime. Someone disguised a retired terminal to look like Sullivan's in the system and—"

"Our guy would have found that."

"Down in the kernels? Only someone really clever puts shit like that there. Besides, if it's Mark, why is someone banging away at that same terminal now, using Mark's ID and password? The bank hasn't reassigned that terminal or ID to another employee. I checked. Now, I know they have a lot of privileges in jail these days, but I doubt Mark can remotely access a secure bank terminal."

D'Nanza paused. "I don't have time for your theories. This trial starts Monday."

Rafe cursed under his breath. "Don't you want to bring the right man to trial? I think you'd have a better conviction rate if you did."

"Are you a fully trained federal investigator now?"

"No, just someone who's willing to look at all the facts in front of him. Someone willing to look beyond the surface, rather than being concerned with taking my next donut break."

"I ought to haul your ass to jail," D'Nanza snarled. "You took money that did not belong to you. End of story. And I did some digging on you. I know all about your sordid little past pranking the CIA."

Rafe's gut clenched, but he kept on with this game of chicken.

"Goody. Then maybe you'll realize I wouldn't resort to such drastic measures if I believed there was a shred of a possibility that Mark Sullivan was guilty."

"You're lucky you've done solid work for one of our assistant directors, Tim Norton, over the years. If he'd given me the slightest indication that you're a thief or a crackpot, buddy, you'd already be standing on concrete looking through bars."

Rafe plugged his laptop into the data port. "Norton's a good guy. At least he realizes that hauling my ass to jail won't solve the problem. You got the wrong guy locked up. Sullivan was set up from start to finish either by his boss, his wife, or his best friend."

"That's your speculation. The fact that Sullivan's sister hired you doesn't compel me."

"She didn't hire me. I looked into it as a favor."

"A favor." He snorted. "Do I want to know what you asked for in return? I've seen her; she's a looker. Maybe I'd like to do a favor or two for her myself."

"Keep your dirty mind off Kerry Sullivan," he growled.

"Is that the way the wind blows?"

Rafe heard the sticky smile in the agent's voice and gritted his teeth. "I'm inside, so I'm not aware of wind blowing, actually. I am aware that if you just looked at what I've dug up—"

"I have more than one case to work on, and my work on this one is done. I'm late for a meeting, so here's the deal: If no one has made a move on that money by this time tomorrow, I'm going to arrest you and bring you up on every charge I can. If someone does make a move on the money, call me. *Maybe* you'll avoid doing time. But personally, I'm looking forward to slapping you in handcuffs and bringing you in."

D'Nanza disconnected the call. Rafe put the phone down, tension knotting his insides.

"Prick," he muttered to the phone, then connected to Standard National's mainframe.

He'd known when he took the money that he'd be sticking his neck on the chopping block. The thought of jail made him shiver. All too well, he remembered the weekend he'd spent there before his old man had bailed him out. It had been cold, winter. The food sucked. Big guys with tattoos thought he was some sort of rich Harvard kid and tormented him. If he hadn't been tall, built broad, worked out . . .

Rafe shook the memories away and browsed Standard National's files. It was quarter after 10 A.M. now, so hopefully all his suspects were at the bank and someone would start looking for the money soon.

Scrolling through the overnight deposits and withdrawals, he sorted his list by terminal ID. *There!* Already someone had accessed terminal 4389 and, using Mark's ID and password, gone on a fishing expedition. Rafe got down to the keystroke level and smiled. Now he was damn glad he'd installed a bit of software that would track the user's keystrokes.

A little prowling through the files had him pumping his fists in the air in triumph. Yeah, the guilty party logged in about twenty minutes ago and had looked everywhere for the money. No doubt whoever it was—and his bet was still on Jason, the lying twit—knew by now that the money had been taken.

And likely knew that Rafe had taken it.

Racing to the phone, he dialed Kerry's number. His heart began to pound. He was going to talk to her. Would she be happy to talk to him? Three rings, four . . . five. Her voice mail. He hung up and scowled.

Had Kerry decided not to speak to him? No, she might be upset about their time together or their parting or whatever, but she'd take a call that might be about her brother. Granted, he didn't know a lot about women in general, except in bed, but he *knew* that much about Kerry. No question, she'd do anything for Mark.

Before he could contemplate anything, his phone rang. He peered at the caller ID. Ah, his faithful assistant.

"Morning, Regina."

"Good morning, Mr. Dawson. I have two urgent phone calls that have come into the office. The first from Mr. Smikins at Standard National Bank. He's threatening nonpayment because the work isn't finished."

"What a putz. I'm basically finished with their files. Their security breach was internal. I'll update their external control measures today. Send him the checklist of internal security recommendations and tell him I'll call later today. He'll pay me."

Or else. Rafe planned to show up on his father's doorstep the day he turned thirty and prove he was worth five million and more successful than the old goat had ever been. Then he'd feel vindicated. His father's voice in his head telling him he was worthless and would never amount to anything for any reason to anyone would stop ringing in his head late at night when he couldn't sleep. He was worthy of happiness, of success, of a warm beautiful woman like Kerry—not that he intended to make anything of their relationship. It was the principle. Rafe wasn't about to give up his five-million-dollar goal for any reason.

Unless you're in jail, a little voice whispered in his head. *Won't Daddy be proud then?*

Telling the unpleasant part of his brain to fuck off, he turned his attention back to Regina. "Who else called? Someone named Kerry Sullivan?"

Rafe heard the note of hope in his voice and thought about biting off his tongue.

Perceptive Regina heard it, too. "No, but she must be something.

The other call was about her. Someone named Jason Bailey. He called you some rather . . . interesting names. Sorry to say, I didn't bother to write them down word for word. None were too polite. The rest of the message indicated that Kerry is crying, and it's your fault. He demanded to know where you're staying."

"Damn it," Rafe muttered. "He went to see her this morning, I'll bet. Son of a bitch."

Because Jason panted so hard after his best friend's sister, he'd called around midnight—rude in itself—to ask when Kerry might be home. And he'd done it with the intent to . . . what? Confront her? Assault her?

Or did he know now that the money was gone and suspect Kerry of having a hand in its disappearance?

"Gotta go. If he calls again or if Kerry herself calls, let me know immediately. Don't you dare tell him where to find me."

"Wouldn't dream of it. What is going on down there?"

Rafe ignored the interest in her voice. "Just call me if you hear from either of them."

"Yes, sir."

Ending the call, Rafe paced, then tried to call Kerry again. On the fifth ring, her voice mail picked up again.

Cursing loudly, he pocketed his BlackBerry. The knot in his gut didn't comfort him. He had no reason to believe Kerry was doing anything but ignoring him. He'd parted company with her hours before because he wanted just to ensure her safety. But something was wrong; he felt it.

He hoped whatever had happened wasn't deadly wrong.

A few keystrokes later, he found Kerry's home address on the Internet and called the front desk for a cab.

The ride there felt like the longest fifteen minutes of his life. The sun shone a bit too brightly through the gray clouds to match well with the worry gnawing his insides. Clouds swirled above, promising an afternoon shower. People came. People went. Traffic sucked. *C'mon, hurry*. He looked at his watch as buildings went by.

Businesses and busy streets gave way to a neighborhood. The cabby steered the car into an older part of town, not quite run down yet, but getting awfully close. Mature trees shaded stucco houses in faded turquoise, terra-cotta, and pink. Shaggy grass, cracked sidewalks, and rust-stained driveways abounded.

Suddenly Rafe smelled something acrid. Smoke? Then he saw it, swarming in an ominous charcoal-colored serpentine above the low roof of an old house at the end of the street. The plumes turned black and menacing as they rose from the tiny building. And the cab was racing toward it. The knot in Rafe's gut clenched so hard he thought he might be sick.

The cab came to a halt—right in front of the burning place. "You sure you want to stop here?"

An explosion rocked the little house. Two windows burst open, scattering shards of glass everywhere. Flames growled and put off enough heat to roast a guy from ten feet away.

"Call 911," he yelled in return.

Scrambling for money, Rafe threw some bills at the cabdriver—he didn't even know how many—and stumbled from the car, up the driveway.

Please be gone, be shopping, be at a movie, be anywhere else.

Kerry's beat-up blue Honda sat in the open garage.

Chapter Thirteen

RAFE charged to the faded yellow door. Smoke furled from the cracks all around. His heart pounded like a kettle drum. Fear thrummed in his veins.

Kerry!

He grabbed the doorknob and tried to turn it. The intense heat inside the house had sizzled the brass into nothing cooler than a fry grill. Fingers singed, he yanked them back with a curse.

Damn, he had to save her. He had to get in the front door! God, what if it was locked? *Break it down, kick it in,* he told himself. *Whatever it takes.*

Pulling his shirttails from his slacks, he doubled the fabric up and tried the doorknob again. Hot, but he'd manage.

Wincing, Rafe gritted his teeth as heat from the brass stung his fingers. Everything inside him urged him to remove his hand before it held a permanent imprint of the knob. He refused.

Roaring, he wrenched the door open.

It had been unlocked.

Rafe rushed into the living room. Smoke oozed everywhere, burning his eyes. They teared, and he swiped the moisture away with a vicious palm. He still couldn't see a damn thing. A drag of air proved to be a mistake when his lungs seized up and he coughed worse than a patient in a tuberculosis ward.

He covered his mouth with his shirt, trying to catch a decent breath, and narrowed his eyes to slits.

"Kerry!" he shouted.

Nothing. No sign of movement. He repeated the call, hoping, praying she answered.

Still nothing.

Dropping to his knees to avoid smoke as thick as cream soup, he crawled across the floor, looking for any sign of Kerry, of life.

Again, he shouted for her as he crept farther into the house. Again, no response.

Forcing himself forward, he edged his way through the living room, down a hallway to a comfortable den. The TV was still on. Rafe ignored the cable talk show and searched the cozy, worn couches and the carpeted floor through the haze of the smoke. He coughed. His skin sizzled in the heat.

No sign of Kerry.

Anxiety rose. Was she trapped or hurt? Passed out . . . or worse? How had this fire started?

From the den, Rafe crawled into the adjoining room to the right. The door was closed. Covering the knob with his shirt, he gritted his teeth and pushed until the door opened. The fire wasn't coming from this part of the house. The much cleaner air and absence of smoke offered a moment's relief. Quickly, he entered the room, clearly her bedroom, and kicked the door closed behind him.

"Kerry!" he shouted past the simple white lace comforter, to the soft peachy-colored walls. Still, no answer.

He darted around a corner, into the adjoining bathroom. The air still hung humid and fragrant with soap. Water droplets clung to the side of the shower stall. Her personal articles—perfume, lipstick, her conglomeration of a key chain—dotted the counter. But no Kerry.

Panic tore into Rafe's gut. She was here. Or she'd been here. Had she escaped on foot? Had she set the fire accidentally and run out of the house?

Or had someone committed a crime and used the fire to cover their tracks? Perhaps even the thief?

Dark fear stabbed at Rafe as he wrenched open the bedroom door, emerged into the blazing part of the little house again and dropped to his knees. The ceiling was ablaze now. Instinct told him to get out. He shoved it aside, refusing to leave. *Just another minute or two . . .*

He began searching the rest of the place, retracing his steps through the den and crawling toward the other adjoining room.

Once he scrambled through a doorway, he'd entered the kitchen. Flames shot upward from the old stove, gas burners flaming high, catching on bits of paper and old cabinets all around the room. On a peeling vinyl floor that was curling and bubbling in the blaze around her, Kerry sat, holding her head in her hands.

His heart squeezed him by the throat.

Rafe scrambled across the room. "Kerry!"

Dazed, she stared at him.

"Rafe?" Her voice sounded like a croak.

She inhaled, then began coughing furiously.

"We have to get out of here," he shouted.

Finally, Kerry became alert. Her eyes focused on him. She nodded, then winced.

Putting an arm around her shoulder, Rafe dragged her to her hands and knees and began crawling.

It felt damn good to hold her, to know she was alive. Her vitality seeped under his skin. But he still had to get her out in one piece. Nothing else mattered.

Sirens roared in the distance as they crept out of the kitchen. They reached the doorway and eased into the living room as an explosion rocked the room behind them. Something burst. Shards of glass hit the wall, the floor.

Suddenly, pain seared his calf. "Argh!"

"What?" Kerry choked into the smoke. Worry furrowed her pale brows.

He gritted his teeth against the pain. "Just keep going."

Ten feet ahead lay the door and safety. The fire had other ideas. The opening between the kitchen and the living room they had occupied only moments ago now flared. Inches from their heels, the fire twisted with deadly hunger, catching quickly on the old wood. As if someone had doused them with gasoline, flames spread to the walls of the living room.

"Oh, God. We're going to die," she cried.

"No, damn it. We're not!"

Rafe swore he'd told her the truth, that they would make it. But in Vegas, he wouldn't have taken these odds. He prayed they would make it to the door before the ceiling collapsed or the walls of fire around them closed in.

"Go!" Rafe shouted, shoving Kerry to the door. "Faster!"

As if spurred on by the danger, she picked up speed, edging on hands and knees. Kerry crossed the threshold, Rafe just behind her.

Sunlight blinded them momentarily as they dragged themselves outside. Kerry lurched to her feet and stood in the driveway, drawing in huge draughts of blessedly fresh air. Panting, Rafe stumbled down to the sidewalk and inhaled his first clean breath in what felt like an eternity. Still, relief and something else that sat heavy in his chest closed his throat. What if he hadn't found her? What if she hadn't come to in time?

When he looked at Kerry, she ran toward him.

Swallowing a lump of tangled emotions, Rafe closed his arms around her and hugged her. Hugged her as if she were a life preserver in an endless sea. Hugged her as if she held his happiness in her hands.

He pushed the thought away and focused on her.

"Thank God you're safe," he whispered, squeezing her tight, as if that alone would fuse them together and always keep her safe.

"You saved me," she murmured into his ear. "I heard you shouting my name and . . . and I—"

She shuddered. A sob rose from her chest. Rafe felt something suspicious sting his eyes, too, as his terrible imagination pictured her trapped, gasping for air, flames circling her . . . What would have happened if he hadn't come to her house on the flimsy excuse that she hadn't answered her phone? What if he hadn't listened to that something inside him that ached beyond all reason to see her again?

"You're fine. You're safe now. Babe, don't cry. It's going to be all right."

Sniffling, she nodded. "I was so scared."

"I know. Me, too."

The sirens were drawing closer now. The crisis was over. Relief slid through his blood, slowly replacing the adrenaline that had sent him charging through the burning house.

"What happened?" He held her shoulders, looked into her eyes. "How did the fire start?"

Easing out of his embrace, she frowned. "I don't know. The last thing I remember is deciding to make a cup of tea. Then . . . I thought I heard something behind me. But before I could turn . . . well, I must have passed out."

Suddenly, she winced and raised her hand to the back of her head. "Ouch."

"Kerry?"

She brought her hand back in front of her. It was wet with fresh blood.

Alarmed, she jerked her gaze to him. "What the . . . ?"

"Did something hit you? Someone?"

"I don't know." She stared into the distance, frowning. "I remember . . . well, the pantry door was open. I didn't remember leaving it open, but often the latch doesn't stay."

"Is it big enough for someone to hide in?"

She nodded. "My stackable washer and dryer are in the back, along with a few shelves against one wall."

"Anyone angry with you this morning?"

Her face fell. "Jason came to visit."

Rafe swore as the fire trucks pulled up to the curb, followed by an ambulance. Firefighters in full gear jumped out and rushed to the house.

"Anyone else inside?" one asked, hose in hand.

Rafe looked at her in question.

"No. No people, no pets," she assured them.

The fireman nodded and went on, blasting the place with a loud torrent of water.

Several others joined the cause, battling the blaze, now spreading through the entire house.

Emergency medical techs leaped out of the ambulance and raced toward them, then assisted them inside the ambulance.

"Are you hurt?" a sturdy woman approaching forty asked, her starched white shirt covering her ample shoulders.

"I just have a bump on the back of my head," Kerry said as she sat inside the vehicle.

"Do you know what day it is?"

She frowned. "Tuesday, May ninth."

The female tech nodded to indicate Kerry hadn't totally lost her marbles, then listened to her lungs with a stethoscope.

"You don't sound as if you inhaled too much smoke, but just in case . . ." She set Kerry under an oxygen mask and examined her wound, cleaning away the blood and treating it with an ice pack.

"This isn't too bad. A bit of a nasty bump that will heal soon. Are you allergic to anything?"

Kerry shook her head.

"Take these and keep the ice on that wound." She handed two brownish tablets to Kerry, following it with a plastic cup of water.

The other tech, a reedy, sandy-haired guy, looked at the gash on

Rafe's calf while pushing an oxygen mask on him as well, cutting off any conversation.

"Might need stitches. Would you like us to take you to the hospital?"

Rafe hesitated, his gray eyes sliding over Kerry. He shook his head.

"You sure?" the tall tech asked.

"Just give me a bandage or something. I'll be fine."

The bleeding stopped. An antibiotic ointment and some butterfly bandages later, Rafe lowered his pant leg down again and the EMTs gave them both clean bills of health.

"Follow up with your doctor in the next few days." The female tech looked at Rafe. "If she has any nausea or vomiting later, or doesn't seem to know when or where she is, anything that would signal a change in mental status, get her to a hospital right away."

Rafe agreed. The ambulance pulled away.

They looked around to see that the firemen had the blaze all but extinguished, but it was obvious that Kerry couldn't stay there.

"Can you tell how the fire started?" she asked one of the firefighters just emerging from the charred house.

"Looks like you might have left a towel or something on the stove when you lit it."

What? She didn't remember doing that.

"You may not recall it. It's not uncommon for something to fall during a fire, and I see you have a head wound." He pointed to the ice pack she held up to her head.

But she remembered everything clearly. "I . . . I—this happened before the fire."

The fireman patted her shoulder gently. "People are often confused after a major trauma like this, especially when they've had a head injury."

"But—"

"You need to rest," Rafe intervened, steering her away. "Come back to my hotel with me. We'll talk about this."

Kerry agreed. After leaving a number where she could be reached, a fireman retrieved her car keys. She and Rafe piled into her beat-up blue Honda, Rafe driving this time. Kerry was too tired, too perturbed. All she smelled was smoke. It lay acrid on her tongue. She wanted a shower and a nap, and to curl up with Rafe. He always made her feel safe in a crazy world.

On that thought, she grabbed his hand as he sped through the streets of Tampa.

He stared at their joined hands for a hard moment, then drove on.

That gave her pause. Did he want her with him, really? Seemed like a silly question when he'd just saved her life and offered her a place to crash. But she'd heard stories of people running into burning buildings to save complete strangers. That didn't equal love, just bravery. And he could pity the fact she had no home now, without *really* wanting her around.

Kerry withdrew her hand. Rafe didn't reach for her again as she continued giving quiet directions.

Oh, she hadn't thought about the fact that her little rental house was gone. It had never felt like home. Most of her mementos were still at Mark and Tiffany's place. What few valuables she had, like her mom's wedding ring, were in a safe-deposit box. But she lamented the loss of a picture of her parents and a few treasured articles of clothing.

The truth was, she had more immediately pressing questions. What the heck had happened this morning? And where would she go now? To Mark's house, she supposed. But if the fire department ruled that the fire had been her fault, she could kiss her thousand-dollar deposit goodbye—an enormous fortune to her. And what if her landlord sued for loss of property?

Kerry clutched her aching head. She couldn't think about it now.

When they reached the hotel, Rafe valeted the car. Kerry walked beside him as they entered the cool lobby of the hotel.

Once inside, he grabbed her hand again as if he wasn't about to let go. She knew it was dangerous, that she was reading too much into a simple gesture after something so harrowing. But he'd come after her, run into a burning building to find her, offered his hotel room. She still hoped he cared, at least a little.

The elevator ride up was silent, and Rafe guided her to his door, palm at her back. Quietly, he closed the door behind them.

Out the window, Kerry saw the Causeway and the Gulf waters beyond, a sludgy blue close to the hotel, then wending out to a sparkling turquoise highlighted by the noontime sun.

"Kerry? Babe, sit down. You look exhausted."

He drew her onto a smallish sofa against one wall, then sat beside her. "Tell me exactly what happened after you left here this morning."

She sighed, trying to get it all straight in her mind. "I went home. I hadn't been there long when Jason arrived. We fought." Regret cramped her belly into a thick knot. "He . . . came on to me, said he never intended to marry Mara. Said he thought about me"—she winced—"about having sex with me all the time. I had no idea."

Rafe looked every bit as furious as he would if someone outlawed computers. "What else did the son of a bitch say?"

Kerry hesitated. "That he wanted to take care of me. When I refused him, he cornered me in the kitchen. He pinned me against the cabinets and . . . he kissed me."

Another bout of anger spread over Rafe's face, tightening his mouth. "I'm going to break his fucking face if I see him again, I swear. Forcing you to kiss him—"

"I broke it off, told him I wasn't interested in him as more than a friend. I think that surprised him for some reason. He cursed at me, then slammed out of the door. I was upset and tense, so I took a hot shower."

"Did you lock the door first?"

Frowning, Kerry sorted through the morning's events in her

head. As vividly as an NFL replay, she realized that she hadn't. "I—I usually do. But I was so distraught . . ."

Losing the man she loved and a trusted friend all within a few hours apparently wreaked havoc on a girl's common sense. What an idiotic mistake!

"Kerry . . ." he growled.

"I know, I know," she huffed. "Anyway, when I came out, I decided to make a cup of tea. That's when something hit me on the head. That's how I remember it, anyway."

Rafe scowled. "That doesn't fit with what the fireman told us."

"True, but I didn't have the stove on yet when I was hit. I didn't have a towel on the stove, either. I just know it. I was still sorting through tea bags when I heard something behind me, from the direction of the pantry. I tried to turn . . . but something—someone?—hit me."

"Jason, I'll bet."

"Maybe." She looked unconvinced. "I just never considered him dangerous. You have to admit, he's not exactly menacing. I can't imagine that he'd actually try to kill me."

"*Someone* tried to kill you. Smikins and Tiffany hadn't just been to your house, hadn't just been rebuffed by you. If your little friend took the money, as I suspected all along, he was probably foaming at the mouth by the time he left your place this morning."

"He wasn't happy," she conceded.

"Hell, I knew he couldn't be trusted," Rafe muttered. "He hadn't locked your door on his way out and probably suspected that you hadn't locked it, either. He could easily have come back in while you took a shower and hidden in your pantry, waited for you. Face it, babe, he had opportunity and motive."

"I . . . I guess. He was angry, but angry enough over my refusal to try to kill me?"

"Maybe not just that. Someone went looking for the money this morning. Someone got on the 'retired' terminal there at the office and started beating around the accounts for that money."

Kerry shook her head. "He hadn't been to the office yet that morning. How could he have known it was missing?"

Rafe scoffed. "He told you he hadn't been to the office yet. Who knows if that's the truth? Maybe he'd been there and realized the money was missing. He knew from the beginning that I was helping you find out how Mark was framed. It's possible this morning, when he saw the money gone and found it shuffled into an account in my name, that he came to you and he was angry."

"Then why come on to me?"

"My guess? He wants you and the money both."

"He never asked me about the money."

Shrugging, Rafe leaned closer. "Why not get close, gain your trust, get a little—or a lot—of ass before you start talking about stolen money? Maybe he wanted you happy and sated before he raised the subject. Besides, would he really tell you if he framed your brother?"

Mentally, Kerry chewed on Rafe's theory. "I don't know. I just don't see him going to the office and leaving, or angry enough after being turned down to try to kill me."

"You didn't see that he was trying to get into your panties, either."

Kerry covered her face with her hands, head reeling. Maybe Rafe was right. Maybe Jason had wanted to get close to her so he could find out what had happened to the money.

She sighed, beyond confused. "It's just . . . I thought I knew him so well. But this morning, I wondered if I knew him at all."

"I know, babe." He squeezed her hand.

Squeezing back, Kerry continued to turn the possibility over in her mind. But something still didn't ring true.

"Wouldn't Jason have brought up the money before just leaving? Why try to kill me before finding out what happened to the money? Any information I had would die with me."

"He's not a stupid guy, but neither is he subtle. He knows where the money is, most likely. But he didn't know where I was. Regina made my hotel arrangements." Rafe grabbed her shoulders, fingers gripping with urgency. "He asked you where I was, didn't he?"

Kerry thought back through the hours that seemed like a whole month ago. "He did, several times. Why does that matter?"

"He can't get to that money without me. I put it in a bank that's nearly as tight as Fort Knox. Working at a bank, he'd know that. So he devised a very smooth plan. Get close to you, find out how to get the money back and who's watching it. That would have been Plan A. When you refused him, he had no choice but to leave and try to hunt me down himself so he could get the money back. Which he did. He asked Regina where I was staying."

"But why try to kill me? That wouldn't gain him anything. It's just risky."

Rafe swiped a hand across his face. "If he can't have you, he doesn't want anyone else to."

She sent him a dubious frown. "That's twisted."

"The guy framed his best friend for embezzlement so he could sleep with said friend's sister. That doesn't make him sound like the most stable of characters."

"Ohmigod!" Kerry gasped as pieces of a puzzle came flying together. "The reason Mark never wanted him to date me . . . When Mark first brought Jason around the house, Mark had been doing some charity work, something to do with a drug treatment center. Jason had just come through rehab. Mark befriended him so that he wouldn't fall back in with old friends and old patterns. Mark helped Jason get the job at the bank. But Mark confided in me once that Jason, when he'd been an addict, had robbed a liquor store with a gun."

Sighing, Rafe grabbed her hand. "Kerry, I know you don't want to see it, but I think you need to reconsider—"

"That Jason might be guilty. I'm thinking about it as we speak."

* * *

SHE'D wanted a shower, and Rafe didn't blame her. He reeked of smoke himself, hair, clothes, skin. It wasn't that he didn't understand her desire.

It was that he didn't understand his own.

Pacing, he stared at the bathroom door, waiting, watching. He gritted his teeth as residual fear pumped through him. What if he'd lost her today? It was one thing to jet home and know she was safe and sound—and eventually with someone who could give her everything her heart desired—here in Florida. In that scenario, he'd never see her again, but she was happy, healthy, loved by some unknown guy Rafe didn't have to picture.

The thought of her dead . . . He swallowed, unable to form thoughts out of the jumble of emotions. It was like a loud buzzing in his head. The mass of feeling was almost too big for his body. Even now, knowing logically that she was all right—that wasn't the same as holding her, looking into those wide green eyes, seeing her smile that could melt metal. Knowing intellectually that she was safe lacked the impact of sliding deep in her heat and feeling her so very alive in his arms.

He was insane. Had to be. Why else did the need to connect with her, feel her in the most elemental way possible, beat at him worse than a group of back-alley thugs?

Raking a grungy hand through his smoky hair, Rafe looked around the room. He needed something to do, something to keep him busy, or he'd yank off all his clothes, jump in the shower with Kerry, and claim her in every way possible.

But he'd given her up, for her own good. For his sanity. He couldn't go back on that now.

Prowling over to his phone, he called Regina.

"Mr. Dawson?"

"I need two things as soon as possible."

"Name it," came her confident reply.

"My flight changed. I don't think I can get out of here before tomorrow, maybe early afternoon. Push out the Fairline Tech job in Jersey until Friday. Offer them ten percent off and my apologies."

"Something wrong with the Standard National job?"

He heard the frown in her voice. "No, it's not the job. Something . . . personal."

"Ah, I see." She hesitated. When he didn't offer anything more, she said, "I'll let you know when I've revised your reservation."

"Thanks. I also need the name of the best criminal attorney in Tampa."

If Mark's case made it to trial, the man deserved more than an overworked public defender. Kerry deserved more. After all, what good was five million dollars if he didn't use it to help someone he lov—

Whoa! Where did that thought come from?

He didn't love Kerry. No. He cared. Yeah, he could do that. Loving her . . . it was too soon. And too difficult. Everything he knew about love, he'd learned from watching his parents, who, with a little more trailer in their blood, could have appeared on Jerry Springer. If he tried to love Kerry, she'd be doomed.

"Criminal attorney? Are you in trouble, boss?"

"No." A smile twisted his mouth when he imagined how the request must have sounded. "Not for me. For a . . . friend."

Regina hesitated. "Miss Sullivan?"

"Not exactly. Long story. Can you let me know when you get that info, too? I want to call the attorney and get it set up before I go."

"Sure thing."

The shower stopped running. Water sloshed. The *whoosh* of the shower curtain against the metal rod told him Kerry was getting out.

"Gotta go. Thanks."

He put his phone down and turned to find Kerry emerging from the little bathroom, her lush body barely wrapped in a skimpy white towel. Wet strands of her dark gold curls clung to her shoulders, rivulets of water running under the terry cloth, between her breasts.

"Kerry?"

At the sound of his voice, she whirled, wide-eyed, to face him. The shock of the day's events bleached her skin white. Scratches marred one of her cheeks. A bruise was forming above her left eye.

Some asshole had done this, nearly ended her life. The need to protect roared with all the subtlety of a tornado inside him.

He swallowed, fisted his hands.

Damn, he was going to explode if he didn't hold her soon, *feel* that she was all right. While part of him ached to have her naked, underneath him, assuring him with every cry and moan that she was real and in one piece, he *needed* to wrap his arms around her and listen to her heart beat.

Okay, hold her, yes, he told himself. *Sex—no dice.* Blood churning through his body, he exhaled. He couldn't make love to her. Their forty-eight hours was up. She owed him nothing. If she had feelings for him, better to end it now, before he really fucked up.

"Shower sounds like a good idea. I'll—um—be back in a few minutes."

The shower, even set to mimic the Arctic, didn't help. He went through the motions quickly. His illogical need to assure himself that she lived and breathed, heaped on top of his insane desire . . . he felt like a rocket ready to explode. Like the adrenaline had never left him. Sure, he could take matters into his own hands, but he'd rather be with Kerry, next to her, even if she just talked and smiled, than self-pleasuring. Being near her was as necessary as air or water right now.

Damn it, what the hell was the matter with him? Next thing he knew, he'd be writing poetry, decorating his own apartment, and trading in his Porsche for a minivan.

With a vicious curse, Rafe yanked on the faucet, cutting off the spray of water. Grabbing a towel, he wrapped it around his waist. He ought to get decent, dry his hair—hell, at least put on underwear—before he stepped out and faced Kerry.

Impatience won. Ignoring the boxer-briefs he'd laid out on the toilet, he turned the knob and emerged into the rest of the room.

Kerry stared out the big bay window, wearing nothing but one of his button-down dress shirts with the streaming sun making the thin cotton transparent . . . and talking on his phone.

* * *

"HELLO?" Kerry whispered, wondering at the wisdom of answering Rafe's phone. But it had rung three times. The caller ID said *Office.* How personal could it be?

After a brief pause, a woman said, "Sorry, must have reached the wrong number."

"Wait! If you're looking for Rafe Dawson, he's in the next room."

Another pause. "Miss Sullivan?"

"Kerry, yes. You're Regina, right?"

"I am."

Frowning into the phone, Kerry asked, "You know who I am?"

"Not exactly, but your name has come up several times lately."

The ironic tone of his assistant's voice made Kerry wince. "I guess Rafe told you I kidnapped him. I swear I didn't hurt him—"

"Kidnapped?" Shock sharpened her voice. "No, he failed to mention that. Why did you kidnap him?"

Then how the heck did she hear my name? It was Kerry's turn to pause. "Do you remember a woman calling you a few weeks ago to talk to Rafe about her brother in jail?"

"That was you?"

"It was. And Rafe helped, more than I believed possible. Your boss is free now and coming home this afternoon."

"Actually, he's leaving tomorrow. He called fifteen minutes ago and asked me to change his flight. If you wouldn't mind, tell him it's done and I'll e-mail the particulars."

"O—okay."

"In the four years I've worked for Mr. Dawson, I've never changed a flight for him for any reason other than weather or shuffling of jobs. He keeps an impeccable schedule."

Kerry had no idea why Regina would say such a thing or how to answer. “Well, he’s been wonderful about helping me with my brother’s case. You work for a great guy.”

“Indeed. Would you also tell Mr. Dawson that Alex Moza will contact him within a few hours?”

Her jaw dropped and her pulse began to stutter. “*The* Alex Moza? The very famous attorney Alex Moza?”

“Yes.”

“Why would Rafe need a high-priced lawyer?” she asked herself as much as Regina.

“Hang up the phone,” Rafe demanded from the doorway to the bathroom.

She whirled to face him. “I—I’m sorry. I just . . . It rang and I—”

“I don’t care.” He grabbed the phone. “Goodbye, Regina.”

Ending the call, he switched the ringer to silent mode, then tossed the little device on the nearest chair.

Then she realized. “You don’t need Alex Moza. You hired him to help Mark?”

“It’s no big deal.”

Kerry paled even as she exploded with tenderness. “Oh, Rafe.” She lifted a trembling hand to her mouth. “It’s a huge deal. Thousands of dollars’ worth of huge. I—I can’t accept. He’s so expensive, he makes Versace dresses seem like bargains.”

“I have the money.”

And he wanted to use it to help her, like he’d used his expertise and his brawn. Kerry didn’t think she could love the man more, but her heart was swelling faster than a hot air balloon. “But—I . . . That’s—”

“For once, don’t argue, okay?”

Afraid she’d simply blurt out the fact she loved him, Kerry merely nodded.

“Are you all right?” he asked, swallowing.

Her face softened. “Thanks to you, yes.”

"Seriously, you're sure?"

Doing her best to smile bright, to hide the love she felt and the fact that her heart was breaking, Kerry whispered, "Seriously, yeah."

"Thank God." Rafe grabbed her, pulled her against him. "I don't think I can wait another second to hold you."

Chapter Fourteen

KERRY threw her arms around Rafe, and that was all the cue he needed to bring her into the circle of his arms. Her lush curves pressed against him, curls soft and damp as they twined around his fingers. A hint of her sugar vanilla scent teased the air around him, diluted by the lingering stench of charred wood and smoke.

She could have died. Someone, most likely Jason, had knocked her unconscious and set her house ablaze. He had *meant* for her to die.

Safe. Here. Mine.

Not yours anymore.

Ruthlessly, he tried to shove the last thought away. But he had given Kerry up, for her own good and his. He was too private, not the kind of man to share more than an evening or two, much less his personal thoughts, his hopes and fears, his very heart. Hell, did he even have one?

Rafe knew himself; it wouldn't be long before the bite in his chest that appeared anytime a woman crowded his personal space gnawed on him and urged him to bolt. Kerry deserved someone who could freely give her all the love her heart could hold.

But while he was here, he could give her the security she needed.

Stroking his hand down her hair, he murmured, "It's all right now. Nothing is going to happen to you. I swear it."

Pulling back a few inches, Kerry stared at him, her shimmering green eyes drowning in a pool of unshed tears. "You can't promise that. No one can. I guess . . . I never thought this person was truly dangerous until today. Devious and mean, yes. Now I'm worried. I may be in over my head, and I don't know who to trust—"

"Me," he growled. "Trust me."

Cupping his face in her trembling hands, she smiled softly. Rafe's heart turned over as she poured out all her trust and affection through that expression. "I always have, but you're leaving tomorrow, going back to your life. I've involved you too much already. You've been nothing but wonderful. Thank you, for going out on a limb for my brother, for not hating me for my crazy scheme, for showing me such passion . . ."

Kerry threw her arms around his neck and clung tight. Her exhalation rasped the sensitive skin just beneath his ear. She shifted against him, sliding her thigh between his, shifting the damp towel wrapped around his hips.

Rafe sucked in a breath as blood stirred in a rising rush. *No, no, no.* He was here to comfort her, assure himself of her well-being, not mount her and reenact all the positions of the *Kama Sutra.*

Easier said than done, Rafe realized when Kerry pressed against him, nestling his stirring cock right between her legs. Oh damn, she felt hot and damp, too. Added to the usual lust was a lingering guilt he couldn't shake that he was leaving Kerry alone to fight a life-or-death battle.

He could only pray it was over by tomorrow morning. Hell, if it wasn't, he'd be in jail himself.

"Don't thank me. I did exactly what I wanted to do, nothing less," he muttered, unable to resist the temptation of her soft neck under his lips.

She groaned at the feel of his mouth on her, and more blood pooled in his cock, now eager to feel her around him, as if he could take her all in at once. As if he could capture the warm, zany, emotion-brimming essence of her.

"Maybe so," her soft whisper contradicted. "But now it's time for me to tend to my problems by myself. No more leaning on Jason or you or Mark."

"Don't you dare think that a little leaning now and then makes you weak. What you did, committing a felony to get your brother out of jail. A little backward in the rationale, but the courage it took to see your plan through makes you strong."

Kerry rewarded him with another watery smile, this one complete with dimples. Would he ever know another woman who could turn him to mush and rev his blood up all with a single smile?

"You committed a crime to help me," she pointed out.

He shrugged. "Illogic must be contagious."

She sailed a mock punch into his shoulder.

A moment later, she murmured, "When you go back to New York, remember what you said to me, that leaning on people doesn't make you weak. Reach out to friends. Tell your secrets. The rewards are rich, and they'll learn what I've figured out: You're good to know."

Her whisper struck down into his heart. He'd never done any of those things. Since his mother's death, when life with his father had become a sharp-tongued battle of wills, he'd shut everyone out. How could he just suddenly change? Sweet of her to think he was capable of more, but Rafe knew better. He was still the asshole who had told his father to get fucked the day he'd turned eighteen.

"You're pretty good to know, too."

Skimming a thumb over his bottom lip, Kerry gazed right up into his eyes. Rafe's heart began to pound, and yet his chest curiously ached at once. His whole body was a chaos of confusion, wants, fear, hope—coming at him so fast he couldn't process it. Kerry stirred him like this. Not knowing what to say or do, he kissed the tip of her thumb.

Her mossy eyes soft, her smile slightly crooked, she murmured, "Make love to me."

Zoom! Wow, four words to breath-stealing, full-blown erection. Kerry was potent.

"Ah, babe." He sighed, trying so hard to resist. "Forty-eight hours is up. I can't make you—"

Kerry placed her fingers over his lips. "You never once coerced me into sex. I volunteered because I *wanted* to. I want to now, bargains and bets be damned."

He gritted his teeth. "I'm trying to do the right thing here. A mad midday romp might not be the best thing for you after such a traumatic morning. Your head—"

"Is fine. The best thing would be for you to make love to me." She frowned, then bit her lip. "That is, if you want to. If you don't, I—"

Rafe cut her off with a kiss.

Moving his mouth gently over Kerry's, he savored the opportunity to taste her.

Her silky lips molded to his, willing, trusting, and he slid his mouth over hers once again before dipping inside to claim her with a soft stroke of his tongue. Against him, she sighed, shifted away, and dropped her hands to the towel around his waist.

An instant later, the damp terry cloth met the carpet, leaving him completely bare.

Then he felt her fingertips caressing a soft trail down his back, igniting his skin with an explosion of tingles. She cupped one palm around the cheek of his ass, slid back to his hip, drifted back up his side. She repeated the process with her other hand. He just about lost his mind.

Yet Rafe didn't want to pounce and devour her. Well, he did. But a conflicting yearning to feast on her, savor her, burn every last touch into his memory, tormented him, too.

Kissing a path from her mouth to her neck, Rafe whispered in her ear, "Don't ever think I don't want you, babe." Gently, he scraped her lobe with his teeth, then edged his over-large dress shirt off her shoulder with an unhurried caress. "I can honestly say I've never wanted any woman as much as I want you. You do something to me . . ."

Kerry caught her breath on a gasp. Then as he smoothed his lips across the silk of her skin to her shoulder, she filtered her fingers through his hair, holding him close.

Suddenly, he found his fingers on the first button of his dress shirt. He looked up at her. "You're sure?"

The smile Kerry sent him was both saucy and sweet as she brushed his hands away.

Slowly, she unbuttoned the shirt herself, inch by inch revealing her rosy skin, the downy valley between lush breasts, the hard, pink-tipped nipples, the flat of her stomach, the enticing indention of her navel, the tops of her thighs . . . the haven behind her pale, damp curls.

Rafe sucked in a breath. He wanted to be strong and resist her. Why take from her again if he was only going away? Because he wasn't that resolute. Life was short, and he'd never been good at self-deprivation. This moment would never come again, and he intended to enjoy every bit of her body she'd allow.

Smoothing his hands over her shoulders, Rafe caressed her and sent his shirt sliding to join his towel on the floor. Kerry stood before him gloriously naked, sunlight streaming over her unblemished skin, lending its rosy tones a golden glow.

The bed was only a few steps away. Lifting her against him, Rafe took those steps. With a jerk of one hand, the bedspread found its way to a heap on the floor. He lay Kerry across the sheets, covered her body with his own, and fused their mouths together.

The sense of connection leapt between them, powerful, undeniable. It was the damndest thing. He felt like an addict, and Kerry was his drug of choice. He couldn't get her out of his system, couldn't leave her alone.

Beneath him, Kerry banded her arms around him and kissed him back with an aching hunger, a silent plea.

She arched into him, breasts like brands on his chest, as she tore her mouth from his to whisper, "Fill me. Complete me."

At her words, lust surged in his belly, coiling, primal. Something new and frantic unfurled in his chest. He swallowed. His insides felt jagged, nerves on the edge. Hunger and a need to do exactly as she asked pounded at him. Kerry was impossible to refuse. He wasn't even going to try.

"All day," he whispered, burying his hands in the riot of her sunshine curls. "All night."

She fit her mouth to his, bottom lip lush, soft. Then she took the offensive, tongue sliding inside his mouth, seeking, destroying his control. Resisting her ranked up there with preventing the sun from rising. Not gonna happen.

He let her shatter him.

With suddenly shaking hands, Rafe urged her thighs apart. She opened to him willingly, planting hot, whispery kisses down his neck, his shoulder. A fresh surge of arousal detonated inside him as he reached to the ground for the pants he'd discarded earlier . . . and the last condom he possessed in his wallet.

He had to sit up to find the damn thing, and Kerry was behind him, wrapping her soft, fragrant body around him. She dragged her tongue across his shoulder blade, and he shivered. He nearly came when she seized his cock with a firm grip and tugged on him with unhurried strokes.

If the woman was trying to drive him insane, she was succeeding like a pro worthy of an MVP award.

Finally, he controlled his unusually clumsy fingers long enough to rip the foil packet open. Kerry rolled the latex down his cock. Once in place, he rounded on her with a growl and tumbled her onto her back. His mouth followed.

Fusing their lips together, he plundered, tasting her, trying to imprint himself on her. And his hands . . . he felt her everywhere. Palming her full breasts, rolling her tender nipples, sliding down the curve of her waist, over the flare of her hips. She writhed and opened to him with a moan. Never had he known any woman so artlessly responsive.

Beneath him, she parted her thighs and bent her knees in welcome. "I want to feel every inch of you."

Her words sizzled down his spine. Rafe sank into her wet heat, plunging in to the hilt. *Damn!* She electrified him, boiled his blood.

Jesus, how was he going to last more than thirty seconds?

Drawing in a deep, desperate breath, he waited—for control, for focus, for something to help him stave off the power Kerry's sweet sugar scent and soft flesh had on his senses.

If he could pull off that trick, he'd make David Copperfield look like an amateur.

Slow, slow, he told himself. His mind somehow made his body obey.

He eased back, nearly to the point of withdrawing. With an unhurried stroke, Rafe tunneled his way back inside. The friction had him gritting his teeth against the mind-boggling pleasure, against the feel of her warmth. But he repeated the process at the same deliberate pace, a lingering dance that had him gasping, his balls tightening, his chest aching with the knowledge this might well be the last time he touched Kerry.

She clung to him, hands wandering his back, curving over his ass as he thrust. And her mouth . . . Dear God, that woman trailed kisses over his lips, down his neck, nibbling on his shoulder. He tasted her want. Her desperation and perspiration blended. Golden sunlight revealed the adoration in her red-rimmed eyes. It should have sent warning bells off in his head, but as he stroked into her body again, shoulders bunching, cock on fire, the sensation that he could sink into her forever wouldn't stop. Her muscles tensed, the clasp of her pussy tightened, her kisses urged him to stay. The bells in his head remained silent.

"Rafe. Oh, yes!"

The flush he knew and loved turned her skin pink. Her nipples swelled.

Suddenly her hazy green eyes connected with his. Her dreamy, tender look punched him in the gut. Even with her eyes dilated, he saw something way beyond lust streaming from her gaze.

Of its own volition, the arousal in his gut ratcheted up another notch, now nearly overwhelming.

"Kerry?" he asked, even as he slid deep into the welcoming depths of her body again.

She moaned throatily, then bit her lip so hard Rafe thought she might draw blood. She closed her eyes, shutting him out.

No! "Look at me," he demanded for a reason he couldn't understand. "Look!"

Her naked lashes fluttered open, giving way to eyes drenched in tears and devotion. It hit him like a knockout punch to the gut. In that single look, Rafe felt fused to her, unwilling to break away, unable to stop thrusting into her body. Powerless to keep his heart untouched.

Her arms tightened around him as her sex fisted his cock so tight, Rafe thought he'd die from the pleasure, from the bond he felt thickening between them.

"Rafe!"

At her cry, he increased the tempo of his strokes. "I'm here."

Her eyes darkened, softened. She pressed her mouth to his, then tore away.

"I love you!"

Her scream echoed in his ears as she fluttered around his cock, then convulsed, gripping him like nothing he'd ever felt. The last sensations he knew—pleasure, substantial and hot, sliding through his veins and his chest exploding with something he didn't understand—propelled him into an orgasm that damn near stole his consciousness. The ecstasy went on and on, longing bubbling up with a last shot of lust to make one hell of a potent reaction. He shouted out his satisfaction as he poured himself into Kerry.

When he stopped moving, Rafe all but collapsed. His arms refused to support him anymore. His eyelids wouldn't even stay open. His chest heaved as if he'd just run a four-minute mile.

But he could think only about Kerry—and the words she'd said.

Suddenly, her breath caught as she lay under him, as if she was . . . Rafe peered down at Kerry's flushed face and her tightly shut eyes. Tears leaked out of each corner.

I love you.

She'd said the three forbidden words guaranteed to send him into a panic. The three words he didn't deserve, since he could never give back a tenth of her devotion. How the hell had this happened?

His own feelings . . . No, he wasn't looking into that snake pit. No sense fooling himself that just because he wasn't quite ready to let go of Kerry, this thing between them could last. He just wasn't the bonding type.

What was he going to do? The last thing he wanted to do was hurt her.

Gut twisting, Rafe backed away from the bed and peeled the condom off. He took the moment needed to throw the prophylactic in the trash and tried to straighten out his stunned brain. He let out a long, shuddering breath, braced his hands on the dresser in front of him.

What an asshole he was. Truly. He'd pushed Kerry to give all, share every bit of her past, her problems, her hopes—and her body. Like a gluttonous jerk, he'd taken everything she'd so trustingly offered. Okay, he'd helped her some in return; he'd admit that. Rafe glanced over his shoulder at Kerry's pale face. But not enough. He couldn't give her the one thing her searching eyes told him she wanted.

His love in return.

Viciously, he swore. How the fuck had he allowed his impulses to override his common sense? Kerry had little way of knowing where all those touching, talking, laughing, and of course, sex-filled hours might lead. She was the novice, and he supposedly the expert in dodging this very thing. If the predicament weren't so alarming—and didn't involve him—he'd be rolling on the floor, laughing his ass off at the schmuck who'd been too enthralled with a woman to read the danger signs.

No use in pretending he hadn't known. Rafe had seen the signs, and ignored them because he didn't want to let Kerry go.

A huge chunk of him *still* resisted the thought.

He cast another glance over his shoulder. She looked tense, stricken, and he swore.

"I'm not expecting anything in return," Kerry whispered, tangled in the sheet across the room, sitting cross-legged on the bed.

Sure. And he was Batman.

Rafe tensed. Maybe . . . "Did it just slip out during the heat of things, or did you mean it?"

After a contrite glance, she looked down at the hands she wrung in her lap. "I'd like to be able to tell you it just slipped out, but I've been aware of my feelings for a while."

Shit.

How was he supposed to respond to that? No denying he'd been thinking about her for a while, too. But Kerry was a white picket fence sort of girl. He could easily picture her in the suburbs with two kids, being PTA president. She'd want to be surrounded by friends and family. She'd want a man who could give her all that, plus friendship, trust, and unconditional love.

Oh, she was so barking up the wrong tree with him. Rafe had never lived outside New York City. The suburbs might as well be Mars. He liked high-rises because the views were great and there was no yard work involved. He'd never given procreating much thought. What did he know about raising kids? What he'd learned from his father would fill a book on how *not* to be a parent. Even if he could put all that aside, the fundamental question was, could he give Kerry what she needed emotionally? Could he share himself fully, since anything less would break her heart?

Highly doubtful. What he knew about commitment would leave a thimble half-empty.

No matter what he did, he was going to hurt her. *Damn it to hell and back.*

"I lived with a girlfriend once," he found himself admitting. "Right after college. It only took five weeks for her to move out. According to her, I wasn't affectionate. I didn't 'check in.' I forgot our anniversary. I rarely came home for dinner. I paid more attention to my computer than her, unless I wanted sex. I never sent flowers. I'm lousy at apologizing. And I have all the emotional warmth of an ice cube at the North Pole."

Rafe sighed, uncomfortably aware that this wasn't a situation money and a good dose of logic could fix. "It would never work, Kerry. My ex-girlfriend . . . I won't even tell you what she called me the last time I bumped into her. Let's just say it made a crowd turn around and gawk, and on the streets of New York, that's really something."

Turning around, Rafe watched Kerry's blanched expression smooth as she carefully arranged it into . . . nothing.

But she couldn't hide the hurt simmering in her eyes, hurt that gouged a hunk out of his heart. Damn it, he'd almost rather be castrated with a dull, rusty knife than know he'd caused that look.

But it was either hurt her some now, or rip her heart out of her chest and eat it raw later. Now would hurt less. At least he hoped so.

Rafe frowned. "I'm just no good for you, babe."

"I didn't ask to be your girlfriend or move in with you. Really, naïve me in New York City? Since I've never seen it, I'd probably turn tail and run back to sunny Florida the first time it snowed." Her choked laughter twisted at his gut.

"Kerry—"

"Really, no biggie. I'm fine."

Yeah? If she'd had Pinocchio's affliction, her nose would be as long as a yardstick.

She reached down for his discarded shirt and, beneath the cover of the sheet, donned it. With forced cheer, she asked, "So how about lunch? I'm starving."

* * *

KERRY had sensed as a girl that Bonnie Raitt could be a wise woman. From Bonnie and her own mother's car radio, she'd learned that a woman couldn't make a man love her if he didn't. That included Rafe. Today, that truth had never seemed wiser.

The song's maudlin piano melody swirled in her head, telling her it was time to give up this fight, before she humiliated herself any further and discomfited him any more.

That reality choked her throat with tears. Her time with Rafe was definitely over. And she'd likely never see the man she loved again.

Ten minutes ago, she'd convinced him she was desperately starving and *needed* a sandwich from the deli across the street. He'd latched on to the excuse to escape the tense hotel room and left. What she really needed was her brother freed, a pint of Ben & Jerry's Karamel Sutra, and a good crying jag.

None of that was going to happen anytime soon. Ben and Jerry, two of the few men in her life until Rafe, weren't conveniently standing by with her sugar fix. The crying would give her a terrible headache and solve nothing, even if it was very tempting. And Mark . . . she'd screwed that up just as bad. The thief might still make a move on the money today and show his hand. But he might not, in which case, she had no backup plan. Rafe had done all he could for her, and she'd repaid him by force-feeding him her love.

Unrequited love. Did you really think a guy with so much going for him was going to fall in love with a crazy, small-town waitress? He deserves a witty woman whose idea of a good time is something beyond drugging and kidnapping, followed by pledges of eternal devotion. Pathetic.

Cursing the voice in her head, Kerry donned a pair of sweat shorts she found in Rafe's suitcase. Looked fab with the oversize dress shirt. She ought to leave them both and buy clothes in the hotel gift shop. But they were Rafe's—the only things she had of him besides memories—and for now she was clinging to them.

The firefighters had managed to find her flip-flops by her back door, thankfully. So, in an ensemble that would have the fashion police calling out the SWAT team, Kerry penned a note with just one word: *Goodbye*. Tears clogging her throat, she set the note next to his humming laptop, slipped out the door, and darted to the elevator.

Her hands shook, her eyes leaked, and she had no doubt her nose looked as pink as a bunny. Well, she'd never thought she was going to win beauty contests anyway. This just clinched it.

But she hadn't thought she'd lose the man she'd love forever just days after finding him.

Once inside her car and away from the hotel, Kerry surrendered to the pending waterworks and let the tears flow. She had to find some peace, get some sleep, before her head exploded and her chest caved in from the pain.

Why had she been stupid enough to surrender her heart to a man more interested in computer viruses than happily ever after?

Blindly, she drove, getting on I-275 and crossing the Howard Franklin Bridge with no particular destination in mind. Why hadn't she thought of the fact her house was in cinders and that one of her best friends wanted to be much, much more before she'd taken off?

Water. That's what she needed. The water always calmed her, helped her think. But a traffic-laden drive to Clearwater Beach proved the area too crowded for a weeping woman. The lively music and flirting of sun worshipers only made her more miserable.

Where to go? Where to go?

Returning to the Love Shack was tempting. A little jaunt south, and seclusion and beachfront luxury could be hers. But it held too many memories of Rafe, of the great times she'd never have with him again. Besides, if Jason truly was trying to cut her life short, he'd know to look for her there.

She wanted the comforts of home. A real home. Something that soothed her, a place where she felt surrounded by love and happy memories.

Exactly!

Turning the car around, Kerry sighed and drove single-mindedly to her destination.

* * *

RAFE felt the emptiness of the room as soon as he walked in. Tossing the sandwiches on the faux mahogany desk, he looked around. Empty bedroom. Empty bathroom. Even though her sugary vanilla scent lingered, Kerry had gone.

Damn it!

Next to his laptop he spotted a white square from the hotel's notepad. Flowing script—a woman's handwriting.

Goodbye.

"That's it?" He crumpled the note into his fist and tossed it into the trash. "That's fucking it?"

Of course that was it. She'd poured her heart out to him. He'd panicked and acted like an idiot, humiliating her. Yes, she had run off.

What would you have done in her place, moron?

He should have insisted on room service, should have listened to his instinct that a woman in the midst of heartbreak needed comfort, not a turkey on rye with light mayo. He'd ignored his gut, thinking they both needed a few minutes alone.

Apparently, what he really needed was to pull his head out of his ass.

But damn it, so did Kerry. He paced the length of the room, raking a hand through his hair. The woman should not have run off when a murderous psycho was after a half-million dollars in electronic deposits, along with her hide.

Rafe returned to the desk and braced his palms on the surface. He stared blankly at his laptop. Where would she go? Not to her house, obviously. Not to Jason's, though he was probably at the bank. He paused. The bank? Maybe . . . but no. It would be closing soon. A hotel?

Hell, he had no idea.

A flashing on his screen caught his attention. The keystroke-tracking software he'd installed on the bank's mainframe popped open on the display.

Rafe clicked the button to open the window, hoping the thief was on and too busy trying to recover the money to snuff Kerry. *Eureka!* His little friend—most likely Jason—realized he'd screwed up with the fire and set Kerry running. He was tapping away at the terminal like a man possessed, trying all sorts of loopholes and back doors to extract the money, to reverse the transaction, to call it back.

He gave a grim smile. Jason could try all he wanted. Not a dime of that money was going anywhere until he was good and ready to give it to the FBI. And from the frantic nature of Jason's searching, it wouldn't be too long before he did something desperate and stupid so the Feds could come in and mop up.

Now if he could just find Kerry. Once he knew she was okay, he could breathe again.

The hotel's phone rang, jangling his nerves. Lurching for it, he damn near knocked his laptop over as he grappled to reach the receiver.

"Kerry?" he demanded.

"No. Guess again."

Jason.

Rafe had never understood the term a "killing rage" until that very moment. A crime of passion, committed in the heat of anger . . . it had all sounded like a lame excuse to toss out self-control and get away with murder. But at this moment, his grasp of the concept snapped into place with crystal clarity. Murdering Jason sounded perfectly sane.

"If you lay one hand on her," Rafe began, "I swear to God, you asshole, they'll have to pick up the pieces of your remains with tweezers."

Silence. Rafe could hear Jason breathing on the other end, but his imagination quaked. Had he already nabbed Kerry? Hurt her? Raped or killed her?

"I assume that Kerry told you I tried to lay a hand on her already. I got the message loud and clear that she's not interested, so you don't have to threaten me. Is she with you?"

"Why?"

"Look, I called because—"

"You're guilty as hell of framing Mark and want to confess? I'm gathering evidence against you left and right," Rafe growled, unable to hold his temper.

"What?" Irritation threaded his tone. "You are a complete loose cannon. I don't know why Kerry thought you could help us, much less why she loves you. Look, just tell me where she is, so I can tell her what I know."

Jason had heard Kerry's admission of love before he had? Not a comforting thought . . .

"Know about what?" Rafe asked, rather than bring up the love thing.

"Smikins."

A lie? A diversionary tactic? "Go on."

He sighed. "Can I come up first? This is too hard to explain over the house phone."

House phone? Why did he feel as if he were the butt of the joke in some comedy of errors? Would the ghosts of Abbott and Costello appear next to start their legendary *Who's on First* routine?

"Where are you?" Rafe barked.

"In the lobby of your hotel. If you'll tell me your room number, because these nice people at the front desk won't, I'll come up and tell you what I know. Then you can tell me where to find Kerry. And we won't have to speak to each other ever again."

Pulse racing, Rafe glanced at his computer. Yep, his culprit was still banging away at the accounts, looking for a way to retrieve the money he'd wired elsewhere. And Jason was standing in the lobby of the hotel?

Impossible.

"2415," he said, deciding to test 'ol Jason. If the guy didn't show up in the next two minutes, he'd—

Before he could finish the thought, the line went dead.

Chapter Fifteen

THREE minutes later, someone pounded on the door. Unless Kerry had suddenly developed the strength of a female wrestler, Rafe figured that someone had to be male. Jason, seriously?

With a scowl, he flung open the door. Sure enough. More mid-sized and moderate than big and bad, Jason stood in the doorway, panting. A glance back at the laptop on the faux wood desk told Rafe the thief was just now shutting down the bank's terminal.

That meant the psycho arsonist with murderous intentions wasn't Jason. *Holy shit!* It also meant the real killer-wannabe could be chasing Kerry again within moments. Unless . . .

What if Jason was up to his ass in crime with a partner, or had decided to finish Kerry off by torching her inside her own house for simply refusing to have sex with him? Possible. Time would tell. If Jason was guilty, he'd quickly be asking for account access information to retrieve the money Rafe had hidden away.

Glaring above Rafe's shoulder, Jason looked around the room, pausing on the rumpled bed. "Where's Kerry?"

"Just left." Rafe saw no surprise on the shorter man's face. Wouldn't a dude who'd executed a plan to kill his best friend's sister be surprised to learn she was still alive?

"Where did she go?" Jason's features said that he had annoyed down pat.

"How did you know to find me here?"

"Is this twenty questions? I went by Kerry's to talk to her. The firefighters said someone set fire to her house. I told them I was her brother, and they told me where to find her. Why isn't she here? Is she okay? What the hell happened?"

The concern seemed genuine, but who knew? "She's fine."

"Tell me where to find her." Jason scowled. "It's urgent."

No shit. There was a killer with an attitude on the loose. Rafe still wondered if Jason was more aware of that than he was letting on. He could be someone's accomplice. Still, Jason hadn't once mentioned account access information or seemed concerned about a missing half-million dollars.

"I'll tell you what I know if you tell me what you know." The clock was ticking, and Rafe hated playing cat and mouse with the wannabe boy toy, but he wasn't trusting just anyone, not until he knew that Jason wasn't Mr. Deranged with an affinity for matches, or said weirdo's assistant. "And if you promise not to corner Kerry again and force her to kiss you."

"You don't want her, but you don't want anyone else to have her? That's it!" Jason loosened his tie, mouth so taut his bottom lip turned white. "I'm going to beat the crap out of you, you arrogant slime."

The shorter man threw a punch, putting most of his body weight behind it. Rafe stepped back a bare instant before the blow connected. Then he stepped up with a jab to Jason's belly, followed by a right cross to the nose. Jason's head snapped back. Blood trickled from his nostril as he cursed and cuffed Rafe with a quick strike to the chin.

Little prick. That hurt.

Why was he fighting when Kerry was by herself, trying to elude a killer?

Again, Jason came at him, this time with the intent to pummel his nose. Rafe blocked the punch, grabbed Jason's wrist, and twisted it behind his back. Jason panted and hissed in between a string of creative curses.

"Let me go or I'm pressing charges," Jason threatened.

"You're in *my* hotel room, so stop threatening or I'll tell the cops you came here to harass me. Here's the deal: After you left Kerry's house this morning, someone hit her on the back of the head, rendered her unconscious, then torched her place with her inside. I found her before the fire got her. We escaped and came here. I went to get her a sandwich. When I came back, she was gone."

He released Jason.

"You—you think someone is trying to kill her?" Jason sputtered as he faced Rafe.

The look of horror, if it wasn't genuine, would win ol' Jason an Oscar.

"No question."

"Why?"

Eyes narrowed, Rafe stared at the other man. "We'll get back to that. Tell me what you know about Smikins."

Jason glared. "I loathe you."

"Thanks for the newsflash. Do you want this killer to get Kerry while you stand here running your mouth?"

As if that finally knocked some sense into him, Jason shook his head. "No." He swallowed, looking genuinely afraid. "No. What I know . . . I found Smikins today in the storage room with the abandoned terminal you asked me about. I saw 4389 written on the front. He had it hooked up in there. Remember the 'office' he let you borrow the day you were at the bank?"

"You *found* Smikins with the terminal?" If Jason was telling the truth, this was huge. More than huge, even. It was damning. It might well free Mark Sullivan.

The shorter man nodded. "About two this afternoon, I went looking for him to approve a large transaction. There he was hunching over the machine, tapping on the keys. When I asked him about it, he told me he'd just been in the closet looking for some old forms and run across the terminal. But he seemed nervous and sweaty. It didn't make sense."

Rafe frowned. "He was supposedly looking for old forms and he got sidetracked by an old terminal?" He had to agree with Jason's assessment: As excuses went, this one was thin. In fact, it was damn near transparent. "Why didn't he ever see the terminal before?"

"Those were exactly my questions. He stammered and claimed ignorance." Jason snorted. "Smikins is ignorant about a lot of things, like managing a bank branch. I just didn't believe he knew nothing about that terminal."

Pay dirt! Mind racing, Rafe sorted through everything Jason had just said. *If* it was true, the implications blew his mind. Smikins had potentially known about the terminal all along and withheld the truth. Why else would he stash the terminal in an unused room unless he had something, perhaps even criminal activity, to hide? It seemed likely that Kerry had been right about Smikins framing her brother to clear his path into Tiffany's good graces and panties. But he couldn't prove it until Smikins made a move on him to get the money back.

"So I said I felt sick and left to tell Kerry," Jason continued. "Why isn't she here and why is someone trying to kill her?"

Jason continued to say all the right things, have all the right reactions. Rafe sighed. Only one way left to prove this theory.

"Did you come in your own car?"

Confusion twisted Jason's face. "Yeah."

"I'll answer your last question on the way to find Kerry. I think she's in terrible danger, and if you had anything to do with this plot to kill her, I swear to God, you won't be able to find a cave remote enough to hide from me." Panic ate at Rafe's gut as he scooped up his shoes, ran out the door to his hotel room, and headed for the stairwell.

Jason followed, yelling, "If I had anything to do—Dude, don't you get it?" he snarled. "I love her and I would *never* harm her. I've loved her for years. I want to love her for the rest of her life. Unlike you. You 'loved' her for a few convenient days, and you'll be hopping a plane soon and leaving her behind. I'll be here to pick up the pieces and I hope to hell I never see your selfish, sorry ass again."

Rafe had won a lot of skirmishes in business by listening to his gut. It now told him that, despite how unlikable Jason was, he wasn't making this up. He did love Kerry. And soon Rafe would be gone. Kerry might turn to this guy for comfort.

The thought made him nearly grind his teeth into powder, but he held his tongue. If he wasn't going to stay and make a future with Kerry, he had no business telling her what to do with hers once he was gone.

"Message received. Start driving," he said as they reached the parking lot and Jason's black Mustang.

"Where to?"

Kerry or the bank terminal first? No contest. "Where do you think Kerry might go?"

"Was she upset when she left the hotel?"

Gee, when hadn't tears constituted upset? "Most likely."

"You broke her heart, didn't you, ass wipe?"

"What are you, my conscience?" Rafe growled. "Just concentrate on driving to wherever you think Kerry might go."

With a scowl, Jason turned the car out of the hotel parking lot and headed east. "We'll try Mark's place. She's always spent a lot of time there."

"Good call. That sounds like Kerry, wanting to be close to family and memories."

"So, you kept your pants zipped long enough to figure that out, huh?"

Rafe wanted to tell Jason that it was unlikely he'd ever have his pants unzipped around Kerry long enough to become acquainted with the sound of her in orgasm. But he didn't. He didn't want to ponder being wrong on that score. Besides, focusing on Kerry and her safety was more important.

"Can we bury this hatchet," *preferably in your head,* Rafe thought, "long enough to focus on why Smikins would hurt Kerry?"

Dodging thickening afternoon traffic, Jason frowned. "Why do you think Smikins set Kerry's house on fire?"

Rafe quickly explained about the money he had rerouted to another bank in order to draw out the thief. "So I suspect Smikins thought Kerry knew too much or something and tried to do away with her."

"Smikins hates Mark. I always suspected he was the one responsible for making sure the 'evidence' against Mark was pat and found its way into the FBI's hands. Maybe he found out that you were helping Kerry and got nervous. Maybe he thought he needed to do away with her, just in case she knew something."

"But why not do away with me, too? After I told him where to find the money, of course. If I'm the one who could find the evidence to free Mark and put Smikins behind bars, why not off me?"

Jason cursed as a red light stopped him. "Maybe he thought killing her would serve as a warning to you? I don't know. I only know you're giving Smikins a lot more credit for logical thought than he deserves."

"I'll buy that. The self-important always delude themselves."

"Exactly. Or maybe he thought or hoped you were there. Did he know where you were staying?"

Rafe sifted back through the day. "No, he apparently called my assistant in New York. She wouldn't tell him what year it was, much less the name of the hotel I chose."

"And knowing Smikins, it's likely he went after Kerry precisely because he couldn't find you." The light turned green, and Jason sped off with a squeal of his tires. "Smikins has an infamous temper."

Not good news on the temper. Rafe knew from experience that a simple Internet search had produced Kerry's street address. Smikins might not be the brightest bulb in the box, but he wasn't illiterate either.

And Rafe had left her at home, alone, unprotected. He swore roundly and wished he had something to hit besides glass and a guy driving a car at sixty miles an hour in a thirty-five zone. Of course, Rafe knew he was the one who deserved a swift kick. What if something had happened to Kerry? What if he hadn't gone to her house or hadn't arrived in time?

What if he was too late this time?

He exhaled and forced his thoughts to slow. If he could find Kerry soon, he'd just explain to her that Smikins was a cross between a kleptomaniac and Norman Bates. Rafe would protect her—with his last breath, if he had to.

"Well, at least we won't have trouble convincing Kerry of Smikins's guilt," Rafe muttered.

"No. She detests the jerk. She's thought he was guilty all along."

"I should have listened a little harder to that."

Maybe if he had listened, Kerry's life wouldn't be in danger right this moment. He only prayed he and Jason caught up with her before Smikins did.

* * *

KERRY let herself into Mark and Tiffany's place with the spare key behind the planter on the front porch. The interior of the house was dark and hot, not unusual for the middle of a workday. The foyer and living room, like the rest of the house, were almost surgically clean. Tiff sure could make a normal girl feel like a slob.

Still, as Kerry shut the door behind her, she could feel Mark here. His strength seemed embedded in these walls. She recalled the day he'd painted the living room that soothing sage color, and nearly dumped most of the paint on himself. She dropped her car keys on the living room table and wandered into the kitchen, feeling a sad smile steal across her face when she spotted the little burn mark on the kitchen counter where Mark had scarred the wood after one of his culinary experiments.

A sob bubbled up inside her. Even if the entire defensive line of an NFL football team had tackled her, Kerry couldn't imagine feeling worse than she did at that moment. She felt like she'd failed her big brother so miserably and completely lost her heart in the process—all while breaking the law. Couldn't forget that. True, the money might still draw the thief out into the open, but with the day mostly gone and no one with five sticky fingers in sight, Kerry was beginning to fear the guilty party was too clever to fall for Rafe's trap. Which meant Mark would stay in jail, and Rafe would join him unless someone in the FBI had a sense of humor.

Her life had been so topsy-turvy lately, Kerry felt sure she'd have better luck predicting the date of California's next major earthquake than guessing her next monkey wrench.

She hated to whine. Really, she did. But why hadn't she fallen in love with someone who could love her back? Why hadn't she listened when Rafe had told her that he was no good for her? And why, why was she powerless to help her brother while he rotted in jail? She was out of answers. She only knew that she'd screwed so many things up. God, if she could go back six months and know then what she knew now . . .

The garage door slammed on the other side of the house. Kerry rose, froze. Who would be coming in the garage door now? A quick glance at the clock showed it was only three-thirty. Tiffany shouldn't be home for at least an hour, maybe longer. With her current lucky streak, whoever had just entered the house was a deranged killer.

Footsteps raced through the laundry room, entered the hall, headed toward the kitchen. Scrambling for a hiding place, Kerry leapt behind the curtains draping the full-length window in the living room.

Moments later, someone breezed into the adjoining kitchen

with a muttered curse . . . one she'd know anywhere. Kerry released the breath she'd been holding.

"Tiff?" She peered through the doorway, into the kitchen, stepping away from the drape.

Squealing, Tiffany jumped, a hand to her slight chest as she entered the living room. "You? Oh my goodness, you scared me! I—I didn't expect to see you."

"Sorry."

Judging from the fact Tiff shared all the same skin tone as a cadaver, Kerry must have really startled her.

"Um . . . no, my fault," Tiff assured her with one of her sweet smiles. "I should have noticed your car outside. Don't know how I missed it. A lot on my mind, I guess."

"Everything okay?"

"Trying day." Tiffany tried to smile. "Before I forget to ask, do you know Mr. Dawson's room number at the hotel? Smikins wants to visit in person, since Mr. Dawson won't return his calls. I can't tell you how angry Smikins is about that. He chewed me out all day long."

Ah, that explained Tiff's terse greeting. Not to mention her askew hairdo and half-tucked blouse. She hated listening to Smikins rant. Then again, who didn't?

"I would have called, but my house . . . caught fire. Actually, I think someone torched it and tried to kill me."

Tiffany's mouth dropped open in horror. "Oh, my! What does the fire department think?"

She snorted. "That I had some sort of kitchen accident."

"You don't think it's possible?"

"I know I'm not a great cook, but I wasn't cooking." She frowned. "I'd planned to make tea but I hadn't even started."

"Tea?" Tiffany frowned. "You only make tea when you're upset. What happened?"

"You mean besides the clock ticking away on my best hope of

uncovering the truth about Mark's supposed crime, being hit on by my brother's best friend, and falling in love with a guy so far out of my league, I'm playing peewee to his pros? Other than that, nothing." The sting of tears cracked her flippant façade.

Tiffany patted her back. "I know it's been tough lately."

Sniffling, Kerry sent her sister-in-law a watery-eyed glance of thanks.

She and Tiffany had never been sister-like close, but Mark's wife had always lent an ear and been patient. She didn't always seem to grasp the big picture, but today, Kerry simply appreciated her listening. In fact, Tiffany's bit of kindness felt like a blowtorch to her plastic composure.

Lack of sleep, coupled with an overload of raw emotions, stress, and fear all caught up with her at once. God, she couldn't cry again. Her eyes were sandpapery, aching sockets, her head a pounding mess. She felt spent, empty, completely wrung out. Surely she didn't have any more grief left to give. Yet she couldn't stop a new flow of tears.

The waterfall started and rivaled those she'd seen in pictures of Hawaii. And damn it, tears just kept coming, along with pain. Loss. Humiliation. Somehow she knew her life would never be the same without Mark around to anchor her and Rafe around to love her. She couldn't hug them, help them, be with them. Reality sucked.

Chin trembling, Kerry stared at the ceiling and desperately tried to rein in her tears. "I'm a total wreck! My life . . . it's just falling apart. My house and most of my stuff are charred to a crisp, someone tried to kill me, and the man I love . . . if he'd shouted the fact he didn't love me, the message wouldn't have been any clearer. And Mark . . . I tried so hard to help him, but I only made a muck out of everything."

Fresh tears drowned out her next few words for the moment.

"All this will go away soon," Tiffany murmured beside her. "I'll help you."

"How?" Kerry turned to look at her sister-in-law with a frown.

"How do I free my brother? How do I get my heart back? I just don't see it." She sniffled again, surrendering to more new tears. "I don't want to cry anymore, but I can't stop. I don't know who to turn to. I don't have Mark's support and I—"

"I know how much you want Mark back and that you'd go to great lengths to see him free, but getting mixed up with that Dawson character? That is who you fell in love with, right?"

Kerry nodded. "How'd you know?"

"Jason. By the way, I'm not surprised he made a pass at you. But you're the kind of girl who wants a man she can rely on. Dawson isn't it. What's his room number so I can give him a piece of my mind? Oh, and I can tell Smikins so that he can give Dawson a piece of his mind, too . . . what little there is of it." She smiled.

Rising to grab a paper towel out of the kitchen, Kerry returned to the living room and dabbed at her swollen eyes. "I wouldn't wish that on my worst enemy."

A tense smile graced Tiffany's fine-boned face. "I know, but I promised Shorty I'd find out today and let him know. He swears he'll fire me if I don't. Can you help me out? Then we'll work on solving all your dilemmas, I promise."

Weighing her sister-in-law's loss against Rafe's inconvenience, Kerry muttered Rafe's room number at the hotel.

"Thanks, honey. You look dead on your feet. Let me get you a sandwich."

Gotta love Tiff. Her answer to all of life's troubles was food. She was lucky to have the metabolism that allowed her to do that without gaining massive pounds. "No thanks, I—"

"Did you even eat today?"

"Well, no." Come to think of it, she really hadn't.

"A quick sandwich will do the trick."

Let her make it, she told herself. It would make Tiffany feel better, if nothing else.

Pausing, Kerry watched her sister-in-law retreat to the kitchen, looking tense and unhappy. And she felt ashamed. She wasn't the only one suffering. Tiffany was a bride without a groom, a woman in love without her man, a well-organized assistant with an asshole for a boss. Things hadn't been all wine and roses for her since the month after she and Mark married.

"Can I help you?" she called after Tiff.

"You sit. You've had a trying day. I'll just be a few minutes," she said, bustling around the kitchen.

A moment later, Tiffany's cell phone rang. She snatched the phone from its holster attached to the waistband of her slacks, her face pulled tight with anxiety. Boy, if that was Smikins, he sure had Tiff under his thumb.

"Hello?" she said, her voice just above a whisper.

A moment later, Tiffany began to ease the door between the kitchen and the living room shut. "I have the necessary information . . ." was all Kerry heard before the door closed completely.

Smikins. What a jerk! He just wasn't happy unless he hounded his staff and called them during their off time. She remembered Mark suffering under the bank manager's awful temper and impatience.

Alone now, Kerry couldn't stop her thoughts from wandering back to Rafe. No doubt, he'd discovered her note by now, realized that she was gone. Was he relieved? Given how seriously he hadn't wanted her to love him, she'd guess yes.

Being this caught up in a man felt wretched, but she could no more change how she felt than she could stop breathing. She was learning the hard way that love was neither convenient nor momentary.

Dabbing her eyes on soft cotton, Kerry realized she was still wearing Rafe's shirt and sweat shorts. Tears welled up anew. Even the sight of his clothing made her cry. How pathetic was that?

No. No more tears. They stopped now. Rafe was gone, and he wasn't coming back. She loved him; he didn't love her. She wasn't going to spend her life pining for a man who didn't want her. At least, she hoped not.

She wouldn't, she promised herself. She'd get over him. Find some other way to help her brother. Somehow, she'd see Mark free. But her new life without Rafe and his wardrobe started now.

* * *

RAFE watched Jason maneuver his way to Mark Sullivan's place, wishing the afternoon traffic wasn't such a bitch. Damn, he was sweating. Heat, nerves, fear. He hated this fucking town right now.

"Did you try Kerry's cell phone?" Jason asked.

"I think it burned in the fire."

Jason cursed, and Rafe couldn't have agreed more. He doubted his gut was going to loosen up so that he didn't feel like puking until he *knew* Kerry was okay.

"How much longer?" he asked, frustrated by the never-ending line of cars in the left-turn lane.

"Ten minutes, tops. Did you call Mark and Tiffany's house?"

"Don't know the number."

Again, Jason cursed. Apparently, his mood was no better.

Reaching for the cell phone strapped to his belt, Jason said, "We can only hope that if Smikins wants to kill Kerry, he won't think to look for her at Mark's house."

But chances were the slimy SOB would. He'd torched her out of her own house. Where else would she go but to family, to the only other place she would consider home?

Before Jason could dial a single number on the keypad, the phone rang. He frowned at the display. "It's the bank. Damn Smikins. Has to be him." He pressed the Talk button. "Hello?"

After a brief pause, Jason said, "Hey, Francine."

Another pause, this one longer. "Now? What the heck is going on?"

The silence this time went on for long, agonizing seconds. Suddenly, Jason's eyes widened with what Rafe could only describe as shock.

"What is it?" Rafe demanded.

Jason waved him away, his face stunned. "Oh my . . . I can't believe it."

The shorter man listened again to the voice on the other end and nodded. "How long ago?" Another brief pause later, he added, "And you saw this yourself?"

Francine's voice blared across the line suddenly. Rafe couldn't hear her words, per se. But her tone was loud and clear: *Panic.*

"Holy shit." Jason raked a hand through his short brown hair. "I can't come to close the bank right now. Do the best you can, and I'll be there as soon as I can."

Another screech through the cell phone.

"No," Jason huffed. "I don't know exactly when that will be. As soon as I can."

With that, Jason hung up on a sputtering Francine.

Rafe turned to him with a questioning gaze.

"We've got to get to Kerry fast."

Jason sped up, barely making the intersection before the light turned red.

"What the hell is going on?" Rafe glared at the other man.

"The mystery terminal I found Smikins next to earlier is missing. So is he."

Chapter Sixteen

RUBBING at the sore, gritty lids of her eyes, Kerry padded from the living room, down the hardwood floor of the hall. Normally, she'd ask Tiffany if she could go into her bedroom and retrieve one of Mark's shirts. But Tiff was on the phone, so why disturb her? Kerry doubted she would mind.

At the end of the hall, the grandfather clock, one of the few keepsakes left from her father's family, said the time neared 4:00 P.M. Thank God the day was ticking away. After a heart-wrenching morning and a harrowing afternoon, she didn't need an evening full of danger and doom. No doubt about it, Kerry had reached her drama quotient for the day.

The door to the garage sat on her left, the car keys on a table beside it. She smiled. Her sister-in-law put them there nearly every day—and then couldn't find them half the time.

As Kerry reached the end of the hall, Tiff's conversation heated up. A strain of insistent whispers reached her ears. Then Tiffany gasped. Frowning, Kerry wondered if Smikins had crossed the line from deluded jerk to outright bully.

Just in case, she listened for sounds of Tiffany in distress, but for a long thirty seconds heard no screams or tears, heard nothing more than the mumble of Tiffany's low conversation through the wall.

With a shrug, Kerry ambled into the master bedroom, intent on finding a shirt that didn't smell like Rafe, didn't remind her of the man she'd always love but never have. Traces of Mark still lingered in the bedroom. The masculine forest-and-taupe-striped bedspread, the heavy knotty pine furniture, pictures of Mark's martial arts instructor—the one who'd been a father figure to him in high school when he'd had no father.

Tiffany's presence was usually understated in this room . . . except today.

Her sister-in-law's clothes were piled everywhere. Lingerie in one stack, shorts and T-shirts in another, dresses strung out across the floor. Weird. Tiff prided herself on fanatic cleanliness.

Puzzled, Kerry rounded the corner into the master bath—and stood stock-still.

Two suitcases crammed to capacity sat beside her vanity, which had been wiped clean of her jewelry box and assorted perfume bottles. *What the . . . ?* Tiffany was going somewhere? But Mark's trial started Monday.

Thoughts scrambled through her brain like lab mice on crack. This didn't make any sense. Why would Tiff take a last-minute trip? She had no other family, so it wasn't that someone back home needed her. The fact she and Mark had both been orphaned as youngsters had been a connecting point for them. So where the hell was she going?

A turn to her left showed her the closet—or rather the empty closet. It looked like Tiffany wasn't just going away, she was leaving for good.

As in moving out? Leaving her brother?

Shock and cold betrayal seeped across her skin. Mark's wife was leaving him on the eve of his trial? Was she ashamed? Did she believe he was guilty and wanted nothing more to do with him?

Kerry whirled around, nearly dizzy with her racing thoughts. *No!* Mark would be crushed if Tiffany left him, especially now and—

Then, on Mark's vanity, Kerry saw an airline itinerary. Quickly, she scooped the page up. It listed a one-way trip for Tiffany from Tampa to Owen Roberts International on Grand Cayman Island. Her flight left at eight.

The paper fell from numb fingers.

Grand Cayman? Why would Tiffany want to go there now, just before the trial? She couldn't possibly be taking a vacation without Mark. She couldn't afford it. Besides, it was a one-way ticket. Why would Tiffany travel there? To the island where all the embezzled funds Mark had been accused of stealing had mysteriously disappeared. Unless . . .

No! Not Tiffany. She couldn't be guilty. She loved Mark.

Didn't she?

Tiffany loves him so much she's leaving, apparently for good, days before his trial starts?

Kerry's blood turned to ice.

Exhaling a series of hard, fast breaths, Kerry felt her pulse accelerate as puzzle pieces snapped into place. Tiffany had had access to Mark's system password. As the assistant who had taken over Smikins's care and feeding after the other had left in a huff, she would likely have known where terminal 4389 was. That put her in a position to hide it. And use it. After all, the previous short skirt hadn't simply snapped her fingers and made it disappear. Tiffany had known Kerry was working with Rafe to free Mark. From that, she could have guessed Rafe had stashed the money electronically in order to draw her out. Her brother's wife had known where Kerry lived, had asked several times that day for the name of Rafe's hotel and his room number, supposedly because Smikins was screaming for the information. But why had Tiff tried to torch her house, with her inside? And the woman had never been a genius, so how had she embezzled the money so cleverly, manipulated the bank's records and computers for her purposes?

Maybe Kerry was jumping to conclusions, but it all seemed to fit.

She didn't have all the answers, but when she read a good mystery, the hairs on the back of her neck stood up when the bad guy appeared. They were doing the same thing now. The info she had before her made her deeply suspicious. Enough to get the hell out of Dodge and call in the cavalry.

Easing out of the bedroom, she tiptoed down the hall. An odd sound sliced its way through the air from the kitchen just then. It sounded like a soft hiss. But with a faintly metallic clink. Kerry picked up her pace down the hall, toward the living room. What was that noise?

Then Kerry realized she'd heard that sound before—just before Mark had chopped meat.

Oh, God. Tiffany had drawn the knife big enough to take the head off Godzilla from its butcher block. A blade that size wasn't necessary to cut a ham and cheese sandwich.

Kerry paused, blood tearing through her veins. Fear crept in a cold chill across her skin. Tiffany meant to kill her? Her brain seemed to go numb with disbelief. She didn't want to know what her sister-in-law might have planned. If Tiffany was guilty of framing her own husband for a felony, Kerry had been horribly guilty of underestimating her. Clenching trembling fists, she realized she couldn't afford to underestimate her sister-in-law again.

Inching her way into the living room, toward her car keys, she stopped short when she realized they no longer sat on the coffee table.

"Looking for these?" Tiffany dangled her car keys in one hand, squarely blocking the front door. Her other hand, looking casually slung on the back side of her hip, was hidden behind her.

Holding the knife?

Play it casual. Be cool. "I just realized that I really need to talk to my insurance company about the fire. If I want to start getting reimbursed for my damage, I'd better go."

She held out her hands for her keys.

Tiffany merely slipped them into her pocket. "Not yet. You look shaken."

Kerry offered her a smile that she hoped didn't look as stilted as a laugh track on a bad sitcom. "Um, long day. I'm fine. I'll just come back in a bit and we can chat more. How's that?"

"Not a good idea."

From the sharp look on Tiffany's face, the bitch wasn't buying Kerry's innocent act, and the bulge in her pants pocket tempted her with the lure of her car keys. But Kerry didn't dare step any closer. That hidden hand behind the double-crossing criminal's back didn't hold a cream puff.

Continuing to play dumb, Kerry said, "It's . . . um, good of you to care, but I'm okay. Really."

Tiffany cocked her head to the side. The gaze she shot Kerry's way could only be called shrewd. "Not until I make all your troubles go away. I promised you that."

Blood stilled in Kerry's veins, chilling her already cold skin. Moments later, as adrenaline pumped, it all reversed. Kerry broke out in a sweat.

Yeah, earlier Tiff had promised to make all her troubles go away. Kerry feared now that her sister-in-law hadn't meant by talking through them.

Tiffany meant to solve all of Kerry's problems by ending her life.

* * *

A scant three minutes had passed when Jason's phone rang again.

Stuck at a red light, Jason took in the caller ID's display with a sigh. "What, Francine?"

As much as he didn't like the little jerk, Rafe understood Jason's impatience. If the woman thought closing the bank was more important than saving a friend's life, she deserved to get chewed on.

"Oh, my God!" Jason uttered. Fear and shock gave gravity to his words, his tone.

That, along with the chalk white pallor of his skin, told Rafe something was dreadfully wrong.

"What?" he snapped.

Jason held up a hand to stay Rafe's words. "No, no. Don't cry. Don't panic. I'll call the police. You handle the employees. I'll be there when I can."

Ending the call with a grim voice, Jason rubbed a thin sheen of sweat from his forehead and uttered a hiss of a curse.

"Out with it, man!"

As Jason began to dial 911, he looked visibly shaken. "Smikins is dead. Someone slit his throat from ear to ear and stuffed the body in the storage closet in the spare office."

Holy shit! Rafe's mind raced, every turn leading him to frightening possibilities. Sure, a lot of people probably wanted the tyrannical Smikins dead. But the timing was too coincidental to be anyone besides the embezzler, the mastermind who'd framed Mark Sullivan. It wasn't Jason. It obviously wasn't Smikins.

"Tiffany!" he shouted, then shouted at Jason, "Where the hell is Tiffany?"

"I—I don't know."

"Call Francine back," he demanded, fear revving his heart like an LS1 V-8 engine on a 'Vette.

Jason cleared his display and hit his speed dial as he gunned the car forward through the green light.

Damn it, Kerry had left his hotel room and walked straight into a murderer's lair. Why the hell hadn't he just told her he had feelings for her that he couldn't comprehend and that scared the shit out of him, instead of crushing her heart with his panic? His crappy relationship skills had sent her fleeing straight into danger.

He was every bit as stupid and selfish as Jason had accused him of being.

Someone finally answered Jason's call because he barked, "Where's Tiffany Sullivan?" After a pause, he exploded, "You don't see her? When was the last time you did?" Jason cursed. "If you don't know, ask someone else."

Tiffany wasn't there because she was the thief who'd framed her own husband for embezzlement, then killed her boss when he—what, discovered her? And now Kerry, sweet, unsuspecting Kerry, had walked trustingly right to Tiffany's door.

"What?" Jason said suddenly. "No one has seen Tiffany in nearly an hour!"

Cold terror slid through Rafe's veins.

Ahead, traffic stopped. Rafe opened the passenger window and looked out. Stalled car in the right lane. Damn it all to hell! He didn't have time for this. The seconds of Kerry's life could be ticking away. She was sitting next to a cold-blooded bitch of a killer and probably had no idea.

"Drive down the shoulder," he demanded of Jason. "I'll call the police."

Jason steered the car onto the shoulder and gunned it. Rafe grabbed his BlackBerry and dialed 911.

Rafe quickly explained the situation both at the Sullivan house and at the bank to the dispatcher.

"What's Mark's address?" he barked at Jason.

Jason recited it. After relaying that information to the dispatcher and giving them a description of Kerry's beat-up car, which should be out front, Rafe was thrilled when the dispatcher promised to send silent squad cars out to Mark's house.

Ending the 911 call, Rafe turned to Jason. "Do you know Tiffany's cell number?"

"Yeah." Jason handed Rafe his phone. Speed dial number five. "Do you think we should call? Won't that tip Tiffany off that we're on to her?"

He was right, Rafe realized. If he called Tiffany, she would smell something very fishy. Lord knew what she would do to Kerry. The woman had already proved that she would stop at nothing—not even murder.

Think! He had to stop the panic racing, clear his head. Shit, how was he supposed to think like a killer? Cursing, Rafe beat a fist on the dashboard. He had to do something. Something that would distract Tiffany but not let her know they were on to her.

"You call." He handed Jason his phone again. "Tell her you're calling to tell her Smikins is dead."

Jason sent him an incredulous glare. "I don't think she'll be surprised by that information."

"I know, but if you act like she should be, she won't suspect anything. Just keep her talking. If she's talking, she can't be killing Kerry."

With a nod, Jason reached for his phone. "And if she doesn't want to talk about Smikins?"

Rafe took a deep breath. He might go to prison for this but . . . "Tell her I'll give her the access codes to the money if she gives me Kerry alive and in one piece."

* * *

KERRY looked for a place to run. Tiffany blocked the front door.

She needed to get out of the house. She needed a car. Her own was locked, and Tiffany had the keys. A neighbor's? No. No one conveniently kept their keys in an unlocked car in plain sight. And she knew as much about hot-wiring a car as she knew about nuclear physics. Absolutely nothing.

"You're getting paler. Sit down," Tiffany invited.

But Kerry heard the underlying demand. *Should I confront her?* No, giving Tiff more reason to demonstrate the various uses of the Ginsu on human flesh wasn't a good idea. Could she play dumb and get the criminal to believe it?

"I . . ."

While she grasped for words, Tiffany's cell phone rang again, slicing through the tense air.

Her sister-in-law flinched as she diverted her gaze just long enough to grasp the phone from the holster at her waist and find the Talk button. "Hello?"

Kerry didn't wait around to see who was on the other end. While she was distracted, Kerry darted down the hallway toward the garage. The thieving bitch was lighter and had been a sprinter in high school. Not to mention the fact she had a weapon and could likely slice and dice Kerry with it before she saw daylight again.

"Can't talk now," Tiffany said.

Looking back, Kerry caught a glimpse of her shoving the phone back in its holster. In the other hand, she held the knife. The stark silver of a four-inch, serrated blade gleamed in the sharp, streaming light. The pound of Tiffany's footsteps down the hardwood floor, now following, echoed in Kerry's ears as she sped toward the nearest way out of the house: the garage.

Terror sped through her body, powering her legs into a sprint so speedy, she'd never accomplished it on her gym's treadmill. A tight ball of fear settled into her stomach, bundled up with nausea. God, was she going to die here, in a house she'd always thought of as a home, at the hand of a woman she'd trusted as family?

Not without one hell of a fight.

Her heart pounded as she reached the end of the hall and spied Tiffany's car keys, still on the little table. She had just one chance to scoop them up at a full-out run. *Don't screw up!* Her life literally depended on it.

As she scurried toward the garage door and what she dearly prayed was freedom, Kerry reached out for the keys. She nearly missed—two fingers closing over one key dangling off the central ring. Still, she grasped it tightly in her knuckles and pulled, knowing that if she didn't succeed, if she dropped them, she was a shish kebab before she even opened the door to the garage.

Yanking the keys off the table and to her chest, Kerry felt a burst of relief. For once today, her luck held. But a quick turn of her head proved that Tiffany was gaining on her, was probably no more than three steps behind.

Praying faster than a repenting sinner on Judgment Day, Kerry reached for the edge of the little table and gave it a push. A crash, a shriek, and thud later, Kerry looked back to see that her brother's traitorous wife had tripped over the lightweight piece of furniture, as Kerry had hoped.

"Damn you! That's going to leave a mark," Tiffany shouted as she struggled to her feet. "Can't you just die quietly?"

Kerry grasped the knob to the garage and swung the door wide. "I've never been good at being quiet."

Then she sprinted inside the hot, shadowy confines of the garage and slammed the door in Tiffany's face.

Safe—for about three seconds. She had no way to lock the murderous witch out.

Blindly, she groped against the wall for the button that would open the garage door. One swipe along the wall. Another. A third. Nothing. *No, no, no! The button has to be right here!*

The doorknob jiggled, warning Kerry that Tiffany was about to open the door. She ducked. Sweat trickled down the back of her neck as she crawled toward Tiffany's car. The garage was damn near black now that the light from the house no longer streamed in. Tiffany's car was every bit as old as her own and had no automatic key locks that would shed a little light, damn it.

God, was she going to die? *No!*

Kerry tried to crouch on the oil-slicked cement and feel her way to the car door, using only the blessed light seeping in around the double garage door at the front of the house as a guide. She held the car keys tightly in her other hand.

With a lurch and a yell, Tiffany burst into the garage and flipped on the overhead light. Kerry saw the driver's-side door. She reached for the handle and gave a frantic yank. *Locked!* She was as good as dead.

Tiffany laughed.

Doom pierced Kerry's gut as her heart beat a frantic tattoo against her chest. She wouldn't have enough time to unlock the door, get in, shut the door behind her, and lock it.

But doomed or not, she wasn't done fighting.

"You shouldn't have gone into my bedroom," snarled Tiffany. "Slitting your silly throat would have been easier if you hadn't figured things out."

Wanting a shirt besides Rafe's had tipped her off to the danger. Now she just hoped she'd done enough to save her life. "Why the hell are you trying to kill me?"

Tiffany stalked to the driver's-side door. Kerry ran to the other side, still keeping the car between them.

"Obviously you've figured out that I took the money from the bank. If I let you leave here, you'll go to the police."

"But I didn't know that when you hit me over the head and set my house on fire."

She shrugged. "I knew you'd figure it out eventually. Easier to get rid of you before you suspected. Jason told me you were due home that morning. I snuck in and waited. After his inept pass"—she rolled her eyes—"you were good enough to leave a voice mail telling me where to find Mr. Dawson. At that point, I thought you were expendable and dangerous to me."

Unreal! The planning, the calculation . . .

"But then I went to Dawson's hotel," Tiffany continued, "and no amount of flirting was going to get me his room number since the desk clerk was a woman. So, in a way, it was helpful of you to come here so that I could persuade you to give me his room number."

"I'm not the only one who knows the truth," Kerry lied. "Rafe knows, too."

Okay, so he suspected Jason. But if Tiffany thought she wasn't the only one standing between herself and a clean getaway, maybe . . . what? Tiffany would drop the knife and leave her alone? No, but maybe she could think of something, some way to negotiate with the would-be killer.

"He's next on my list, don't worry. Once I'm done with you, I should have no trouble slitting his throat like I did Smikins. Men don't really see women as a threat."

Kerry gasped. "You—you killed Smikins?"

"What do you care? Even if I let you live, you wouldn't miss him. He figured me out and he was in my way."

Just like me. Oh, this was bad. It was one thing to think Tiffany might kill her. Another to know for sure that she was actually capable of such a thing.

"Everyone underestimated me, I think." Tiffany grinned, then she widened her eyes, taking on an insipid, somewhat vacant expression. "It's so easy to be overlooked when everyone thinks you're a harmless little bimbo."

Then the intelligence and feral anger slipped back into Tiffany's gaze. A foreboding chill skittered down Kerry's spine. The criminal bitch was both calculating and serious. She had to do something, think of something. Maybe if she could keep Tiffany talking, she could formulate a plan.

"Why did you frame my brother? He loved you. He would have done anything for you. Anything."

"He's a great guy, good looking, well put together, good in bed, even. Unlike most jerks, he has a big heart . . . just not a big enough wallet."

Tiffany lunged in her direction. Kerry ran in the other, until they had the full length of the car between them.

This was surreal—being hunted down like prey, hearing the woman her brother had given his heart and his name to admit she had framed him for the money. What next?

"He gave you the roof over your head," Kerry protested. "You had a decent life with Mark."

"Decent? By your standards, maybe. I wasn't meant to work as an assistant to some asshole in a little bank, scraping by to pay off someone else's medical bills, barely having enough money to eat out once a month. Forget shopping or vacations, nice cars or new clothes from anywhere but Wal-Mart." She grimaced. "I grew up dirt poor. The daughter of a traveling preacher in Arkansas with eleven kids. I shared everything in a run-down camper with all my siblings. The minute I realized men liked the way I looked, I left. No more Ruthie Jo for me. I changed my name, lost my accent, learned how to give a great blow job and convince men I was harmless. It's worked for the last twelve years, sweetie. Mark was no different to me than all the others."

"You bitch! I'd love to get my hands on your scrawny neck."

"Come and get it."

Kerry wanted to. The urge to jump over the car and strangle the conniving witch thrummed in her veins, pulsing hot and strong. But in a fight against Tiff and her friend, Mr. Knife, Kerry knew she'd lose. Now that she'd heard Tiffany's confession, she had to stay alive long enough to free Mark—and keep the dangerous woman away from Rafe.

Damn it, Mark had achieved his black belt. Why hadn't she listened more closely when he'd tried to teach her self-defense? Time for Plan B.

Too bad her Plan B's always sucked.

"Nice try," Kerry went on. "So did you marry him just to set him up?"

Tiffany suddenly sprinted toward the back of the car. Kerry charged toward the front.

"Of course," said the duplicitous redhead. "This is a great scam. Or it will be once I get my hands on that money. How do I get those access codes?"

"What scam?"

"I don't have time for this."

"Then I'm not telling you how to get the money." As if she knew, Kerry thought.

With a long-suffering sigh, Tiffany said, "If it makes you feel better before you die . . . money laundering. I'm cleaning money for some crime boss back East and taking part of the cut. And if I don't find them their money soon, they will come kill us all. They've called me five times in the last two days to remind me."

That made sense. Kerry remembered the phone call yesterday at the bank that had shaken Tiffany. The liar had claimed the caller was a nasty customer, but she'd looked awfully pale. Then just a while ago in the kitchen, the whispers, the low voices, the sudden need to kill.

The Mafia meant business—but so did Kerry.

"So you married my brother for his bank access and his passwords so that you could launder some crime boss's drug and prostitution money?"

"Are you just slow today? I've already said that."

The insistent burn of anger started creeping up on her fear. "And the computer knowledge? Where did you come by that?"

"That was easy." She waved the technical feat away as if it was nothing. "A continuing fling with a programmer I met a few months back. You know what they say, 'Men are like floor tiles. Lay them right the first time and you can walk on them for a lifetime.' "

"You cheated on Mark?" Somehow, that horrified her almost as much as knowing Tiffany had lied when speaking her wedding vows.

Her reaction made Tiffany laugh. "Spoken like a little virgin wearing rose-colored glasses."

"Yeah? That's better than being a deceitful, two-timing killer."

Tiffany arched an auburn brow. "When this is all said and done, I'll be set financially for a long while, and living on one of the most beautiful islands in the world. All I have to do is destroy the mainframe terminal I used, which is in the trunk of my car, and hop a plane by eight o'clock to enjoy a life of luxury. What would you have if I let you live? A job waiting on hicks at a greasy spoon and memories of a rich guy who gave you your first taste of cock, which you confused with love." Tiffany looked at the knife in her hand, then glanced back at Kerry. "Sex is a transaction. You have something men want, and men have something you want. When the something you want becomes sex or love, you're their slave. I learned that fast. Too bad you won't get a chance to put my good advice to use. Now enough flapping our jaws. How do I get the money?"

"Are you going to spare me if I tell you?"

She cocked her head as if considering. "I might."

But Kerry knew, just like she'd known Mark was innocent, that Tiffany was lying.

"Go to hell!"

"You first. The only thing standing between me and what I want are the access codes to the bank account Dawson moved the money into—and you."

With that, Tiffany charged. Kerry tripped over the lawn mower and fell. Her knees crashed onto unyielding cement, but she didn't dare stop to feel the pain.

As Kerry rose, she glanced over her shoulder and found Tiffany charging toward her. The redhead bared her teeth, eyes gleaming fury as she raised the large knife clutched in her hand. Scrambling away as fast as her feet would take her, Kerry's back soon hit her brother's tool bench, which was wedged against the wall. The impact jarred the car keys out of her hand. They skittered out of reach.

Now what?

Turning quickly, she grabbed the first thing from the squatty, red-legged table that resembled a weapon: a crowbar.

Clutching her new weapon in her hand, Kerry whirled around in time to sidestep the first plunge of Tiffany's knife. Well, almost. Kerry felt a slice crease her forearm. She pushed aside the stinging sensation and gripped the crowbar tighter, raising it to meet the next attack. That's when she saw the blood seeping a thin line through her skin, beading at the end before plopping onto the grimy cement.

Lord, Tiffany really meant to kill her. Logically, she'd known that, but to actually see blood . . . The moment felt crystal clear, yet slow. Danger dried out her mouth, made her palms damp. This really could be the end—before she could see Mark again, before she could kiss Rafe one last time.

No!

The psycho bitch growled and came at Kerry again. Prepared this time, she raised the crowbar to meet the blade, the clash of metal on metal resounding through the garage. The heavy metal bar in her hands held.

The good thing about outweighing someone by thirty pounds, Kerry discovered next, was that she could push her attacker away.

Tiffany stumbled back, nearly tripping on her own feet, then looked up at Kerry with a malicious gleam in her eye. "I never liked you. You're the kind of woman who makes men think we're weak and easily manipulated. I can't wait to end your worthless life."

Fury poured through Kerry like lava down the side of a volcano. This bitch was going down!

As Tiffany charged toward her again, she swung out with her crowbar and struck the scrawny slut's shoulder.

"Ouch!" the redhead protested, glaring at Kerry.

"I don't like you either. You're the kind of woman who makes men believe they can't trust us. You're not going to kill me. I won't let you get away with any of this."

Gathering her strength, Kerry came at Tiffany swinging, right giving her might. Kerry vowed that she'd stop the schizoid from hurting Rafe, from framing Mark. Tiff's next destination wouldn't be a tropical beach but a cold eight-by-eight cell in some scary federal locale.

With a guttural yell, Kerry launched at Tiffany, her crowbar making a wide arc. Tiffany stumbled back, retreating. She tried to lean away, blue eyes as wide as swimming pools. Her skin paled in surprise, making every freckle stand out.

Then the crowbar struck Tiffany's wrist. The brutal knife in her hand went flying. Tiff gasped, clutching her wrist as she dove for the knife skittering across the oily floor.

"Bitch!" she screamed as she reached for the blade.

Kerry kicked it out of the way and leaped on Tiffany, pinning her to the ground. Thanking her love of all things chocolate again for her superior weight, she straddled the skinny wretch, pinned her down, and thrust the crowbar across her neck.

"Oh, I think that honor is all yours. I can't wait to see you wearing prison-issue orange jumpsuits, accessorized by handcuffs."

A commotion at the door from the house to the garage brought Kerry's head up. Two men rushed in. She'd never been so happy to see black uniforms and shiny badges in her life. Rising to her feet, she let the officers close in.

"Police! Hands up!" one shouted at Tiffany, gun drawn.

The other opened the garage door to the late afternoon sun—and another four officers waiting with guns drawn. Rafe and Jason stood just behind them.

"The police?" the criminal redhead screeched. "No!"

"Looks like the people who can make your worst fashion nightmare come true have arrived," Rafe drawled to Tiffany as he walked in behind the police. "Hope you enjoy your new clothes from somewhere besides Wal-Mart."

Rafe is safe! Kerry thought in relief. He was safe.

"They have no proof of anything!"

"We all heard your entire confession from the other side of the garage door, Ruthie Jo."

Relief burst through Kerry's heart at Rafe's mocking words. The nightmare, the danger, the threat to her brother—it was over. Really, truly over. Everyone was safe. Soon, her brother would be free. And she'd get to touch Rafe one more time.

Within moments, two policemen flanked Tiffany, cuffed her, read her her rights, and dragged her away.

Chapter Seventeen

STICKY with sweat and bone tired, Kerry stared as Tiffany disappeared with her police escort. Despite her exhaustion, elation flowed through her, along with a complex mix of pride and lingering adrenaline. And huge doses of relief. Finally, the real culprit was going down for embezzlement, and her beloved brother would be free. Life would be normal again.

Except that normal meant that the man she loved would be gone from her life in a few short hours. Tears pricked at Kerry's eyes.

As the other officers began securing the crime scene and calling for detectives, Rafe took Kerry's hand and led her into the house. In the kitchen, he pulled her against the sanctuary of his broad chest, his fingers stroking through her curls. His heartbeat resounding in her ears, he held her tight. She felt safe, whole, cared for. She wanted that feeling to last.

It's an illusion, she told herself. Yes, he was strong, capable, caring in his own gruff way. He simply wasn't hers to keep. She eased back.

"Are you all right?"

At her nod, Rafe glanced at the slash Tiffany's knife had made into Kerry's forearm and swore. He guided her to the sink and washed her cut with gentle fingers. It didn't look deep enough for stitches, but it stung like a bitch. After, he wadded up some paper towels and pressed them over her bleeding forearm. As his gentleness undid her, Kerry judiciously avoided looking at Rafe. It was either that or boo-hoo like a sap at a three-hankie movie.

"Thank God that's the worst of it." He cupped her cheek, looking at her with haunted eyes. "I was seriously afraid I wouldn't get here in time. I worried that you wouldn't suspect Tiffany until it was too late."

Rafe cared. She knew it, could feel it in the protective grip of his gaze, hear it in his sandpaper voice. But that didn't make anything different between them. Two hours ago he'd been telling her that he wasn't into commitment. She needed to stop hoping for a Hollywood ending.

"I figured it out before she pounced. If I hadn't . . ."

Neither of them finished that sentence.

His grip on her tightened. "I can't believe that Tiffany framed Mark and tried to kill you. You trusted her like family."

Kerry nodded. "I did. But Tiffany married Mark with every intention of making sure he went to prison for her crimes. She betrayed my trust, yes. But Mark gave her his entire heart."

"Bitch," he muttered. "He had no idea?"

"None of us did. The truth is going to kill him."

Anger tightened Rafe's face. "At least she won't be doing this to anyone else anytime soon."

"True. Between our statements, and all the police who overheard her ranting in the garage, that should be more than enough to put her away." She sent him a wobbly smile. "So we did it."

"Yeah, babe. We did. You more than me."

He threaded his fingers through her curls again, broad palms cradling her head as if she were a treasure to keep close to his heart.

Kerry melted. She never felt more right, more whole, than when she was with him.

How would she get past the gaping hole in her heart—in her life—once he returned to New York?

"You were so brave," he murmured close to her ear. "I'm sorry it took me a while to get here with reinforcements."

"I'm just thrilled you did. Thank you for not giving up." Kerry bit her lip as she eased back, appalled to feel a tear slipping down her cheek. She swiped it away with an impatient hand. "Thank you for all your help."

He brushed away another tear scalding a path over her skin. The tenderness, intensity, and hot possession in his gray eyes swirled like a whirlpool. She drowned in the feeling of caring, of security, of being desired. When she looked at him, her world felt right. With Tiffany soon behind bars and Mark soon to be released, everything was as it should be—or almost.

Rafe dipped his head and took gentle possession of her mouth. His kiss tasted of worry and gladness . . . and goodbye.

Kerry's heart shattered. Her life would be incomplete without him. How would she ever heal without her other half? She stepped away, fresh tears prickling her aching eyes, closing up her throat.

He cursed, regret clouding his potent gaze. "Look, I—"

"Mr. Dawson," called one of the officers from the edge of the kitchen. "You'll need to come with us now. We need your statement."

"I'll be right there."

"And Ms. Sullivan, an officer will come to take your statement momentarily. Do you need an EMT to look at that arm?"

"No," she whispered. "Thanks."

Nodding, the officer left the room and exited the house via the front door.

Pain slammed Kerry in the awkward silence. She wanted to ask Rafe to stay. Beg him. But she couldn't make him love her, couldn't cure his fear of commitment, couldn't stop him from leaving. She'd only hurt them both if she tried.

"They'll, um, be wanting your statement, too, in a minute, it seems."

"Yeah." She nodded, desperately fighting the tears boiling behind her eyes. "Your flight leaves in the morning, right?"

Rafe paused, then said, "About eleven."

As she nodded, he grabbed her arms and pulled her closer, against the taut, whipcord heat of his body. "I don't have any right to ask you this, but . . . I want to see you again before I go. I suspect we'll be with the police most of the night, but tomorrow, I've reserved the hotel limo. Would you ride to the airport with me?"

It would be hard. It would hurt like hell, but she couldn't say no. This would be her last chance to store up memories of him, of them together. "I'll be there."

"Thank you." Squeezing her arms, he planted a quick, deep kiss on her mouth. "See you."

Then he was gone.

As soon as his retreating form disappeared through the door, Kerry gave in to the pressure of the searing tears that had built behind her eyes. She clutched her stomach as the pain ripped through, and she let the tears fall. After today and the endless crying, she was going to look like a bunny permanently, with the swollen nose and red-rimmed eyes. And she really didn't care.

"I'm sorry."

She turned to find Jason in the kitchen entry from the hall. She had no idea how long he'd been there. With hands shoved deep in his pockets and his mouth flattened in a grim line, he looked taut and pensive.

"You really do love him," he said, as if the concept were as novel as walking in space.

"Yes." She sniffled. "And . . . you've been a good friend."

His tart smile seemed to mock his feelings as he approached. "That's me, all-around great guy. But if you ever have a change of heart . . ."

Certainly, life would be easier for her if she did, but she wouldn't.

"Ms. Sullivan," called one of the female officers. "We'll need you to come with us so we can get your statement."

"Go on," he said, caressing her shoulder. "I'm sure they'll be wanting my statement soon, too. After we get Mark free, we'll sort all this out."

With another sniff, Kerry shoved back more tears and left with the officer, knowing in her head that getting Mark out of jail would be the end to many problems and the beginning of a new life. But her heart knew that by eleven o'clock tomorrow morning, that new life would have lost its best chance at happiness.

* * *

TUESDAY had nearly expired into Wednesday before Rafe finished with the police. Endless questions about his involvement in Mark Sullivan's case had exhausted him. He'd hated like hell to have to admit to having a sexual relationship with Kerry. It was no one's business but theirs. The police, however, had been insistent to understand how he'd started working on the case and why he'd resorted to means so drastic as to steal in order to trap a thief. He'd either had to tell the truth or flat-out lie. Lying wouldn't go over well when this case went to court.

Then Robert D'Nanza, his oh-so-understanding pal over at the FBI, had been called. After Rafe provided the access codes and the money had been recovered, everyone had finally stopped treating him like an accomplice.

One more thing to do. One last thing he could do for Kerry before he left her.

In the midst of giving his statement, he'd taken a call and made a few. That had expedited the process, of course. Now, at his side, his cell phone rang again, and he answered.

"It's Alex Moza. I'm done."

"Quick work. Thank you."

"Finding the right people at this time of night proved an interesting feat but . . ." Rafe heard the shrug in Moza's voice. "What's life without a good challenge?"

Despite being dead-dog tired, Rafe smiled. "I assume you'll send me an astronomical bill?"

"Count on it."

Then Moza gave him directions to his destination. "I'll be waiting."

Rafe caught a cab from the precinct, wondering what the hell he was going to say. Why was he worried?

He didn't have long to plan. Traffic was nonexistent now, the streetlights a yellowed blur against the backdrop of the urban night as the taxi sped through town just after midnight.

A few minutes later, a short, fifty-something Hispanic man, impeccably dressed in a tailored designer suit, emerged through a heavy door into a waiting area at the county's central jail. Alex Moza, for sure. Behind him strode a tall blond hulk of a guy who looked around with wary eyes.

Kerry hadn't been kidding when she described her brother as a Viking. Mark Sullivan had to be six-foot-five, and likely outweighed Rafe by forty pounds. He had a tattoo of a Celtic knot around his bulging biceps. Wide shoulders tapered to a flat belly and narrow hips, shouting of an athletic life. Golden hair, as straight as Kerry's was curly, hung nearly to his shoulders.

This is a guy who nearly died of cancer? Mark Sullivan no longer looked sickly; more like a man no sane person would want to meet in a back alley.

Shit, he hoped the guy wasn't in the mood for a fight, given what Rafe had been doing to his sister. After all, he'd done his best to help free Mark.

He was nervous about what he would say exactly, Rafe realized a moment later. He wanted Mark Sullivan to like him. In fact, he was sweating like a teenage boy meeting his prom date's father.

At that, Rafe frowned. He hoped the brother of the woman he had deflowered and planned to leave would approve?

Yeah, that would happen as soon as the Cubs won the World Series.

Hoping to keep the situation neutral, he approached the attorney first. "Mr. Moza."

"Mr. Dawson."

The two shook hands.

"Everything is set?"

Moza nodded his salt-and-pepper head. "I'll start filing paperwork in the morning to have the charges dismissed. It should be formalized by Friday, I'm guessing. Oh, and I've introduced myself to Mark and apprised him that I'll be representing him now."

"Great. Thanks again." Rafe stuck out his hand.

The attorney shook it, told Mark he'd be in touch, and departed.

"Not to be rude," said Mark as soon as Moza was out of sight, "but what the hell is going on? How is it possible that my charges are being dismissed?"

As he'd instructed, Moza hadn't told Mark anything. That was for the best. The truth about Tiffany and her perfidy would come as a shock. The information needed to come from someone Mark loved and trusted—like Kerry—not a total stranger.

"It's all going to work out," Rafe evaded. "The good news is that you'll be free soon. Mr. Moza will see to it."

Confusion clouded his expression as he stared at Rafe. "Are you the one responsible for sending me an attorney I can't afford? Because I know my wife and sister don't have that kind of money."

"I am. Rafe Dawson."

He stuck out his hand, and his gut clenched in apprehension. Pointless, really, to worry about whether Mark Sullivan would like him. He wouldn't. And after tomorrow, it wouldn't matter. Still, the hope wouldn't go away.

Hesitantly, Mark shook his hand.

"You're paying Moza's fees?"

"Yes."

More confusion furrowed Mark's forehead. "And you're putting up the cash to bail me out?"

Seeing additional questions forming behind Mark's hazel eyes, Rafe held in a wince. "Yes."

"Not to seem ungrateful, but why?"

"As a favor to your sister."

Mark crossed his arms over his wide chest. "You know Kerry? She's never mentioned you."

Rafe resisted the urge to loosen his already out-of-place tie. "We met last Thursday. I'm the e-security consultant Standard National hired. After a little digging around, it was easy to see you weren't guilty."

Rafe smiled, wondering what the odds were that Mark Sullivan would settle for the abridged version of events. His guess? They sucked.

"I'm glad you found what the FBI didn't, but how did Kerry get involved?"

Damn it, Rafe hated being right.

"Kerry . . . persuaded me to look into your situation."

"And you agreed? Just like that? Why?"

Mark's tone told Rafe the man would sooner buy oceanfront property in Nebraska than the half-story he was concocting. But Rafe wasn't saying any more. If Kerry wanted to tell her brother the whole truth, that was her prerogative. It wasn't his place to spill information about Kerry's sex life to her brother.

"Look, the important thing is that you're out and it's over."

"You're right. I just can't quite get past the part where my sister *persuaded* you." Mark's hazel eyes pinned him with a frankly unfriendly stare. "I'd bet my last dime that you're not gay."

He sighed. "You'd win that bet."

"Then I can only think of one reason a slick Manhattan dude like you would be interested in Kerry."

Anger pumped through Rafe at Mark's accusation. At one time, maybe that was true, but now . . . "You're selling your sister short, man. I'd be lying my ass off if I said I didn't think she was sexy. But she's more. Kerry is an amazing woman—warm, fun, and caring. She shares her thoughts and feelings fearlessly. I don't know anyone more loyal. She risked so much to see you freed, I'm still mind-boggled. Kerry has a lot to offer a man."

Mark's hazel gaze mellowed from hostile to thoughtful. "But not you?"

Rafe bit back the urge to stake his verbal claim here and now. To take Kerry and run, keep her in his life and in his bed for as long as he could. Then he'd have her warmth, sexy submission, and impromptu birthday parties all to himself. He could spend monstrous amounts of time devoted to her pleasure, to seeing her eyes light up at things like Rockefeller Center at Christmas or fireworks over the Statue of Liberty.

Then his imagination supplied him a vision of Kerry standing by his front door, suitcases in hand, devastated by heartbreak and calling him a bastard for "shutting her out." She'd damn him for crushing her heart, getting wrapped up in work, burying his feelings. She was important—he couldn't imagine a time when he would think otherwise. But Rafe simply didn't know how to prove it in the ways that mattered to a woman over days, months, and years. To believe that the answers that had eluded him since his first girlfriend would magically appear . . . he'd just be putting everyone through hell.

"Not me," Rafe said finally. "She deserves better."

* * *

AT nine the next morning, Rafe emerged from the hotel's elevator to find Kerry standing in the hotel lobby. The sight of her was like a punch in the gut. From the sunny curls haphazardly clipped to the back of her head to the black spike-heeled sandals on her feet, she appealed to him. A body-hugging black tank top straining across her award-winning breasts and a short purple skirt didn't hurt her cause either.

In the end, though, what he'd miss about her most wasn't her appearance. He'd miss her sense of adventure, her laughter, the unabashed way she cared. Most of all, he'd miss the way he felt—smarter, more connected to the world, more alive—when he was with her.

With a long stride, he approached her, itching to be near her. What he saw in her sad smile and red-rimmed eyes ripped the heart out of his chest. He shouldn't have asked her here. The request to see her had been selfish and stupid . . . and impossible to deny.

"Good morning, beautiful," he murmured.

A soft flush pinkened her cheeks. "All ready, I see."

He answered with a tight nod. What more could he say?

Wordlessly, they headed to the hotel's limo, waiting out front as scheduled. The driver opened the back door of the gleaming white stretch vehicle. With a hand at the small of Kerry's back, Rafe guided her inside.

Okay, so he could have taken the hotel's shuttle van to the airport for free, rather than paying for the prima donna treatment. But he'd wanted some privacy when he talked to Kerry. He needed to make sure she understood that he wasn't leaving because he didn't care.

He was leaving because he did.

Rafe climbed into the limo behind her, planting himself so close, he doubted air molecules could squeeze between them.

The driver shut the door and climbed into the front seat. Rafe raised the privacy partition. It was now or never.

But the words he'd rehearsed this morning, the ones that had sounded so convincing, simply wouldn't come. Which was exactly the point. He sucked at meaningful conversation.

The silence grew thick as they left the hotel's parking lot.

"Thank you for bailing Mark out." She grabbed his hand, and her touch jolted him to his toes. "It was stunningly generous. You didn't have to do it, and I know you fronted a lot of money so that he could come home early—"

"It's no big deal." Rafe shrugged, drinking up the adoration in her gaze. God, if he was a better man, he'd love looking into those eyes forever. "I just made a few phone calls. Once the charges are officially dropped, I'll have the money back, so it's nothing."

"It was everything to me. When Mark came through the door, we hugged, I cried." She smiled, radiance transcending her fatigue. "It's wonderful to have my brother home. Thank you so much."

Rafe shrugged. "So, did he mention meeting me?"

Kerry winced.

"I suspected he didn't like me much." Rafe tried to ignore the disappointment swirling in his gut.

"I didn't have a very good answer for how I persuaded you to help me. He already guessed the truth, anyway."

"Great. If he comes to New York for any reason, call me so I can get a bodyguard first."

Her tinkling laughter sounded in his ears as her dimples danced. Kerry was truly beautiful when she smiled.

"I owe you that much."

"So how is Mark this morning?" he asked.

"Locked in his room." Her sad smile turned into a frown. "He took the news of Tiffany's guilt hard. He tried to find excuses, reasons why I had to be wrong about his wife. Once I proved it, though, he just stared blankly at the wall for a while, then went to his room and locked the door."

"No guns or sharp objects in there, I hope."

"He's not like that. But once he accepted the truth . . . I've never seen his anger run so deep."

"He needs time. It hasn't even been a day yet."

"Knowing Mark, it could be years before he lets it go."

Rafe related to that. Who would get over a wife's betrayal of that enormity in a week or two? Hell, who would blame the guy if he hung on to the sting of her duplicity until he was old enough to collect Social Security?

"He's lucky to have you around to help him," he murmured.

With a frown, Rafe realized that line was a perfect segue for his speech. Now, if he could just make the words come out and make sense . . .

"Kerry, I . . . I think I should explain—"

"Don't say anything." She closed her eyes. "We both knew from the start that it wasn't going to last. I let myself get too carried away in the fantasy. My fault, not yours."

When she opened those green, green eyes again, she reached out, cupped his cheek, skimmed her thumb over his lips. A charge of power struck deep in his chest on its way down to his cock. How was it possible that he wanted to hold her close and pound into her all at once?

"The truth is," she went on, "I got way more out of this arrangement than you. I got my brother and my life back. You just got laid."

He gritted his teeth and gripped her shoulders. "You listen to me. I didn't just get laid. I met a great woman who made me think a lot about my life and what's important. I won't forget that."

"But the sex was good?" She bit her lip, as if uncertain.

He snorted at her understatement. "The sex was so great it nearly sent me into meltdown."

A bittersweet smile lifted the corners of her mouth as her cheeks flushed pink again.

Rafe couldn't resist the urge to take her hand and thread her fingers through his.

Kerry glanced out the window, and Rafe's gaze followed hers as the limo merged onto the freeway. Then she turned back to him, a hint of mischief dancing in her eyes.

"That good, huh?"

"Damn straight."

She drew in a deep breath and looked him in the eyes. "I'm not wearing any panties. On purpose."

Using their threaded fingers, she drew his palm over her breasts. No bra, either. He groaned.

Shit. "Kerry, I'm leaving."

At those words, she sobered. "I know."

"I don't want to take advantage—"

"You're not."

He swallowed, resisting the urge to just pounce on her and forgo the questions. "Why?"

"I want you. Just one more time."

She squeezed her hand over his as his fingers curled around her breast. Rafe felt the rising nipple scorching his palm. He started to sweat, despite the chilled air emerging from the vents above. How the hell was he supposed to resist something he wanted so badly, his brain was nearly fried in his head? Already, his cock was hard and eager and more than ready. The thought of holding her again, having her again, sent him to the edge.

But it would be unfair to make her hope they could work things out, to take more from her when he had nothing else to give.

"We used my last condom yesterday."

Kerry reached into the little purse at her side and dug out a foil packet. With a flick of her wrist, she tossed it into his lap. One pristine condom, waiting just for him. *Holy shit.*

"I'm prepared. Don't say no. Besides"—she grinned—"I owe you a little something for the action you missed out on the last time we were in the back of a limo together."

God, he wanted her so much. His brain whirled with images of impaling her on his cock, of breathing in her sugar sunshine scent again as she came, of memorizing the feel of her against him. It probably made him a bastard of mythic proportions, but he couldn't refuse her.

In fact, he couldn't get to her fast enough.

He grabbed both arms and hauled her onto his lap, locking his mouth over hers. He took possession of her lips as he positioned her on top of him. His tongue dove deep, wanting more of her, wanting all she offered. Sweetness. Warmth. Sunshine. Pure decadence.

Kerry opened to him, yielding. She met his kiss perfectly, parry to his thrust, driving him out of his mind.

As he settled her on his lap, his hips parted her thighs around him. Her skirt slid up, up, up. She hadn't been lying. Not a bikini, thong, or boy short separated his gaze from the damp, gold curls shielding the soft lips of her pussy. A quick drag of his finger up her swollen cleft proved she was every bit as wet as she looked.

The reality sent him into a blind frenzy.

Latching on to her mouth again, he plunged past her lips to get more of her taste on his tongue while he pulled her brief tank top up her waist, over her ribs, sliding it above her breasts. He broke the kiss in order to shove the top over her head, onto the floorboard, and get a good look at paradise. Thank God for tinted windows.

Hard rosy nipples jutted inches from his face. He swallowed as another bolt of lust jolted his cock like a live wire.

Taking one point between his thumb and forefinger, he laved the other with his tongue. With her groan crashing into his ears, he sucked her nipple into his mouth, gently nibbling with teeth. A soothing swipe of his tongue followed. He repeated the process with her other nipple.

Getting enough of this lush, vibrant woman was impossible. What the hell was he going to do back in New York with all the models and socialites whose bodies could double for coatracks? Whose personalities most resembled dead houseplants?

When Kerry started unbuttoning his dress shirt with fevered hands and rocking her hips so that her cleft nudged the ridge of his cock, he was gratified that her impatience matched his.

Together, they peeled off his shirt. Kerry took it from him and hung it from some hook to her left. As she did, Rafe discovered he had just enough room between their bodies to shove his pants down to his thighs.

Then he grabbed her hips and pulled her flush against him. Her soft, wet folds bracketed an ever-hardening clit. He guided her to slick them against his naked cock, focusing on the sensitive ridge below the head.

"Give me your lips," he demanded, feeling his blood churn with fire.

Kerry leaned in, crushing hard-tipped breasts against him, and consumed his mouth with a kiss that both yielded and demanded. Her tongue stroked inside his mouth, danced, flirted, and teased before retreating. Blood roared in his ears. She nudged against his dick again, now soaked and hot and wild. Rafe threw back his head and hissed at the pleasure sizzling up his spine, down his legs.

On either side of his hips, Kerry's thighs began to tremble. He could feel her juices flowing, coating his cock as she swelled with pleasure while she rocked against him. Damn, the woman made him feel hotter than a fire with a never-ending supply of gasoline.

She picked up the pace, urging her hips against his more rapidly. Her breath began to catch at the back of her throat. A flush splotched the skin from her breasts to her neck. She threw her head back in abandon.

Rafe nibbled at her neck, breathing on a sensitive spot just behind her ear. "You're going to come, aren't you, babe?"

"Yeah."

Her weak, trembling voice made him smile even as it tightened the coil of his need to be inside her. Deciding that if she could fan his flames, he could return the favor, he pulled at one of her nipples with his thumb and forefinger, rolling, pinching, listening to her gasp. The other hand he feathered down the cleft of her ass, just enough to wake up all the nerves and leave her tingling.

He swallowed her first moan, then her next.

"Come for me, babe. I love the way your skin turns pink and you cry out my name."

"Rafe!"

On the underside of his cock, he felt gentle flutters of sensation, followed by a drenching rush of her juices. *Holy mother of . . .* He blew out a deep breath, did his best to keep his composure, despite the warning tingles brewing at the base of his spine.

Sated for the moment, she sank against him. He stroked a hand down the damp skin of her back, fighting the urge to hammer into her.

He lost the battle.

Rafe grabbed the condom from the seat beside her, tore it open, and rolled it on. "Got to be inside you. Need you now."

Green eyes, wide and beseeching, latched on to his face as she raised herself up. "Yes, now."

Clutching her hips, he guided her down until he impaled her. He felt her stretching to accommodate him. She writhed, trying to fit him all inside. She rose up once, twice, removing all but the most sensitive part of his head, then she slammed back down. Finally, she sheathed him fully, and Rafe felt her everywhere. Wet beyond his dreams and fist tight, she surrounded every inch of him. He ground into her, stimulating her clit with his pelvis, the head of his cock touching the mouth of her womb.

Then he swallowed her gasp with a deep kiss.

Rafe let her establish the rhythm, for now anyway. But her choice pleased the hell out of him. Slow, dragging, friction-filled, each stroke caused maximum impact. Desire tore through his blood, coursing like a raging river. And at the bottom of each stroke, he rose, making sure his body had contact with that distended clit.

But the effort was costing him in control.

"Babe," he rasped. "You're killing me here. Can't hold out much longer."

"Harder. Need . . . Just a little . . ."

Happy to oblige, Rafe grasped her hips tighter and crushed her down onto him. He took a nipple in his mouth, rolled it around on his tongue—and felt her contract around him.

She cried out, pulsing around him, milking him of every last drop of energy, semen, and, he feared, the ability to want anyone but her.

* * *

THEY'D barely righted their clothes when the limo pulled up curbside. Her days, her nights, her time with Rafe in general, all at an end now.

"Have a good flight," Kerry murmured, holding back tears boiling behind her eyes.

That beat the heck out of saying, *Have a nice life*. That just seemed too flippant . . . too final.

She looked at him, his cheeks still sporting the remnants of a flush of desire, his mouth as tempting as ever. Biting her lip, she drank in the sight of him for the last time. She'd miss his quiet strength, his brash ways, his willingness to listen, the way he always helped, even when he didn't think he did.

He pressed a card into her hand. "This has my office and home numbers, along with my cell number and address. If you need anything, if something goes wrong with Moza or the proceedings . . . or whatever, call me."

The edges of the card sliced against Kerry's finger as she grasped it.

"Ah, babe. Don't look at me like that. I'm trying to do the right thing." He clutched her shoulders. "I wish I could be a better man for you. I want you happy. In the long run, I just can't give you what you want. Don't hate me." He gave a self-deprecating grunt. "I'm already pretty pissed at myself."

She filtered her fingers through the soft, inky blackness of his hair. "I think you're wonderful the way you are. I've never been happier than when I'm with you, Rafe."

He frowned. "This is an anomaly. This isn't me. Away from here, from you, I'm a snarling, sarcastic workaholic. No one likes being with me. Trust me, you're better off."

"Maybe you're different with me," hope made her blurt.

At the resignation that crossed Rafe's features, Kerry wished she'd bitten her tongue instead.

"I can't afford to gamble your heart on that, babe. You shouldn't want to, either."

And he'd go on believing he was incapable of a relationship, even if she told him a hundred times that she loved him just the way he was. He didn't see himself as successful soul mate material. All the pleading in the world wasn't going to change his mind—not unless he decided to change it. She knew just how stubborn Rafe could be.

Defeat drooped her shoulders.

"I love you," she whispered finally. And she couldn't hold the tears back. "Don't forget that."

Eyes squeezed shut with pain and regret, he looked away. "I know. And I don't know how to love you back the way you deserve to be. I'm sorry."

And he was too afraid to try, she realized.

Rafe caressed her cheek, brushing away fresh tears, and shot her a lingering glance that clearly showed all his grief and confusion. Then he turned away and exited the limo—and her life.

Tears fell in earnest then, her stomach twisting with anguish. She'd saved her brother . . . but in the end, she'd lost her heart.

Chapter Eighteen

MAY eighteenth dawned. His thirtieth birthday. Whoop-de-frickin'-doo.

As Rafe ducked out of his posh apartment building on the east side of Central Park in the upper eighties, he swore and dragged on his overcoat. It wasn't supposed to be fifty degrees this time of year. Had someone forgotten to tell Mother Nature that spring had sprung?

Both elevators in the modern high-rise he called home had been unavailable this morning. The first because it had been broken. The second because one of his stupid neighbors two floors down had passed out in there after an all-night party, leaving behind the pungent odor of vomit.

You'd think that if someone was paying four thousand a month for an apartment, he would be more responsible than a teenager at his first keg party.

Shaking his head, Rafe walked down twenty-four flights of

stairs, which made him realize he'd better get his ass back to the gym. He just hadn't had the energy since leaving . . . Florida last week.

A guy in a charcoal suit juggled his briefcase and glasses—and promptly spilled hot coffee on Rafe's left shoe—before walking on. The shoe, now ruined, squeaked when he walked. A biting wind whipping off the East River seeped under his skin. He shivered.

What a hellacious morning.

It was supposed to be eighty-six degrees in Tampa today. He'd looked at three this morning when he'd been unable to sleep. Again.

Rafe sighed as he stepped into the subway. Damn, he'd seen cleaner public restrooms at gas stations. And why did *everyone* have to talk on the cell phone, rather than pay attention to where they were going?

Once sandwiched on the subway between a model-shaped brunette giving him the eye and some Rasta dude who needed a shower, Rafe settled in for his ride to Midtown.

At least he had the FBI off his back. Alex Moza had notified him that all of the charges against Mark Sullivan had been dropped the previous week. Standard National Bank had paid him promptly. For finding the real culprit, they'd sent him a bonus.

Had he kept it and smiled? Rafe snorted. Nope. He'd gone fucking soft in his old age. He'd sent the excess back with a note indicating that he'd rather see Mark Sullivan reinstated in his job and the enclosed amount applied to his back pay. The bank had readily agreed.

So everyone should be happy now. The Sullivan siblings were together again, Mark had his job and his freedom, even if he was minus a wife, while Rafe had his five million dollars and his bachelorhood intact.

Whoop-de-frickin'-doo.

Why was he so damn miserable?

Maybe he needed to get laid. He hadn't since . . . Florida.

"Good morning," said the cool brunette on his left. Her smile held interest.

Rafe glanced. Nice smile, great tits under a tight blue sweater. Legs up to her armpits. A vision many guys could relate to having a wet dream about.

His libido didn't even make a halfhearted jump.

What the hell was the matter with him? He'd imagined the decade of his thirties would change him, yeah. But not on his first day. He hadn't expected it to kill his sex drive, either.

Nodding the brunette's way, Rafe extracted his BlackBerry and pretended to look at his calendar. He hopped off at Fiftieth and walked the rest of the way.

Along the way, he took a call from Regina and ran a few errands. Still, all too soon Rafe found himself entering a familiar Gramercy Park apartment building. Dragging up two flights of stairs, he arrived in front of the square black door he hadn't knocked on in several years.

After a perfunctory rap, the jingle of chains and the turn of a dead bolt made Rafe's stomach knot. If he'd bothered with breakfast, or even a single good meal in the last few days, he might have tossed it all up.

He swallowed the nausea down. Damn it, he was here for a purpose. He'd waited six years for this day. Worked long, tough hours tending bar and doing freelance work after a full day of college classes. Starved until he'd built up his business. Lived in an apartment building that housed more rats than people. Nothing was going to fuck this up, especially not some melancholy he hadn't been able to shake since . . . Florida.

The door was flung wide, and Rafe found himself staring at his father.

Wearing a blue silk robe belted around his slightly paunching middle, Benton Dawson III stared at Rafe. He knew this expression—

the one that told him he was as welcome as a swarm of mosquitoes. Well, today he planned to be just as pesky.

"You."

Rafe plastered on an acidic smile. "I'm here for a long-overdue father-son visit. I know you've missed them."

Shooting him a resentful glare, his father reluctantly shuffled back, smoothing a hand down his thick graying blond hair. Rafe stepped inside. Yep, it still smelled like a distillery. The hardwood floors were sticky under his loafers. Clothes were strewn across the couch, over the breakfast bar. A nearly empty bottle of gin sat on the coffee table in front of the TV.

He walked to the rectangular bottle and lifted it. "Last night's party, or just starting early this morning?"

"I don't have any coffee made yet. Say what you came to say and go."

"Gosh, I'm feeling the love today, Dad. I've missed you, too."

Benton Dawson III drew himself up and gritted his teeth. "Must you continue in this juvenile method of torture? You really are more like your mother than you know."

"Well, since she was capable of human feeling and decency, I'll take that as a compliment."

His father snorted. "She also came from a worthless peasant family."

A white-hot tread of anger sizzled through him. "Apparently, she was good enough for you to seduce."

Red flags of anger appeared on his father's pale, unshaven cheeks. Blue eyes boiled. If looks could kill . . .

"Well, Alondra certainly wasn't good enough to birth any offspring I'd want to claim."

Rafe held in a wince. That one shouldn't hurt him, but it did. He shoved the feelings aside. "Oh, you are feisty this morning. I haven't heard that particular nasty insult since I was about sixteen."

"Maybe I should remind you more often."

Damn, why was it always the same with his father? Ugly, unkind, sarcastic. And he'd even started it today. Behavior like that would garner him a soft lecture that would make him feel about three inches tall if he were still with . . . well, in Florida.

Dad grunted. "No one in that family ever amounted to anything."

Not even you. Rafe heard the unspoken words loud and clear.

"Why are you convinced I'm just the last in a long line of bad seeds, huh?"

"Do you want me to start listing the reasons? We'd be here all damned day."

"Humor me."

His father eased down onto the couch with a superior glance. "You were born defying me. For some reason foreign to logic, you turned down a perfectly good opportunity to go to Harvard."

"Last I heard, Columbia wasn't a school for slackers. They gave me a great scholarship. It was close to my apartment. What does it matter that I didn't attend your alma mater if I'm so worthless, anyway?"

"Just the principle." He sniffed. "And if it weren't for a few good graces and pulled strings, you could have spent all your college years and more in prison."

Rafe sat on a bar stool across the room and steepled his hands. "I never claimed that my CIA stunt in college was smart. It wasn't. I learned from it. But you never forgave me."

"Because you spend all day tinkering with those damned computers. You'll never get a real job."

"That is my real job!" He rose to his feet with a sigh. "Did you know that I'm thirty today?"

His father stilled, saying nothing.

"And with the job I finished last week, I've made over five million dollars in the last six years. All on my own."

The older man's expression turned hostile. "What do you want, a pat on the back?"

Maybe. He'd wanted a reaction. Something. All along, Rafe had imagined that he'd wanted to throw his success into the face of his father, who'd lost most of the multimillion-dollar fortune he'd inherited.

With anger rattling his composure and regret twisting his gut, Rafe realized that what he'd wanted was for his father to be proud of him. Just once.

He stared at his father with hot, dry eyes, feeling his throat tighten. "How about happy birthday and congratulations? Could we not try being civil for once?"

Were those words actually coming out of his mouth?

Contempt curled his father's lip. "You don't know how to be civil to anyone unless they're giving you money or a piece of ass."

A perfect retort danced on the tip of his tongue, sharp and cutting. Rafe stilled it. Slicing into his father, waiting for him to strike back, seeing who would draw first blood—it all seemed pointless suddenly. This ongoing war wasn't changing anything, just entrenching resentment on both sides. Why hadn't they ever just . . . talked?

"You know, you're so busy telling me what's wrong with my life and not looking at yours. You say Mom wasn't good enough for you. At least she parented. At least she tried. You only blamed her for your entire life going wrong. No one forced you to take her to bed. They only asked you to live up to your responsibility once you did."

"That's enough!"

"It's the truth. Then you threw yourself a thirty-year pity party. You curled up in a bottle and stopped living and pissed away most of your old-money fortune. To an outsider, I know whose life would look more fucked up." Rafe figured that little comment was going to send his father into the stratosphere, but he couldn't seem to stop talking. "Are you even capable of caring about anyone but yourself?"

"What's the point?" His brow furrowed with disdain. "Who needs someone else's approval or affection?"

One look at his father's mocking expression told Rafe that his father believed he had no need for him—for anyone. Nothing he ever did or said to his father would change anything, unless Benton Dawson III wanted to climb down from his high horse. Any attempt to please the man would only end in misery.

God, wouldn't he have saved himself years of hurt if he'd only seen it sooner? Rafe shook his head, sadness and anger winding through him for what would never be.

"Most people need someone," Rafe said softly.

His father scoffed. "Other people don't change who you are or what you make of your life."

Didn't they? Rafe remembered the happiest times of his life as those few months when just he and his mother had lived together. He'd also been happy . . . in Florida. Last week, he'd been making a choice to aid someone for a greater cause, to improve an innocent man's life, help get a family back on track. Granted, he'd been heartily compensated for his time and effort. But Rafe suddenly realized he'd come out the winner, too. He'd done something he'd been proud of, all because of the warmth and encouragement of one woman.

His father waved a dismissive hand through the air. "Everyone eventually leaves anyway. Why pretend otherwise?"

"They leave because you drive them away with your biting sarcasm and surly attitude. Mom actually loved you at one point. You reminded her every day that she wasn't good enough for you. She might be alive now if you hadn't driven her to seek an annulment."

"You think you're any better than me, you little shit? Thirty years old, no wife, no kids, no girlfriend, I'll bet. The only difference between us is that I accept the truth and don't hide from it and pretend. You sit here and tell yourself that I'm just an asshole." He shook his head, eyes narrowed in arrogant contempt. "You're no different."

Rafe opened his mouth to protest. Then he stopped. Damn, it wasn't true. It couldn't be.

Last week had shown him glimpses of joy, possibilities of more to life. He'd enjoyed—no, loved—the connection, the closeness of being with a woman more than sexually. His father had never managed that in his entire cynical life.

Smiling, Rafe faced his father proudly . . . before he remembered that he'd walked away from the closeness, the woman who had shown him something more, because he'd thought he couldn't really *be* with her, wouldn't be good for her.

Because they'd be like his parents. On that subject, confusion, doubt, anger pounded at him. Could they be different? Could *he*?

When it came to his father, however, Rafe knew one thing: Nothing was going to change between them, not unless the old man wanted it to. Until that day, he could only put the pain and the past behind him and hope his father would someday do the same.

"Call me if you're ever tired of fighting." He strode for the door. "Goodbye, Dad."

* * *

THREE hours later, Rafe wandered out of his office, into Dawson Security Enterprises' lobby. It was lunchtime—past actually. Not that he was hungry. "Unsettled" was a better word. When he wasn't working, he wanted to be. When he was working, he wanted to be home. When he was with people, he wanted to be alone. But after being holed up in his office for the last hour in complete silence, staring sightlessly out the floor-to-ceiling windows at his great view of midtown, he wanted to climb the walls. All morning, his father's snarling voice rang in his ears.

You're no different.

"Boss?" Regina prompted softly, dark hair brushing her jaw.

Rafe blinked and found himself staring at a glass and chrome table centered before a black leather sofa. How long had he been standing in the middle of the room and staring at the furniture like an idiot?

"Yeah, just thinking."

"Anything in particular? Something I need to do?"

He wished there was something she could do to help him. Hell, he didn't know how to help himself. This out-of-sorts shit really annoyed him. It was stupid to let anything his father said crawl under his skin and yet . . .

No wife, no kids, no girlfriend. You're no different than me.

Rafe had never thought he wanted any of the above, really. He'd always told himself that relationships were nuisances, that he didn't need anyone.

Yet, since leaving . . . Florida, he'd never felt so lonely and empty in his life.

Regina rose to her feet and walked around to the front of her desk. Her gaze of concern looked almost motherly. "Boss, are you okay?"

"Yes," he said automatically. Then he shook his head. "No. Hell, I don't know."

"Anything I can do?"

Voices swirled in his head: Regina's quiet concern, his father's sneer . . . then the soft, feminine voice he couldn't get out of his head, telling him to reach out to his friends.

He swallowed, took a breath, and blurted out, "Have you had lunch?"

Regina smiled. "No. Actually, I was hoping you'd emerge from your office so I could take you to lunch for your birthday."

"You remembered?"

"Not every day your boss turns thirty."

"Do you . . . can you go now?"

Laughing, she told him to pick a place and lead the way.

Twenty minutes later, they sat in a corner booth at one of his favorite Italian holes in the wall. After giving the waiter their drink order, Regina turned to him with a smile.

"Happy birthday, boss."

"Thanks." He hesitated, not sure where to start or what to say. Maybe he should just shut up and smile through lunch.

But a hundred thoughts assailed him. Different sensations streaked through his gut. He was a mess. It felt like shit. But after a week of it, Rafe knew it wasn't going away on its own.

"Have I been a bastard to work for?"

The question clearly surprised her, as her brown eyes widened. "No. Demanding, sometimes. You want what you want and you want it done right. But that's not unreasonable. It's what you pay me for."

"I—I mean . . . personally."

At that question, she hesitated. "Not a bastard, you just keep to yourself. I figured out pretty quickly that you're not one for personal chitchat, and that's okay."

Her polite way of saying that he'd rebuffed her attempts at being friendly. Which he had.

He swallowed, faintly embarrassed. All this time, he'd been standoffish and vaguely rude, just by being himself. Why did he cut people off? Because he was too much like his father?

Was being such a loner just a piss-poor choice?

"I'm sorry if I was rude. I've never been good at . . . connecting with people. You know, on a personal level."

She shrugged. "You're a private man."

"Maybe too private. But you always talked about your husband and your kids. I'm ashamed to say I smiled and nodded and didn't really listen."

"I know." She sent him a crooked smile. "But I kept talking, hoping you'd open up. I've been pretty sure for a while that you didn't have anyone in your life."

"No. That was by choice." Where to start? What to say? What did he even want from this conversation?

"Your folks live anywhere nearby?"

"My mom died when I was eleven. My dad still lives in the city." He cleared his throat. "We hate each other."

Regina recoiled in surprise. "I'm sorry. I had no idea. Brothers? Sisters?"

"No. My parents loathed each other, so it's a miracle I was ever conceived." He heard his voice coming out all hoarse and scratchy. He tried to talk normally but emotions clutched at his throat, closing it up.

"You need someone to talk to." It wasn't a question.

Rafe nodded, relieved that she'd brought it up. Even if he didn't know her well, he knew after years together that he could trust her.

"Kind of. Yeah. Do you mind?"

She squeezed his hand in motherly encouragement. "For a long time, I've wanted to help you. I've sensed how lonely you are. But I knew you wouldn't welcome my help, or anyone else's. What changed that?"

Everything. His birthday, accomplishing his goal, his revealing altercation with his father today. But in the end, the cause boiled down to one person.

Suddenly, the woman whose name he'd avoided even thinking about for the past week whizzed through this brain, lighting him up. *Kerry*. The sound of her name warmed him deep inside. *Kerry*. The sting of tears was like a fire at the backs of his eyes, and he ground his teeth together to keep them from falling.

Kerry.

"In Florida, I . . . um, I think I fell in love. I know I fucked it up."

"Kerry Sullivan?

Hearing her name was like a blow to his gut. He gave a jerky nod. "She told me she loved me and I . . ." He shook his head. "I just left her."

"Why?"

Back to the eternal question. The one he thought he knew the answer to when he'd boarded the plane to New York. Now, he didn't know squat.

"I told myself—told her—that I just didn't connect with people, that I couldn't be the kind of man she'd need. She's . . ." The damn tears were back, and Rafe lifted his face toward the ceiling, hoping they would stop. A deep breath later, he said, "She's like sunshine. Warm. God, I've never known anyone who just gives with their whole heart. When I was with her, I felt everything. She made me mad, made me laugh. She made me want to wrap her in my arms and protect her from all the crap in her life. I enjoyed just . . . being near her. I wanted to make all her days good, to fix her wrongs." He laughed. "Hell, I even committed a federal offense to help her."

Regina gasped.

"I won't be arrested. It was part of a . . . never mind. It's all good now. The Feds and I are cool again."

Relief visibly relaxed her features. "But you still left her?"

"She never asked for my love, but I know she wanted it. I could shoot myself for hurting her, but I kept telling myself that I'd only hurt her more if I stayed because I'm such a bastard in relationships."

"I think that's crap."

Rafe jerked his gaze to her in shock. Regina had never spoken a single four-letter word. Even a mild one.

"Did you ever try in a relationship?"

"Not really. That's my point. I don't know how!" He sighed. "My father told me this morning that I'm just like him, incapable of caring about anyone."

"I hope you know that's even worse crap."

A smile tugged at the corners of his mouth, despite the emotions careening through him. "I've never heard that language from you."

"And you never will in the office, and you really need to cut down on your use of the F-word, but I'll let it slide today."

With a tip of his head, he acknowledged her kindness.

"But you wouldn't be sitting here talking to me if you were truly like your dad. You wouldn't be near tears over this girl if you didn't care."

He winced. "You noticed that? I'd hoped it was too dark to see."

"I noticed. Just like I noticed that you've been very different since you returned from Florida. In the past, you always seemed vaguely lonely. This week, misery just bounced off you. You love this girl."

"Yeah, I do," he acknowledged. And deep down, admitting it felt right. He felt good.

"So why did you leave her?"

The waiter set their drinks and salads in front of them, then shuffled away. There went his excuse to stall for time so he could think.

Rafe grabbed his fork, his brain still churning. "I left her because . . . because I was scared." He sighed. "I was scared by how much I wanted her, by how much she made me feel. I thought I'd hurt her. I pretended the feelings didn't exist until she told me that she loved me. Then . . . I don't know. I panicked."

"Exactly. Because you haven't cared that much about anyone . . . since when?"

He paused to ponder that. "My mother. Her death hurt bad. Being with Dad was no bed of roses, so I just shut everyone out. Clean, easy."

"Empty."

"Yeah," he acknowledged in a rough syllable, scrubbing a hand across his face.

"Still afraid?"

"Hell, yeah. But I'd rather be afraid with Kerry than without her."

Smiling, Regina squeezed his hand. "I knew you were a smart man. All along, I suspected you were a good one, too."

"Thanks." He leaned over and kissed her cheek. "Would you be offended if I left right this minute?"

A smile lit up her face. "No."

"Thanks. Get me on the next flight to Tampa and clear my calendar. I need to pack a bag, make a stop. I'll call you later." He grinned. "Much later, if I'm lucky."

"Go get her, boss."

Chapter Nineteen

THE Thursday night dinner rush mercifully ended—after she'd botched three orders, spilled iced tea on an elderly man, tripped over a child searching for her crayons on the floor, and neglected to shut the refrigerator door after cutting a cuddling couple a piece of key lime pie. No wonder tips had been lousy. All in all, not Kerry's best night as a waitress.

Not her best night, period.

Her mind lingered on Rafe, now in New York. He'd made love to her, helped her free her brother, saved her life, and left as suddenly as he arrived. He'd wanted her, had fun with her. But he hadn't loved her. All along, Rafe had warned her that he wasn't into relationships. She had listened not with her ears but her fairy-tale dreams.

Now, she was back to being a pumpkin. Reality and cutting loneliness set in.

Across the room, Mark brooded in a corner booth, staring out the window, to the dimly lit parking lot. Her heart ached for him. If she'd been hurting this past week, he must feel utter torture. Kerry had known all along that falling for Rafe would only lead to heartbreak, but she'd done it anyway. Mark had married a woman, believing he'd spend the rest of his life with her, have a family with her, only to find out she'd deceived him on every level.

Sidling over to his table with a piece of coconut crème pie, Mark's favorite, she set the pastry in front of him. "Eat up. It's on the house."

He turned exhausted, red-rimmed hazel eyes on her. His expression was . . . nothing. Empty. Void. And she didn't buy it for a minute. She'd been staying with him all week, since her house was still in cinders. She heard him up at two in the morning, knew he'd been working long hours at the bank now that he'd been reinstated and given Smikins's job as branch manager.

"No thanks."

"You have to eat. You barely touched your dinner."

"Same for you."

"I'm working."

"Eat the pie." He pushed it in her direction.

She pushed it back toward him. "Can't. Still have tables to bus and a few customers to wrap up before closing."

"It'll wait until you get back."

Sighing, Kerry grabbed Mark's hand. "I know the last week has been a blur for you, and that you're hurt and confused. But you have to eat. You have to sleep. You'll be no good for work, for life, if you don't."

A grim smile lifted one corner of his mouth. "You might take your own advice, little sister. Granted, I've been gone for a while, but purple smudges under your eyes didn't used to be part of your look, and I never recall you not eating for entire days in the past. Or being clumsy. Though I'm sure that old guy got a thrill when you tried to pat the iced tea from his crotch."

Kerry stood and swatted her brother's shoulder. "Stop. I didn't mean to. I just . . ."

"Had your mind elsewhere." The grin cracking his bleak face disappeared. "I hear you."

Suddenly, Mark's cell phone rang. With a frown, he unclipped it from his belt.

"At least try the pie," she implored.

Wondering if it was Mark's divorce attorney again, Kerry gave him some privacy by tending to the customers who needed a coffee refill across the room.

Mark shot her an absent nod. Kerry refilled drinks and sent a curious glance at her brother. His confusion had turned to an outright scowl. He growled something low into the phone, but she couldn't hear the words. What the heck was that about?

Before she could return to his side, her boss called from the kitchen, "Kerry, can you lock the front door for the night?"

"Sure, Pops. I'll let out the customers as they're ready to go."

With a wink, the owner and cook disappeared to his offices in the back, his nearly bald head reflecting the bright overhead light.

Hand in hand, the cuddling couple left a moment later as she locked the front door and flipped the OPEN sign to read CLOSED.

Her gaze lingered as they walked to their car. Kerry's heart kicked her in the chest like Superman on steroids. She wished that could have been her with Rafe, sharing a sweet with her sweetie, holding hands, making plans . . .

"It's not in the cards for me, and I need to get over it," she muttered to herself, hoisting dirty dishes off the couple's table and scooping up her tip.

The lights shut off in the kitchen. The last of her customers made their way toward the door. As she thanked them with a plastic smile and let them out, Kerry glanced back at her brother. The scowl had vanished, replaced by a low murmur and a nod. Then he flipped his phone shut.

"You 'bout done here?" Mark asked.

"Let me throw these dishes in the sink and grab my stuff."

"I'll go out and bring the car around."

"Thanks for waiting on me. Hopefully I'll get my car out of the shop tomorrow."

"No sweat."

Mark leaned down, a long way, given his height, and dropped a kiss on her cheek. "Thanks for everything. I know I've said it before, but I wouldn't be free if it wasn't for you. You deserve every happiness in the world."

Smiling, she grabbed his hand. "I owed you for being such a great big brother. I'd do anything for you."

"Same here." He squeezed her fingers and left.

Kerry finished up her last-minute routine, turning off lights, grabbing her purse. "Pops," she called to the back. "I'm gone."

"Good night," he shouted from his office. "I'll finish the last of the dishes and lock up behind you."

"Thanks. See you Saturday."

Kerry made her way toward the front of the restaurant. She peered out the wall of windows on her left, searching for Mark and his car. Instead, she saw her brother leaning down to talk to someone through the window of a sleek black limousine.

Who would be coming to Pop's Coffee Stop in a limousine, especially at closing time? Someone had to be lost.

With a shrug, Kerry let herself out and rounded the corner, just as Mark straightened away from the limo's window and reached down to shake a hand that emerged from the gleaming car's dark confines. In his free hand, Mark held a rectangular scrap of paper.

"Mark?"

He whirled around. The gleam in his eyes took her aback. He wore an actual smile. A real one. What in the heck was happening here?

"There's someone here to see you," her brother said, then walked away, heading into the dark parking lot.

Before she could say a word, the back door of the limousine opened. Out stepped the last person she ever thought she'd see again.

Rafe Dawson.

She gasped, then covered her hand with her mouth. She blinked, twice, just to make sure her eyes weren't deceiving her.

They weren't.

There he stood, all solid and real—and watching her intently. Kerry's insides malfunctioned. She forgot how to breathe. But her heart . . . it pounded ninety to nothing. To say nothing of the wave of dizziness.

With his dark hair spiked in its usual muss, his gently wrinkled white dress shirt rolled up over powerful forearms, and charcoal slacks molding to lean hips, he looked amazing. His gray eyes glimmered with something she couldn't understand. How could the sight of one man make her want to faint?

"Hi, Kerry."

He'd come back. *He'd come back!* Kerry searched Rafe's beloved, familiar face for some sign of his feelings. If anything, he looked apprehensive.

What did that mean? Nothing, likely. In fact, he looked like a man contemplating a root canal. She had to stop wishing that things would be different between them.

"What . . . Why are you here?" she asked cautiously.

"Can I talk to you? In the limo?"

Kerry's gaze trailed into the depths of the dark car. She wanted to talk to him . . . But to get in there, alone with the man whose most casual touch would set her head spinning? Where memories of their last limo ride together would chip away at her composure? He'd already broken her heart once and had the power to unravel the fragile mending she'd barely started.

"It's not a good idea. If you came to check on me or whatever, I . . . I'm all right. I heard you before you left. Don't worry. I won't turn stalker or anything. I won't even call if I have another loved one in jail."

She sent him a stilted smile.

Rafe didn't laugh at her joke. "Please. Three minutes."

And after three minutes, he'd return to New York. Or worse, what if he just wanted another scorching weekend? Or another wild ride in the backseat? Being in his arms, burning against his skin, she'd fall deeper under his addictive, seductive spell. Her brief glimmer of hope that he could love her would die a death worthy of the worst Hollywood gore flick, and she'd be left alone to try to mend yet another wound in her heart.

"Kerry," he implored.

She screwed her eyes shut. She wanted to heed that thick, rough voice. God knew she did. She'd never been good at denying the man anything, especially since realizing that she loved him. But if he'd come here with some idea to start another brief fling because they had great chemistry . . .

"I just can't," she choked out. "My heart can't take it."

Rafe winced. Then with a slow nod, he turned away.

Kerry's heart fell as he leaned into the limousine. Now he was going to leave again, this time for good. Something in her wanted to call back to him, promise him anything—everything—if he'd stay just one more night.

She held her tongue. *Be strong. Be determined.*

To her surprise, Rafe emerged from the limo again, holding something in his hands. It glimmered silver in the moonlight, but his large palms covered the object too well for her to identify it.

Until he slapped a silver handcuff around first one of her wrists, then the other.

She sputtered, too shocked to scream. Then he bent, wrapped his arms around her thighs, and lifted her feet from the ground, tossing her over his shoulder in a fireman's carry.

"What are you doing?" she squealed, her cheek resting on his back. "Put me down!"

Three steps later, she felt the limo's smooth leather riding up underneath the short skirt of her green polyester waitress's uniform as he settled her on the seat.

Rafe tucked her into the car, climbed in after her, and slammed the door. With the flick of a button, he raised the privacy partition between them and the faceless driver.

Then he turned to face her. "Kerry—"

"What the hell are you doing?"

"I'm kidnapping you."

"Kidnapping . . . Are you serious? I already told you I wouldn't come after you and—"

"That's why I'm here," he said softly.

Kerry peered at him, trying to understand. He didn't want her, so she wasn't following him and that meant he had to kidnap her because . . . ?

"If you're here to pick up where we left off last week, I can't do it. I'm not up for fun and games, sex for sex's sake—"

"As much as I enjoy making love to you, that's not what I want. Scratch that," he stopped himself. "That's not the reason I'm here."

Frowning, she tried to decipher what he wanted, besides sex. "I'm lost. Can you tell me what the heck you came here to say, then let me get home?"

Before you break my heart again and confuse me to lunacy?

Rafe said nothing for the longest minute. He just stared, his eyes seeming to trace every curve of her face. Finally, slowly, something softened his features.

"Ah, babe . . . I suck at words. I had a speech, but I can't remember a damn word of it now. I just . . ." He sighed. "You wouldn't leave my head once I got back to New York. The harder I tried to block you out, the more you stayed with me. Your smile, your thoughtfulness, your warmth. I just couldn't stay away."

A breath lodged itself in her chest. There went the ol' heartbeat again, chugging away until she was sure her chest was bruised. And that pesky pixie, hope, had returned. Did he, by chance, want her for more than a fling?

"What are you saying?" she whispered.

He hesitated, then flipped on a muted light in the limo's interior. "Look at the chain between your handcuffs."

At the chain . . . Certainly he hadn't come all this way to ask her for her opinion on the latest in all things bondage?

Then she saw something dangling sparkle, twinkle in the cool light of the limousine. Was that a . . . ?

"A ring?" She jiggled her wrists until the ring turned around on the chain. "A diamond ring?"

"Princess cut, set in platinum. The jeweler says it's a great stone and a popular cut, and the setting reminded me of you, but if you don't like it—"

Like it? She loved it! Slightly whimsical with filigree around the center stone, solid without being flashy. She fell in love instantly.

"Are you . . . ?" Kerry swallowed, her heart picking up yet more steam. "Are you asking what I think you're—no, that's not possible."

Maybe this was his weird way of assuaging his conscience. Certainly, this wasn't a proposal. It couldn't be . . . could it?

"I'm fucking this up." He sighed. "I'm sorry."

He grabbed her wrists and pulled her closer. Without the use of her hands, Kerry fell off balance and onto Rafe's broad chest. He clasped her against him, so warm, smelling so familiar and yummy, Kerry couldn't decide whether to burrow against him or jump his bones.

Listen to the man instead!

Rafe grasped either side of her face and stared straight into her eyes. "I know I'm bad with words. I know I said a lot of stupid things before I left here last week. But since then, I realized that I'm not happy without you. I'm not whole without you. Ah babe, I'm not perfect, and I'm sure I'll piss you off more than once." He swallowed. "But I love you."

Gasping, Kerry felt her eyes widen until she was sure the lids darted over her brows. *I love you,* the words repeated in her head. Tears pooled in her eyes.

"Rafe . . ." Her voice caught as one hot tear tracked down her cheek.

"I love you even though I thought I couldn't. So much I think I might explode sometimes." He tangled his fingers in her curls. "That ring means exactly what you think. Tell me I'm not too late. Say yes." He caressed her cheek. "Marry me."

"You're serious?"

He nodded, cheeks taut, gaze decidedly nervous. "Marry me."

"You're sure?"

"Yes. Marry me."

"You're not just teasing—"

"Damn it, woman. Marry me."

Rafe wanted to marry her. *Her!*

"That's a romantic proposal."

"Is that a yes?"

Kerry smiled through her tears. "Yes!"

She pressed her lips to his. He responded enthusiastically by slanting his mouth over hers, invading the recesses of her mouth with his tongue and staying a good, long while.

When he finally eased away, Kerry's head swam and her heart floated. "I thought I'd never see you again."

"Babe, I couldn't stay away. I didn't know how much I needed you, how much you make me feel, until I'd already left."

"You were gone more than a week."

"Just proves how stubborn I can be."

"Ain't that the truth." Kerry laughed, joy lighting every corner of her heart, washing away the pain of the last week and leaving her with only love.

When he unscrewed a loose link in the chain between the cuffs, the ring dropped into his palm. Silently, he slipped it onto her finger. It fit perfectly, and her world felt right.

"Wow, married," she breathed. "Should we plan for a ceremony this late this summer? I think it's too late for a June wedding, but August—"

"I was thinking more like Saturday."

"*What!*"

"Once I tap on the privacy partition, the limo will take us to the airport. I've chartered a plane to take us to Vegas."

Getting married in Las Vegas in two days? The idea boggled the mind. "I don't have a dress."

"You can get one tomorrow. Regina helped me arrange a chapel, a photographer, and flowers. Your brother has a plane ticket for a flight that leaves Friday after work."

"Pretty sure of yourself, huh?"

Rafe paused. "Why do you think I brought the handcuffs?"

"You would have abducted me?"

Wearing a grin, Rafe leaned in and planted a kiss on her lips. "Why not? It worked for us the first time."

"True." She laughed. "Well, now that I've said yes, what should we do with the handcuffs?"

Rafe tapped on the privacy partition and the car sped away. Then he sent her a smile infused with pure sin. "We'll think of something."

About the Author

Shayla Black (aka Shelley Bradley) is the *New York Times* and *USA Today* bestselling author of more than thirty sizzling contemporary, erotic, paranormal, and historical romances for multiple print, electronic, and audio publishers. She lives in Texas with her husband, munchkin, and one very spoiled cat. In her "free" time she enjoys watching reality TV, reading, and listening to an eclectic blend of music.

Shayla's work has been translated into approximately a dozen languages. She has also received or been nominated for the Passionate Plume, the Holt Medallion, the Colorado Romance Writers Award of Excellence, and the National Reader's Choice Awards. RT Book Club has twice nominated her for Best Erotic Romance of the year and awarded her several Top Picks and a KISS Hero Award.

A writing risk-taker, Shayla enjoys tackling writing challenges with every book. Find Shayla at www.ShaylaBlack.com or visit her on her Shayla Black Author Facebook page.

Be on the lookout for

STRIP SEARCH

by Shayla Black
writing as Shelley Bradley

Now available from Heat Books

"ARE YOU READY FOR THE 'HOTTEST' READ OF THE SUMMER?"*

If the Feds want to nail a thug with ties to the Mafia, they need a slick trap to catch him. Enter Mark Sullivan, totally built for the job—to go undercover as a male stripper in the Vegas club where the mobster works. The perk? The club's owner. Sure, she's got some unsavory connections, but how can anyone with those legs be all bad?

When it comes to business, Nicola DiStefano's a pro. As for pleasure, she's been out of commission too long to care. If anyone can strip her of her inhibitions it's the new guy who's stirring her wildest fantasies. But Mark and Nicki have more in common than sizzling sexual chemistry. They each have their share of secrets, and with the mob closing in, what gets exposed is as irresistible as it is dangerous.

"[A] BOOK YOU DO NOT WANT TO MISS."

—**Romance Readers Connection*